THE VETERAN
AND OTHER STORIES

Frederick Forsyth

CORGI BOOKS

THE VETERAN
A CORGI BOOK: 0 552 14923 3

Originally published in Great Britain by Bantam Press,
a division of Transworld Publishers

PRINTING HISTORY
Bantam Press edition published 2001
Corgi edition published 2002

1 3 5 7 9 10 8 6 4 2

Set in 10½/12½ pt Palatino by
Falcon Oast Graphic Art Ltd.

Corgi Books are published by Transworld Publishers,
61–63 Uxbridge Road, London W5 5SA,
a division of The Random House Group Ltd,
in Australia by Random House Australia (Pty) Ltd,
20 Alfred Street, Milsons Point, Sydney, NSW 2061, Australia,
in New Zealand by Random House New Zealand Ltd,
18 Poland Road, Glenfield, Auckland 10, New Zealand
and in South Africa by Random House (Pty) Ltd,
Endulini, 5a Jubilee Road, Parktown 2193, South Africa.

Printed and bound in Germany by
Elsnerdruck, Berlin.

For Sandy,
who somehow still manages to put up with me

CONTENTS

THE VETERAN

It was the owner of the small convenience store on the corner who saw it all. At least, he said he did.

He was inside the shop, but near the front window, rearranging his wares for better display, when he looked up and saw the man across the street. The man was quite unremarkable and the shopkeeper would have looked away but for the limp. He would testify later that there was no-one else on the street.

The day was hot beneath a skim of grey cloud, the atmosphere close and muggy. The hysterically named Paradise Way was as bleak and shabby as ever, a shopping parade in the heart of one of those graffiti-daubed, exhausted, crime-destroyed housing estates that deface the landscape between Leyton, Edmonton, Dalston and Tottenham.

When it was opened thirty years earlier with a grandiose civic ceremony, the Meadowdene Grove estate was hailed as a new style of low-budget council housing for working people. The name alone should have given the game away. It was not a meadow, it was not a dene and it had not seen a grove since the Middle Ages. It was, in fact, a grey poured-concrete gulag commissioned by a borough council that flew the red flag of world communism above the town hall and designed by architects who, for themselves, preferred honeysuckle-twined cottages in the country.

Meadowdene Grove then went downhill faster than the Tour de France coming off the Pyrenees. By 1996 the warren of passages, underpasses and alleys that linked the grim residential blocks were crusted with filth, slick with urine and came alive only at night when gangs of local youths, unemployed and unemployable, roamed their manor to 'score' from the area drug peddlers.

Working-class pensioners, fiercely respectable, trying to cling to the old moralities, the comforting certainties of their own younger days, lived behind barricaded doors, fearful of the wolf packs outside.

Between the blocks, each seven storeys high, each door fronted by an open passage with greasy stair-wells at either end, were patches of what had been green grass. A few rusted and abandoned cars, stripped to shells, crouched beside the inner roads that traversed the squares designed for public recreation and from which narrow passages ran through to Paradise Way.

The main shopping parade had once bustled with retail commerce, but most of the shops had finally closed, their proprietors exhausted by the struggle against pilfering, shoplifting, wilful damage, broken windows and racist abuse. More than half were now boarded up with defaced ply board or steel shutters and the few that stayed open for business tried to protect themselves with wire-mesh defences.

On the corner, Mr Veejay Patel soldiered on. As a ten-year-old he had come with his parents from Uganda, expelled by the brutalities of Idi Amin. Britain had taken them in. He was grateful. He still loved his adopted country, abided by the law, tried to be a good citizen, puzzled by the steady degeneration of standards that characterized the Nineties.

There are parts of what London's Metropolitan Police call the north-east quadrant where a stranger is unwise to roam. The limping man was a stranger.

He was barely fifteen yards from the corner when two men emerged from a concrete passage between two boarded shops and confronted him. Mr Patel froze and watched. They were different, but equally menacing. He knew both types well. One of them was beefy, with a shaven skull and porcine face. Even at a distance of thirty yards, Mr Patel could see a ring glint in the left ear lobe. He wore baggy jeans and a soiled T-shirt. A beer belly sagged over his broad leather belt. He took up station foursquare in front of the stranger, who had no choice but to stop.

The second man was slimmer, in pale drill trousers and a grey zip-fronted windcheater. Lank, greasy hair fell just below his ears. He slipped behind the victim and waited there.

The beefy one raised his right fist, close to the face of the man to be mugged. Mr Patel saw

11

the glint of metal on the fist. He could not hear what was said, but he saw the beefy one's mouth move as he spoke to the stranger. All the victim had to do was hand over his wallet, watch and any other valuables he might be carrying. With luck the muggers would grab the loot and run; the victim might survive unscathed.

He was probably silly to do what he did. He was outnumbered and outweighed. To judge from his grey hair, he was middle-aged and clearly his limp indicated he was not fully mobile. But he fought back.

Mr Patel saw his right hand come up from his side, moving extremely fast. He seemed to sway slightly at the hips, turning his shoulders to add force to the blow. The beefy one took it full on the nose. What had been a silent mime was pierced by a shout of pain that Mr Patel could hear even through his plate-glass window.

The beefy one staggered back, throwing both hands to his face, and Mr Patel saw the gleam of blood between the fingers. When he made his statement, the shopkeeper had to pause to recall clearly and in sequence what happened next. Lank Hair swept in a hard punch to the kidneys from behind, then kicked the older man in the back of his good knee. It was enough. The victim went down to the pavement.

On the Meadowdene Grove estate footwear was either trainers (for speed) or heavy boots (for kicking). Both these assailants had boots. The man on the pavement had doubled himself into the embryo position to protect his vitals, but there were four boots going for him and the beefy one, still clutching his nose one-handed, went for the head.

There were, the shopkeeper later estimated, about twenty kicks, maybe more, until the victim had ceased to twist and turn. Lank Hair bent over him, flicked open his jacket and went for the inside pocket.

Mr Patel saw the hand come back out, a wallet held between forefinger and thumb. Then both men straightened, turned and ran back up the concrete passage to disappear in the warren of alleys that riddled the estate. Before they went, the beefy one tore his T-shirt out of his jeans and held it up to staunch the blood pouring from his nose.

The shopkeeper watched them disappear, then scuttled back behind his counter where he kept the telephone. He dialled 999 and gave his name and address to the operator, who insisted she could not summon any emergency service until she knew who was calling. When the formalities had been accomplished, Mr Patel asked for police and an ambulance. Then he returned to the front window.

The man still lay on the opposite pavement, quite inert. No-one tended him. This was not the sort of street where people wanted to get involved. Mr Patel would have crossed the road to do what he could, but he knew nothing of first aid, feared to move the man and make a mistake, feared for his shop and that the muggers might come back. So he waited.

The squad car was first and it took less than four

minutes. The two police constables inside had by chance been less than half a mile away on the Upper High Road when they took the call. Both knew the estate and the location of Paradise Way. Both had been on duty during the spring race riots.

As the car screeched to a halt and the wail of the siren died away, one of the PCs emerged from the passenger door and ran over to the figure on the pavement. The other remained at the wheel and used the radio to confirm that an ambulance was on its way. Mr Patel could see both officers looking across the street towards his shop, checking the address source of the 999 call, but neither of them came over to him. That could wait. The officers' gaze turned away as the ambulance, lights flashing and siren wailing, came round the corner. A few gawpers had congregated up and down Paradise Way, but they kept their distance. The police would later try to interview them for witnesses, but merely waste their time. On Meadowdene Grove you watched for fun, but you did not help the fuzz.

There were two paramedics, skilled and experienced men. For them, as for the police, procedures are procedures and must be followed to the letter.

'It looks like a mugging and a kicking,' the constable kneeling beside the body remarked. 'Possibly a bad one.'

The paramedics nodded and went to work. There was no blood flow to staunch, so the first priority was to stabilize the neck. Victims of crash and beating trauma can be finished off there and then if the cervical vertebrae have already been damaged and are then abused even more by unskilled man-handling. The two men quickly fitted a semi-rigid collar to prevent the neck from wobbling side to side.

The next procedure was to get him onto a spine board to immobilize both neck and back. That was done right there on the pavement. Only then could the man be lifted onto a gurney and hefted into the back of the ambulance. The paramedics were quick and efficient. Within five minutes of swerving into the kerbside they were ready to roll.

'I'll have to come with you,' said the constable on the pavement, 'he might make a statement.'

Professionals in the emergency services know pretty exactly who does what and why. It saves time. The paramedic nodded. The ambulance was his territory and he was in charge, but the police had a job to do, too. He already knew that the chances of the injured man uttering a word were out of the window, so he just muttered, 'Stay out of the way. This is a bad one.'

The constable clambered aboard and sat well up forward, close to the bulkhead of the driving compartment; the driver slammed the doors and ran to his cab. His partner bent over the man on the gurney. Two seconds later the ambulance was racing down Paradise Way, past the staring onlookers, its high-pitched siren scream clearing a path as it swerved into the traffic-choked High Road. The constable clung on and watched another pro at work.

Airway, always clear the airway. A blockage of

blood and mucus in the windpipe can choke a patient to death almost as fast as a bullet. The paramedic used a suction pump which yielded a small amount of mucus, the sort a smoker might contain, but little blood. Air passage free, breathing shallow but sufficient to sustain life. To be safe, the paramedic clamped an oxygen mask with attached reservoir bag over the swollen face. It was the rapid swelling that worried him; he knew the sign too well.

Pulse check: regular but already too fast, another possible sign of cerebral trauma. The Glasgow Coma Scale measures the alertness of the human brain on a scale of 15. Fully awake and completely alert gives 15 over15. A test showed the patient was eleven over fifteen and falling. A figure of three is deep coma, under that – death.

'Royal London,' he shouted over the wail of the siren. 'A and E plus neuro.'

The driver nodded, went through a major crossroads against the lights as cars and trucks pulled over, then changed tack towards Whitechapel. The Royal London Hospital in Whitechapel Road has an advanced neurosurgical unit; one nearer to the ambulance's position did not, but if 'neuro' were needed, the extra few driving minutes would pay dividends.

The driver was talking to his control, giving his exact position in South Tottenham, estimated time of arrival at the Royal London, and asking for a complete Accident and Emergency trauma team to be ready and waiting.

16

The paramedic in the back was right. One of the possible call signs of major head injury, particularly after an assault, is that the soft tissue of the entire face and head swells rapidly to a great, bloated, unrecognizable gargoyle. The face of the injured man had begun swelling back on the pavement; by the time the ambulance swerved into the A and E bay at the Royal, the face was like a football. The doors crashed open; the gurney was lowered into the care of the trauma team. There were three doctors under the command of the consultant, Mr Carl Bateman; these were an anaesthetist and two juniors; there were also three nurses.

They enveloped the gurney, lifted the patient (still on the spine board) onto one of their own trolleys and wheeled him away.

'I'll need my spine board back,' shouted the paramedic, but no-one heard him. He would have to collect it the next day. The policeman scrambled out.

'Where do I go?' he asked.

'In there,' said the paramedic, 'but don't get in the way.'

The constable nodded obediently and trotted through the swing doors, still hoping for a statement. The only one he got was from a senior staff nurse.

'Sit there,' she said, 'and don't get in the way.'

Within half an hour Paradise Way was a buzz of activity. A uniformed inspector from the Dover Street police station, known simply in those parts as the Dover 'nick', had taken charge. The street up and down from the attack site had been cordoned off with striped tape. A dozen officers were quartering the area, concentrating on the shops along the parade and the six floors of flats that stood above them. The apartments across the road from the scene of the crime were of particular interest, for anyone looking out and down might well have seen it all. But it was uphill work. Reactions varied from genuine apology through bovine denial to outright abuse. The door-knocking went on.

The inspector had quickly called for a fellow-rank officer from CID, for it was clear this was a job for detectives. At the Dover nick DI Jack Burns had been summoned from a half-drunk and much-treasured cup of tea in the canteen to the presence of Detective Superintendent Alan Parfitt to be told to take over the Paradise Way mugging. He protested that he was handling a chain of car thefts, a hit-and-run and was due in court the next morning. To no avail. Shortage of staff, he was told. August, bloody August, he growled as he left.

He arrived at the scene with his partner Detective Sergeant Luke Skinner just about the same time as the POLSA team. The Police Search units do an unlovely job. Dressed in heavy-duty overalls and protective gloves, their task is to search the areas round crime scenes for clues. Clues are not always obvious at first glance so the general rule is to grab it, bag it and find out what it is later. The job can also be very mucky, involving crawling on hands and knees in some rather unpleasant places. The Meadowdene Grove estate was not a pleasant place.

'There's a missing wallet, Jack,' said the uniformed inspector who had already spoken to Mr Patel. 'And one of the assailants had his nose bloodied. He was holding the hem of his T-shirt to his face as he ran off. May have sprayed blood on the floor.'

Burns nodded. While the POLSA searchers scoured the smelly passages of the concrete blocks on hands and knees and the uniformed men tried to find another eyewitness, Jack Burns entered the shop of Mr Veejay Patel.

'I am Detective Inspector Burns,' he said, offering his warrant card, 'and this is DS Skinner. I gather you were the one who made the 999 call?'

Mr Patel surprised Jack Burns, who came from Devon and had been three years with the Met, the whole time at Dover nick. In his native county he was accustomed to citizens helping the police where, when and as they could, but north-east London had been a shock. Mr Patel reminded him of Devon. He really wanted to help. He was clear, concise and precise. In a lengthy statement taken down by DS Skinner, he explained exactly what he had seen, and gave clear descriptions of the assailants. Jack Burns warmed to him. If only all cases included a witness like Veejay Patel of Entebbe and Edmonton. Dusk was settling over Meadowdene Grove when he signed DS Skinner's handwritten statement.

'I would like you to come down to the station and look at some photographs, if you would, sir,' said Burns at last. 'You might be able to spot these two men. It would save an awful lot of time if we knew who we were looking for exactly.'

Mr Patel was apologetic.

'Not tonight, if you please. I am alone in the shop. I close at ten. But tomorrow my brother returns. He has been on holiday, you see. August. I could get away in the morning.'

Burns thought. Court appearance at ten thirty. Formal remand. He would have to leave it to Skinner.

'Eleven o'clock? You know the Dover Street station? Just ask for me at the front desk.'

'Not often you meet that sort,' said Skinner as they crossed the road to their car.

'I like him,' said Burns. 'When we get those bastards, I think we might have a result.'

On the drive back to Dover Street DI Burns discovered by radio where the injured man had been taken and which constable was watching over him. Five minutes later they were in contact.

'I want everything he possessed – clothes, effects, the lot – bagged and brought to the nick,' he told the young officer. 'And an ID. We still don't know who he is. When you've got it all, call up and we'll send a replacement for you.'

Mr Carl Bateman was not concerned either for the name and address of the man on the trolley, or yet who had done these things to him. His concern was keeping him alive. From the docking bay, the trolley had come straight through to the resuscitation room where the A and E team went to work. Mr Bateman was sure there were multiple injuries inflicted here, but the rules were clear: life-threatening first, the rest can wait. So he went through the ABCD procedure.

A is for airway. The paramedic had done a good job. Airway was clear, despite a slight wheezing. The neck was immobilized.

B is for breathing. The consultant had the jacket and shirt torn open, then went over the chest area both front and back with a stethoscope.

He detected a couple of cracked ribs but they, like the mashed knuckles of the left hand and the broken teeth in the mouth, were not life-threatening and could wait. Despite the ribs, the patient was still breathing regularly. There is little point in performing spectacular orthopaedic surgery if the patient decides to stop breathing. The pulse worried him; it had left the normal 80 mark and climbed above 100. Too fast: a probable sign of inner trauma.

C is for circulation. In less than a minute, Mr Bateman had two intravenous catheters in place. One drained off 20 millilitres of blood for immediate analysis; then, while the rest of the examination proceeded, a litre of crystalloid fluid went into each arm.

D is for disability. This was not good. The face and head were hardly recognizable as belonging to a human being and the Glasgow Scale showed the man was now 6 over 15 and fading dangerously. There was serious cerebral damage here, and not for the first time Carl Bateman thanked the unknown paramedic who had spent a few extra minutes getting the man to the Royal and its neuro unit.

He called up the scanner unit and told them he would have his patient there in five minutes. Then the consultant called his colleague Mr Paul Willis, the senior neurosurgeon.

'I think I must have a major intra-cranial haematoma here, Paul. Glasgow is now at five and still dropping.'

'Get him in as soon as you have a scan for me,' said the neurosurgeon.

When he was knocked down the man had been wearing socks and shoes, underpants, shirt – open at the neck, trousers held up by a belt, jacket and a light raincoat. Everything below the waist was not a problem and had simply been pulled down. To prevent jolting of the neck and head, the raincoat, jacket and shirt were just cut off. Then everything was bagged, pocket contents still in place, and given to the delighted constable waiting outside. He was soon replaced and able to take his trophies back to Dover Street and an expectant Jack Burns.

The scanner confirmed Carl Bateman's worst fears. The man was haemorrhaging into the brain cavity. The blood was pressing upon the brain itself with a force that would soon prove lethal or irreversible.

At eight fifteen the patient entered brain surgery. Mr Willis, guided by the scans that showed exactly where the intra-cranial pressure was being exerted, could reach the haematoma with a single insertion. Three small holes were drilled in the skull, then linked with saw-cuts to create a perfect triangle, the standard operation.

With this triangle of bone removed, the haematoma was drained of the blood causing the pressure, and the damaged arteries leaking into the brain cavity were tied off. With the blood sacs gone, the pressure was eased and the brain was able to expand back into the full space that had been its natural area.

The triangle of bone was replaced and the flap of scalp stitched over it. Heavy bandaging would keep both in place until nature could take its course and heal. Despite the damage, Mr Willis was hopeful that he had been in time.

The body is a weird contraption. It can die from bee stings or recover from massive trauma. When a haematoma is removed and the brain allowed to expand back to its full cavity size, patients can simply recover consciousness and perform quite lucidly within days. No-one would know for twenty-four hours, until the anaesthesia wore off. By day two, without recovery, there would be cause for concern. Mr Willis scrubbed off, changed and went home to St John's Wood.

'Bugger all,' said Jack Burns, staring at the clothes and personal effects. The latter included a half-smoked pack of cigarettes, half a box of matches, assorted coins, a soiled handkerchief and a single key on a ribbon, apparently for a house door somewhere. These had come from the trousers. From the jacket, nothing. Whatever else the man had carried, the wallet must have contained it all.

'A neat man,' said Skinner, who had been

examining the clothes. 'Shoes, cheap and patched, but an effort has been made at a shine. Trousers, cheap, worn, but a crease down each front leg, made by an iron. Shirt, frayed at neck and cuffs, but also ironed. A man with no money, but trying to keep up appearances.'

'Well, I wish he'd kept a credit card or a letter addressed to himself in a back trouser pocket,' said Burns, who was still plodding through the endless form-filling required of today's policeman. 'I'll have to log him as a UAM for the moment.'

The Americans would call him a John Doe. The London Met refers to an Unidentified Adult Male. It was still warm, but the night was pitch-black when the two detectives locked away the paper-work and saw they had time for a quick pint before going home.

A mile away, the neat man lay face up in the intensive care unit of the Royal London, breathing shallow but regular, pulse still too high, checked every now and then by the night sister.

Jack Burns took a long draught of his beer.

'Who the hell is he?' he complained to no-one in particular.

'Don't worry, guv, we'll find out soon enough,' said Luke Skinner. But he was wrong.

DAY TWO – WEDNESDAY

For DI Jack Burns it was a brutally busy day. It brought two triumphs, two disappointments and a host of still unanswered questions. But that was par

24

for the course. Rarely is a detective blessed with a case wrapped up like a Christmas parcel simply being delivered to his desk.

His first success was with Mr Patel. The shop-keeper was at the front desk on the dot of eleven, as eager to help as ever.

'I would like you to look at some photographs,' said Burns when they were seated in front of what looked like a TV screen. In his younger days the Criminal Records Office photos, known through-out the force as the mug shots, were contained in a large album, or several such, shielded behind plastic sheeting. Burns still preferred the old way, for the witness could flip forward and back until he had made his choice. But the process was now electronic, and the faces flashed up on the screen.

There were 100 to start with, and they covered some of the 'hard cases' known to the police in the immediate north-east quadrant of London. Not that 100 was the limit, not by a long way, but Burns began with a selection all known to the Dover nick. Mr Veejay Patel turned out to be a detective's dream.

As number 28 flashed up he said, 'That one.'

They were staring at a brutish face combining considerable stupidity with equal malevolence. Beefy, shorn skull, earring.

'You are sure? Never seen him before? Never been in your shop, for example?'

'No, not this one. But he was the one who took the blow to the nose.'

Mark Price, said the caption, and there was an identification number. At 77, Mr Patel got his second, the one with a long sallow face and lank hair falling to the ear lobes on each side. Harry Cornish. He had no doubt on either face and had not even paused for more than a second or two for any of the other faces. Burns closed the machine down. The CRO would come up with the full files on each man.

'When I have traced and arrested these men, I shall ask you to attend an identification parade,' said Burns. The shopkeeper nodded. He was willing. When he had gone, Luke Skinner remarked, 'Strewth, guv, we could do with a few more like him.'

While waiting for the CRO computer to come up with the full files on Price and Cornish, Jack Burns put his head round the corner of the CID squad room. The man he wanted was poring over a desk. More form-filling.

'Charlie, got a minute?'

Charlie Coulter was still a detective sergeant, but older than Burns, and he had been on the plot at Dover nick for fifteen years. When it came to local villains he knew them all.

'Those two?' he snorted. 'Right animals, Jack. Bags of form. Not local; moved in about three years ago. Mostly small, low-intelligence stuff. Bag-snatching, mugging, pilfering, brawling, football hooligans. Plus some actual bodily harm. Both done time. Why?'

'This time it's grievous bodily harm,' said Burns.

26

'Kicked some old man into a coma yesterday. Got an address for them?'

'Not offhand,' said Coulter. 'The last I heard they shared a squat somewhere off the High Road.'

'Not on the Grove?'

'Don't think so. That's not normally their patch. They must have been visiting, on the off chance.'

'Do they run with a gang?'

'Nope. Loners. They just hang around with each other.'

'Gay?'

'No record of it. Probably not. Cornish was done for an indecent assault. On a woman. It fell through. She changed her mind. Probably frightened off by Price.'

'Druggies?'

'Not known for it. Boozers, more like it. Pub brawls a speciality.'

At that point Coulter's phone rang and Burns left him alone. The CRO files came through and gave an address. Burns went to see his Chief Super, Alan Parfitt, and got permission for what he wanted. By two p.m. a magistrate had signed a search warrant for the named premises, two licensed officers had drawn sidearms from the armoury. Burns, Skinner and six others, one toting a door-rammer, made up the team of ten.

The raid was at three. The house was old and scrofulous, destined for demolition once the developer had acquired the entire row; in the interim, it was boarded up and services had been cut off.

The peeling door sustained one very perfunctory

knock, then the rammer splintered the lock and they were running up the stairs. The two thugs lived on the first floor up, in a pair of rooms that had never been much but were now a tip of considerable squalor. Neither man was at home. The two Armed Response officers holstered their guns and the search began.

The rummage team were looking for anything and everything. A wallet, former contents thereof, clothing, boots . . . They were not especially gentle. If the place had been a tawdry squat when they arrived, it was hardly home-sweet-home when they left. But they came up with only one trophy. Rolled up and tossed behind a shabby old sofa was a grubby T-shirt, its front crusted with blood. It was bagged and tagged. All other items of clothing went the same way. If forensic could find fibres on anything that must have come from the victim's clothing, that match would put the thugs on the spot, at the time, and in physical contact with the limping man.

While the searchers did their business, Burns and Skinner quartered the street. Most neighbours knew the two thugs by sight, none spoke favourably of them, mainly because of their habit of rolling home drunk and noisy in the small hours, and no-one knew where they were or might be in the middle of an August afternoon.

Back at the station Jack Burns started on the telephone. He asked for an 'all points' on the missing men, made one quick call with a simple enquiry to Mr Carl Bateman, the A and E surgeon at the Royal

28

London, and then rang around the A and E departments at three other hospitals. A junior doctor at the St Anne's Road hospital came up trumps.

'Gotcha,' shouted Burns as he put the phone down. There is a hunter instinct in a good detective, the knowledge of a nice adrenalin rush when the evidence is coming together. He turned to DS Skinner.

'Get down to St Anne's. Find a Dr Melrose in A and E. Get a full signed statement. Take a photo of Mark Price for identification. Get a photocopy of the accident log for the whole of yesterday afternoon. Then bring it all back here.'

'What happened?' asked Skinner, catching the mood.

'A man answering to Price's description wandered in there yesterday with a sore nose. Dr Melrose discovered it was broken in two places. When we find him, that hooter will be reset and heavily strapped. And Melrose will give us a firm ID.'

'When was this, guv?'

'Guess. Just on five p.m. yesterday afternoon.'

'Three hours after the punch in Paradise Way. We're going to get a result on this one.'

'Yes, lad, I think we are. Now get over there.'

While Skinner was away, Burns took a call from the sergeant who had led the POLSA team. It was disappointing. Before sundown the previous day they had scoured every inch of that estate on hands and knees. They had crawled into every nook and cranny, examined every passage and alley, culled

29

every patch of weary grass and every slick gutter. They had removed and emptied the only five public garbage cans they could find.

They had a collection of used condoms, dirty syringes and greasy food wrappings typical of such a place. But they had no blood and no wallet.

Cornish must have stuffed the stolen wallet into one of his own pockets until he could examine the prize at his leisure. Cash he would have taken and spent, the rest he would have thrown away somewhere, but not on the Meadowdene Grove estate. And he lived half a mile away. That was a big area, too many trash cans, too many alleys, too many builders' skips. It could be anywhere. It could, O blessed joy, still be in one of his pockets. Neither he nor Price would ever be contestants on *Mastermind*.

As for Price, stuffing his T-shirt over his bleeding nose must have kept the blood from falling to the pavement until he was well clear of the estate. Still, one superb eyewitness and the evidence of the broken nose at St Anne's just three hours after the punch was not bad for a day's work.

His next call was from Mr Bateman. That, too, was a slight disappointment, but not disastrous. His last call was a beauty. It came from DS Coulter, who had more snouts out in the territory than anyone else. A whisper down the line had told him Cornish and Price were playing pool at a hall in Dalston.

Luke Skinner was entering the front lobby as Burns came down the stairs. He had a complete statement from Dr Melrose, positive ID and a copy of the treatment log in which Price had identified himself under his true name. Burns told him to lock up the evidence and join him in the car.

The two thugs were still playing pool when the police arrived. Burns kept it short and businesslike. He had back-up in the form of a police van with six uniformed men who now protected all the doors. The other pool players just watched with the engaged curiosity of those not in trouble observing someone who is.

Price glared at Burns with piggy eyes flanking a broad band of plaster over the bridge of his nose.

'Mark Price, I am arresting you on suspicion of grievous bodily harm on an unidentified adult male at or about two twenty p.m. yesterday afternoon at Paradise Way, Edmonton. You do not have to say anything, but it may harm your defence if you do not mention when questioned something which you later rely on in court. Anything you do say may be given in evidence.'

Price shot a panicky glance at Cornish, who evidently passed for the brains of the outfit. Cornish gave a slight shake of his head.

'Piss off, filth,' said Price. He was spun around, cuffed and marched out. Two minutes later Cornish followed. Both went into the van with the six constables and the small cavalcade returned to Dover nick.

Procedures, always procedures. In the car on the way back, Burns asked for the FMO (force medical officer) to be summoned as a matter of emergency.

31

The last thing he needed was a later claim that police brutality had in any way contributed to that nose. Also, he needed a blood sample to compare with the blood on the T-shirt. If there was any of the victim's blood on that shirt, that would do it.

As he awaited the arrival of a blood sample from the man in the coma, he pondered the disappointing reply from Mr Bateman to his query concerning the right fist.

It was going to be a long night. Arrest had been at 7.15 p.m. That gave him twenty-four hours before either his chief superintendent gave him twelve further hours, or the local magistrates gave him a further twenty-four.

As arresting officer, he would have to fill out yet another report, signed and witnessed. He would need a sworn statement from the FMO that both men were fit enough to be questioned. He would need every stitch of their clothing and the contents of all pockets, plus blood samples for elimination.

Luke Skinner, watching like a hawk, had already made sure neither man jettisoned anything from their pockets as they were arrested and marched out of the pool hall and into the van. But no-one had been able to prevent Cornish telling the police constables that he wanted a lawyer, and fast. Until then, he was saying nothing. This message was not for the policemen; it was for his thick accomplice. And Price got the message, loud and clear.

The procedures took over an hour. Dusk was descending. The FMO departed, leaving behind his statement as to the fitness of both men to be questioned, and the state of Price's nose at the time of arrest.

Both thugs were lodged in separate cells, both dressed in paper one-piece overalls. Both had had a cup of tea and would later receive a canteen fry-up. By the book, always by the book.

Burns looked in on Price.

'I want a brief,' said Price. 'I ain't saying nothing.'

Cornish was the same. He just smiled and insisted on a lawyer.

The duty solicitor was Mr Lou Slade. He was disturbed over his supper, but insisted he wished to see his clients before turning in for the night. He arrived at Dover Street just before nine. He met both his new clients and spent half an hour closeted with them in an interview room.

'You can now conduct the interviews in my presence if you wish, Detective Inspector,' he said when he emerged. 'But I have to say my clients will make no statement. They deny the charge. They say they were nowhere near the place in question at the time in question.'

He was an experienced lawyer and had handled similar cases. He had got the measure of his clients and believed not a word, but he had a job to do.

'If you wish,' said Burns. 'But the case is very strong and building steadily. If they went for an admission, I might even believe the victim hit his head on the pavement as he fell. With their records . . . say, a couple of years in the Ville.' Pentonville was known locally as the 'Ville'.

Privately, Burns knew there were a score of kick

marks on the injured man, and Slade knew he knew.

'Stinking fish, Mr Burns. And I'm not buying. They intend to deny. I shall want all you have got under the disclosure rules.'

'In due course, Mr Slade. And I shall need any claim of alibi well in time. But you know the rules as well as I.'

'How long can you keep them?' asked Slade.

'Seven fifteen tomorrow night. Twelve hours extra from my super would not be enough. I'll almost certainly want an extension in custody from the magistrates tomorrow, around five p.m., the last hearing of the evening.'

'I shall not oppose,' said Slade. He knew not to try and waste time. These were two thugs and they had half-killed a man. The magistrates would extend the custody remand without a blink. 'As for your interviews, I suppose you will insist, even though on my advice they will say nothing.'

''Fraid so.'

'Then as I am sure we both have homes to go to, may I suggest nine tomorrow morning?'

It was agreed. Slade went home. Price and Cornish were locked up for the night. Burns had one last call to make. When he was connected to the Royal London he asked for the duty nurse in the ICU. The injured man might, just might, have come to.

Mr Paul Willis was also working late that night. He had operated on a young motorcyclist who seemed to have tried to break the land-speed record coming down Archway Hill. The neurosurgeon had done his best, but privately he gave the motorcycle rider a fifty-fifty chance of seeing out the week. He heard about Burns's call after the staff nurse had put the phone down.

The twenty-four hours since anaesthetic was administered had elapsed. With its effects gone, he would have hoped for the first signs of stirring. Before heading home he went to look again at the limping man.

There was no change. The monitors indicated a regular heartbeat, but the blood pressure was still too high, one of the signs of brain damage. On the Glasgow Scale the patient still hovered around 3 over 15, deep coma.

'I'll give it another thirty-six hours,' he told the staff nurse. 'I was hoping to get away this weekend, but I'll come in on Saturday morning. Unless there is a happy sign of recovery, in which case, not. Would you leave a note that I be informed of a change for the better, either here or at home? If there's no change by Saturday, nine a.m., I'll want a rescan. Please book it for me.'

The second day ended with Price and Cornish, stuffed with fried food, snoring ox-like in their cells at Dover Street nick. The victim lay on his back wired to three monitoring machines under a low blue light, locked into some faraway private world.

Mr Willis cast thoughts of patients from his mind for a while and watched an old Clint Eastwood spaghetti western in his elegant house in St John's Wood Terrace. DS Luke Skinner was just in time for a date with a very pretty drama student from the Hampstead School whom he had met in the crush bar at a Beethoven concert a month earlier. This was the sort of taste (Beethoven, not girls) that he emphatically did not discuss in the Dover nick canteen.

DI Jack Burns returned to rustle up some baked beans on toast in an otherwise empty house in Camden Town, wishing that Jenny and the boys would return from their holiday at Salcombe, in his native Devon, where he dearly wished he could have joined them. August, he thought, bloody August.

DAY THREE – THURSDAY

The interviews with Price and Cornish turned out to be useless. It was not Jack Burns's fault; he was a skilled and experienced interrogator. He took Price first, knowing him to be the more dense of the two. With Lou Slade sitting quietly by his client's side, Burns took the line of sweet reason.

'Look, Mark, we've got you bang to rights. There's a witness, saw it all. Everything. Start to finish. And he is going to testify.'

He waited. Nothing.

'For the tape, my client declines to make a statement,' murmured Slade.

'Then he hit you right on the nose, Mark. Broke your ruddy hooter. No wonder you lost your rag. Why on earth did an old guy like that do it?'

Price might have muttered, 'I dunno,' or, 'Stupid

old git.' That would have gone down well with the jury. Admission of presence at the scene. Bang goes any alibi. Price glared but stayed silent.

'Then there's your blood, Mark. Pouring out the broken nose. We've got samples, laddie.'

He was careful not to say he only had blood from the T-shirt, not the pavement, but he did not tell an untruth. Price shot a panicky glance at Slade, who also looked worried. Privately the lawyer knew that if samples of his client's blood, proved by DNA tests to be Price's blood and no-one else's, had been found on the pavement close to the beaten man, there would be no defence. But he still had time for a change of plea, if necessary. Under the disclosure rules, he would insist on everything Burns had got, and long before any trial. So he just shook his head, and Price's silence went on.

Burns gave each defendant an hour of his best efforts, then packed it in.

'I shall need to make an application for extension of police custody,' he told Slade when Price and Cornish were back in their cells. 'Four this afternoon?'

Slade nodded. He would be present, but say virtually nothing. There would be no point.

'And I am setting up two identity parades for tomorrow morning at St Anne's Road. If I get two results, I shall go for a formal charge and then a remand in custody,' he added. Slade nodded and left.

As he drove back to his office, the duty solicitor had little doubt this was not going to go his clients' way. Burns was good at his job: meticulous, thorough, not given to silly mistakes that the defence could exploit. He also thought privately that his clients were guilty as hell. He had seen their record sheets and so would the magistrates that afternoon. Whoever the mystery witness was, if he was a respectable person and stuck to his guns, Price and Cornish would not be seeing much daylight for a long time.

Years before, the police used to carry out identity parades inside the station. The new method was to have Identification Suites dotted at various places around the city. The nearest to Dover nick was in St Anne's Road, just down the pavement from the hospital where Dr Melrose worked and Price had had his nose attended to. It was a more efficient system. Each suite was equipped with the latest in parade platform, lighting and one-way mirrors through which the identification could be made without the chance that a real hard case could 'eyeball' the witness and terrify him into silence without a word being said. The suites also had an on-call panel of men and women of different sizes and aspects to make up the parade at short notice. These volunteers were paid £15 to appear, stand in line and then walk out again. Burns asked for two parades, giving careful descriptions of his prisoners, for eleven a.m. the next day.

Luke Skinner was left to handle the media, to whom Burns had a deep aversion. Anyway, the DS did it better. He was that fairly rare phenomenon, the public-school-educated policeman, with a polish much mocked in the canteen, but very useful on occasion.

All press enquiries had to funnel through Scotland Yard, which had an entire bureau dedicated to public affairs, and they had asked for a brief statement. It was still a low-interest case, but apart from a serious wounding there was also a missing-person angle. Skinner's problem was that he had no good description and certainly no picture, because the injured man was simply unsketchable with his bloated head swathed in bandage.

So Skinner would simply appeal for anyone who had gone missing from home or work in the Tottenham/Edmonton area the previous Tuesday and had not been seen since. A man who walked with a pronounced limp, between fifty and fifty-five, short grey hair, medium height, medium build. August was a thin month for news; the media might carry the item, but not intensively.

Nevertheless, there was one paper that might give the item a good run and he had a contact on it. He had lunch with the reporter on the *Edmonton and Tottenham Express*, the local rag that covered the whole area of the Dover Street nick. The reporter took notes and promised to do what he could.

The civil courts may go into recess for a long vacation in the summer, but the network of criminal courts never ceases to labour. Over 90 per cent of lawbreaking is handled by the magistrates' courts and the processes of the law have much to go on seven days a week and every week in the year. Much of the day-to-day work is carried out by lay magistrates who take no pay but work as a civic duty. They handle the mass of minor offences – traffic violations, issuing of warrants for arrest or search, drinking-licence extensions, minor theft, affray. And the granting of extensions to police custody or remands to prison to await trial. If a serious case comes before the magistrates' court, it is the modern custom for a paid stipendiary magistrate, a qualified lawyer, to take the bench, sitting alone.

That afternoon, Court No. 3 at the Highbury Corner court was in the charge of three lay magistrates, chaired by Mr Henry Spellar, a retired headmaster. The issue was so simple it took but a few seconds.

When it was over, Price and Cornish were led away and driven back to Dover Street. Burns reported to Detective Superintendent Parfitt.

'How's it going, Jack?' asked the head of the whole CID branch at Dover Street.

'Frustrating, sir. It started fast and well, with an excellent witness who saw it all. Start to finish. Respectable shopkeeper across the road. Good citizen. No hesitation at ID and prepared to testify. I am short of the missing wallet taken from the victim. Plus forensics linking Price and Cornish to the time and the place. I've got Price's broken nose and the treatment of that nose in St Anne's just three hours later. It tallies perfectly with the eye-witness statement.'

'So what is holding you?'

'I need the wallet, linkage to the thugs; I need forensics to hurry up, and I'd like to ID the victim. He's still a UAM.'

'Are you going to charge them?'

'If Mr Patel picks them out of the line tomorrow, yes, sir. They mustn't walk on this one. They're both guilty as hell.'

Alan Parfitt nodded.

'All right, Jack. I'll try and chivvy forensics. Keep me and the CPS informed.'

At the Royal London dusk fell again but the man in ICU did not see it. It had been forty-eight hours since the operation; the effects of the anaesthetics were long gone, but he did not flicker. He was still far away in his own world.

DAY FOUR – FRIDAY

The newspaper came out and it had given Luke Skinner a good spread. The story was the second lead, front page. The reporter took the angle: Limping Mystery Man – Who Is He? Police Ask. There was a description of the assault and reference to two local men who were 'helping the police with their inquiries'. This is one of those much-used phrases comparable with hospital bulletins that describe people in absolute agony as being 'comfortable'. It means the opposite and everyone knows it.

The reporter gave a good description of the victim, his height, build, short grey hair and that giveaway limp, then ended with a query in bold capital letters: DID ANYONE SEE THE LIMPING MAN? DS Skinner grabbed a copy and took it to his canteen breakfast. He was pleased with the coverage. A small sidebar mentioned the renewal of custody and a further twenty-four hours.

At eleven, Price and Cornish were taken by van to the St Anne's Road ID suite. Burns and Skinner followed, with Mr Patel. There were two parades, each with the suspect and eight others of roughly similar appearance. Due to the state of Price's nose, the other eight burly men in his parade had a strip of plaster across the bridge.

Mr Patel did not hesitate. Within twenty minutes he had positively identified both men and again confirmed he would testify to what he had said in his statement. Burns was happy. Neither thug had seen him, neither ran with a gang; with luck Mr Patel would remain unintimidated.

They drove him back to his shop. The volunteers were paid and left. Price and Cornish were restored to the cells where Burns intended to charge them formally when he returned.

He and Skinner were entering the nick to do precisely that when the desk sergeant called out.

'Jack, there was a call for you.' He studied a notepad. 'A Miss Armitage. A florist.'

Burns was puzzled. He had ordered no flowers. On the other hand, Jenny was returning in another week. A bunch of flowers might help with the romantic side of things. Good idea.

'Something about a limping man,' said the sergeant.

42

Burns took the address and went back to the car with Skinner.

The Misses Armitage, twin sisters of many summers, ran a small flower shop on the Upper High Road. Half of their wares were inside the shop, half displayed on the pavement. The latter blooms fought a battle for survival with the billowing clouds of fumes from the juggernauts heading south towards Highbury or north to the industrial Midlands.

'It might be the man,' said Miss Verity Armitage. 'He seems to answer the description. You did say Tuesday morning, did you not?'

DI Burns assured her that Tuesday morning would have been about right.

'He bought a bunch of flowers. Not an expensive one, in fact about the cheapest in the shop. Oxeye daisies, half a dozen. From his appearance he did not have much money, poor dear. And the paper says he has been injured.'

'Badly hurt, ma'am. He cannot speak. He is in a coma. How did he pay?'

'Oh, cash.'

'In coins, from his trouser pocket?'

'No. He produced a five-pound note. From a wallet. I recall that he dropped it and I picked it up for him because of his leg.'

'What kind of wallet?'

'Cheap. Plastic. Black. And then I gave it back to him.'

'Did you see where he put it?'

'In his pocket. Jacket pocket. Inside.'

'Could you show me a bunch of oxeye daisies?'

They lunched back at the Dover Street canteen. Burns was glum, disappointed. A credit card would have left a record: name, and from the credit company an address or a bank account. Anything. But cash . . .

'What would you do, on an afternoon in August, with a bunch of flowers?' he asked Skinner.

'Take it to a girlfriend? Give it to your mum?'

Both men pushed their plates aside and frowned over the mugs of tea.

'Sir?'

The voice was timorous and came from further down the long table. It was from a WPC, very young, just arrived from training school. Jack Burns looked down the table.

'Mmm?'

'It's just an idea. Are you talking about the limping man?'

'Yes. And I could use a good idea. What's yours?'

She blushed a fetching pink. Very new PCs do not usually interrupt detective inspectors.

'If he was walking where he was, sir, he would have been heading for the High Road five hundred yards ahead. And the buses. But five hundred yards behind him is the cemetery.'

Burns put down his mug.

'What are you doing now?' he asked the girl.

'Sorting files, sir.'

'That can wait. We're going to look at a cemetery. Come along.'

Skinner drove, as usual. The WPC, who came

44

from the borough, directed. It was a big cemetery, hundreds of graves, in rows. Council owned and ill maintained. They started at one corner and began to patrol, taking a row of headstones each. It took nearly an hour. The girl found it first.

They were withered, of course, but they were oxeye daisies, dying in a jam jar of stale water. The headstone indicated that it covered the earthly remains of Mavis June Hall. There was a date of birth, the date of death and the letters RIP. She had been dead twenty years and even then she would have been seventy.

'Look at the date of birth, guv. August 1906. Last Tuesday was her birthday.'

'But who the hell was she to the limping man?'

'His mum, perhaps.'

'Maybe. So perhaps his name is Hall,' said Burns.

They drove back past the Armitage flower shop and Miss Verity identified the daisies as almost certainly hers. At the Dover nick, Skinner contacted the Missing Persons Bureau for the name Hall. There were three, but two were women and one a child.

'Someone must have known this bugger. Why don't they report him missing?' fumed Burns. It was getting to be one frustration after another.

The pretty and bright WPC went back to her files. Burns and Skinner went down to the cells where Price and Cornish were formally charged with inflicting grievous bodily harm on an unidentified adult male. At quarter to four they set off for Highbury Corner, where the chief clerk had exceptionally managed to find a last-minute slot in the sitting schedule. This time, the two thugs would not be returning to Dover Street. Burns intended that they should be lodged in a real prison on a week's remand, probably Pentonville.

Things had changed at the court. They were in Number 1 this time, where the prisoner's dock is dead centre, facing the bench, rather than in one corner. The magistrate was now a stipendiary, or 'stipe', in the form of the experienced and highly qualified Mr Jonathan Stein.

Price and Cornish arrived by police van again, but another van in the livery of HM Prison Service was on standby to take them to jail. Mr Lou Slade was at his table facing the bench, but for the CPS a young barrister would make the remand submission.

Years ago, it was the police who handled their own prosecutions up to and through the magistrates' courts and many old-timers preferred it that way. But for a long time all prosecutions have been handled from the first appearance to the final trial, if any, by the unified structure of the Crown Prosecution Service. Among their tasks is to assess whether a police-prepared case has a realistic chance of a conviction before a judge and jury. If the CPS thinks not, the case is withdrawn. More than one disgruntled detective, seeing a case on which he has worked long and hard against a real villain withdrawn from the lists, has referred to the CPS as the Criminal Protection Service. It is not always a happy relationship.

A big problem with the CPS is that it is under-funded, overstretched and pays in peanuts. As a predictable result, it is sometimes regarded as a mere stepping stone for the young and inexperienced before they move into private practice and on to better things.

Miss Prabani Sundaran was very bright and very pretty, the apple of her Sri Lankan-born parents' eye. She was also on her first major case. But this should not have been a problem.

The remand in custody was going to be a formality. There was no way Mr Stein was going to grant bail to Price and Cornish. Their records for violence were appalling and he had them in front of him. Remands can only last for a week, so there would be several more yet to come before the defence was chosen, engaged, prepared and ready. Then would come the process of committal, when the prosecution evidence would be produced in full and the magistrate would commit the thugs for trial at the Crown Court, complete with judge and jury. By then, Miss Sundaran would be assisting a full-fledged Treasury Counsel, possibly even a Queen's Counsel, who would be engaged by the CPS to try to achieve a conviction. All she had to do was go through the motions. The procedures, just the procedures.

At a nod from Mr Stein she rose and, reading from her notes, gave the briefest outline of the charge. Slade rose.

'My clients will deny the charge and in due course will enter a full defence,' he said.

'We seek a remand in custody for one week, sir,' said Miss Sundaran.

'Mr Slade?' The stipe was asking if Mr Slade intended to ask for bail. Slade shook his head. Mr Stein gave a wintry smile.

'Very wise. Remanded in custody for one week. I shall . . .' He peered at both lawyers over his half-moons. 'Put this down to be heard before me next Friday morning.'

The entire court knew perfectly well that he meant he would listen to, and grant, a further remand in custody for another week, and so on until both prosecution and defence were ready for committal to Crown Court.

Price and Cornish, still handcuffed but now flanked by prison officers, disappeared below decks in the direction of the Ville. Mr Slade went back to his office knowing that by Monday morning he would have an answer to his application for Legal Aid. His clients clearly had no assets with which to pay for their own defence, and he would have to try to find a barrister from one of the four Inns of Court to take the case for pretty small pickings.

He already had in mind a couple of chambers whose all-powerful chief clerks would consider it, but he knew he would probably get a freshly qualified sprog who needed the experience or an old blowhard who needed the fee. No matter. In an increasingly violent world a GBH does not set the Thames on fire.

Jack Burns returned to Dover Street. His desk

was full. He still had a huge workload, now forming a backlog. And on the matter of the limping man he had some problems to solve.

DAY FIVE — SATURDAY

Mr Paul Willis came in at nine a.m. on the Saturday as promised. There had been no change in his patient and he was becoming worried. The rescan was quickly effected and the surgeon studied the results acutely.

There was certainly no fresh haematoma to account for the continuing coma. The blood vessels he had tied off remained leak-proof. No blood was pressing on the brain. It had expanded quickly to its full and usual size. No fresh leaks had developed to create pressure from a different source.

And yet, intra-cranial pressure remained too high, and blood pressure was the same. He began to fear the neurosurgeon's nightmare. If there had been catastrophic and diffuse axonal injury inflicted by those kicks, it would not show up, even on the scan. But if the brain stem or cortex was damaged beyond self-repair, the man would remain in a permanent vegetative state until the life-support system was switched off, or he would simply die. He resolved to do brain-stem tests after the weekend. Meanwhile, his wife was much looking forward to the lunch party in Oxfordshire with the people they had met in Corfu and she was waiting downstairs in the car. He looked down at his patient once again and left.

The adoo were coming out of the dead ground near the old stone fort and there were scores of them. He had seen them before on his tour with B Squadron in this bitter and secret war, but they had been distant figures against the dun brown hills and appearing in ones and twos. This was a full-scale mass attack and the fanatical bastards were swarming everywhere.

There were only ten of them, him and his mates; plus about fifty mixed askaris from the north, local gendarmes and some levies, the untrained and wild-firing firgas. Among his mob there were two 'Ruperts', two sergeants, a lance corporal and five troopers. He put the adoo already at over 200 and they were coming from all sides.

Lying flat on the roof of the Batthouse, he squinted down the sights of his SLR and slotted three adoo before they even knew where the fire was coming from. Not surprising, the roar of mortars and shells, the chatter of small arms was unremitting.

Had it not been for that single shot as the rebs swept over the outpost at Jebel Ali an hour earlier, they would have been finished already. The alert had given them a few minutes to take position before the first wave of attackers swept towards the wire. As it was, sheer numbers were moving the situation from piss-poor to desperate.

Down below, he could see the body of an askari face down on the muddy track that passed for Main Street. Captain Mike was still trying to cover the

400 yards to where Corporal Labalaba, the fiercely brave Fijian with half his jaw shot away, was firing the obsolete 25-pounder field gun over open sites at point-blank range into the oncoming waves of tribesmen.

Two keffiyeh-covered heads came out from behind the DG fort to his right, so he blew them both off. Three more came over the low ridge to his left. They were trying to drop the ducking and dodging captain in the open ground. He gave them the rest of his magazine, slotted one and discouraged the other two.

He rolled over to change magazines and a bloody great rocket from a Carl Gustav screamed over his head. Ten inches lower and he would have been hamburger steak. Below the rafters on which he lay, he could hear his own 'Rupert' on the radio to base, asking for a Strikemaster hit and to hell with the low cloud. With a new magazine, he caught another couple of adoo in the open and dropped them both before they could get Captain Mike, who had just disappeared into the gunpit with Medical Orderly Tobin to try to help the two Fijians.

He could not know then, but would learn later, that the fearless Labalaba had just taken a second bullet, this time through the forehead and was dead; nor that Tobin was mortally wounded just after patching up Trooper Ti, who had taken three bullets but would still somehow live. By luck, he saw the terrorist who was manning the Carl Gustav that had nearly killed him. The adoo was between two hummocks of sand just by the torn and sagging

51

perimeter wire. With precision, he put a nice cupro-nickel-jacketed 7.62 NATO round straight through his throat. The Carl Gustav went silent, but the numbing blasts from the mortars and one remaining 75mm recoilless rifle the adoo were using went on.

At last, somehow, the Strikemasters came, racing in off the sea below cloud no more than 100 feet up. Bombs and strafing finally broke the will of the adoo to carry on. The attack wavered and then fell apart. They began to run, carrying their wounded and most of their dead with them. Later he would learn that he and his mates had fought off between 300 and 400 of them, and sent about a 100 to paradise.

Lying on his roof as the firing died, he began to laugh with relief and wondered what Auntie May would think of him now.

In the ICU unit of the Royal London, the limping man was still far, far away.

DAY SIX – SUNDAY

Jack Burns was a man of simple pleasures and one of them was his Sunday morning lie-in. That day he did not get it. The phone rang at seven fifteen. It was the desk sergeant at Dover nick.

'There's a man just come in here who takes his dog for a walk early in the morning,' said the sergeant.

Burns wondered blearily just how long, if he really put his mind to it, it would take to strangle the sergeant.

52

'He's clutching a wallet,' said the sergeant. 'Says his dog found it on waste ground, about half a mile from the housing estate.'

Burns came awake fast. 'Cheap, plastic, black?'

'You've seen it?'

'Keep him there. Do not let him leave. I'll be there in twenty minutes.'

The dog-walker was a pensioner, Mr Robert Whittaker, upright and neat, nursing a cup of tea in one of the interview rooms.

Mr Whittaker gave and signed his statement, then left. Burns called the POLSA team and asked the grumpy team leader for an inch-by-inch search of the half-acre of waste ground. He wanted his report by sundown. It had not rained for four days but the sky looked heavy and grey; he did not want any wallet contents degraded by a good soaking.

Finally he studied the wallet. He could see slight indentations made by the dog's teeth, a slick of canine saliva. But what else might it yield? With tweezers, he lifted it into a plastic evidence bag and called Fingerprints. Yes, I know it is a Sunday, he said again, but this is a rush job.

During the day the searchers filled eight binliners of rubbish from the patch of waste ground and sere grass alongside Mandela Road and the examination of it lasted into the night.

But nothing turned up that could have come from the wallet which, as Mr Whittaker had stated and Burns had confirmed, was completely empty.

He lay huddled and fearful in the near darkness, a single flickering night light at the end of the room casting strange moving shadows towards the ceiling. Down the length of the orphanage dormitory he could hear the other boys murmuring in sleep and occasionally a whimper from a bad dream. He did not know where he would go, what he would become, now that Mum and Dad were gone. He only knew that he was alone and frightened in this new environment.

He might have dozed but he came awake again when the door opened, and there was an oblong of light from the passage outside. Then she was bending over him, gentle hands tucking the sheet and blankets tighter round him, soothing his sweat-damp hair back from his face.

'Now, now, lad. Not asleep yet? Now, you go to sleep like a good boy, and God and all his angels will look after you until Auntie May comes back in the morning.'

Thus comforted, he slipped away into the long, warm darkness of the endless night.

It was the duty staff at the ICU in the Royal London. She had tried the Dover nick, but Burns had earlier given the ICU his personal number for emergency calls.

'DI Burns? Royal London. I am sorry to have to inform you that the patient you were interested in – the unidentified man in intensive care – he died at ten past six this morning.'

Jack Burns put down the phone facing another full day. He now had a murder case. At least it would go straight up the priority ladder. There would be a post-mortem and he would have to attend it. The two animals in the Ville would have to be brought back to Highbury and recharged.

That meant that the Clerk to the Magistrates would have to be informed, and the defending solicitor, Lou Slade. Procedures, more procedures, but they had to be done and done right. There could be no question of Price and Cornish walking away on a technicality discovered by a clever-dick lawyer. Burns wanted them inside grey stone walls for years and years to come.

The Royal London has its own small mortuary and pathology department, and it was here that the PM took place at midday. It was conducted by Home Office pathologist Mr Laurence Hamilton.

Odd birds, forensic pathologists, was Burns's private opinion. They did a job that disgusted him. Some were effulgently cheerful, given to light banter as they cut and sawed a body into bits. Others were more professorial, regarding what they found with boyish enthusiasm, as a lepidopterist finding an amazing new butterfly. Others were dour and spoke in monosyllables. Mr Hamilton was of the first variety. For him, life could not be better nor his job more wonderful.

Jack Burns had attended several in his career, but the smell of ether and formaldehyde almost always made him gag. When the disc saw bit into the skull he turned away and looked at the charts on the wall.

'Good Lord, he's taken a beating,' said Hamilton as they surveyed the pale and bruise-covered body lying face up on the slab.

'Kicked to death. Last Tuesday,' said Burns. 'Just took him six days to die.'

'Unfortunately "death by kicking" is not quite the result I shall have to produce,' said Hamilton genially. He began to cut, dictating what he found to his theatre sister and the microphone linked to a tape recorder that she held out to him as he moved around the table.

It took a good hour. There was a lot of damage and Mr Hamilton spent time on the old wound, the right femur and hip shattered long ago, held together with steel pins, which had caused the man to limp for the rest of his life.

'Looks as if he was hit by a truck,' said Hamilton. 'Terrific damage.' He pointed out the scars where the bones had come through the flesh and the neater one where the surgeon had opened the victim to get access to the damage.

Everything else, and there was much, stemmed from the previous Tuesday: crunched left hand, stamped into the pavement, smashed front teeth, three cracked ribs, broken cheekbone. Burns checked the right fist, but Carl Bateman had been right. There was no damage. Puzzling.

'Cause of death?' he asked at length.

'Well, Mr Burns, it will all be in my official report.' Of course. He would be a major prosecution witness at the trial. 'But between you and me, massive axonal damage to the brain. The neurosurgeon did all he could, but he would not have seen this. It doesn't show on a scan. Assisted by general trauma due to multiple injuries which, though not individually life-threatening, would have had a collective effect. I'll put him back together for the relatives. Are there relatives?'

'I don't know,' said Burns. 'I don't even know who he was.'

He spent the afternoon covering all the formalities for the next day: the Clerk to the Magistrates, Pentonville Prison. Lou Slade was suitably regretful. His Legal Aid had come through and he had spent the morning trying to find a barrister to take the case. Like Burns, he had run into the August syndrome; half the people he rang were away. But he thought he had a young junior from King's Bench Walk who would take it. At least with a murder he would now excite more interest. It is an ill wind . . .

'I still have to defend them,' he said.

'Don't try too hard, Mr Slade,' said Burns and put the phone down.

There was bad news in the afternoon, but it was superseded by the good news. Chivvied by Detective Chief Superintendent Parfitt to hurry up, forensics came back with their results. There was nothing in the way of blood or fibre samples on the clothes of Price and Cornish to link them physically with the dead man. The blood on the T-shirt was uniquely from one source, and that was its owner, Price.

Burns was philosophical. If the men had wrestled

57

body to body there would have been fibre traces passing from fabric to fabric. Price and Cornish would have been too stupid to be aware of the extraordinary advances in forensic technology of the past twenty years. Clues showed up nowadays that could never have been seen when Burns was a copper on the beat at Paignton.

But the limping man had been felled by a punch and a kick behind the knee. On the ground only toecaps had hammered into his body and after twenty-four hours the boots removed from Price and Cornish had been scuffed and dust-covered by a day's extra use, and yielded nothing that would stand up in court.

But the call from Fingerprints made up for it all. There was the dog saliva and three sets of prints. One matched those of the dead man, clearly the owner of the wallet. One set matched those of Mr Whittaker, who had dutifully agreed to have his prints taken after making his statement. The third set were those of Harry Cornish. Burns was so excited that he stood up, phone in hand.

'You're sure? No chance of error?'

'Jack, I need sixteen points of similarity for a perfect match. I've got twenty-one. It's over a hundred per cent.'

The technician from Fingerprints would also be a crucial trial witness. Burns thanked him and put the phone down.

'Gotcha, you bastard,' he told the potted plant.

There was still one remaining problem and it nagged him. Who was the dead man? What brought him to Edmonton? Was it just to put cheap flowers on the grave of a woman long dead? Did he have family, perhaps away at the coast like his own Jenny? Did he have a job and colleagues? Why had no-one noticed him missing? How could he deliver such a smashing blow to Price's nose and sustain no bruising to the knuckles? And why did he fight back at all, for a miserable wallet with at most a few notes in it?

It was Luke Skinner who came up with an idea.

'The first constable who reached the scene. He bent over the man and saw his face before it began to swell. And the first paramedic, the one who tended him on the pavement and in the ambulance. If we put them together with a police artist . . .?'

Burns traced the paramedic through the London Ambulance Service and the man, hearing his patient had died, agreed to help. He was on an early shift the next day, but could be free after two p.m. and would happily give his time.

The police constable was right there in Dover Street station and was traced through the duty roster and incidents log. A skilled police sketch artist agreed to come up from Scotland Yard the next day at two.

Burns finished his day in a long tactics session with Alan Parfitt. The chief of detectives examined every scrap of evidence Burns laid before him and finally agreed.

'We can get a result here, sir. We have the evidence of Mr Patel, two identifications of the men by Patel, the blow to the nose, the repair three hours later by Dr Melrose and the wallet. We can send them down for life.'

'Yes, I think we can,' said Parfitt. 'I'll back you. I'll be seeing a senior bod at the CPS tomorrow and I think I can persuade him that this one will go all the way.'

There were statements, statements and more statements. The file was two inches thick. The full reports from the post-mortem and the fingerprints department had yet to come in and be added. But both men agreed it was a 'go' and Parfitt was sure he could persuade the CPS of the same.

DAY EIGHT — TUESDAY

Price and Cornish were back in the dock at Number 1 court, Highbury Corner the next day and Mr Stein presided. Miss Sundaran represented the Crown, and her parents beamed with pride behind the glass panel shielding the public gallery as she handled her first murder case. Mr Slade looked somewhat glum.

Mr Stein kept it short and efficient. The clerk read out the new charge, murder, and Mr Slade rose to say again that his clients denied the charge and reserved their defence. Mr Stein raised an eyebrow at Miss Sundaran, who asked for a new remand in custody for one week.

'Mr Slade?' he asked.

'No application for bail, sir.'

'Then granted, Miss Sundaran. Hearing is set for next Tuesday at eleven a.m. Take them down.'

Price and Cornish were led away to the prison van. Miss Sundaran now had the entire file and was pleased with what she had. Back at her office she had been told that this would almost certainly go to trial and that she would be involved. Hopefully the file would be passed by the CPS to Mr Slade in the next twenty-four hours. Then preparation for the defence could begin.

'Some ruddy defence,' thought Slade, even this early in the case. 'I'm going to need a genius in a wig to get them off this one.'

The sketching session went well. The paramedic and the constable agreed on the approximate appearance of the man on the pavement a week earlier and the artist went to work. It was a team effort. The artist sketched, erased, sketched again. A face came into view. The cast of the eyes, the short-back-and-sides grey hair, the line of the jaw. Both men had seen the man only with his eyes closed. The artist opened the eyes and a man was looking at them, a man that once was, now battered and sawn meat in a refrigerated drawer.

Luke Skinner took over. He had a senior contact in the Scotland Yard press office and he wanted a spread in the *Evening Standard* for the following day. The pair of them met the chief crime correspondent later that evening. They all knew August was the 'silly season'. News was thin. This was a story. The crime correspondent took it. He could see his headline. 'BEATEN TO DEATH. DID YOU KNOW HIM?' There would be a panel to accompany the sketch, with a full description, stressing the once-shattered right leg and hip, the pronounced limp. It was, Skinner knew, about as good as they were going to get, and the last chance.

DAY NINE – WEDNESDAY

The *Evening Standard* is London's only evening newspaper and covers the capital and most of the South-East pretty intensively. Skinner was lucky. News through the night had been exceptionally light, so the *Standard* ran the sketch of the staring man on the front page. 'DID YOU KNOW THIS MAN?' asked the headline above it, then came a note to turn to more details inside.

The panel gave approximate age, height, build, hair and eye colour, clothes worn at the time of the attack, the belief that the man had been visiting the local cemetery to place flowers on the grave of one Mavis Hall and was walking back to the bus route when he was attacked. The clincher was the detail of the leg shattered about twenty years earlier and the limp.

Burns and Skinner waited hopefully through the day, but no-one called. Nor the next, nor the next. Hope faded.

A brief coroner's court was formally opened and immediately adjourned. The coroner declined to grant the borough the right to bury in an unmarked grave, lest someone might yet come forward.

'It's odd and very sad, guv,' said Skinner to Burns as they walked back to the nick. 'You can live in a bloody great city like London, with millions of people all around you, but if you keep yourself to yourself, as he must have done, no-one even knows you exist.'

'Someone must,' said Burns, 'some colleague, some neighbour. Probably away. August, bloody August.'

DAY TEN – THURSDAY

The Hon. James Vansittart QC stood in the window bay of his chambers and gazed out across the gardens towards the Thames. He was fifty-two and one of the most notable and successful barristers at the London Bar. He had taken silk, become a Queen's Counsel, at the remarkably early age of forty-three, even more unusual in that he had only been at the bar for a total of eighteen years. But fortune and his own skill had favoured him. Ten years earlier, acting as junior for a much older QC who had been taken ill during a case, he had pleased the judge, who did not wish to abandon the case and start again, by agreeing to proceed without his leader. The senior QC's chambers had taken a gamble, but it paid off with a triumphant acquittal of the defendant. The Bar agreed it was Vansittart's forensic skill and oratory that had turned the jury, and the later evidence that showed the defendant was not guilty did no harm.

The following year, Vansittart's application for silk had met little opposition from the Lord Chancellor's office, which was then in the hands of a Conservative government. His father, the Earl of

63

Essendon, being a Tory whip in the House of Lords, was probably not unhelpful either. It was generally thought at the Bar and the clubs of St James's that the second son of Johnny Essendon was the right stuff. Clever, too, but that could not be helped.

Vansittart turned from the window, walked to his desk and pressed the intercom for his chief clerk. Michael 'Mike' Creedy ran the affairs of the thirty barristers in these chambers with oiled precision and had done so for twenty years. He had spotted the young Vansittart shortly after he came to the bar and had persuaded his then head of chambers to invite the young man to join. His judgement had not been wrong; fifteen years later the former new junior had become deputy head of chambers and a star in the legal firmament. A charming and talented portrait-painting wife, a manor in Berkshire and two boys at Harrow completed a pretty successful picture. The door opened and Mike Creedy entered the elegant, book-panelled room.

'Mike, you know I seldom take Legal Aid cases?'

'Seldom is good enough for me, sir.'

'But now and again? Once a year, say? Sort of paying one's dues, good for the image?'

'Once a year is a good average. No need to over-egg the pudding, Mr Vee.'

Vansittart laughed. Creedy was in charge of the finances and though this was a very wealthy set of chambers, he hated to see 'his' barristers taking peanuts for a Legal Aid brief. Still, whims are whims and have to be indulged. But not too often.

'You have something in mind?'

'I'm told there is a case at Highbury Corner. Two young men accused of mugging and killing a pedestrian. They claim they didn't do it. Could even be true. The names are Price and Cornish. Could you find out who their solicitor is and ask him to take my call?'

An hour later Lou Slade sat and stared at the telephone as if it had suddenly turned into gold studded with diamonds.

'Vansittart?' he whispered. 'James bloody Vansittart?'

Then he collected himself and readdressed the phone, at the other end of which was Mike Creedy.

'Yes, indeed. Well, I am most honoured. And surprised, I admit. Yes, I'll hold on.'

Seconds later the call was transferred and the QC came on.

'Mr Slade, how good of you to take my call.'

The voice was easy, confident, courteous and beautifully modulated. Eton, maybe Harrow, oh and Guards, thought Slade.

It was a brief talk, but covered all that needed to be. Slade would be delighted to instruct Mr Vansittart in the matter of Regina versus Price and Cornish. Yes, he had the prosecution file, it had arrived that very morning and he would be happy to come to the Temple for a first tactical discussion with his clients' new barrister. The meeting was fixed for two p.m.

Vansittart turned out to be all Slade had expected: urbane, charming and courteous, plying his guest with tea in bone china and, spotting a slight yellow stain on the two first fingers of the right hand, offering a silver box of Balkan Sobranie. Slade lit up gratefully. A good East End lad, these bastards made him nervous. Vansittart looked at the file, but did not open it.

'Tell me, Mr Slade, how do you see this case? Just run over it for me.'

Not unnaturally, Slade was flattered. It had already been quite a day. He ran over the events of the past eight days, since he had been called to the Dover Street nick while eating his supper.

'So, it would seem that Mr Patel is the key and yet only witness,' said Vansittart when he had finished. 'The rest is forensic or circumstantial. And it's all in here?'

'Yes, it's all there.'

Slade had had one hour in his office and a further hour in the taxi to flick through the CPS file, but it had just been enough.

'But I think it is pretty strong. And the clients have no alibi except each other. They claim they were either in bed at their squat or mooching around the streets together.'

Vansittart rose, forcing Slade to put down his half-drunk cup and stub out his butt before doing the same.

'It's been more than kind of you to come personally,' said Vansittart as he ushered Slade to the door, 'but I always feel that if we are going to work together an early personal meeting is best. And I am grateful for your advice.'

He said that he intended to read the entire file

that evening and would call Slade in his office the next day. Slade explained that he had court work all morning, so the call was fixed for three p.m.

DAY ELEVEN — FRIDAY

The call was precisely at three.

'An interesting case, Mr Slade, wouldn't you say? Strong, but not, perhaps, impregnable.'

'Strong enough, if the witness statement of Mr Patel holds up, Mr Vansittart.'

'Precisely my conclusion. Tell me, have our clients offered any explanation for either the prints on the wallet or the treating of the broken nose just three hours after the mugging?'

'No. They just keep repeating "Dunno" and "Can't remember". They are not all that bright.'

'Ah well, can't be helped. But I think we do need a couple of reasonable explanations. I feel our first consultation is in order. I would like to see them at the Ville.'

Slade was jolted. This was damned quick.

'I am afraid I am in court all day on Monday,' he said. 'Tuesday is the further remand in custody. We could see them in the interview room at Highbury Corner before they are taken away.'

'Y-e-e-e-s. I had hoped to make an intervention on Tuesday. Better if I could know the nature of the ground under my feet before then. I hate to interfere with a chap's weekend, but would tomorrow suit?'

Slade was jolted again. Intervention? He had no

idea a high-flying QC would even want to be present for a formal renewal of remand in custody. The meeting at Pentonville Jail was agreed for ten o'clock the next day. Slade would make the arrangement with the prison authorities.

DAY TWELVE — SATURDAY

There must have been some confusion. Mr Vansittart was at the prison at a quarter to nine. To the prison officer at visitor reception he was polite but insistent. The appointment was for nine o'clock, not ten, and he was a busy man. The solicitor would doubtless come along later. After conferring with higher authority, the man asked a colleague to show the barrister to an interview room. At five after nine the two prisoners were shown in. They glowered at the lawyer. He was not fazed.

'I'm sorry Mr Slade is a bit late,' he said. 'But no doubt he will be along later. Meanwhile, my name is James Vansittart and I am your defending barrister. Do sit down.'

The escorting warder left the room. Both men sat across the table from Vansittart. He took his seat and produced the prosecution file. Then he flicked a packet of cigarettes and a book of matches across the table. Both men lit up greedily. Cornish pocketed the pack. Vansittart gave them a genial smile.

'Now you two young men have got yourselves in a bit of trouble here.'

He flicked through the file as they both watched him through a haze of smoke.

'Mr Cornish . . .' he glanced up at the lank-haired Harry Cornish, 'one of our problems is the wallet. Apparently it was found last Sunday morning by a dog-walker, lying in waste ground, deep in the grass, just over the fence from Mandela Road. No question it belonged to the dead man; it had his prints on it. Unfortunately, it also had yours.'

'Dunno,' said Cornish.

'No, well, memory fades when you are busy. But there has to be an innocent explanation. Now, I suppose you are going to tell me that on the Wednesday morning, the day after the attack, you were walking along Mandela Road to get some lunch at a caff when you saw a wallet lying in the gutter?'

Cornish may have been the brains of the outfit, but he was not really clever, just sly. Nonetheless, something gleamed in his eyes.

'Yeh,' he agreed, 'thass wot 'appened.'

'And if that is what you wish to tell me, then as your brief I shall, of course, believe it. And no doubt your version is that, as anyone would naturally be, you were curious to see a wallet in the gutter, so you bent down to pick it up, thus putting your prints on it.'

'Right,' said Cornish. 'Thass wot I done.'

'But unfortunately, the wallet was empty? Not a damn thing in it. So, without thinking, a man might just spin it like a playing card high in the air, over the fence into the waste ground, where it lay in the grass until a dog discovered it. Something like that?'

'Right,' said Cornish. He was beginning to like his new brief. Clever geezer. Vansittart produced a sheaf of sheets of lined legal paper from his brief-case. He speedily wrote out a statement.

'Now, I have taken notes of this explanation. Please read them through and if you agree that this is what really happened, well, that would be a pretty fair defence. So you could sign it.'

Cornish did not read fast, but he scrawled a signature anyway.

'Now, our second problem is your nose, Mr Price.'

The plaster had gone, but the nose was still swollen and sore.

'The records show that you went to have it patched up at St Anne's Road hospital around five on the afternoon that this unfortunate man was attacked in Paradise Way. The prosecution are trying to make a big thing of this.'

'Well, it 'urt,' said Price.

'Do you two ever go out for a few beers?'

They nodded.

'Went out on the Monday night?'

They looked blank. Then Cornish nodded.

'King's 'Ead, Farrow Street.'

'And there you were seen drinking, by others, including the barman?'

They nodded again.

'Monday evening, the night before the attack?'

Nods.

'Now, it could be that you are going to tell me that Mr Price had more than a skinful. That on your

70

way home he wanted to pee in the gutter, but tripped over an uneven kerbstone and crashed face down onto a parked car, busting his nose as he did so?'

Cornish jabbed Price with his elbow.

'You remember, Mark. Thass exactly wot 'appened.'

'So, now we have a busted nose, bleeding all over the street. So, you take off your T-shirt and hold it to your face until you got home and the bleeding had stopped. Then, being well drunk, you fell asleep until about midday on the Tuesday?'

Cornish grinned.

'Thass it exactly. Innit, Mark?'

'But there are still five hours between then and going to the hospital. No doubt you are going to tell me that you didn't want to make a fuss, didn't realize the nose might be broken, and it was only your pal who finally persuaded you to get medical attention when it just kept on hurting. So, around five, you went to the hospital for a check-up.'

Price nodded eagerly.

'But of course that was after lunch. Perhaps you had a fry-up in a working man's caff somewhere, sitting there from one o'clock until half past two? Found a copy of the *Sun* on the table, studied the racing pages, that sort of thing? Can't remember the name of the caff, can you?'

They both shook their heads.

'No matter. There are scores of them spread all over that manor. But you never went near Meadowdene Grove all day?'

'Nah,' said Cornish, 'we just went into this caff and 'ad egg and chips till about 'arf past two.'

'Not one of your usual lunch places?'

'Nope. Just wandered in off the street. Can't remember the name.'

'Well, that seems pretty persuasive. Jury ought to believe that. So long as you stick to it. No changes. Keep it short and simple. Got it?'

They nodded. Mr Vansittart wrote a second statement on legal paper with Price's version of events concerning his nose. Price could hardly read. He signed anyway. The lawyer tucked both statements into the bulging file. A rather bewildered Lou Slade came in. Vansittart rose.

'My dear Mr Slade. I am most dreadfully sorry about the mix-up. I thought you said nine. But never mind. Our clients and I are just finishing.'

He turned to Price and Cornish with a friendly beam.

'We'll see each other in court on Tuesday, but we won't be able to talk. As for anyone you share a cell with, say absolutely nothing. Some of them are narks.'

He offered the disgruntled solicitor a lift home in his Bentley. On the ride, Slade read the two new statements.

'Better,' he said, 'a lot better. Two very strong defences. I'm surprised they didn't tell me all this. It leaves Patel—'

'Ah yes, Mr Veejay Patel. An upright man. An honest man. Perhaps honest enough to admit he might, just might, have made a mistake.'

Mr Slade had his doubts, but then he recalled that in cross-examination Vansittart had a reputation second only to George Carman. His day began to look a bit brighter. And the barrister intended to show up at Highbury Corner on Tuesday. Unannounced. That ought to rattle some cages. Slade began to smile.

DAY FIFTEEN — TUESDAY

Cages were indeed rattled. Miss Prabani Sundaran was at her place at the long table fronting the bench when James Vansittart entered the court and seated himself a few feet away, where the defending solicitors sit. She blinked several times. The barrister gave her a friendly nod and a smile.

On the bench, Mr Jonathan Stein had been writing notes from the previous case. Years of training caused him to restrain a flicker of expression. Lou Slade sat behind Vansittart.

'Put up Price and Cornish,' called the chief clerk.

The two thugs were led up into the dock, cuffed and flanked by prison officers. Vansittart rose.

'May it please the court, I am James Vansittart and I represent the accused, assisted by my friend Mr Louis Slade.'

He sat. The stipe contemplated him thoughtfully.

'Mr Vansittart, I understand this hearing is for a further remand of the accused for one week more in custody.'

He almost used the word 'mere'. Vansittart bobbed back up.

73

'Indeed it is, sir.'

'Very well. Ms Sundaran, you may proceed.'

'Thank you, sir. The Crown would like to apply for a further week on remand in custody in the case of Mark Price and Harry Cornish.'

Jonathan Stein glanced at Vansittart. Surely he was not going to suggest . . .?

'No application for bail, sir,' said the barrister.

'Very well, Ms Sundaran. Granted.'

Stein wondered what on earth all this had been about. But Vansittart was back on his feet.

'But the defence would like to make another application to the court.'

'Very well.'

'The defence wishes to know, sir, whether there are any further matters that the prosecution needs to investigate, or whether the Crown's case, as made available to the defence under the rules of disclosure, is now complete.'

He sat down and gazed at Miss Sundaran. She kept her composure, but inside she was a mass of butterflies. She was accustomed to a preordained script as taught at law school. Someone had just torn it up.

From behind her DI Jack Burns leaned forward and whispered in her grateful ear.

'I understand, sir, that the deceased has not yet been identified and inquiries in that direction are still proceeding.'

Vansittart was back up.

'May it please the court, the defence does not deny that a man has tragically been brought to his death. For that reason he could not now recover and give evidence or contribute in any way to the case. His precise identity is not therefore germane. The defence must therefore repeat its question: is the Crown ready to proceed to committal?'

There was silence.

'Ms Sundaran?' asked Stein gently.

She was like a trainee pilot on first solo flight. Her engine had just blown up and someone was asking her what she intended to do about it.

'I believe the Crown case is complete, sir.'

Vansittart was back up.

'In that case, Mr Stipendiary, I would like to apply for full committal proceedings this day week. We will both be aware of the adage "justice delayed is justice denied". My clients have been locked up for two weeks now, for a crime they will vigorously claim they did not commit. With Crown and defence now ready to proceed, we ask for no further delay.'

Jonathan Stein pondered. Vansittart was going for a high-risk strategy. At committal, the job of the magistrate is not to find the accused innocent or guilty; it is simply to judge whether a prima facie case exists, whether there is enough evidence to send the case onwards and upwards to full trial at the Central Criminal Court, the famous Old Bailey. Habitually, barristers did not appear until that point. If the formidable Vansittart QC had deigned to appear at Highbury Court, it looked as if he was going for a 'no case to answer' tactic.

'Then, granted,' he said. 'Today week.'

'Sir, the defence will ask, nay asks now, that the Crown will produce all its witnesses for cross-examination at that time.'

So, it was going to be a full dress rehearsal. When a defence barrister cross-examines, he reveals the thrust of the defence. Habitually it is the prosecution that must reveal to the defence all that it has got, while the defence can keep its strategy secret until the trial. Only the production by the defence of a sudden alibi which the police have no time to check is not allowed.

'Granted. Miss Sundaran, you have a week to prepare your witnesses and bring them to court.'

DAY SIXTEEN — WEDNESDAY

Prabani Sundaran was in a panic and had taken her fears to a senior officer at the CPS.

'Sir, I need an experienced barrister to lead me next Tuesday. I can't take on Vansittart.'

'Prabani, you're going to have to,' said her department chief. 'Half my team are still away. It's bloody August you know. Everyone else is up to their eyebrows.'

'But, sir, Vansittart. He's going to grill the prosecution witnesses.'

'Look, it's only a committal. A formality. He's going for a high-risk strategy and it's too high risk. The court record will give us his entire defence. Wonderful. I wish it happened every time.'

'But supposing Mr Stein throws it out?'

'Now look, Prabani, you are going too far, but

you have to keep your nerve. Stein won't throw it out. He knows a strong case when he sees one. We've got the identifications by Mr Patel and his rock-solid statement. If he stands up, Stein will send it to the Bailey. Without Patel we wouldn't have a case, anyway. Now, just handle it.'

That afternoon it got worse. The Chief Clerk to the Magistrates came on. There had been a fall-through. The whole of Friday was free. Could she take it on then? Prabani Sundaran thought fast. Apart from witnesses, Mr Patel and the dog-walker Mr Whittaker, all on her side were professionals. They would have to make the time. She asked for an hour and phoned around. At four she phoned the clerk to agree.

James Vansittart took the call at five. He, too, agreed. Pentonville Jail was informed. Friday, ten a.m. Court No. 1. Mr Jonathan Stein presiding.

DAY EIGHTEEN — FRIDAY

The Crown had eleven witnesses and they began with the first constable to reach the scene. He testified that he had been with a colleague in a parked squad car just after two p.m. on that Tuesday when a call came from the control room requiring them to attend an assault victim on the pavement at Paradise Way. This they had done, arriving four minutes after the call. He had tended to the man on the pavement as best he could while his partner called for back-up. Within five more minutes an ambulance had arrived and removed the victim to hospital. In fifteen further minutes a uniformed inspector had arrived and taken control.

James Vansittart smiled at the young man.

'No questions,' he said and the relieved constable took his place at the back of the court. The second witness was the uniformed inspector. He, too, was led by Ms Sundaran through his statement. At the end, Vansittart rose.

'Inspector, at the time of your arrival on the scene, had some spectators gathered in the street?'

'Yes, sir.'

'Did you have other police officers with you?'

'Yes, sir. There were, in all, ten in attendance.'

'Did you instruct them to interview everyone present with a view to finding any possible eyewitnesses of the assault?'

'I did, sir.'

'Did you also have your ten colleagues visit every flat and house that could possibly have overlooked the scene, with the same aim in mind?'

'Yes, sir.'

'Penetrating the estate itself, down the passage through which the attackers had escaped, did your colleagues continue inquiries to try to find an eyewitness?'

'Yes, sir.'

'In all, how many hours were spent on this exercise?'

'I called the team off as dusk fell, about eight o'clock.'

'So, your ten men were intercepting pedestrians

in the estate and knocking on doors for nearly six hours?'

'Yes, sir.'

'In that time, did they come up with one single eyewitness who either saw the attack or saw two men answering the description of my clients running through the estate?'

'No, sir.'

'So, after, what? over a hundred inquiries, you found not one shred of evidence to link my clients to the time and the place?'

'No, sir.'

'Thank you, Inspector. No further questions.'

Jack Burns was next. He was led through his lengthy statement from the first call in the canteen to the final formal charging of Price and Cornish with murder. Then Vansittart rose.

'You have conducted a very thorough investigation, Mr Burns?'

'I hope so, sir.'

'Left no stone unturned?'

'I would like to think so.'

'How many officers were in the search team, the POLSA?'

'About a dozen, sir.'

'But they found no trace of Mr Price's blood at or near the crime scene?'

'No, sir.'

'So here is a badly broken nose, streaming blood in a fountain, and not one single droplet fell to the pavement?'

'None was found, sir.'

Burns knew better than to allow a lawyer to bait him.

'You see, Mr Burns, my client will say that none of his blood was found there because he did not break his nose at that place, because he was never there that Tuesday. Now, Mr Burns . . .'

Vansittart had made a mini speech in place of a question. He knew there was no jury present to be impressed. He was talking to Stipendiary Magistrate Jonathan Stein, who looked at him expressionlessly and made notes. Miss Sundaran scribbled furiously.

'Penetrating the estate itself, did your POLSA team search for anything else the miscreants might have dropped?'

'Yes, sir.'

'And how many binliners did they manage to fill?'

'Twenty, sir.'

'And were the contents searched with the finest of toothcombs?'

'Yes, sir.'

'And in twenty binliners, was there one shred of evidence linking my clients to the time and the place?'

'No, sir.'

'Yet, by noon the next day you were actively looking for Mr Price and Mr Cornish with a view to arresting them. Why was that?'

'Because between eleven and twelve the next day I had established two positive identifications.'

'From the CRO photographs, the so-called mug book?'

'Yes, sir.'

'And made by a local shopkeeper, Mr Veejay Patel?'

'Yes, sir.'

'Tell me, Inspector, how many photographs did Mr Patel examine?'

Jack Burns consulted his notes.

'Seventy-seven.'

'And why seventy-seven?'

'Because the twenty-eighth photograph he positively identified as Mark Price and the seventy-seventh as Harry Cornish.'

'Is seventy-seven the total of youngish white males who have ever come to the attention of the police in the north-east quadrant of London?'

'No, sir.'

'The figure would be higher?'

'Yes, sir.'

'How many photographs did you have at your disposal that morning, Mr Burns?'

'About four hundred.'

'Four hundred. And yet you stopped at seventy-seven.'

'The identifications were absolutely positive.'

'And yet Mr Patel never had the opportunity to look at the remaining three hundred and twenty-three?'

There was a long silence.

'No, sir.'

'Detective Inspector Burns, my client, Mr Price, seen from the neck up, is a beefy, mid-twenties white male with a shorn head. Are you telling this court there are no others like that among your four hundred photos?'

'I cannot say that.'

'I suggest there must be a score. Nowadays, beefy young men who choose to shave their skulls are two a penny. Yet, Mr Patel never had the opportunity to compare Mr Price's photograph with any similar face further down the list of four hundred?'

Silence.

'You must answer, Mr Burns,' said the stipendiary, gently.

'No, sir, he did not.'

'Then there might have been another face, further on, remarkably similar to Mr Price, but Mr Patel had no chance to make a comparison, go back and forth, stare at both of them, before making his choice?'

'There might have been.'

'Thank you, Mr Burns. No further questions.'

It had been damaging. The reference to beefy young men with shorn heads being 'two a penny' had scored with Mr Stein. He, too, watched television and saw coverage of football hooligans at play.

Mr Carl Bateman was purely technical. He simply described the arrival of the unconscious man at the Royal London and all he had done for him before the patient went to neurosurgery. Nevertheless, when he had finished, Vansittart rose.

'Just one very brief issue, Mr Bateman. Did you at any point examine the right fist of the patient?'

Bateman frowned, puzzled.

'Yes, I did.'

'At the time of admission or later?'

'Later.'

'Was this at someone's request?'

'Yes.'

'And whose, pray?'

'Detective Inspector Burns.'

'And did Mr Burns ask you to look for knuckle damage?'

'Yes, he did.'

'And was there any?'

'No.'

'How long have you been in Accident and Emergency?'

'Ten years.'

'A very experienced man. You must have seen the results of many violent blows delivered with the fist, both to the human face and to the fist itself?'

'Yes, I believe I have.'

'When a human fist delivers a blow of such force as to shatter the nose of a much bigger man, would you not expect to find knuckle damage?'

'I might.'

'And what would be the chances of such damage occurring? Eighty per cent?'

'I suppose so.'

'Abrasions to the skin of the knuckles? Bruising over the metacarpal heads, the thin and fragile bones that run up the back of the hand between the knuckles and the wrist?'

'More likely the metacarpal bruising.'

'Similar to the Boxer's Injury?'

'Yes.'

'But there was none on the right fist of the man now tragically dead?'

'No.'

'Thank you, Mr Bateman.'

What Carl Bateman could not know was that when the limping man smashed Price in the face, he did not use a bunched fist, but a much more dangerous blow. He employed the hard heel of the hand, driving upward from the waist, hammering into the nose from the underside. Had Price not been of almost ox-like strength and an accustomed brawler, he would have been knocked flat and possibly senseless.

The brain surgeon, Mr Paul Willis, gave his evidence and left the witness box with no questions from Vansittart, but not Dr Melrose of St Anne's Road Hospital.

'Tell me, Dr Melrose, when you examined Mr Price's nose between five and five thirty on the afternoon of last Tuesday fortnight, was there blood in the nostrils?'

'Yes, there was.'

'Crusted or still liquid?'

'Both. There were crusted fragments near the end of the nostrils, but it was still liquid further up.'

'And you discovered the nose bone to be fractured in two places and the cartilage pushed to one side?'

'I did.'

'So you set the bone, reshaped the nose and

84

strapped it in order to let nature take its course?'

'Yes, I did.'

'If the patient, before coming to the hospital, had very foolishly and despite the pain tried to reset his own nose, would that have caused fresh bleeding?'

'Yes, it would.'

'Bearing that in mind, can you say how many hours before you saw the nose the injury had been inflicted?'

'Several hours, certainly.'

'Well, three? Ten? Even more?'

'That is hard to say. With complete accuracy.'

'Then let me put to you a possibility. A young man goes out on the Monday evening, gets lamentably drunk in a pub, and on the way home wishes to urinate in the gutter. But, stumbling over an uneven paving stone, he falls heavily forward and smashes his nose into the tailboard of a jobbing builder's lorry parked by the kerb. Could that have inflicted the injury you saw? The previous night?'

'Possibly.'

'Well, Dr Melrose, yes or no? Is it possible?'

'Yes.'

'Thank you, Doctor. No further questions.'

Vansittart was speaking to Jonathan Stein; in code, but it came through loud and clear. What he said was: that is exactly my client's story and if he sticks to it, we both know the prosecution cannot disprove it.

At the back of the court Jack Burns swore inwardly. Why could not Melrose simply have insisted the injury could not possibly have occurred more than four hours before he tended it? No-one would ever have known. Damn scrupulously honest doctors.

Mr Paul Finch was the head of forensics. He was not a police officer, for the Met has for years used civilian scientists on contract for its forensic work.

'You received into your possession a large quantity of items of clothing taken from the flat shared by the accused?' Vansittart asked.

'Yes, I did.'

'And every stitch of clothing worn by the victim during the attack?'

'Yes.'

'And you examined everything with the latest state-of-the-art technology to see if any fibres from the one set could be found on the other set?'

'Yes.'

'Were there any such traces?'

'No.'

'You also received a T-shirt soaked in dried blood?'

'Yes.'

'And a sample of blood from my client, Mr Price?'

'Yes.'

'Did they match?'

'They did.'

'Was there anyone else's blood on that T-shirt?'

'No.'

'Did you receive samples of blood taken from the pavement in the area of Paradise Way or the streets of the Meadowdene Grove estate?'

'No.'

'Did you receive samples of blood taken from beneath and around a builder's truck in Farrow Road?'

Mr Finch was totally bewildered. He glanced at the bench, but received no help. DI Burns had his head in his hands. Miss Sundaran was looking out of her depth.

'Farrow Road? No.'

'Precisely. No further questions.'

Mr Hamilton presented his post-mortem report with cheerful self-confidence. Cause of death, he pronounced, was due to severe axonal damage to the brain stem caused by repeated and heavy blows to the skull, compatible with blows administered by boots.

'Did you,' asked James Vansittart, 'examine every inch of the body during post-mortem?'

'Of course.'

'Including the right hand?'

Mr Hamilton referred to his notes.

'I have no reference to the right hand.'

'Because there was no damage to it?'

'That would be the only reason.'

'Thank you, Mr Hamilton.'

Unlike the professionals, Mr Whittaker, the elderly dog-walker, was slightly nervous and had taken some trouble with his dress. He wore his blazer with the Royal Artillery badge; he was entitled: in his National Service he had been a gunner.

There had already been a pleasing stir at the Over Sixties Club when it was learned he would be a witness in a murder trial, and a grateful but bewildered Mitch had received a lot of petting.

He described to the bench, led by Miss Sundaran, how he had taken Mitch for his daily walk just after dawn, but how, fearing rain was coming, he entered the walled-off waste ground via a missing panel and headed for home by a short cut. He explained how Mitch, running free, had come back to him with something in his mouth. It was a wallet; so, recalling the appeal in the Friday paper, he had taken it to Dover Street police station.

When he had finished, the other man rose, the one in the West End suit. Mr Whittaker knew he represented those bastards in the dock. They would have been hanged in the witness's younger days, and good riddance. So this man was the enemy. But he smiled in a most friendly fashion.

'Best hour of the day on a summer's morning? Cool, quiet, no-one about?'

'Yes. That's why I like it.'

'So do I. Often take my Jack Russell for a walk about then.'

He smiled again, real friendly. Not such a bad cove after all. Though Mitch was a lurcher cross, Mr Whittaker had had a Jack Russell when he was on the buses. The blond man could not be all bad.

'So you are walking across the waste ground and Mitch is running free?'

'Yes.'

'And there he is, suddenly back beside you, with something in his mouth?'

'Yes.'

'Did you see exactly where he found it?'

'Not exactly, no.'

'Could it have been, say, ten yards from the fence?'

'Well, I was about twenty yards into the field. Mitch came up from behind me.'

'So he could have found the wallet about ten yards from the sheet-metal fence?'

'Yes, I suppose so.'

'Thank you, Mr Whittaker.'

The elderly man was bewildered. An usher beckoned him down from the witness stand. Was that it? He was led to the back of the court and found a seat.

Fingerprints is another discipline the Met contracts out to civilian experts and one of these was Mr Clive Adams.

He described the wallet that had been delivered to him; the three sets of prints he had found; how he had eliminated those of the finder, Mr Whittaker, and those of the owner, now dead. And how he had matched the third set exactly to those of Harry Cornish. Mr Vansittart rose.

'Any smudges?'

'Some.'

'How are smudges caused, Mr Adams?'

'Well, one fingerprint imposed over another will cause a smudge that cannot be used in evidence. Or rubbing against another surface.'

'Like the inside of a pocket?'

'Yes.'

'Which were the clearest prints?'

'Those of Mr Whittaker and Mr Cornish.'

'And they were on the outside of the wallet?'

'Yes, but two prints from Cornish were inside, on the inner faces.'

'So, those of Mr Whittaker were imposed on the plastic when he held the wallet in his hand and never smudged by being shoved inside a tight pocket?'

'So it would seem.'

'And those of Mr Cornish were also imposed in the same way and also remained clear because after that point the wallet was not rubbed against the fabric of an inside pocket?'

'So it would seem.'

'If a man, running from the scene of a mugging, opened the wallet, plucked from it all its contents, then shoved the wallet into the rear pocket of his jeans, it would have his clear prints on the outer cover of the plastic?'

'Yes, it would.'

'But would the denim fabric, the tightness of jeans pockets and the running motion, blur those prints within, say, half a mile?'

'That might be the effect.'

'So, if our runner half a mile later plucks the empty wallet from his rear pocket with forefinger and thumb in order to throw it away, he would leave just that forefinger and thumb print for you to find?'

'Yes.'

'But if a finder came along and so covered the plastic surface with his own prints, could he not over-smudge the forefinger and thumb?'

'I suppose he might.'

'You see, your report says that there were some smudges, over-covered by fresher prints, that could have come from another hand.'

'They are only smudges. The prints under the smudges could also be those of the owner or Cornish.'

In the back of the court Jack Burns's stomach turned. Miss Verity Armitage. She had picked up the fallen wallet from the floor of her flower shop.

'Mr Adams, the wallet was plucked from the deceased's pocket just after two last Tuesday fortnight. By the same hour on Wednesday or shortly afterwards, Mr Cornish was in police custody. He must have put his prints on that wallet within that twenty-four-hour period?'

'Yes.'

'But the wallet was only found on Sunday morning. It must have lain in that grass for between four and a half and five and a half days. Yet the prints were clear.'

'There was no sign of water damage, sir. In fine dry conditions that is perfectly possible.'

'Then can you say precisely whether Mr Cornish's prints were impressed onto the plastic on Tuesday afternoon or the Wednesday morning?'

'No, sir.'

'Wednesday morning two young men are walking down Mandela Road when they see, lying in the gutter, a wallet. With quite normal curiosity, one of them stops to pick it up. He opens it to see what it contains. But there is nothing, neither money nor papers. It is a cheap wallet, worth nothing. He flicks it high over the sheet-metal fence separating Mandela Road from some waste ground; it lands some ten yards into the area and lies in the long grass until discovered by a dog on the Sunday. Feasible?'

'I suppose so.'

'Yes or no, Mr Adams. Would the prints then match the ones you found?'

'Yes.'

Another message for Jonathan Stein. That is what Harry Cornish is going to insist happened, and it is a complete explanation of his prints on that wallet. Mr Jonathan Stein stared down thoughtfully and made notes.

There remained Mr Veejay Patel. His two identifications and his statement were completely unambiguous. Miss Sundaran led him through his evidence stage by stage. At the back, Burns relaxed. He would get his committal. Vansittart rose.

'Mr Patel, you are an honest man.'

'I hope so.'

'A man who, if he thought, just thought, that he might have made a mistake, would not be too arrogant to admit the possibility?'

'I hope not.'

'You say in your statement that you saw Mr Price quite clearly because he was facing towards you.'

'Yes. He was to my right, from the shop window, facing three-quarters towards me.'

'But he was also facing the victim. So the victim was facing away from you. That was why you could not later help in the identification of his face.'

'Yes.'

'And you say the second mugger, whom you believe to be Mr Cornish, was standing behind the victim. Surely he also was facing away from you?'

'Well, yes.'

'Then how did you see his face?'

Mr Patel looked worried.

'I did not do so, then. Only when they began to circle the man on the ground, kicking him.'

'Mr Patel, if you were kicking someone on the ground, where would you look?'

'Well, at the man.'

'Meaning, downwards?'

'Yes.'

'If I may crave the court's indulgence, sir. Mr Cornish, would you stand up?'

In the dock, Harry Cornish rose, as did the prison officer to whom he was handcuffed. Mr Stein looked startled, but Vansittart would not pause.

'Mr Cornish, would you please look down at a spot in front of your feet.'

Cornish did so. His lank hair fell in a screen covering any sign of his face from the court. There was a stunned silence.

'Sit down, Mr Cornish,' said Vansittart. He addressed the Indian shopkeeper quite gently.

'Mr Patel, I suggest you saw a thin, sallow-faced man with ear-length hair at a distance of thirty yards. The next day when you saw a photo of a thin, sallow-faced man with ear-length hair you assumed it must be the same man. Could that be what happened?'

'I suppose so,' mumbled Veejay Patel. Burns tried vainly to catch his eye. He would not make eye contact. He's been got at, thought Burns in despair. Someone has been on the blower to him, a quiet voice in the middle of the night, mentioning his wife and daughter. Oh God, not again.

'Now, regarding Mr Price. Do you ever go to watch Arsenal at Highbury, Mr Patel?'

'No, sir.'

'You see, looking across that road on that terrible day, you saw a beefy young white man with a shorn skull, did you not?'

'Yes.'

'And if you went to Highbury, you would see a hundred of them. And if you look behind the windscreens of fifty per cent of the white vans that cut up other drivers on the roads of north London every day, you would see another hundred. And do you know what they wear, Mr Patel? Blue jeans, usually grubby, leather belts and a soiled T-shirt. It is almost a uniform. Have you ever seen men like that before?'

'Yes.'

'All over the streets of London?'

'Yes.'

'On television when we are all shamed by the spectacle of foreign policemen trying to cope with English football hooligans?'

'Yes.'

'Mr Patel, the victim could not have punched his

attacker with the force you describe. It would have grazed his right knuckles, probably bruised the bones of his hand. I suggest you saw him raise his right hand, probably to ward off a blow to his face he thought was coming. Could that be what you saw?'

'Yes, I suppose it could.'

'But if you could make a mistake like that, could you not also make a mistake about a human face at thirty yards?'

Burns held his head in his hands. Whoever had briefed the frightened shopkeeper had done a good job. Patel had not withdrawn all co-operation from the police, for then he could have been treated as a hostile witness. He had just changed 'absolutely' to 'possibly' and 'definitely' to 'maybe'. Maybe is not enough; a jury cannot convict on maybe.

When the abject Mr Patel had left the witness box, Miss Sundaran said to Mr Stein, 'That is the case for the prosecution, sir. We would ask for a committal to Crown Court on a charge of murder.'

The stipendiary raised an eyebrow to James Vansittart. Both knew what was coming. One could have heard a pin drop.

'Mr Stipendiary, we both know the meaning and the significance of the Law's Test. You have to have before you sufficient evidence upon which, if uncontradicted . . .' Vansittart dragged the last word out slowly to stress how unlikely this was, '. . . a reasonable jury, properly directed, could safely convict.

'It just is not there, sir. The Crown had three real

pieces of evidence. Mr Patel, the broken nose and the wallet. Mr Patel, clearly a thoroughly honest man, has come to the view that he could, after all, have picked two men bearing a similarity, but no more, to the ones he saw that afternoon.

'That leaves the matter of the broken nose of Mr Price and the fingerprints of Mr Cornish upon an empty and discarded wallet. Although you here today, sir, are not strictly concerned with what may, or may not, be said at another date in another court, or indeed with the obvious lines of defence which arise in this case, it must be clear to you from your considerable experience that in due course the allegations regarding both nose and wallet will be comprehensively and indeed compellingly refuted.

'There is a perfectly logical explanation both to the broken nose and the wallet. I think we both know that a jury cannot safely convict. I must ask for a dismissal.'

Yes, thought Jonathan Stein, and a jury will see your clients looking spruce and clean, shirt, jacket and tie; the jury will never see the records of these two homicidal thugs. You will get your acquittal and waste a deal of public time and money.

'It is with the most considerable reluctance that I must concur with Mr Vansittart. The case is dismissed. Let the accused be discharged,' he said. Thoroughly disgusted by what he had had to do, he left the bench.

'All rise,' shouted the clerk, a bit late, but most of those present were rushing for the doors. Cornish and Price, uncuffed, tried to reach from the dock to shake Vansittart's hand, but he stalked past them towards the corridor.

It takes time to get from the second to the ground floor: the several lifts are usually busy. By chance, Jack Burns made it first and was staring gloomily and angrily.

Price and Cornish, free citizens, swaggering, swearing and snarling, came out of a lift and walked towards the doors. Burns turned. They faced each other across twenty feet.

In unison, both thugs raised rigid middle fingers and jerked them up and down at the detective.

'So much for you, filth,' screamed Price. Together they swaggered out into Highbury Road to head back to their squat.

'Unpleasant,' said a quiet voice at his elbow. Burns took in the smooth blond hair, the lazy blue eyes and languid, self-confident manner and felt a wave of loathing for Vansittart and all his type.

'I hope you are proud of yourself, Mr Vansittart. They killed that harmless old man as surely as we are standing here. And thanks to you they are out there again. Until the next time.' His anger boiled over and he did not even make an attempt at courtesy. 'Christ, don't you make enough taking cases for the mega-rich down in the Strand? Why do you have to come up here for Legal Aid peanuts to set those animals free?'

There was no mockery in Vansittart's blue eyes, but something very like compassion. Then he did something strange. He leaned forward and whispered into Burns's ear. The detective caught a whiff of an expensive but discreet Penhaligon essence.

'This may surprise you, Mr Burns,' the voice murmured, 'but it has to do with the triumph of justice.'

Then he was gone, out through the revolving doors. A Bentley with a driver at the wheel swept up as if on cue. Vansittart threw his attaché case onto the rear seat and climbed in after it. The Bentley eased away and out of sight.

'Triumph of my arse,' snarled Burns.

It was the lunch hour. He decided to walk the two miles back to the nick. He was halfway there when his pager sounded. It was the station. He used his mobile. His colleague on the front desk came on.

'There's an old boy here wants to see you. Says he knows the deceased.'

He turned out to be an old-age pensioner and a Londoner to his boot heels. Burns found him in one of the interview rooms, quietly enjoying a cigarette beneath the 'No Smoking' notice. He took to him at once. His name was Albert Clarke, 'but everyone calls me Nobby.'

Burns and Nobby Clarke sat facing each other at the table. The DI flicked open his notebook.

'For the record, full name and address.'

When he reached the borough where Nobby lived, he stopped.

'Willesden? But that's miles away.'

'I know where it is,' said the pensioner. 'I live there.'

'And the dead man?'

'Of course. That's where we met, dinwee?'

He was one of those cockneys who feel obliged to turn statements into questions by adding an unnecessary interrogative at the end.

'You came all this way to tell me about him?'

'Seemed only right, 'im being dead an' all,' said Nobby. 'You got to get the bastards what did that to 'im. Bang 'em up.'

'I got them,' said Burns. 'The court just let them go.'

Clarke was shocked. Burns found an ashtray in a drawer and the old man stubbed out.

'That's well out of order. I don't know what this bloody country's coming to.'

'You're not the only one. Right, the dead man. His name?'

'Peter.'

Burns wrote it down.

'Peter what?'

'Dunno. I never asked him.'

Burns counted slowly and silently from one to ten.

'We think he had come this far east on that Tuesday to put flowers on a grave in the local cemetery. His mum?'

'Nah. He didn't have no parents. Lost them as a small child. Orphan boy. Raised at Barnardo's. You must mean his Auntie May. She was his house mother.'

Burns had an image of a small boy, bereft and bereaved, and of a kindly woman trying to put his shattered little life back together. Twenty years after her death, he still came on her birthday to put flowers on her grave. Eighteen days ago it was an act that cost him his life.

'So where did you meet this Peter?'

'The club.'

'Club?'

'DSS. We sat side by side, every week. They give us chairs. Me, with the arthritis, 'im with the gammy leg.'

Burns could imagine them sitting in the Department of Social Security waiting for the crowd of applicants to thin out.

'So while you sat and waited, you chatted?'

'Yeah, a bit.'

'But you never asked his surname?'

'No, and 'e never asked me mine, did 'e?'

'You were there for your pension? What was he there for?'

'Disability money. 'E had a thirty per cent disability pension.'

'For the leg. Did he ever say how he got it?'

'Certainly. 'E was in the army. In the Paras. Did a night jump. Wind caught him and smashed him into a rock pile. The chute pulled him through the rocks for 'arf a mile. By the time his mates got to him, his right leg was in bits.'

'Was he unemployed?'

Nobby Clarke was contemptuous.

'Peter? Never. Wouldn't take a penny wot wasn't due to him. 'E was a nightwatchman.'

Of course. Live alone, work alone. No-one to report him missing. And the chances were the company he worked for had closed down for August, bloody August.

'How did you know he was dead?'

'Paper. It was in the *Stennit*.'

'That was nine days ago. Why did you wait so long?'

'August. Always go to my daughter on the Isle of Wight for two weeks in August. Got back last night. Good to be back in the Smoke. All that wind off the sea. Catch me death, I nearly did.'

He had a comforting cough and lit up again.

'So how did you happen on a nine-day-old newspaper?'

'Spuds.'

'Spuds?'

'Potatoes,' said Nobby Clarke, patiently.

'I know what spuds are, Nobby. What have they got to do with the dead man?'

For answer Nobby Clarke reached into a side pocket of his jacket and pulled out a torn and faded newspaper. It was the front page of the *Evening Standard* of nine days ago.

'Went down to the greengrocer this morning to buy some spuds for me tea. Got 'ome, unwrapped the spuds and there 'e was staring at me from the kitchen table.'

An old-fashioned greengrocer. Used newspaper to wrap potatoes. From the paper, grimed with stains of earth, the limping man stared up. On the reverse side, page two, was the panel with all the details, including the reference to Detective Inspector Burns of the Dover Street nick.

'So I come straight over, din't I?'

'Want a lift home, Nobby?'

The pensioner brightened.

''Aven't been in a police car in forty years. Mind you,' he added generously, 'we 'ad real rozzers in those days.'

Burns called Luke Skinner, told him to grab the key on the ribbon that was taken from the pocket of the dead man and bring the car to the front.

They dropped Nobby Clarke at his sheltered accommodation, having taken details of the local Social Security office, and went there. They were about to close and the staff was accessible. Burns flashed his warrant card and asked for the supervisor.

'I'm looking for a man. First name, Peter. Surname unknown. Medium height, medium build, grey hair, aged about fifty to fifty-five. Pronounced limp, collected a thirty per cent disability pension. Used to sit . . .' He glanced round. There were several seats by the wall. 'Over there with Nobby Clarke. Any ideas?'

DSS offices are not very chatty places, at least not between the staff behind their bars and grilles and the applicants outside. Finally one of the female clerks thought she recalled such a man. Peter Benson?

The computer did the rest. The supervisor punched up the file on Peter Benson. Due to extensive benefit fraud, photographs of applicants have been required for years. It was a small passport-sized photograph, but it was enough.

'Address?' asked Burns, and Skinner took it down.

'He hasn't been in for about three weeks,' said the clerk. 'Probably on holiday.'

'No, he's dead,' said Burns. 'You can close the file. He won't be coming again.'

'Are you sure?' asked the supervisor, clearly worried by the irregularity of it all. 'We ought to be officially informed.'

'He can't do that,' said Burns. 'Inconsiderate of him.'

The two detectives found the address by using the *London A–Z* and asking a few neighbours. It was another housing estate and the small one-bedroom flat was on the fourth floor. Walk up; lift broken down. They let themselves in.

It was shabby, but neat. There was three weeks of dust and some dead flies on the window sill, but no mouldy food. Washed plates and cups were on the draining rack beside the sink.

A bedside drawer yielded bits of army memorabilia and five military medals, including the MM, awarded for courage in combat. The books on the shelf were well-thumbed paperbacks and the pictorial decorations were prints. Burns finally stopped by a framed picture on the sitting-room wall.

It showed four young men, staring at the camera, smiling. In the background was what looked like a stretch of desert and the edge of an old stone fort. Beneath the picture was printed 'Mirbat, 1972'.

'What's Mirbat?' asked Skinner, who had come to stand beside him.

'A place. A small village. Dhofar, eastern province of Oman, at the end of the Saudi peninsula.'

The young men were all in desert cammo. One wore a local Arab keffiyeh of chequered cloth, held in place by two rings of black cord. The other three had sand-coloured berets with a badge at the front. Burns knew that if he had a magnifying glass he would make out the emblem of a winged dagger with three letters above it and three short words beneath.

'How do you know?' asked Skinner.

'The Queen came to Devon once. I was on Royal Protection duty. There were two from that regiment attached to us. Bodyguard duty involves long periods of waiting. We all began to reminisce. They told us about Mirbat.'

'What happened there?'

'A battle. There was a war going on. A secret war. Communist terrorists were being sent over the border from Yemen to topple the Sultan. We sent down a British Army Training Team, the BATT. One day a force of between three and four hundred terrorists attacked the village and garrison at Mirbat. There were ten men from that regiment and a group of local levies.'

'Who won?'

Burns jabbed a finger at the photograph.

'They did. Just. Lost two of their own, downed over a hundred terrorists before they finally broke and ran.'

Three of the men were standing, the fourth was on one knee at the front; twenty-four years ago, in a forgotten desert village. The one at the front was the trooper; behind him were a sergeant, a corporal and their young officer, or 'Rupert'.

Skinner leaned forward and tapped the crouching trooper.

'That's him, Peter Benson. Poor bugger. To go through all that and end up kicked to death in Edmonton.'

Burns had already identified the trooper. He was staring at the officer. The smooth blond hair was covered by the beret and the arrogant blue eyes were creased by the glare of the sun. But that young officer was going to go home, leave the army, attend law school and a quarter of a century later become one of the great advocates of his country. Skinner had made the connection with a sharp intake of breath near Burns's ear.

'I don't understand,' said the detective sergeant. 'They kicked his mate to death and he went out of his way to get them off.'

Burns could hear the public-school voice murmuring in his ear.

'This may surprise you, Mr Burns . . .'

Staring at the faces of the four young warriors of a generation gone by, Jack Burns realized too late that the deceptively languid lawyer was not talking of the justice of the Old Bailey, but of the Old Testament.

'Guv,' said the troubled young man at his side, 'with Price and Cornish back on the streets, what will happen if that sergeant and that corporal ever come across them?'

'Don't ask, laddie. You really do not want to know.'

A burial took place at the private plot of the Special Air Service Regiment near their base at Hereford. The body of an old soldier was laid to rest. There was a bugler who played the Last Post and a salvo over the grave. About a dozen attended, including a noted barrister.

That evening, two bodies were recovered from a lake near Wanstead Marshes, east London. They were identified as those of Mr Mark Price and Mr Harry Cornish. The pathologist recorded that both men had died of ligature strangulation and that the instrument, most unusually, appeared to be piano wire. The file on the case was opened, but never closed.

THE ART OF THE MATTER

The rain came down. It fell in a slowly moving wall upon Hyde Park and, borne by a light westerly wind, drifted in grey curtains of falling water across Park Lane and through the narrow park of plane trees that divides the northbound and southbound lanes. A wet and gloomy man stood under the leafless trees and watched.

The entrance to the Grosvenor House Hotel ballroom was brightly lit by several arc lights and the endless glare of camera flashes. Inside was warm, snug and dry. Under the awning before the door was an area of only damp pavement and here the uniformed commissionaires stood, gleaming umbrellas at the ready, as the limousines swept up, one by one.

As each rain-lashed car drew up by the awning one of the men would run forward to shield the descending star or film celebrity for the two-yard dash, head down, from car to awning. There they could straighten up, plaster on the practised smile and face the cameras.

The paparazzi were either side of the awning, skin-wet, shielding their precious equipment as best they could. Their cries came across the road to the man under the trees.

'Over here, Michael. This way, Roger. Nice smile, Shakira. Lovely.'

The great and the good of the film world nodded benignly at the adulation, smiled for the lenses and thus for the distant fans, ignored the few anorak-clad autograph hunters, strange persistent voles with pleading eyes, and were wafted inside. There they would be led to their tables, pausing to beam and greet, ready for the annual awards ceremony of the British Academy of Film and Television Arts.

The small man under the trees watched with unrequited longing in his eyes. Once he had dreamed that he too might be there, a star of the film world in his own right, or at the very least a recognized journeyman at his trade. But he knew it was not to be, not now, too late.

For more than thirty-five years he had been an actor, almost entirely in films. He had played in over a hundred, starting as an extra, with no spoken words, moving to tiny bit parts but never being cast in a real role.

He had been a hotel porter while Peter Sellers walked past and on screen for seven seconds; he had been the driver of the army lorry that gave Peter O'Toole a lift into Cairo; he had held a Roman spear, rigid at attention, a few feet from Michael Palin; he had been the aircraft mechanic who helped Christopher Plummer into a Spitfire.

He had been waiters, porters, soldiers in every known army from the Bible to the Battle of the Bulge. He had played cab-drivers, policemen, fellow-diners, the man crossing the street, the wolf-whistling barrow boy and anything else one could think of.

But always it was the same: several days on the set, ten seconds on screen and goodbye chum. He had been within feet of every known star in the celluloid firmament, seen the gents and the bastards, the kindly and the prima donnas. He knew he could play any part with utter conviction and con-vincingly; he knew he was a human chameleon, but no-one had ever recognized the talent he was sure he had.

So he watched in the rain as his idols swept past to their evening's glory and later to their sumptu-ous apartments and suites. When the last had gone in and the lights had faded he trudged back through the rain to the bus stop at Marble Arch and stood, dripping water in the aisle, until he was deposited half a mile from his cheap bedsitter in the hinterland between White City and Shepherd's Bush.

He stripped off his soaking clothing, wrapped himself in an old towel robe liberated from a hotel in Spain (*Man of La Mancha* starring Peter O'Toole and he had held the horses) and lit a single-bar fire. His wet clothes steamed quietly through the night until by morning they were merely damp. He knew he was flat broke, skint. No work for weeks; a profession vastly overcrowded even with short, middle-aged men, and nothing in prospect. His phone had been cut off and if he wished to speak to his agent, yet again, he would have to go and visit in person. This, he decided, he would do on the morrow.

He sat and waited. He always sat and waited. It was his lot in life. Finally the office door opened and someone emerged whom he knew. He jumped up.

'Hallo, Robert, remember me? Trumpy.'

Robert Powell was caught by surprise and clearly could recall nothing of the face.

'*The Italian Job*. Turin. I drove the cab; you were in the back.'

Robert Powell's unquenchable good humour saved the day.

'Of course. Turin. Been a long time. How are you, Trumpy? How are things?'

'Pretty good. Not too bad, can't complain. Just popped by to see if you-know-who might have something for me.'

Powell took in the frayed shirt and shabby mac.

'I'm sure he will. Good to see you again. Good luck, Trumpy.'

'Ditto, old boy. Chin up, what?'

They shook and parted. The agent was as kind as he could be, but there was no work. A costume drama was going to shoot at Shepperton, but it was already cast. A very overcrowded profession whose only inexhaustible fuel was optimism and the chance of a great part tomorrow.

Back at his flat Trumpy forlornly took stock. Social Security provided a few pounds a week but London was expensive. He had just had another confrontation with Mr Koutzakis, his landlord, who once again had repeated that rent was in arrears and his patience not quite as limitless as the sun of his native Cyprus.

Things were bad; in fact things could not get much worse. As a watery sun disappeared behind the tower blocks across the yard the middle-aged actor went to a cupboard and retrieved a package wrapped in hessian. Over the years he had often asked himself why he clung on to the dratted thing. It was not to his taste anyway. Sentiment, he supposed. Thirty-five years earlier, when he was a stripling of twenty, a bright and eager young actor in provincial repertory convinced of stardom to come, it had been bequeathed to him by his great-aunt Millie. He unwrapped the item from its hessian swathes.

It was not a large painting, some twelve inches by twelve, excluding the gilt frame. He had kept it wrapped through all the years, but even when he got it, it had been so dirty, so crusted with grime, that the figures in it were vague outlines, little more than shadows. Still, Great-aunt Millie had always sworn it might be worth a few pounds, but that was probably just the wishful romanticism of an old woman. As to its history, he had no idea. In fact the small oil had quite a story.

In the year 1870 an Englishman of thirty, seeking his fortune and having some knowledge of the

Italian language, had emigrated to Florence to try his luck with a small endowment from his father. This was at the pinnacle of Britain's Victorian glory and Her Majesty's gold sovereign was a currency to open many doors. Italy by contrast was in its habitual chaos.

Within five years the enterprising Mr Bryan Frobisher had achieved four things. He had discovered the delicious wines of the Chianti hills and begun to export them in great vats to his native England, undercutting the accustomed French vine-vintages and laying the foundations of a tidy fortune.

He had acquired a fine town house with his own coach and groom. He had married the daughter of a quite minor local nobleman, and, among many other decorations for his new house, he had bought a small oil painting from a second-hand shop on the quay near the Ponte Vecchio.

He did not buy it because it was well known or well presented. It was covered in dust and almost hidden at the back of the shop. He just bought it because he liked it.

For thirty years, as he became British Vice-Consul to Florence and Sir Bryan, KBE, it hung in his library and for thirty years, each evening, he smoked his after-dinner cigar beneath it.

In 1900 a cholera epidemic swept Florence. It carried away Lady Frobisher, and after the funeral the sixty-year-old businessman decided to return to the land of his fathers. He sold up and came back to England, buying a handsome manor in Surrey and employing a staff of nine. The most junior was a local village girl, one Millicent Gore, who was engaged as a parlourmaid.

Sir Bryan never remarried and died at the age of ninety in 1930. He had brought almost a hundred packing crates back from Italy and one of them contained a small and by now discoloured oil painting in a gilt frame.

Because it had been his first gift to Lady Lucia and she had always loved it, he hung it again in the library where the patina of smoke and grime dulled the once-bright colours until the images of the figures became harder and harder to discern.

The First World War came and went, and in passing changed the world. Sir Bryan's fortune became much depleted as his investments in the Imperial Russian railway stock vanished in 1917. After 1918 Britain had a new social landscape.

The staff diminished, but Millicent Gore stayed. She rose from parlourmaid to under-housekeeper, and from 1921 onwards the housekeeper and only member of inside staff. In the last seven years of his life she looked after the frail Sir Bryan like a nurse and on his death in 1930 he remembered her.

He left her a cottage tenancy for life and a capital sum in trust to provide an income on which she could live modestly. While the rest of his estate was realized at auction, there was one item not included: a small oil painting. She was very proud of this; it came from a strange place called Abroad, so she hung it in the tiny sitting room of her tied cottage, not far from the open wood-burning range. There it became dirtier and dirtier.

Miss Gore never married. She busied herself with village and parish works and died in 1965 at the age of five and eighty. Her brother had married and produced a son and he in turn had sired a boy, the old lady's only great-nephew.

When she died she had little to leave, for the cottage and the capital fund reverted to the estate of her benefactor. But she left the painting to her great-nephew. Thirty-five more years went by until the dirty, stained, crusted old artefact saw the light of day again when it was unwrapped in a musty bed-sitter in a back street off Shepherd's Bush.

On the following morning its owner presented himself at the front desk of the prestigious House of Darcy, fine arts auctioneers and valuers. He clasped a hessian-wrapped package to his chest.

'I understand that you offer a service of valuation to members of the public who may have an item of merit,' he said to the young woman behind the desk. She too took in the frayed shirt and grubby mackintosh. She waved him towards a door marked Valuations. The interior was less lush than the front lobby. There was a desk and another girl. The actor repeated his query. She reached for a form.

'Name, sir?'

'My name is Mr Trumpington Gore. Now, this painting—'

'Address?'

He gave it.

'Phone number?'

'Er, no phone.'

She gave him a glance as if he had said that he lacked a head.

'And what is the item, sir?'

'An oil painting.'

Slowly the details, or lack of them, were teased out of him as her expression became more and more weary. Age unknown, school unknown, period unknown, artist unknown, country – presumed Italy.

The woman in Valuations had a huge crush on a young blade in Classic Wines and she knew it was the hour of mid-morning coffee in the Caffé Uno just round the corner. If this boring little man with his awful little daub would go away, she could slip out with a girlfriend and coincidentally bag the table next to Adonis.

'And finally, sir, what value would you put on it?'

'I don't know. That was why I brought it in.'

'We must have a valuation from the customer, sir. For insurance purposes. Shall I say a hundred pounds?'

'Very well. Do you know when I may expect to hear?'

'In due course, sir. There is a large number of pieces already in the storeroom waiting to be studied. It takes time.'

It was plain her personal view was that a glance would be enough. God, the junk some people passed over her desk, thinking they had discovered a Ming dish in the lavvy.

Five minutes later Mr Trumpington Gore had signed the form, taken his copy, left the hessian package and was back on the streets of Knightsbridge. Still stony broke. He walked home.

The hessian-wrapped painting was consigned to the basement store area, where it was given an identification tag: D 1601.

DECEMBER

Twenty days went by and still D 1601 stood against the wall in a basement store in its hessian wrappings, and still Trumpington Gore waited for an answer. There was a simple explanation: backlog.

As with all the great art auction houses, well over 90 per cent of the paintings, porcelain, jewellery, fine wines, sporting guns and furniture that the House of Darcy offered for sale was from sources known to them and easily verified. A hint of source or 'provenance' often appeared in the pre-sale catalogue. 'The property of a gentleman' was a frequent introduction to a fine item. 'Offered by the estate of the late . . .' was not uncommon.

There were some who disapproved of the practice of offering the general public a free valuation service on the grounds that it brought in too much time-consuming dross and too few items Darcy would even wish to offer for sale. But the service had been devised by the founder, Sir George Darcy, and the tradition survived. Just occasionally some lucky hopeful from nowhere discovered that Grandpa's old silver snuff box really was a rare Georgian treasure, but not often.

In Old Masters there was a fortnightly session of

the Viewing Committee, chaired by the department director, the fastidious and bow-tied Sebastian Mortlake, assisted by two deputies. In the ten-day run-up to Christmas he decided to clear the entire backlog.

This housekeeping turned out to cost five days of almost continuous session until he and his colleagues were tired of it.

Mr Mortlake relied on the fat sheaf of forms filled at the moment of deposit of the picture. Top of his preferences were those where the artist was clearly identifiable. That at least would give the eventual catalogue-writers a name, something close to a date and the subject matter was of course obvious at a glance.

Those he selected as possible for sale were set aside. A secretary would write to the owner to ask if he wished to sell, bearing in mind the suggested valuation. If the answer was 'yes' then a condition on the original form specified that the painting could not be taken elsewhere.

If the answer was 'no' the owner would be asked to collect the work without delay. Storage costs money. Once the selection was made and authority from the owner received to proceed with sale, Mortlake could select the forthcoming auction for the picture's inclusion and the catalogue could be prepared.

For minor works by minor artists that had just scraped past Sebastian Mortlake's watery gaze, the blurb would include phrases like 'charming', meaning 'if you like that sort of thing', or 'unusual', meaning 'he must have done this after a very heavy lunch'.

After viewing almost 300 canvases Mortlake and his two fellow assessors had broken the back of the 'off the street' offerings. He had selected only ten, one of them a surprising piece from the Dutch van Ostade school, but alas not by Adriaen himself. A pupil, but acceptable.

Sebastian Mortlake never liked to choose for the House of Darcy anything with a valuation at sale of less than £5,000. Large premises in Knightsbridge do not come cheap, and the seller's commission on less than that would not make much of a dent in the overheads. Lesser houses might handle canvases offered at £1,000, but not the House of Darcy. Besides, his forthcoming late-January sale would already be a big one.

As the hour of lunch approached on the fifth day, Sebastian Mortlake stretched and rubbed his eyes. He had examined 290 examples of pictorial dross, looking in vain for that hint of undiscovered gold. But ten 'acceptables' seemed to be the limit. As he told his junior staff, 'We must delight in our work, but we are not a charity.'

'How many more, Benny?' he called over his shoulder to the young under-valuer behind him.

'Just forty-four, Seb,' replied the young man. He used the familiar first name that Mortlake insisted on to create the friendly spirit he valued in his 'team'. Even secretaries used first names; only porters, though addressed by their first names, called him 'guv'.

'Anything of interest?'

'Not really. None with attribution, period, age, school or provenance.'

'In other words, family amateurs. Are you coming in tomorrow?'

'Aye, Seb, I thought I would. Tidy up a bit.'

'Good lad, Benny. Well, I'm off to the Directors' Lunch and then down to my place in the country. Just handle them for me, would you? You know the score. A nice polite letter, a token valuation, have Deirdre knock them out on the processor and they can all go in the last batch of mail.'

And with a cheery 'Happy Christmas boys and girls' he was off. Minutes later his two assistants at the viewing sessions had done the same. Benny saw to it that the last batch of paintings just viewed (and rejected) were taken back to the store and the last forty-four brought up to the much better lit viewing room. He would look at some that afternoon and the final batch the next day before departing for Christmas. Then he fished some lunch vouchers from his pocket and headed for the staff canteen.

He managed thirty of the remaining 'off the street' hand-ins that afternoon and then went home to his flat in the northern, that is, cheaper, end of Ladbroke Grove.

The presence of Benny Evans, aged twenty-five, at the House of Darcy was in itself a triumph of tenacity over prospects. The front-office staff, those who actually met the public and sashayed through the viewing galleries, were beautifully suited and languid-voiced exquisites. The distaff side was made up of young and very presentable female equivalents.

Among them moved the uniformed commission-aires and ushers, and the overalled porters, they who lifted and carried, hefted and trolleyed, brought and removed.

Behind the arras were the experts, and the aristocracy of these were the valuers, without whose forensic skills the whole edifice would collapse. Theirs were the sharp eyes and retentive memories that could tell at a glance the good from the ordinary, the real from the phoney, the worthless from the mother lode.

Among the senior hierarchs the Sebastian Mortlakes were minor monarchs and were permitted their several eccentricities because of all that knowledge gained by thirty years in the business. Benny Evans was different and the deceptively shrewd Mortlake had spotted why, and this explained Benny's presence.

He did not look the part, and playing the part is integral and indispensable in the London art world. He had no degree, he had no polish. His hair emerged from his head in untidy tufts that no Jermyn Street stylist could have done much to improve even if he had ever been to one.

When he arrived in Knightsbridge the broken nosepiece of his plastic National Health spectacles had been mended with Elastoplast. He did not need to dress down on Fridays; that was the way he always dressed. He spoke with a broad Lancashire accent. At the interview Sebastian Mortlake had gazed in fascination. It was only when he tested the lad on his knowledge of Renaissance art that he took him on, despite appearances and the rib-digs of his colleagues.

Benny Evans came from a small terraced house in a back street of Bootle, the son of a mill-worker. He did not shine at primary school, achieved some modest GCSEs and never took advanced level at all. But at the age of seven something happened that made it all unnecessary. His art teacher showed him a book.

It had coloured pictures and for some reason the child gazed at them in wonderment. There were pictures of young women, each holding a small baby, with winged angels hovering behind. The little boy from Bootle had just seen his first Madonna and Child by a Florentine Master. After that his appetite became insatiable.

He spent days in the public library staring at the works of Giotto, Raphael, Titian, Botticelli, Tintoretto and Tiepolo. The works of the giants Michelangelo and Leonardo da Vinci he consumed as his mates devoured cheap hamburgers.

In his teens he washed cars, delivered papers and walked dogs, and with the savings hitch-hiked across Europe to see the Uffizi and the Pitti. After the Italians he studied the Spaniards, hitching to Toledo to spend two days in the cathedral and the church of Santo Tomé staring at *El Greco*. Then he soaked up the German, Dutch and Flemish schools. By twenty-two he was still broke, but a walking encyclopedia of classical art. That was what Sebastian Mortlake had seen as he led the young applicant for a job through the galleries off the main hall. But even the foppish and clever Mortlake had missed something. Gut instinct: you either have it, or you do not. The scruffy boy from the back streets of Bootle had it, and no-one knew, not even he.

With fourteen hand-ins left to examine, he came in to work the next day in an almost empty building. Technically it was still open; the commissionaire was at the door but he had few to greet.

Benny Evans went back to the viewing room and began to look at the last of the hand-ins. They came in various sizes and an assortment of wrappings. Third from last was one wrapped in hessian sacking. He noted idly that it was D 1601. When he saw it he was shocked at its condition, the layers of grime that covered the original images beneath. It was hard to make out what they had once been.

He turned it over. Wood, a panel. Odd. Even odder, it was not oak. The Northern Europeans, if they painted on wood, used mainly oak. The Italian landscape had no oak. Could this be poplar?

He took the small painting to a lectern and trained a bright light on it, straining to see through the gloom of the patina caused by over a century of cigar and coal smoke. There was a seated woman, but no child. A man was bending over her, and she was looking up at him. A small, even tiny, rosebud of a mouth, and the man had a round, bombé forehead.

His eyes hurt from the light. He altered the angle

of its beam and studied the figure of the man. Something jogged a faint chord of memory: the posture, the body language ... The man was saying something, gesturing with his hands, and the woman was transfixed, listening with rapt attention.

Something about the way the fingers curled. Had he not seen fingers curl like that before? But the clincher was the face. Another small pursed mouth, and three tiny vertical crease lines above the eyes. Where had he seen small vertical, not horizontal, lines on a forehead before? He was sure he had, but could not recall where or when. He glanced at the hand-in sheet. A Mr T. Gore. No phone. Damn. He dismissed the last two pictures as worthless rubbish, took the sheaf of forms and went to see Deirdre, the last remaining secretary in the department. He dictated a general letter of regret and gave her the forms. On each was the valuation price of the submitted but rejected picture, as was also the name and address of the owner.

Although there were forty-three of them, the word processor would get every name and valuation different, yet the rest of the text identical. Benny watched for a while in admiration. He had the sketchiest knowledge of computers. He could just about set one up and peck at the keys but the finer points eluded him. After ten minutes Deirdre was doing the envelopes, fingers flying. Benny wished her a merry Christmas and left. As usual he took the bus to the top end of Ladbroke Grove. There was a hint of sleet in the air.

The clock by his bedside told him it was two in the morning when he woke. He could feel the sexy warmth of Suzie beside him. They had made love before sleeping and that usually guaranteed a dreamless night. And yet he was awake, mind spinning as if some deep-buried thought process had kicked him out of slumber. He tried to think what had been on his mind, apart from Suzie, as he drifted into sleep three hours earlier. The image of the hessian-wrapped picture came into his thoughts.

His head shot off the pillow. Suzie grunted in sleepy annoyance. He sat up and delivered three words into the surrounding blackness.

'Bloody, fooking 'ell.'

He went back to the House of Darcy the next morning, 23 December, and this time it really was closed. He let himself in by a service entrance.

The Old Masters library was what he needed. The access was by an electronic keypad and he knew the number. He was an hour in there, and emerged with three reference books. These he took to the viewing room. The hessian-wrapped package was still on the high shelf where he had left it.

He borrowed the powerful spotlight again, and a magnifying glass from Sebastian Mortlake's private drawer. With the books and the glass he compared the face of the stooping man with others known to have come from the brush of the artist in the reference books. In one of these was a monk or saint: brown robe, tonsured head, a round bombé forehead and three tiny vertical lines of worry or deep thought, just above and between the eyes.

When he was done he sat in a world of his own as one who has tripped on a stone and may have discovered King Solomon's Mines. He wondered what to do. Nothing was proved. He could be wrong. The grime on the picture was appalling. But at least he should alert the top brass.

He replaced the picture in its wrapping and left it on Mortlake's desk. Then he entered the typing pool, switched on Deirdre's word processor and tried to work out how it functioned. Within an hour he had begun, finger by finger, to type a letter.

When he had finished he asked the computer, very politely, to run off two copies and this it did. He found envelopes in a drawer and hand-addressed one to Sebastian Mortlake and the other to the Vice-Chairman and Chief Executive Officer, the Hon. Peregrine Slade. The first he left with the picture on his departmental chief's private desk, the second he pushed under the door of Mr Slade's locked office. Then he went home.

That Peregrine Slade should return to the office at all so close to Christmas was unusual but well explained. He lived only round the corner; his wife, the Lady Eleanor, was almost permanently at their Hampshire place and by now would be surrounded by her infernal relatives. He had already told her he could not get down until Christmas Eve. It would shorten the purgatory of the Christmas break playing host to her family.

That apart, there was some snooping on senior colleagues he wished to accomplish and that needed privacy. He let himself in by the same

125

service entrance that Benny Evans had left an hour earlier.

The building was pleasantly warm – there was no question of turning off the heating during the break – and certain sectors were heavily alarmed, including his own suite. He disconnected the system for his office, passed through the outer office of the absent Miss Priscilla Bates and into his own inner sanctum.

Here he took off his jacket, took his laptop computer from his attaché case and plugged into the main system. He saw he had two items of e-mail, but would deal with them later. Before that, he wanted some tea.

Miss Bates would usually make this for him, of course, but with her gone he had to force himself to make his own. He raided her cupboard for the kettle, Earl Grey, bone china cup and a slice of lemon. He found one piece of that fruit and a knife. It was while he was looking for a socket for the kettle that he saw a letter on the carpet by the door. As the kettle brewed he tossed it onto his desk.

Bearing his cup of tea at last he returned to his own office and read the two e-mails. Neither was so important that it could not wait until the New Year. Logging on with a series of private access codes, he began to prowl through the database files of his department heads and fellow board members.

When he had trawled enough, his thoughts turned to his private problems. Despite a very handsome salary, Peregrine Slade was not a rich man. The younger son of an earl, hence the handle to his name, he had nevertheless inherited nothing.

He had married the daughter of a duke, who turned out to be a pettish and spoiled creature, convinced she was entitled as of right to a large manor in Hampshire, an estate to surround it and a string of very pricey horses. Lady Eleanor did not come cheap. She did however give him instant access to the cream of society, which was often very good for business.

He could add to that a fine flat in Knightsbridge, but he pleaded that he needed this for his work at Darcy. His father-in-law's influence had secured him his job at Darcy and eventual promotion to vice-chairman under the starchy and acerbic Duke of Gateshead, who adorned the chair of the board.

Shrewd investments might have made him wealthy but he insisted on managing his own and this was the worst advice he could have taken. Unaware that foreign exchange markets are best left to the geeks who know about them, he had invested heavily in the euro currency and had watched it tumble 30 per cent in under two years. Worse, he had borrowed heavily to make the placement and his creditors had delicately mentioned the word 'foreclosure'. In a word, he was in a hole of debt.

Finally there was his London mistress, his very private peccadillo, an obsessional habit he could not break, and hideously expensive. His eye fell on the letter. It was in a Darcy envelope, therefore in-house and addressed to him in a hand he could not recognize. Could not the fool use a computer or find a secretary? It must have appeared during the course of this day or Miss Bates would have seen it last night. He was curious. Who worked through the night? Who had been in before him? He tore it open.

The writer was clearly not good with a word processor. The paragraphs were not properly inset. The 'Dear Mr Slade' was in handscript and the signature said Benjamin Evans. He did not know the man. He glanced at the letterhead. Old Masters department.

Some wretched staff complaint, no doubt. He began to read. The third paragraph held his attention at last.

'I do not believe it can be a fragment broken from some much larger altarpiece because of the shape and the absence from the edges of the panel of any sign of detachment from a larger piece.

'But it could be a single devotional piece, perhaps contracted by a wealthy merchant for his private house. Even through the murk of several centuries of grime and stain, there appear to be some similarities with known works of . . .'

When he saw the name, Peregrine Slade choked violently and spilled a mouthful of Earl Grey all over his Sulka tie.

'I feel the precaution may be worthwhile, despite the expense, of having the picture cleaned and restored and, if the similarities are then more clearly visible, of asking Professor Colenso to study it with a view to possible authentication.'

Slade read the letter three more times. In the building off Knightsbridge his light alone burned out into the blackness as he thought what he might do. On his computer he accessed Vendor Records to see who had brought it in. T. Gore. A man with no phone, no fax, no e-mail address. A true address in a penurious district of cheap bedsitters. Ergo, a pauper and certainly an ignoramus. That left Benjamin Evans. Hmmmm. The letter ended, below the signature, with the words: cc Sebastian Mortlake. Peregrine Slade rose.

In ten minutes he was back from the Old Masters department holding the hessian package and the duplicate letter. The latter could be incinerated later. This was definitely a matter for the vice-chairman. At that point his mobile phone rang.

'Perry?'

He knew the voice at once. It was prim but throaty and his mouth went dry.

'Yes.'

'You know who this is, don't you?'

'Yes, Marina.'

'What did you say?'

'Sorry. Yes, Miss Marina.'

'Better, Perry. I do not like my title being omitted. You will have to pay for that.'

'I am really very sorry, Miss Marina.'

'It has been over a week since you came to see me. Mmmmm?'

'It has been the Christmas rush.'

'And in that time you have been an extremely naughty boy, haven't you, Perry?'

129

'Yes, Miss Marina.'

His stomach seemed to be running water, but so were his palms.

'Then I think we shall have to do something about that, don't you, Perry?'

'If you say so, Miss Marina.'

'Oh but I do, Perry, I do. Seven o'clock sharp, boy. And don't be late. You know how I hate to be kept waiting when I have my little ticklers out.'

The phone went dead. His hands were trembling. She always frightened the daylights out of him, even with a voice down a phone line. But that, and what came later in the schoolroom, was the point.

JANUARY

'My dear Perry, I am impressed and intrigued. Why such a sumptuous lunch, and so early in the year? Not that I am complaining.'

They were at Peregrine Slade's club off St James's Street. It was 4 January, a self-indulgent country was staggering back to work, Slade was the host and Reggie Fanshawe, proprietor of the Fanshawe Gallery in Pont Street, eyed with approval the Beychevelle Slade had ordered.

Slade smiled, shook his head and indicated that there were other lunchers a mite too close for absolute privacy. Fanshawe got the message.

'Now I am even more intrigued. I must wait, consumed with curiosity, until the coffee?'

They took their coffee quite alone in the library upstairs. Slade explained succinctly that six weeks earlier a complete unknown had walked in off the street with an unutterably filthy old painting that he thought might have some value. By a fluke and pressure of overwork in the Old Masters department it had come under the gaze of only one man, a young but evidently very clever junior valuer.

He slipped the Evans report across to the gallery owner. Fanshawe read, put down his glass of Special Reserve port, lest he spill it, and said, 'Good God.' In case the Almighty had missed the appeal, he repeated it.

'Clearly you must follow his suggestion.'

'Not quite,' said Slade. Carefully he explained what he had in mind. Fanshawe's coffee went cold and his port remained untouched.

'There is apparently a duplicate letter. What will Seb Mortlake say?'

'Incinerated. Seb left for the country the previous day.'

'There'll be a record on the computer.'

'Not any more. I had an IT wiz come in yesterday. That part of the database has ceased to exist.'

'Where is the painting now?'

'Safe in my office. Under lock and key.'

'Remind me, when is your next Old Masters sale?'

'On the twenty-fourth.'

'This young man. He'll notice, he'll protest to Seb Mortlake, who might even believe him.'

'Not if he is in the north of Scotland. I have a favour up there that I can call in.'

'But if the painting was not rejected and returned to owner, there would have to be a report and a valuation.'

'There is.'

Slade drew another sheet from his pocket and gave it to Fanshawe. The gallery owner read the anodyne text, referring to a work, probably early Florentine, artist unknown, title unknown, no provenance. Valued at £6,000 to £8,000. He leaned back, raised his port glass in a toast and remarked, 'Those beatings I gave you at school must have had some effect, Perry. You're as straight as a sidewinder on speed. All right, you're on.'

Two days later Trumpington Gore received a letter. It was from the House of Darcy on headed paper. There was no signature, but a stamp from the Old Masters department. It asked him to sign an enclosed form authorizing the auctioneers to proceed with the sale of his painting, which they valued at £6,000 to £8,000. There was a return-addressed envelope with stamp. Though he did not know it, the address would bring the letter, unopened, to Peregrine Slade's desk.

He was ecstatic. With even £6,000 he could stagger on for another six months, which surely would include further acting work. Summer was a favoured time for film-making on outside locations. He signed the authority form and sent it back.

On the 20th of the month Peregrine Slade rang the director of Old Masters.

'Seb, I'm in a bit of a bind and I wonder if you could do me a favour.'

132

'Well, of course, if I can, Perry. What is it?'

'I have a very old friend with a place in Scotland. He's a bit absent-minded and he clean forgot about the expiry of the insurance cover on his paintings. Reinsurance is due at the end of the month. The swine in his insurance company are cutting up rough. They won't reissue without an up-to-date revaluation.'

The valuation for insurance purposes of substantial or even not-so-substantial art collections was a service regularly performed by all the great art houses of London. There was of course a useful fee involved. But advance notice was habitually much longer.

'It's a bugger, Perry. We've got the big one in four days and we're working our tails off down here. Can't it wait?'

'Not really. What about that young lad you took on a couple of years ago?'

'Benny? What about him?'

'Would he be mature enough to handle it? It's not a huge collection. Mainly old Jacobean portraits. He could take our last valuation, add a bit and bingo. It's only for insurance.'

'Oh, very well.'

On the 22nd Benny Evans left on the night train for Caithness in the far north of Scotland. He would be gone a week.

On the morning of the sale, which Slade would be taking himself, he mentioned to Mortlake that there was one extra lot, not in the catalogue, an afterthought. Mortlake was perplexed.

'What extra lot?'

'A small daub that could be Florentine. One of those off-the-street things that your young friend Master Evans handled. The tail-end jobs that he had a look at after you had left for Christmas.'

'He never mentioned it to me. I thought they had all been returned to owner.'

'My fault entirely. Slipped my mind. Must have slipped his as well. I happened to be in to clear up some details just before Christmas. Saw him in the corridor. Asked him what he was doing. He said you had asked him to look at the last forty-odd of the hand-ins.'

'True, I did,' said Mortlake.

'Well, there was one he thought might be worth a try. I took it off him to have a look, got distracted, left it in my office and forgot all about it.'

He offered Mortlake the modest valuation that purported to come from Benny Evans and certainly bore his signature, let the director of Old Masters read it, then took it back.

'But do we have authority?'

'Oh yes. I called the owner yesterday when I saw the damn thing still in my office. He was more than happy. Faxed the authority through last night.'

Seb Mortlake had a lot more on his plate that morning than an anonymous daub with no attribution and a valuation close to his personal basement price of £5,000. His star offering was a Veronese, along with an exceptional Michele di Rodolfo and a Sano di Pietro. He grunted his assent and hurried to the auction room to supervise the running order. At ten a.m. Peregrine Slade mounted his rostrum, took his gavel in hand and the auction began.

He loved taking the most important auctions. The elevated position, the command, the control, the waggish nods to well-known dealers, bidders and pals from the inner coterie of the fine-art circuit of London, and the silent recognition of agents he knew would be there to represent some really mega player in the circus who would never dream of appearing personally.

It was a good day. Prices were high. The Veronese went to a major American gallery for more than double the estimate. The Michele di Rodolfo caused a few muted gasps as it went for four times the estimate.

As the last twenty minutes came into view he noticed Reggie Fanshawe slip into a seat at the rear and, as agreed, well to one side. As the last lot in the catalogue went under the hammer, Slade announced to a depleted hall: 'There is one extra item, not in your catalogues. A latecomer, after we had gone to press.'

A porter solemnly walked forward and placed a very grubby painting in a chipped gilt frame on the easel. Several heads craned forward to try to make out what it represented through all the grime covering the images.

'A bit of a mystery. Probably Florentine, tempera on board, some kind of a devotional scene. Artist unknown. Do I hear a thousand pounds?'

There was a silence. Fanshawe shrugged and nodded.

'One thousand pounds I have. Any advance on a thousand?'

His eyes swept the room and at the far side from where Fanshawe sat he found a signal. No-one else saw it, for it did not exist, but as the blink of an eye can constitute a bid, no-one was surprised.

'One thousand five hundred, against you, sir, on the left.'

Fanshawe nodded again.

'Two thousand pounds. Any advance on . . . two thousand five hundred . . . and three thousand . . .'

Fanshawe bid against the fictional rival to clinch the purchase at £6,000. As a known gallery owner his credit was good, and he took the picture with him. Three days later, much faster than usual, Mr Trumpington Gore received a cheque for just over £5,000, the hammer price minus commission and VAT. He was delighted. At the end of the month Benny Evans came back to London, utterly relieved to be free of the bleak fastness of a freezing castle in Caithness in January. He never mentioned the grubby painting to Seb Mortlake and presumed from Mortlake's silence that his chief had disagreed with him and that silence implied rebuke.

APRIL

Quite early in the month the sensation hit the art world. The window of the Fanshawe Gallery was dressed entirely in black velvet. Alone behind the glass, on a small easel, delicately but brightly lit by two spotlamps and guarded night and day by two big and muscled Group Four security guards, was a small painting. It had lost its chipped gilt frame.

The painting, tempera on poplar board, was much as the artist would have finished it. The colours glowed as fresh as when they were applied over 500 years before.

The Virgin Mary sat, gazing upwards, entranced, as the Archangel Gabriel brought her the Annunciation that she would soon bear in her womb the Son of God. Ten days earlier it had been authenticated without hesitation by Professor Guido Colenso, by far and away the world's leading authority on the Siena School, and no-one would ever gainsay a judgement by Colenso.

The small notice below the painting simply said: SASSETTA 1400–1450. Stefano di Giovanni di Consolo, known as Sassetta, was one of the first of the giants of the early Italian Renaissance. He founded the Siena School, and influenced two generations of Sienese and Florentine Masters who came after him.

Though his surviving works are few in number and comprise mainly panels from much larger altarpieces, he is valued beyond diamonds. At a stroke the Fanshawe Gallery became a world player, attributed with discovering the first single-work Annunciation painted by the Master.

Ten days earlier Reggie Fanshawe had clinched a sale by private treaty for over £2,000,000. The divvy-up was done quietly in Zurich and the personal financial position of each man was transformed.

The art world was stunned by the discovery. So was Benny Evans. He went back through the catalogue of the 24 January sale but there was no trace. He asked what had happened and was told about the last-minute addition. The atmosphere inside the House of Darcy was poisonous and he intercepted a lot of accusing stares. Word gets around.

'You should have brought it to me,' hissed a humiliated Sebastian Mortlake. 'What letter? There was no letter. Don't give me that. I've seen your report and your valuation to the vice-chairman.'

'Then you must have seen my reference to Professor Colenso.'

'Colenso? Don't mention Colenso to me. That shit Fanshawe hit upon the idea of Colenso. Look, laddie, you missed it. It was evidently there. Fanshawe spotted it, but you missed it.'

Upstairs an emergency board meeting was taking place. The acidulous Duke of Gateshead was in the chair but Peregrine Slade was in the dock. Eight other directors sat around the table pointedly studying their fingertips. No-one was in the slightest doubt that not only had the mighty House of Darcy lost about a quarter of a million in commission, but it had had in its hands a real Sassetta and had let it go to a sharper pair of eyes for £6,000.

'I run this ship, and the responsibility is mine,' said Peregrine Slade quietly.

'I think we all know that, Perry. Before we reach any conclusions, would you be kind enough to tell us exactly how this happened?'

Slade took a deep breath. He knew he was

speaking for his professional life. A scapegoat would be needed. He did not intend that it should be he. But he also knew that to be shrill or to whinge would have the worst possible effect.

'I am sure you all know that we offer the public a free valuation service. Always have. A tradition of the House of Darcy. Some agree with this, others not. Whatever one's view the truth still is that it is immensely time-consuming.

'Occasionally a real treasure is indeed brought in by a member of the public, identified, authenticated and sold for a large sum, with of course a substantial fee for us. But the vast majority of the stuff brought in off the street is junk.

'The sheer burden of work, and especially in the heavy pre-Christmas period, means that what appears to be the worst of the junk has to be seen by junior valuers, lacking the experience of thirty or more years in the business. That is what happened here.

'The painting in question was handed in by a complete nonentity. He had no idea what it was or he would never have brought it in. It was in a simply appalling state, so dirty the painting beneath the grime was almost invisible. And it was seen by a very junior valuer. Here is his report.'

He distributed copies of the valuation at £6,000 to £8,000 that he had himself prepared, pecking away at the computer keys in the dead of night. The nine board members read it glumly.

'As you will see Mr Benny Evans thought it might be Florentine, circa 1550, by an unknown artist and of modest value. Alas, he was wrong. It was Sienese, circa 1450 and by a Master. Under all that grime he just did not spot it. That said, his examination was clearly rather cursory, even slipshod. However, it is I who now offer my position here to the board.'

There were two who pointedly stared at the ceiling but six shook their heads.

'Not accepted, Perry. As for the slipshod young man, perhaps we should leave him to you.'

Peregrine Slade summoned Benny Evans to his office that afternoon. He did not offer the young man a seat. His tone was contemptuous.

'I don't have to explain to you the nature or extent of the disaster that this affair has visited on the House of Darcy. The papers have had a field day. They have said it all.'

'But I don't understand,' protested Benny Evans. 'You must have got my report. I put it under your door. All that about my suspicion it might really be a Sassetta. About having it cleaned and restored. About consulting Professor Colenso. It was all there.'

Slade icily proffered him a single sheet of headed paper. Evans read it without comprehension.

'But this isn't mine. This is not what I wrote.'

Slade was white with rage.

'Evans, your carelessness is bad enough. But I will not tolerate mendacity. No-one who attempts to offer me such pathetic lies has any place in this house. You will find Miss Bates outside. She has your cards. Clear your desk and be gone within an hour. That is all.'

Benny tried to have a word with Sebastian Mortlake. The kindly director listened for a few moments, then led the way to Deirdre's desk.

'Pray punch up the report and evaluation file for the twenty-third and twenty-fourth of December,' he said. The machine obediently regurgitated a sheaf of reports, one for Item D 1601. It was what Benny Evans had just seen in Slade's office.

'Computers don't lie,' said Mortlake. 'On your way, lad.'

Benny Evans may have had no A levels and little knowledge of computers, but he was no fool. By the time he hit the pavement he knew exactly what had been done and how. He also knew every man's hand was against him and that he would never work again in the art world.

But he still had one friend. Suzie Day was a cockney, not a classic beauty, and with her punky hairstyle and green fingernails there were some who would not have appreciated her. But Benny did, and she him. She listened for the hour it took him to explain exactly what had been done and how.

What she knew about fine art could have filled an entire postage stamp, but she had another talent, the precise opposite of Benny. She was a child of the computer generation. If you drop a new-hatched duckling into water, it will swim. Suzie had dipped her first forefinger into cyberspace with computer games at school and found her natural environment. She was twenty-two and could do with a computer what Yehudi Menuhin used to do with a Stradivarius.

141

She worked for a small firm run by a former and reformed computer hacker. They designed security systems to protect computers from illegal entry. Just as the best way to get through a padlock is to ask a locksmith, the best way to break into a computer is to ask someone who designs the defences. Suzie Day designed those defences.

'So what do you want to do, Benny?' she asked when he was finished.

He might have come from a back street in Bootle, but his great-granddad had been one of the Bootle Lads who went to the recruiting booths in 1914. They ended up in the Lancashire Fusiliers and in Flanders they fought like tigers and died like heroes. Of the 200 who went, Benny's great-grandpa and six came back. Old genes die hard.

'I want that booger Slade. I want him dead in the water,' he said.

It was that night in bed that Suzie had an idea.

'There must be someone else out there as angry as you are.'

'Who?'

'The original owner.'

Benny sat up.

'You're right, lass. He's been swindled out of two million quid. And he may not even know it.'

'Who was he?'

Benny thought hard.

'I saw the hand-in ticket briefly. Someone called T. Gore.'

'Phone number?'

142

'None listed.'

'Address?'

'I didn't memorize it.'

'Where would it be logged?'

'In the databank. Vendor Records or Storage lists.'

'Do you have access? A personal password?'

'Nope.'

'Who would?'

'Any senior executive, I suppose.'

'Mortlake?'

'Of course. Seb would be able to enquire for anything he wanted.'

'Get up, Benny luv. We're going to work.'

It took her ten minutes to log on to the Darcy database. She posed her query. The database asked for an identification of the enquirer.

Suzie had a list beside her. How exactly did Sebastian Mortlake identify himself? Did he use just 'S' or 'Seb' or the full Sebastian? Lower case, upper case or a mix? Was there a dot or a hyphen between first and second names, or nothing at all?

Each time Suzie tried a different format and got it wrong the Darcy database rejected her. She prayed there was not a maximum limit to the erroneous formats, followed by an alarm at Darcy that would close down the contact. Fortunately the IT expert who had set up the system had presumed that some of Darcy's art freaks were so naïve about computers that they would possibly forget their own codes. The link stayed open.

At the fifteenth try she got it. The director of Old

143

Masters was seb-mort: all lower case, first name shortened, hyphen, surname cut in half. The Darcy database accepted that seb-mort was on the line and asked for his password.

'Most people use something close and dear to themselves,' she had told Benny. 'Wife's name, pet dog's name, borough where they live, a famous figure they admire.'

'Seb is a bachelor, lives alone, no pets. He just lives for the world of pictures.'

They started with the Italian Renaissance, then the Dutch/Flemish school, then the Spanish Masters. At ten past four on a sunny spring morning Suzie got it. Mortlake was seb-mort and GOYA. The database asked what she wanted. She asked for the owner of storage item D 1601.

The computer in Knightsbridge scoured its memory and told her. Mr T. Gore, of 32 Cheshunt Gardens, White City, W.12. She obliterated all trace of her incursion and closed down. Then they grabbed three hours' sleep.

It was only a mile and they puttered through the waking city on Benny's scooter. The address turned out to be a shabby block of bedsitters and Mr T. Gore lived in the basement. He came to the door in his old Spanish bathrobe.

'Mr Gore?'

'I am he, sir.'

'My name's Benny Evans. This is my friend Suzie Day. I am . . . was with the House of Darcy. Are you the gentleman who offered a small old painting in a chipped gilt frame for sale about November last?'

Trumpington Gore looked worried.

'Indeed I did. Nothing wrong I hope? It was sold at auction in January. Not a fake, I hope?'

'Oh no, Mr Gore, it wasn't a fake. Just the reverse. It's chilly out here. Could we come in? I have something to show you.'

The hospitable Trumpy offered them both a share of his morning pot of tea. Since his windfall of more than £5,000 three months earlier he no longer needed to use the tea bags twice. While the two youngsters drank he read the page-long spread in the *Sunday Times* that Benny had brought with him. His jaw dropped.

'Is that it?' He pointed at the full-colour illustration of the Sassetta.

'That's it, Mr Gore. Your old painting in its brown hessian wrapping. Cleaned, restored and authenticated as a genuine and very rare Sassetta. Siena, about 1425.'

'Two million pounds,' breathed the actor. 'Oh, calamity. If only I had known. If only Darcy had known.'

'They did,' said Benny. 'At least they suspected. I was the valuer. I warned them. You have been swindled and I have been destroyed. By a man who cut a private deal with this art gallery.'

He began at the beginning, with a last group of hand-ins and a director impatient to get away for his Christmas break. When he had finished the actor stared at the picture of the Annunciation in the paper.

'Two million pounds,' he said quietly. 'I could

145

have lived comfortably for the rest of my life on that. Surely, the law—'

'Is an ass,' said Suzie. 'The record will show that Darcy made a mistake, an error of judgement, and that Fanshawe acted on a hunch and came up a winner. It happens. There is no recourse in law.'

'Tell me something,' said Benny. 'On the form you filled out, it said as profession "actor". Is that true? Are you an actor?'

'Thirty-five years in the profession, young man. Appearances in almost a hundred films.'

He forbore to mention that most of these appearances had lasted a few seconds.

'I mean, can you pass as someone else and get away with it?'

Trumpington Gore drew himself up in his chair with all the dignity a tatty old bathrobe would allow.

'I, sir, can pass for anything, in any company, and get away with the impersonation. It is what I do. Actually, it is all that I do.'

'You see,' said Benny, 'I have an idea.'

He spoke for twenty minutes. When he had done the impoverished actor pondered his decision.

'Revenge,' he murmured. 'A dish best eaten cold. Yes, the trail has gone cold. Slade will not be expecting us. I think, young Benny, if I may, that you have just gained a partner.'

He held out his hand. Benny took it. Suzie placed her own over theirs.

'One for all, and all for one.'

'Aye, I like it,' said Benny.

'D'Artagnan,' said Trumpy.

Benny shook his head. 'I were never much good at the French Impressionists.'

The rest of April was very busy. They pooled their funds and completed the research. Benny needed to invade the private correspondence file of Peregrine Slade, having access to all his private e-mails.

Suzie elected to go into the Darcy system via Slade's private secretary, Miss Priscilla Bates. Her e-identity was not long in coming. She was P-Bates as far as the database was concerned. The problem was her password.

MAY

Trumpington Gore followed Miss Bates like a shadow, in such a variety of disguises that she suspected not a thing. Having secured her private address in the borough of Cheam, it was Benny who by night raided her garbage bin and took away a binliner full of rubbish. It yielded little.

Miss Bates lived a life of blameless rectitude. She was a spinster and lived alone. Her small flat was as neat as a pin. She commuted to work on the train and underground to Knightsbridge and walked the last 500 yards. She took the *Guardian* newspaper – they tried 'Guardian' as a password, but it did not work – and she holidayed with a sister and brother-in-law at Frinton.

They discovered this from an old letter in the trash, but 'Frinton' did not work either. They also found six empty tins of Whiskas.

'She has a cat,' said Suzie. 'What's its name?'

Trumpy sighed. It meant another trip to Cheam. He appeared on the Saturday, knowing she would be in, and masqueraded as a salesman of pet paraphernalia. To his joy she was interested in the scratching post for bored cats, who otherwise shredded the loose covers.

He stood in the doorway, false buck teeth and heavy glasses, and a piebald tom emerged from the sitting room behind her to stare contemptuously at him. He enthused over the beauty of the animal, calling it 'puss'.

'Come here, Alamein, come to Mummy,' she called.

Alamein: a battle in North Africa in 1942 where her father had died when she was a baby of one. In Ladbroke Grove Suzie logged on again and punched it up. For the Darcy database Miss Priscilla Bates, private and confidential secretary to Peregrine Slade, was P-Bates ALAMEIN. And she had right of access to all her employer's private e-mails. Pretending to be her, Suzie downloaded a hundred personal letters.

It was a week before Benny made his selection.

'He has a mate on the Arts pages of the *Observer*. There are three letters here from the same man, Charlie Dawson. Occasionally Dawson hears of things going on at Christie's or Sotheby's and tips Slade off. He'll do.'

Using her cyber-skills, Suzie created a letter from Charlie Dawson to Peregrine Slade for later use. Benny was meanwhile studying the catalogue for the next major Darcy sale. Dutch and Flemish Old Masters, scheduled for 20 May. After a while he tapped the illustration of one small oil on paper, laid on canvas.

'That one,' he said. Suzie and Trumpy peered at it. A still life showing a bowl of raspberries: a blue and white Delft bowl and beside it several seashells. An odd composition. The bowl stood on the edge of an old and chipped table.

'Who the hell is Coorte?' asked Trumpington Gore. 'I've never heard of him.'

'Not many have, Trumpy. Quite minor. School of Middleburg, Holland, mid-seventeenth century. But a tiny life's work, barely more than sixty pictures worldwide. So ... rare. Always painted the same sort of stuff. Strawberries, raspberries, asparagus and sometimes seashells. Boring as hell, but he has his fans. Look at the estimated price.'

The catalogue suggested £120,000 to £150,000.

'So why Coorte?' asked Suzie.

'Because there is a Dutch lager billionaire who is obsessed by Coorte. Been trying for years to corner the world market in his fellow countryman. He won't be there, but his representative will. Holding a blank cheque.'

On the morning of 20 May the House of Darcy was humming with activity. Peregrine Slade was again taking the sale personally and had gone down to the auction hall when Miss Bates noted that he had incoming mail. It was nine a.m. The sale started at ten. She read the message for her employer and, suspecting from what it said that it

149

might be important, she used the laser-jet printer to run off a copy. With this in her hand she locked the office and scurried after him.

Slade was checking the position and function of his microphone on the podium when she found him. He thanked her and scanned the letter. It was from Charlie Dawson and could be exceedingly helpful.

'Dear Perry, I heard over dinner last night that a certain Martin Getty blew into town. He is staying with friends and hopes to remain incognito.

'You probably know he has one of the leading thoroughbred studs in Kentucky. He also has a very private, never seen, art collection. It occurred to me he might be in town for that reason.

'Cheers, Charlie.'

Slade stuffed the letter in his pocket and walked outside to the table of paddle girls in the lobby. Unless a bidder at one of these auctions is well known to the auctioneer, it is customary to fill out a form as an intending bidder and be issued with a 'paddle', a plastic card with a number on it.

This can be raised to signify a bid, but more importantly to identify a winning bidder, who will hold it up for the clerk to note the number. That gives name, address and bank.

It was still early, nine fifteen. There were only ten filled-out forms so far, and none mentioned a Martin Getty. But the name alone was enough to set Slade's tastebuds watering. He had a quick word with the three lovely girls behind the table and went back to the hall.

It was a quarter to ten when a shortish man, not particularly smart, approached the table.

'You would like to bid, sir?' said one of the girls, drawing a form towards her.

'I surely would, young lady.'

The Southern drawl was lazy as molasses.

'Name, sir?'

'Martin Getty.'

'And address?'

'Over here or back home?'

'Full residential, if you please.'

'The Beecham Stud, Louisville, Kentucky.'

When the details were complete the American took his paddle and wandered into the saleroom. Peregrine Slade was about to mount the podium. As he reached the bottom step there was a deferential tug at his elbow. He looked down. Her bright eyes were alight.

'Martin Getty. Shortish, grey hair, goatee, shabby coat, dressed down.' She glanced around. 'Third row from back, on the centre aisle, sir.'

Slade beamed his pleasure and continued his climb to his own Olympus. The auction began. The Klaes Molenaer at Lot 18 went for a tidy sum and the clerk below him noted all the details. The porters brought the masterpieces, major and minor, to the easel beside and below the podium one after the other. The American failed to bid.

Two Thomas Heeremans went under the hammer and a fiercely contested Cornelis de Heem fetched double the estimate, but still the American failed to bid. Slade knew at least two-thirds of those present and he had spotted the young dealer from Amsterdam, Jan de Hooft. But what was the mega-rich American there for? Dressing down in a shabby coat, indeed. Did he think he could fool the ace he faced, the supreme Peregrine Slade? The Adriaen Coorte was Lot 102. It came up just after eleven fifteen.

At the outset there were seven bidders. Five had gone by £100,000. Then the Dutchman raised his hand. Slade glowed. He knew exactly whom de Hooft represented. Those hundreds of millions made from foaming lager beer. At £120,000 one of the bidders dropped out. The remaining one, a London agent, contested with the impassive Dutchman. But de Hooft saw him off. He had the bigger cheque book and he knew it.

'At one hundred and fifty thousand, any advance on one hundred and fifty thousand?'

The American raised his head and his paddle. Slade stared. He wanted the Coorte for his Kentucky collection. Oh joy. Oh unbridled lust. A Getty versus Van Den Bosch. He turned to the Dutchman.

'Against you, sir. I have one hundred and sixty thousand on the aisle.'

De Hooft did not blink. His body language was almost contemptuous. He glanced at the figure on the aisle and nodded. Inside himself Slade was in a transport of delight.

'My little Dutch Johnny,' he thought, 'you haven't the faintest idea who you are taking on.'

'One hundred and seventy thousand, sir, any . . .'

The American flicked his paddle and nodded. The bidding went up and up. De Hooft's demeanour lost its at-ease attitude. He frowned and tensed. He knew his patron had said 'Acquire it' but surely there were limits. At half a million he drew a small mobile from his pocket, jabbed twelve numbers into it and spoke in low, earnest Dutch. Slade waited patiently. No need to intrude into private grief. De Hooft nodded.

By £800,000 the hall was like a church. Slade was going up in modules of £20,000. De Hooft, a pale man when he entered the hall, was now paper-white. Occasionally he muttered into his mobile and went on bidding. At £1,000,000 sanity in Amsterdam finally prevailed. The American raised his head and nodded slowly. The Dutchman shook his.

'Sold for one point one million pounds, paddle number twenty-eight,' said Slade. There was a collective exhalation of breath. De Hooft switched off his mobile, glared at the Kentuckian and swept from the hall.

'Lot one hundred and three,' said Slade with an imperturbability he did not feel. 'Landscape by Anthonie Palamedes.'

The American, cynosure of all eyes, rose and walked out. A bright young beauty accompanied him.

'Well done, sir, you got it,' she burbled.

'Been quite a morning,' drawled the Kentuckian. 'Could you tell me where Ah would find the men's washroom?'

'Oh, the loo. Yes, straight down and second door on the right.'

She watched him enter, still carrying the tote bag he had had all morning, and maintained her position. When he came out she would accompany him to the accounts department for the boring details.

Inside the washroom Trumpington Gore took the calfskin attaché case from the tote bag, and extracted the black Oxford shoes with the Cuban heels. In five minutes the goatee beard and grey wig were gone. Ditto the tan slacks and shabby coat. All went into the tote bag which was dropped out of the window into the courtyard below. Benny caught it and was away.

Two minutes later the very pukka London businessman emerged. He had slicked-back thin black hair and gold-rimmed glasses. He was two inches taller, in a beautifully cut, but rented, pinstripe suit, Thomas Pink shirt and Brigade of Guards tie. He turned and walked straight past the waiting girl.

'Damned good auction, what?' He just could not resist it. 'See that American fella got his piece.'

He nodded towards the door behind him and strode on. The girl kept staring at the lavatory door.

It took a week before the fertilizer really hit the fan but when it did it went all over the place.

Repeated enquiries revealed that though the Getty dynasty contained many family members it did not contain a Martin and none of them had a Kentucky stud. When word got around, Darcy in general and Peregrine Slade in particular became a laughing stock.

The hapless vice-chairman tried to persuade the underbidder, Jan de Hooft representing Old Man

Van Den Bosch, to settle at a million. Not a chance.

'I would have had it for a hundred and fifty thousand but for your impostor,' the Dutch dealer told him down the phone. 'So let's settle for that.'

'I'll approach the vendor,' said Slade.

The seller was the estate of a lately departed German nobleman who had once been an SS tank officer in Holland during the war. This unhappy coincidence had always cast a shadow over the issue of how he came by his Dutch collection in the first place, but the old Graf had always protested that he had acquired his Dutch Masters before the war, and had beautifully forged invoices to prove it. The art world is nothing if not flexible.

But the estate was represented by a firm of Stuttgart lawyers and it was with these that Peregrine Slade had to deal. A German lawyer in one hell of a temper is seldom a pretty sight, and at six feet and five inches senior partner Bernd Schliemann was pretty formidable when happy. The morning he learned the full details of what had happened to his client's property in London and the offer of £150,000, he moved into a towering rage.

'*Nein,*' he roared down the phone to his colleague who had gone over to negotiate. '*Nein. Völlig ausgeschlossen.* Withdraw it.'

Peregrine Slade was by no means a complete fool. The empty lavatory, eventually penetrated by a male colleague after half an hour, started the suspicions. The girl gave a good description of the only man who had come out. But that made two descriptions, both completely different.

Charlie Dawson had been stunned when taxed with his part in the matter. He had sent no letter, never heard of any Martin Getty. His e-mail letter was shown to him. Identification showed it purported to come from his word processor, but the installer of the entire Darcy system admitted that a real wizard in the cyberworld could forge that provenance. That was when Slade knew for certain that he had been well tupped. But by whom, and why?

He had just issued instructions for the Darcy computer system to be turned into Fort Knox when he received a curt summons to the private office of the Duke of Gateshead.

His Grace may not have been as noisy as Herr Schliemann, but his anger was as intense. He stood with his back to the door as Peregrine Slade responded to the command to 'Enter.' The chairman was staring out of the window at the roofs of Harrods 500 metres away.

'One is not happy, my dear Perry,' he said. 'Not happy at all. There are a number of things in life one does not like, and one of them is being laughed at.'

He turned and advanced to his desk, placing splayed fingertips on the Georgian mahogany and leaning slightly to fix his deputy with baleful blue eyes.

'A chap goes into his club and a chap is laughed at. Openly, don't you see, dear old bean.'

The term of endearment was like a dagger in the sun.

'And you blame incompetence,' said Slade.

'Should I not?'

'This was sabotage,' said Slade and offered five sheets of paper. The duke was slightly taken aback but he fished spectacles from a top pocket and read them quickly.

One was the phoney letter from Charlie Dawson. The second was a sworn affidavit that he had never sent it, and the third a statement from the best computer expert available to the effect that a near-genius in computer technology could have created it and inserted it into Slade's private e-mail system.

The fourth and fifth papers were from two girls in the saleroom that day, one detailing how the supposed Kentuckian had introduced himself and the other describing how he had vanished.

'Have you any idea who this rogue could be?' asked the duke.

'Not yet, but I intend to find out.'

'Oh, you do that, Perry. Do it without delay. And when you have him, ensure he spends a long time behind bars. Failing that, ensure he is spoken to in such a manner that he will never come within a mile of us again. In the meantime, I shall try to pacify the board – again.'

Slade was about to go when His Grace added an afterthought.

'After the Sassetta affair, and now this, we need something pretty spectacular to restore our image. Keep eyes and ears open for such an opportunity. Failing that, and a resolution of this impersonation business, the board may have to consider a little . . . restructuring. That is all, my dear Perry.'

When he left the room the nervous tic near Slade's left eye, that always flared when he was under extreme stress or in the grip of powerful emotions, was flicking like a panicky Aldis lamp.

JUNE

Slade was not as lost for thoughts as he had pretended. Someone had wreaked immense damage on the House of Darcy. He looked for motive. Gain? But there had been none, except that the Coorte was now going to another auctioneer. But would a rival do this?

If not gain, then revenge. Who would have such a rage against him, and enough knowledge to guess that an agent acting for Van Den Bosch would be present in the hall with a big enough cheque to hike the Coorte to such ludicrous levels?

His thoughts had already settled on Benny Evans, who would have had both. But the 'Martin Getty' he had stared at was not Benny Evans. Yet he had been briefed. He had sat silent until that single picture came under the hammer. So . . . a fellow conspirator. A mere hireling, or another with a grudge?

On 2 June he sat in the chambers in Lincoln's Inn of one of the most eminent lawyers in England. Sir Sidney Avery laid down the brief and pinched the bridge of his nose.

'Your query is: did this man commit an offence in criminal law?'

158

'Precisely.'

'He masqueraded as someone who does not even exist?'

'He did.'

'That, alas, is not an offence in law, unless it was done for the purpose of fraudulent gain.'

'The masquerade was supported by a clearly forged letter of introduction.'

'Actually, a tip-off, but admittedly forged.'

Privately, Sir Sidney thought the scam hilarious. It was the sort of thing that always went down hugely well at the Benchers' dinners in hall. But his expression indicated he was contemplating mass murder.

'Did he at any time claim he was a member of the famously wealthy Getty family?'

'Not exactly.'

'You presumed he was?'

'I suppose so.'

'Did he at any time attempt to take this Dutch picture, or any other picture, with him?'

'No.'

'Have you any idea who he was?'

'No.'

'Can you think of any thoroughly disgruntled ex-employee who might have dreamed this up?'

'Only one, but it was not he in the hall.'

'You dismissed the employee?'

'Yes.'

'On what grounds?'

The last thing Slade intended was to describe the Sassetta swindle.

'Incompetence.'

'Was he a genius with a computer?'

'No. He could hardly use one. But a walking encyclopedia on Old Masters.'

Sir Sidney sighed. 'I am sorry to be discouraging, but I don't think the boys in blue are going to want to know about this. Nor the Crown Prosecution Service. Question of proof, you see. Your actor fellow can be a grey-haired Kentuckian with goatee, American accent and shabby coat one minute, and a crisply spoken ex-Guards officer in pinstripes the next. Whoever you might think you have traced, can you prove who it was? Did he leave fingerprints? A clear signature?'

'An illegible scrawl.'

'Precisely. He denies it all, and the police are nowhere. Your dismissed encyclopedia only has to say he does not know what you are talking about and ... same thing. Not a shred of proof. And somewhere in the back there seems to be a computer wizard. I'm sorry.'

He rose and held out his hand. 'If I were you, I would drop it.'

But Peregrine Slade had no intention of dropping anything. As he emerged into the cobbled yards of one of London's four Inns of Court, a word Sir Sidney Avery had used stuck in his mind. Where had he seen or heard the word 'actor' before?

Back at his office he asked for the details of the original vendor of the Sassetta. And there it was: profession, actor. He engaged a team from London's most discreet private investigation agency. There were two in the team, both ex-detective inspectors of the Metropolitan Police, and they were on double rate for quick results. They reported back in a week but brought little news.

'We followed the suspect Evans for five days but he seems to lead an uneventful life. He is seeking work in a menial capacity. One of our younger colleagues got talking to him in a pub. He appeared completely ignorant of the affair of the Dutch picture.

'He lives at his old address with a punk-style girlfriend, enough metal in her face to sink a cruiser, peroxide hair in spikes, hardly your computer-literate type.

'As for the actor, he seems to have vaporized.'

'This is the year 2000,' protested Slade. 'People cannot vaporize any more.'

'That's what we thought,' said the gumshoe. 'We can trace any bank account, any credit card, car document, driving licence, insurance policy, social security number – you name it, we can find the address of the owner. But not this one. He is so poor, he hasn't got any.'

'None?'

'Oh, he collects Unemployment Benefit, or he used to, but not any more. And the address the Social Security people have for him is the same you gave us. He has an actor's union Equity card; same address. As for the rest, everyone is computerized nowadays except this Mr Trumpington Gore. He has gone straight through some crack in the system and disappeared.'

'The address I gave you. You went to it?'

'Of course, sir. First port of call. We were men from the borough council, enquiring about arrears of council tax. He's quit and gone. The bedsit has been taken over by a Pakistani minicab driver.'

And that, for Slade, was the end of a very expensive trail. He presumed that with £5,000 in his trousers the invisible actor had gone abroad, which would account for every detail the private investigators had, or more accurately had not, brought him.

In fact Trumpington Gore was two miles away in a café off Portobello Road with Benny and Suzie. All three were becoming worried. They were beginning to understand the sort of levels of pressure an angry and wealthy Establishment can generate.

'Slade must be onto us,' said Benny as they nursed three glasses of cheap house wine. 'Someone struck up a conversation with me in a pub a few days ago. My age, but reeking of private fuzz. Tried to bring up the affair of what happened to Darcy at the saleroom. I played dumb as a brick. I think it worked.'

'I've had two following me,' said Suzie. 'Alternating. I had to stay away from work for two days. I think they've left off.'

'How do you know you shook them?' asked Trumpy.

'I finally turned on the younger one and offered 'im a blow job for twenty quid. He went down that street like a ferret on skates. I think that persuaded them I'm not much with a computer. Not many computer people are on the game.'

'And I fear I have had the same,' murmured Trumpington Gore. 'Two private dicks' (the phrase sounded strange in the voice of Sir John Gielgud) 'came round to my humble abode. Claiming to be from the council. By a mercy I was practising my craft. I was in role as a Pakistani minicab driver at the time. But I think I should move.'

'That apart, we are running out of money, Trumpy. My savings are gone, the rent is due, and we can't take any more off you.'

'Dear boy, we have had our fun, we have taken a sweet revenge, perhaps we should pack it in.'

'Yes,' said Benny, 'except that the shit Slade is still there, sitting on my career and a million of your money. Look, I know it's a lot to ask, but I have an idea...'

JULY

On 1 July the Director of British Modern and Victorian paintings at the House of Darcy received a polite letter, apparently from a schoolboy of fourteen. The youth explained that he was studying art for his GCSE exams and was particularly interested in the Pre-Raphaelite school. He asked where he could see the best works of Rossetti, Millais and Holman Hunt on public display.

Mr Alan Leigh-Travers was a courteous man and dictated a prompt reply answering the youthful query in full. When it was typed up, he signed it personally in his own hand: Yours sincerely, Alan Leigh-Travers.

The most prestigious institute in London for the study, identification and authentication of works of art was undoubtedly the Colbert Institute, and deep in its basement lay the scientific laboratory with its formidable array of investigative technology. The Chief Scientist was Professor Stephen Carpenter. He too received a letter. It purported to come from a graduate student preparing her thesis.

The writer explained that she had chosen as her subject the great attempted art frauds of the twentieth century, and the gallant role of science in exposing the work of the fraudsters.

Professor Carpenter was happy to reply and to suggest she read his own work on that very subject, available through the institute's bookshop in the foyer. He too signed his letter personally.

By the 7th of the month Benny Evans had two genuine signatures and samples of handwriting.

Suzie Day knew her boss had once been one of the country's most skilful computer hackers before he did his spell in prison, turned legitimate and started to create security systems aimed at preventing or frustrating attempts to hack into his clients' systems.

Suzie asked him over lunch one day if he had ever, during his period as a guest of Her Majesty, come across another certain type of fraudster. He shrugged in ignorance and pretended that he had no such knowledge. But the man had a mischievous sense of humour and a long memory.

Three days later Suzie Day found a piece of paper tucked into the keys of her personal machine in the office. It simply said: Peter the Penman. There was a phone number. Nothing else was ever said.

On the 10th of the month Trumpington Gore let himself into the back door of the House of Darcy, the one approached from the rear loading yard. It was a self-closing door, operated from the outside only by a keypad, but Benny still remembered the number. He had often gone in and out that way to reach the cheap café where he occasionally took his lunch breaks outside the building.

The actor was wearing a buff dust coat with the logo of Darcy on the breast pocket, exactly like all the other porters, and he carried an oil painting. It was the lunch hour.

A dust-coated porter carrying a painting, walking through the corridors of an art auction house, is about as noticeable as a raindrop in a thunderstorm.

It took Trumpy ten minutes and several apologies before he found an empty office, went inside, locked the door behind him and went through the desk drawers. When he left, the way he had come, he was also carrying two sheets of genuine headed writing paper and two logo-bearing envelopes.

Four days later, having visited the Colbert Institute as a tourist to note the type of dust coats worn there, he reappeared as a Colbert porter and did exactly the same. No-one even turned a head.

By the end of July Peter the Penman, for a modest £100, had created two beautiful letters and a laboratory report.

Benny spent most of the month tracking down a man of whom he had heard years before, a name whispered with horror in the corridors of the art world. To his great relief he found the old man still alive and living in poverty in Golders Green. In the annals of art fraud, Colley Burnside was a bit of a legend.

Many years earlier he had been a talented young artist moving in that Bohemian post-war society of Muriel Belcher's Colony Club and the artists' haunts around Queensway and the studios of Bayswater.

He had known them all in their collective youth: Freud, Bacon, Spencer, even the baby Hockney. They had become famous, he had not. Then he had discovered that he had a forbidden talent. If he could not create his own original works that people would buy, he could create someone else's.

He studied the techniques of centuries ago, the chemicals in the paints, the egg yolk in the tempera and the effect of centuries of ageing that could be recreated with tea and wine. Unfortunately, though he left the tea alone, he started to indulge in the wine.

In his time he passed off to the greedy and the gullible over a hundred canvases and oil-on-boards from Veronese to Van Dyck. Even before they caught him it was reckoned he could run you up a pretty good Matisse before lunch.

After lunch was a problem because of what he called his 'little friend'. Colley's bel amour was ruby in colour, liquid and normally grown on the slopes of Bordeaux. He tripped up because he tried to sell something he had painted after lunch.

An outraged and humiliated art world insisted on the full rigour of the law and Colley was taken away to a large grey building with bars where the screws and the hard men treated him like a favourite uncle.

It took the art world years to work out how many Burnsides were hanging on their walls, and he secured a considerable reduction in his sentence by telling all. When he came out of durance vile, he faded into oblivion, making a thin living dashing off sketches for tourists.

Benny took Trumpy to meet the old man because he thought they would get on, and they did. Two rejected talents. Colley Burnside listened, gratefully savouring the Haut Médoc that Benny had brought, a welcome change from his habitual Chilean Merlot from Tesco.

'Monstrous, dear boy, utterly monstrous,' he spluttered when Benny had finished and Trumpy had confirmed his missing two millions. 'And they called me a crook. I was never in the same league as some of these sharks. But as to the old days, I'm out of it now. Too long in the tooth, over the hill.'

'There would be a fee,' said Trumpy.

'A fee?'

'Five per cent,' said Benny.

'But five per cent of what?'

Benny leaned over and whispered in his ear. Colley Burnside's rheumy eyes lit up. He had a vision of Château Lafitte glowing like garnets by the light of the fire.

'For that kind of fee, dear boy, I will produce you a masterpiece. Nay, not one but two. Colley's last stroke. Gentlemen, to hell with them all.'

There are some paintings which, though extremely old and painted on ancient timber boards, have been so destroyed that hardly a fragment of the original paint remains and they are then valueless. Only the old timber board retains a small value, and it was one of these that Benny acquired after scouring a hundred old shops that claimed to sell antiques but in fact stocked only ancient junk.

From a similar emporium he acquired for £10 a Victorian oil of surpassing ugliness. It showed two dead partridge hanging from a hook, and a double-hammer shotgun propped against the wall. It was titled *The Game Bag*. Colley Burnside would have little trouble copying it, but would have to force himself to make it as devoid of talent as the original.

On the last day of July a ginger-whiskered Scot with a pretty impenetrable accent walked into the branch office of the House of Darcy in Bury St Edmunds, county of Suffolk. It was not a large office but covered the three counties of East Anglia.

'I have here, lassie,' he told the girl behind the counter, 'a work of great value. Created these hundred years ago by my own grandfather.'

He triumphantly showed her *The Game Bag*. She was no expert but even she thought the partridge looked as if they had been hit by a truck.

'You wish to have it valued, sir?'

'Aye, that I do.'

The Bury office had no facility for valuations, which could only be carried out by the London staff, but she could take the painting in and note the vendor's details. This she did. Mr Hamish McFee claimed to live at Sudbury and she had no reason to believe that this was not so. In fact the address was that of a small newsagent whose proprietor had agreed to take in and keep all mail for Mr McFee until further notice, for a consideration of £10 a month in his back pocket. In the next van the Victorian daub was sent down to London.

Before leaving the office Mr McFee noted that his grandfather's genius had been tagged with a storage identification number: F 608.

AUGUST

The month of August swept over the West End of London like a pint of chloroform. The tourists took over and those who lived and worked in the city tried to get away. For the upper crust of the House of Darcy that meant a variety of choice destinations: villas in Tuscany, manors in the Dordogne, chalets in Switzerland, yachts in the Caribbean.

Mr Alan Leigh-Travers was a passionate amateur yachtsman and kept his own ketch in the British Virgin Islands where it was boarded during the non-use periods at a boatyard behind Trellis Island. He intended to spend his three weeks away cruising as far south as the Grenadines.

Peregrine Slade might have thought he had made

the Darcy computer as safe as Fort Knox but he was wrong. The IT expert he had called in used one of the systems invented and developed by Suzie's boss. She had helped perfect some of the system's finer points. One who has developed a system can circumvent it. She did. Benny needed all the holiday rosters for August along with destinations and emergency contact addresses. These she had downloaded.

Benny knew that Leigh-Travers would be cruising the Caribbean, and that he had left two contact numbers: his worldwide mobile phone number and the listening frequency to which he would tune his yacht's radio. Suzie altered both numbers by one digit. Though unaware of it, Mr Leigh-Travers was going to have a really tranquil vacation, with no disturbances at all.

On 6 August the ginger Scotsman swept into the London office and demanded his oil painting back. There was no objection. He was helpful enough to identify it by storage number, and in ten minutes a porter had retrieved it from downstairs and handed it over.

By nightfall Suzie noted that the computer records had logged the painting as having been brought in to the Bury St Edmunds office for valuation on 31 July, but withdrawn by owner on 6 August.

She altered the last part. The new records showed it had been collected by arrangement by a van from the Colbert Institute. On the 10th Mr Leigh-Travers, who had never heard of *The Game Bag*, let alone seen it, left for Heathrow and Miami, there to take a connector flight to St Thomas and Beef Island where his ketch was waiting for him.

The Hon. Peregrine Slade was one of those who preferred not to travel in August. The roads, airports and resorts were a congested nightmare in his view. Not that he stayed in London; he retired to his country seat in Hampshire. Lady Eleanor would depart for her friends' villa at Porto Ercole and he could be alone with his heated pool, broad acres and small but adequate staff. His contact numbers were also on the holiday rosters log, so Benny knew where he would be.

Slade left for Hampshire on the 8th. On the 11th he received a letter, handwritten and posted at Heathrow. He recognized the writing and signature immediately: it was from Alan Leigh-Travers.

'My dear Perry, in haste from the departure lounge. In all the bother of trying to get away and leave the department shipshape for the September sale there was a matter I forgot to mention to you.

'Ten days ago some unknown brought a picture into the Bury office for valuation. When it reached London I had a glance at it. Frankly, a quite ghastly late-Victorian oil showing a couple of dead partridge and a gun. Utterly talentless and normally it would have gone straight back. But something about it seemed odd. It intrigued me.

'You will know the late Victorians painted both on panel and on canvas. This was on a panel that seemed extremely old, several centuries before the Victorian period.

171

'I have seen such panels before, usually in Seb's department. But not oak, that was what intrigued me. It looked a bit like poplar. So it occurred to me that some Victorian vandal might have painted over a much earlier work.

'I know it will cost a few quid and if it is all a waste of time, a big "sorry". But I have sent it to the Colbert to ask Steve Carpenter if he will have a look and give it an X-ray. Because I shall be away and Steve told me he is trying to get off as well, I asked him to send you his report direct to Hampshire.

'See you at the end of the month, Alan.'

Peregrine Slade lay on a lounger by the pool and read the letter twice while sipping his first pink gin of the day. He too was intrigued. Centuries-old poplar wood was never used by the British, even when they painted on panel. Northern Europe used oak. The Italians used poplar, and broadly speaking the thicker the panel the greater its age because the sawing techniques of centuries ago made thin panels almost impossible to cut.

Using someone else's old painting and painting over it was not uncommon, and it was quite well known in the history of art for some talentless idiot to overpaint an earlier work of genuine merit.

Thankfully modern technology had made it possible to age and date tiny fragments of wood, canvas and paint, to identify not only the country of source but sometimes even the school from which they came, and to X-ray an overpainting to see what lay underneath.

Leigh-Travers was right to do what he did, just in

case. Slade intended to go up to London the next day for an exquisitely painful visit to Marina; he thought he would also pop into the office to check the records.

The records confirmed everything the letter from Heathrow had said. A certain Hamish McFee had blown into the Bury office and left behind a Victorian still life entitled *The Game Bag*. It had been accorded a storage number of F 608.

The storage records showed that the oil had arrived in London on 1 August and been collected by the Colbert on the 6th. Slade closed down the system, reflecting that he would await with interest the report from the legendary Stephen Carpenter, whom he did not personally know.

Glancing at his watch he saw it was six p.m. in London or one p.m. in the Caribbean. He spent an hour trying to raise Leigh-Travers on his mobile or his marine radio, but kept finding himself speaking to someone else. Finally, he gave up and went off to his rendezvous with Marina.

On the 18th a shortish porter in the dust coat of the Colbert Institute walked through the front door of the House of Darcy and presented himself at the front desk. He bore a small oil painting in protective bubble wrap.

'Morning, luv. Delivery from the Colbert as arranged.'

The young woman behind the desk looked blank. The delivery man fished out a docket from his pocket and read from it.

'Darcy storage number F 608,' he read. Her face

cleared. She had a number for the computer on the table behind her.

'One moment,' she said, turned and consulted the fount of all wisdom. The oracle explained matters to her. She saw that this item had left the store for examination at the Colbert on the authority of the absent director of British Modern and Victorian art. And now it was being returned. She rang for a porter of her own.

Within minutes she had signed the Colbert man's receipt form and the wrapped painting had been taken back to store.

'If I spend any more time in that building,' thought Trumpington Gore as he emerged onto the hot pavement, 'I ought to start paying them rent.'

On the 20th Professor Stephen Carpenter's report arrived by recorded delivery at Peregrine Slade's manor in Hampshire. He took delivery of it over a late breakfast after a pleasing swim in the pool. As he read it his eggs went cold and his coffee formed a film of skin. The letter said:

'Dear Mr Slade, I am sure you will know by now that before he departed on holiday Alan Leigh-Travers asked me to have a look at a small oil painting purporting to be of the late-Victorian period and executed in this country.

'I have to say that the task turned out to be most challenging and finally very exhilarating.

'At first sight this picture, apparently titled *The Game Bag*, seemed to be of impressive ugliness and lack merit. A mere daub by a talentless amateur about a hundred years ago. It was the wooden

174

panel on which it was painted that caught Alan's attention and therefore it was to this that I turned my principal attention.

'I removed the panel from its Victorian frame and studied it closely. It is undoubtedly of poplar wood and very old. Along its edges I discovered traces of ancient mastic or glue, indicating that it was probably a fragment panel, once part of a much bigger work such as an altarpiece from which it has been broken away.

'I took a tiny sliver of wood from the rear of the panel and subjected it to tests for age and place of probable origin. You will know that dendrochronology cannot be used for poplar, since this tree, unlike oak, has no rings to denote the passing years. Nevertheless, modern science has a few other tricks up its sleeve.

'I have been able to establish that this piece of wood is consistent with those used in Italy in the fifteenth and sixteenth centuries. Further examination under a spectromicroscope revealed tiny nicks and cuts left by the blade of the cross-saw used by the sawyer. One minuscule irregularity in the blade created marks identical to those found on other panels of the period and the place, again consistent with fifteenth- and sixteenth-century Italian work.

'The Victorian painting of two dead partridge and a shotgun has beyond any doubt been painted over a much earlier work. I removed a tiny fragment of the oil, too small to detect with the naked eye, and established that the paint beneath is not oil but tempera.

'Taking an even smaller piece of the tempera for further spectro-analysis, I found it revealed the exact combination of ingredients used by several of the Masters of the period. Finally I X-rayed the painting to see what lies beneath.

'There is a tempera painting beneath, and only the crude thickness of the paint applied by the anonymous Victorian vandal prevents greater clarity.

'In the background is a rural landscape of the period mentioned, including several gentle hills and a campanile. The middle ground seems to have a road or track emerging from a shallow valley.

'In the foreground is a single figure, evidently of the sort to be found in the Bible, staring straight at the viewer.

'I am not able to give precise identification of the artist but you may have here a hidden masterpiece that comes straight from the time and place of Cimabue, Duccio or Giotto.

'Yours sincerely, Stephen Carpenter.'

Peregrine Slade sat transfixed, the letter lying on the table in front of him. Cimabue . . . Oh God. Duccio . . . Jesus wept. Giotto . . . bloody hellfire.

The nervous tic by his left eye began to flicker again. He reached up a forefinger to stop the trembling. He wondered what he should do.

He thought of two recent discoveries, both made (to his considerable frustration) by Sotheby's. In an old armoire in a manor on the Suffolk coast one of their valuers had discovered just such a panel and had spotted the hand of a Master. It had turned out to be by Cimabue, rarest of them all, and had sold for millions.

Even more recently another Sotheby's man had been valuing the contents of Castle Howard. In a portfolio of overlooked and low-rated drawings he had spotted one of a grieving woman, head in hands, and had asked for more expert examinations to be carried out. The drawing, unsuspected for 300 years, turned out to be by Michelangelo. Asking price? £8,000,000. And now it seemed that he too had a priceless treasure masquerading as two dead partridge.

Clearly another swindle with Reggie Fanshawe would never work. Getting rid of the very junior Benny Evans was one thing. Alan Leigh-Travers was quite another. The board would believe Alan, even though he might have no copy of the airport letter. Anyway, Fanshawe could never be used again. The art world was not *that* gullible.

But he could and would make his name and reputation and restore the House of Darcy to its original pillar of respect. If that was not worth a six-figure Christmas bonus, nothing would be. Within an hour he was washed, dressed, at the wheel of his Bentley Azure and eating up the miles to London.

The picture store was empty and he was able to rummage at his leisure until he had found the item logged as F 608. Through the bubble wrap he could make out the forms of two dead partridge on a hook. He took it to his office for further examination.

God, he thought as he looked at it in his room,

but it is ugly. And yet, beneath it . . . Clearly there was no question of letting it go for a song in the auction hall. It would have to be bought by the House, and *then* discovered by accident.

The trouble was, Professor Carpenter. A man of integrity. A man who would have filed a copy of his report. A man who would protest in outrage if some miserable plebeian, the original owner of the daub, was cheated by a certain Peregrine Slade.

On the other hand, he had not said that the hidden painting was certainly a masterpiece, only that it might be. There was no rule against an auction house taking a gamble. Gambles involve risks and do not always pay off. So if he offered the owner a fair price, taking into account the lack of certainty . . .

He punched up Vendor Records and traced Mr Hamish McFee of Sudbury, Suffolk. There was an address. Slade wrote, stamped and despatched a letter offering the miserable McFee the sum of £50,000 for his grandfather's 'most interesting composition'. To keep the matter to himself he included his personal mobile phone number as a means of contact. He was quite confident the fool would take it, and he would run the bill of sale to Sudbury personally.

Two days later his phone rang. There was a broad Scottish accent on the line and a deeply offended one at that.

'My grandfather was a magnificent artist, Mr Slade. Overlooked in his lifetime, but then so was van Gogh. Now I believe that the world will finally recognize true talent when it sees his work. I cannot accept your offer, but I will make one of my own. My grandfather's work appears in your next auction of Victorian Masters early next month or I shall withdraw it from sale and take it to Christie's.'

When Slade put the phone down he was trembling. Van Gogh? Was the man a retard? But he had no choice. The Victorian sale was slated for 8 September. It was too late for the catalogue, which had gone to press and would be available in two days. The miserable partridge would have to be a late entry, not uncommon. But he had the copy of his letter and offer to McFee and had taped the recent phone conversation. The offer of £50,000 would go a long way to appeasing Professor Carpenter, and the board of Darcy would back him to the hilt against any later flak.

He would have to buy the painting 'for the House' and that would mean a bidder in the hall to do exactly what he was told yet not look like a Darcy executive. He would use Bertram, the head porter, a man on the threshold of retirement, utterly loyal after forty years' service and with the imagination of an earwig. But able to obey orders.

At the other end of the phone Trumpington Gore had hung up and turned to Benny.

'Dear boy, do you really know what you are doing? Fifty thousand pounds is a hell of a lot of money.'

'Trust me,' said Benny. He sounded more confident than he was. Hourly he was praying to the cynical god of Old Masters that Slade would be too greedy to reveal what he intended to do into the ear of the rigorously honest Professor Carpenter.

By the end of the month all the senior executives were back in-house and preparations were in full swing for the first major sale of the autumn, the Victorian Masters of 8 September.

SEPTEMBER

Peregrine Slade remained silent on the matter of his own intentions for that day, and was pleased that Alan Leigh-Travers was also a model of discretion, refusing even to mention the subject. Nonetheless, every time they passed in a corridor Slade gave him a broad wink.

Leigh-Travers began to worry. He had always thought the vice-chairman a mite too foppish for his tastes, and had heard that men in middle years with a frigid marriage occasionally turned to the idea of playing an away game. As a father of four he earnestly hoped Slade had not started to fancy him.

The morning of the 8th produced the habitual buzz of excitement, the adrenalin rush that compensates in the art world for all the drudgery and the chore of examining the dross.

Slade had asked the venerable head porter Bertram to be in early and had briefed him to the last detail. In his years of service with the House of Darcy, Bertram had seen five changes of ownership. As a young man, just back from military service, following in his father's footsteps, he had been at the retirement party of old Mr Darcy, the last of the line. A real gent, he was; even the newest porter was invited to his party. They did not make them like that any more.

He was the last man in the building to wear a bowler hat to work; he had in his time carried masterpieces collectively worth billions up and down the corridors and never once put his foot through one.

Nowadays he sat in his tiny office, straining endless cups of tea through his walrus moustache. His orders were simple. He would sit at the back in his blue serge suit, armed with a bidding paddle, and he would bid for only one work. Just so that he would not mistake it for any other still life, he had been shown the two bedraggled partridge hanging from their hook. He had been told to memorize the title *The Game Bag* which Mr Slade would announce in clear tones from the podium.

Finally, just to make sure, he had been told by Slade to watch his face. If Slade wanted him to bid, and there was any hesitation, he would give a quick wink of his left eye. That was the signal for the old retainer to raise his paddle. Bertram went off for a cup of tea and to empty his bladder for the fourth time. The last thing Slade needed was to see his stooge shuffling off to the loo at the crucial moment.

Alan Leigh-Travers had selected a worthy menu of pictures. Stars of the show were two Pre-Raphaelites, a Millais from the estate of a recently deceased collector and a Holman Hunt that had not

181

been seen in public for years. Close behind them were two equine paintings by John Frederick Herring and a sailing ship in stormy weather from the brush of James Carmichael.

The sale started on the dot of ten o'clock. Bidding was brisk and the hall full; there were even some against the back wall. Slade had three still-life oils involving game and shotguns, and he decided to bring in the Scottish work as an unlisted fourth to this batch. No-one would be surprised, and the matter would be over in minutes. When he greeted the assembled throng he was at his most genial.

Everything went well. At the back Bertram sat and stared ahead, paddle in lap.

On the podium Peregrine Slade exuded good humour, even joviality, as the lots went for close to, or above, the upper estimate. He could recognize most of the bidders by sight but there were a dozen he did not know. Occasionally one of the overhead lights flashed off the pebble glasses of a dark-suited man three rows from the back.

During a brief pause as one picture was carried out and another placed on the easel, he beckoned one of the attendant girls to his side. Leaning down from the podium, he muttered: 'Who's the Jap three rows from the back, left-hand side?' The girl slipped away.

At the next picture-change she was back and put a small slip of paper into his hand. He nodded his thanks. Opening it on the podium he saw:

'Mr Yosuhiro Yamamoto, the Osaka Gallery, Tokyo and Osaka. He has presented a letter of credit drawn on the Bank of Tokyo for one billion yen.'

Slade beamed. About £2,000,000 to spend. Not a problem. He was certain he had heard or read the name Yamamoto before. He was right. That was the admiral who bombed Pearl Harbor. He was not to know that a namesake was back in Knightsbridge on a similar mission, or that the letter from the Bank of Tokyo was one of Suzie Day's computer creations.

Mr Yamamoto bid several times for offerings in the early part of the sale but never pursued, and withdrew in favour of others before the canvas was finally sold. Still, behind his impenetrable pebble lenses, he had established his bona fides as a genuine bidder.

The first of the four still lifes arrived. The three listed ones were all by relatively minor artists and went for between £5,000 and £10,000. As the third was removed Slade said with roguish humour: 'There is a fourth still life, not in your catalogues. A late arrival. A charming little piece by the Highland artist Collum McFee.'

Colley Burnside had not been able to resist the temptation to put at least part of his first name into the title of the artist. It was the only recognition he was ever going to get.

'Entitled *The Game Bag*,' Slade said clearly. 'What am I bid? Do I hear a thousand?'

Bertram raised his paddle.

'A thousand at the back. Do I have an advance on a thousand?'

Another paddle went up. The man must have been short-sighted. The rest of the bidders, dealers, collectors, agents and gallery owners were staring in something close to disbelief.

'It's against you, sir, at two thousand pounds,' said Slade, looking fixedly at Bertram. He lowered his left eyelid a fraction. Bertram raised his paddle.

'Three thousand pounds,' said Slade. 'Do I hear four?'

There was silence. Then the Japanese nodded. Slade was confused. He could see the thick black hair flecked with grey, but the almond eyes were masked by the bottle-thick lenses.

'Was that a bid, sir?' he asked.

'*Hai*,' said Mr Yamamoto and nodded again. He sounded like Toshiro Mifune in *Shogun*.

'If you would be kind enough to raise your paddle, sir,' said Slade. The man from Tokyo said clearly, 'Ah, so,' and raised his paddle.

'Four thousand pounds,' said Slade. His composure was still intact though he had never expected anyone to want to outbid the stolid Bertram. On cue, Bertram raised his paddle again.

The bemusement in the hall was nothing to that felt by Alan Leigh-Travers, who was leaning against the back wall. He had never seen or heard of *The Game Bag*, and if he had it would have been on its way home to Suffolk in the next van. If Slade wanted to introduce an extra lot into his sale, wildly post-catalogue, he might have mentioned it. And who was McFee? He had never heard of him. The ancestor of some shooting pal of Slade,

184

perhaps. Still, it had already made £5,000, God knew how, so no matter. A respectable price for anything and a miracle for this daub. The commission fee would keep the directors in decent claret for a while.

In the next thirty minutes the composure of Leigh-Travers was knocked sideways. The Japanese gallery-owner, the back of whose head he could see, kept nodding and saying '*Hai*' while someone out of sight behind a pillar further up the back wall kept raising him. What the hell did they think they were doing? It was a wretched daub of a painting, anyone could see that. The room had lapsed into utter silence. The price went through £50,000.

Leigh-Travers shuffled and jostled his way down the back wall until he came to the pillar and had a look round it. He almost sustained a heart attack. The mystery bidder was Bertram, for Pete's sake. That could only mean Slade was buying in, for the House.

Ashen-faced, Leigh-Travers caught Slade's glance across the length of the hall. Slade grinned and gave him another lascivious wink. That confirmed it. His vice-chairman had gone certifiably insane. He hurried from the hall to where the paddle girls sat, seized an internal phone and rang the chairman's office, asking Phyllis to put him through to the Duke of Gateshead as a matter of urgency.

Before he got back to the hall, the bidding had climbed to £100,000 and still Mr Yamamoto would not back off. Slade was raising now in multiples of £10,000 and beginning to worry badly.

He alone knew that millions of pounds lay beneath the two partridge, so why was the Japanese bidding? Did he also know something? Impossible, the painting was a walk-in from Bury St Edmunds. Had Professor Carpenter shot his mouth off somewhere in the Far East? Equally impossible. Did Yamamoto simply like the painting? Had he no taste at all? Did he think the tycoons of Tokyo and Osaka were going to flock to his galleries to buy this rubbish at a profit?

Something had gone wrong, but what? He could not refuse to take the bids from Yamamoto, not in front of the entire hall, but knowing what lay beneath the partridge he could not indicate to Bertram to stop, either, and thus let the work head for Japan.

The rest of the bidders realized something extremely weird was afoot. None of them had ever seen anything like it. Here was an appalling daub on display that normally should never have appeared in anything above a car-boot sale, and two bidders were driving it through the roof. One was an old codger in a walrus moustache and the other was an implacable samurai. The first thought that occurred to all of them was 'inside knowledge'.

They all knew that the art world was not for the squeamish and that some of the tricks of the trade would have made a Corsican knifeman look like a vicar. Every veteran in the hall recalled the perfectly true tale of the two dealers attending a miserable sale in a decrepit old manor house when one of them spotted a still life of a dead hare, hanging in the stairwell. Not even on display. But they backed a hunch and bought it. The dead hare turned out to be the last recorded painting ever done by Rembrandt. But surely old Harmenszoon on his deathbed and gripped by palsy could not have delivered those awful partridge? So they peered and peered, looking for the hidden talent, but could see none. And the bidding went on.

At £200,000 there was a disturbance in the doorway as people gave way and the wuthering height of the Duke of Gateshead slipped in. He stood against the back wall like a condor alert for a bit of living flesh to peck.

By £240,000 Slade's self-control was beginning to disintegrate. A sheen of sweat beaded his forehead and reflected the glare of the lights. His voice had gone up several octaves. Something inside him screamed for this farce to stop, but he could not stop it. His carefully scripted scenario was completely out of control.

At a quarter of a million the tic near his left eye began to act up. Across the hall old Bertram saw the endless winking and just went on bidding. By this point Slade wanted him to stop, but Bertram knew his orders: one wink, one bid.

'Against you, sir,' Slade squawked at the pebble glasses from Tokyo. There was a long pause. He prayed the nightmare would finally end. In a clear voice Mr Yamamoto said, '*Hai*.' Slade's left eye was going like the front end of a speeding ambulance, so Bertram raised his paddle.

At £300,000 Leigh-Travers whispered furiously in

the duke's ear and the condor began to move pur-
posefully down the wall towards his employee
Bertram. In the silent hall all eyes were on the
Japanese. He suddenly rose, placed his paddle on
his seat, bowed formally to Peregrine Slade, and
walked towards the door. The crowd parted as the
Red Sea before Moses.

'Going once,' said Slade weakly, 'twice.'

His gavel banged on the block and the room
erupted. As always with the ending of unbearable
tension, everyone wanted to say something to his
neighbour. Slade recovered somewhat, wiped
his brow, handed over the rest of the sale to Leigh-
Travers and descended his podium.

Bertram, released from his duty, headed for his
cubbyhole to brew a nice cup of tea.

The duke bent his head to his vice-chairman and
hissed: 'My office. Five minutes, if you please.'

'Peregrine,' he began when they were alone in
the chairman's suite. No more 'Perry' or 'dear old
bean'. Even the façade of amiability was gone. 'May
I ask exactly what the devil you thought you were
doing down there?'

'Conducting an auction.'

'Don't patronize me, sir. That appalling daub of
two partridge, it was junk.'

'At first sight.'

'You were buying it in. For the House. Why?'

From his breast pocket Slade retrieved the two-
page letter and report from Professor Carpenter at
the Colbert.

'I hope this explains why. I should have had it for

£5,000, maximum. But for that lunatic Japanese, I would have.'

The Duke of Gateshead read the report carefully in the sunlight from the window, and his expression changed. His ancestors had murdered and plundered their way to prominence, and, as with Benny Evans, old genes die hard.

'Different complexion, old bean, entirely different complexion. Who else knows about this?'

'No-one. I received the report at my home last month and kept it to myself. Stephen Carpenter, me, now you. That's it. Fewer the better, I thought.'

'And the owner?'

'Some idiot Scot. To cover our backs, I offered him £50,000. The fool turned it down. I have my letter and the tape of his rejection. Now, of course, I wish he had taken it. But I could not foresee that crazy Japanese this morning. Damn near robbed us of it.'

The duke thought for several moments. A fly buzzed on the pane, loud as a chainsaw in the silence.

'Cimabue,' he murmured. 'Duccio. Good God, we haven't had one of those in the House for years. Seven, eight million? Look, settle up with this owner without delay. I'll sanction. Who do you want for the restoration? The Colbert?'

'It's a big organization. Lots of staff. People talk. I'd like to use Edward Hargreaves. He's among the best in the world, works alone and is silent as the grave.'

'Good idea. Get on with it. In your court. Let me know the moment the restoration is complete.'

Edward Hargreaves did indeed work alone, a dour and secretive man with a private studio in Hammersmith. In the restoring of damaged or overpainted Old Masters, he was peerless.

He read the Carpenter report and thought of contacting the professor for a conference. But the senior restorer at the Colbert would be less than human if he were not deeply offended that the fascinating commission had gone to someone else, so Hargreaves decided to stay silent. But he knew the Colbert stationery and the professor's signature, so he could use the report as a base for his own labours. He informed Slade, when the Vice-Chairman of Darcy delivered the Scottish still life to his studio personally, that he would need two weeks.

He set it on an easel beneath the north light and for two days he simply stared at it. The thick Victorian oil paint would have to come off with extreme delicacy so as not to damage the masterpiece beneath. On the third day he began to work.

Peregrine Slade took his call two weeks later. He was agog.

'Well, my dear Edward?'

'The work is finished. What lay beneath the still life is now fully exposed to view.'

'And the colours? Are they as fresh as the day they were painted?'

'Oh, beyond a doubt,' said the voice down the phone.

'I'll send my car,' said Slade.

'I think perhaps I should come with the painting,' said Hargreaves carefully.

'Excellent,' beamed Slade. 'My Bentley will be with you in half an hour.'

He phoned the Duke of Gateshead.

'Splendid work,' said the chairman. 'Let's have an unveiling. My office, twelve hundred hours.'

He had once been in the Coldstream Guards and liked to pepper his talk to subordinates with military phrases.

At five to twelve a porter set up an easel in the chairman's office and left. At twelve sharp Edward Hargreaves, carrying the tempera-on-panel wrapped in a soft blanket and escorted by Peregrine Slade, entered the room. He placed the painting on the easel.

The duke had cracked open a bottle of Dom Perignon. He offered a glass to each guest. Slade accepted, Hargreaves demurred.

'So,' beamed the duke, 'what have we? A Duccio?'

'Er, not this time,' said Hargreaves.

'Surprise me,' said Slade. 'A Cimabue?'

'Not exactly.'

'Can't wait,' said the duke. 'Come on, lift the blanket.'

Hargreaves did so. The painting was indeed as the letter apparently from the Colbert had described it. Beautifully executed and precisely in the style of the early Renaissance of Florence and Siena.

The background was a medieval landscape of

gentle hills with, in the distance, an ancient bell tower. In the foreground was the single living figure. It was a donkey, or Biblical ass, staring forlornly at the viewer.

Its organ hung limply towards the ground as if recently and thoroughly pulled.

In the middle ground was indeed a shallow valley with a track down the centre. On the track, emerging from the valley, was a small but perfectly identifiable Mercedes-Benz.

Hargreaves contemplated a point in space. Slade thought he might succumb at once to a fatal heart attack, then hoped he would, then feared that he might not.

Inside the Duke of Gateshead five centuries of breeding grappled for control. Finally the breeding won and he stalked from the room without a word.

An hour later the Hon. Peregrine Slade left the building on a more permanent basis.

EPILOGUE

The remainder of September was an eventful period.

In response to daily phone calls, the Sudbury newsagent had confirmed a second embossed letter awaited Mr McFee. Disguised as the ginger-whiskered Scot, Trumpy had gone up by train to collect it. The envelope contained a cheque from the House of Darcy for £265,000.

Using some beautifully crafted e-documents from Suzie, he opened an account with Barclays

Bank in St Peter Port, Guernsey, Channel Islands, one of Britain's last no-tax havens. When the cheque was cleared and credited he went over for the day by air and opened another account in the name of Trumpington Gore with the Royal Bank of Canada, just down the street. Then he went to Barclays and transferred the lot from Mr Hamish McFee to Mr Gore down the road. The deputy manager at Barclays was surprised at the speed of the opening and closing of the Scotsman's account, but made no demur.

From the Canadians, who did not give a damn about British mainland tax laws, Trumpy extracted two banker cheques.

One, for £13,250, went to Colley Burnside, who could contemplate a twilight to his life floating contentedly on a sea of vintage claret.

Trumpy withdrew £1,750 in cash for himself as 'getting-by money'. The second cheque was for Benny Evans and Suzie Day jointly, in the sum of £150,000. With the balance of £100,000 the helpful Canadians were happy to create a long-term high-yield annuity fund capable of paying Trumpington Gore about £1,000 a month for the rest of his days.

Benny and Suzie married and returned to Benny's native Lancashire, where he opened a small art gallery and she became a freelance computer programmer. Within a year she had grown out the peroxide, removed the facial metal and had twin boys.

Trumpy got home from the Channel Islands to find a letter from Eon Productions. It told him that

Pierce Brosnan, with whom he had had a tiny role in *Goldeneye*, wished that he have a much larger part in the next Bond movie.

Someone tipped off Charlie Dawson, who, with the amused help of Professor Carpenter, secured the art-scandal scoop of the decade.

The police continue to search for Hamish McFee and Mr Yamamoto, but at Scotland Yard hopes are not high.

Marina sold her memoirs to the *News of the World*. Lady Eleanor Slade promptly had a lengthy conference with Fiona Shackleton, doyenne of London's divorce lawyers. A settlement was agreed in which the Hon. Peregrine was allowed to keep his cufflinks.

He left London and was last heard of running a louche bar in Antigua. The Duke of Gateshead still has to buy his own drinks at White's.

THE MIRACLE

The sun was a hammer in the sky. It beat down on the clustered roofs of the walled Tuscan city and the medieval tiles, some pink but mostly long baked to umber or ashen grey, shimmered in the heat.

Shadows dark as night were cast along upper windows by the overhanging gutters; but where the sun could touch, the rendered walls and ancient bricks gleamed pale, and wooden sills cracked and peeled. In the deep and narrow cobbled alleys of the oldest quarter there were restful pools of further shade and here the occasional sleepy cat sought refuge. But of local humans there was no sign, for this was the day of the Palio.

Down one such alley, lost in a maze of tiny cobbled ways, hardly wider than his own shoulders, the American tourist hurried, red as beef. Sweat trickled down to soak his short-sleeved cotton shirt, the tropical-weight jacket felt like a blanket dangling from his shoulder. Behind him his wife tottered painfully on unsuitable platform sandals.

They had tried to book far too late for a hotel

inside the city, in this of all seasons, and had finally settled for a room in Casole d'Elsa. The rented car had overheated on the road, they had eventually found a parking slot beyond the city walls and now scurried from the Porta Ovile towards their goal.

They were soon lost in the labyrinth of alleys dating back 500 years, stumbling on the hot cobbles, feet on fire. From time to time the Kansas cattleman cocked an ear towards the roar of the crowd and tried to head in that direction. His well-upholstered wife sought only to catch up and fan herself with a guidebook at the same time.

'Wait for me,' she called as they hurried down yet another defile of brick between town houses that had seen Cosimo of Medici ride by, and been old even then.

'Try to hurry, honey,' he called over his shoulder. 'We're going to miss the parade.'

He was right. A quarter-mile away the massed crowds in and around the Piazza del Campo were straining to catch the first glimpse of the Comparse, the parade in medieval costume of the seventeen great guilds of Siena who once ruled and administered the town. According to tradition, ten of the seventeen Contrade would race their horses that day for the honour of carrying away to their guild-hall the painted banner, the Palio itself. But first, the parade.

The American had read aloud from the guide-book to his wife in their hotel bedroom the previous evening.

'The Contrade or Districts of Siena were created

between the end of the twelfth and the beginning of the thirteenth century,' he read.

'That was before Columbus,' she objected, as if nothing had happened before the great Cristobal sailed from the Tagus estuary to head west into oblivion or glory.

'Right. That was in 1492. This was three centuries before Columbus. It says here they started with forty-two Contrade, reduced three hundred years later to twenty-three, then in 1675 to the seventeen we will see marching tomorrow.'

Out of sight, the first ranks of the hundreds of brightly caparisoned drummers, musicians and standard-bearers of the Comparse pageant were emerging into the Campo itself. Its sixteen palaces were hung with banners and ensigns, crammed with the privileged at every window and balcony, as 40,000 of the populace roared inside the race-ring.

'Hurry, honey,' he called behind him as the tumult ahead rose in volume. 'We've come a long way for this. I can see that darn tower at last.'

And indeed the tip of the Mangia Tower was just visible above the roofs ahead. That was when she tripped and fell, her ankle twisted by the cobbles and the shoe. She cried out and collapsed in a heap upon the stones. Her husband turned and ran back to her.

'Aw, honey, what have you done?' He was creased with concern as he bent over her. She clutched one ankle.

'I think I twisted it,' she said and started to cry.

It had started out so good and turned into such a bad day.

Her husband looked up and down the alley but the ancient timber doors were locked and barred. A few yards away was an arch in a high wall that enclosed the alley on one side. Sun shone through as if there was an open space there.

'Let's get you in there, see if we can find a place to sit,' he said.

He hauled her off the cobbles and she limped down to the arch. It gave onto a flagged yard, with tubs of roses and, Lord be praised, a stone bench in the shade of the wall. The American helped his spouse to the cool stone, where she sank with great relief.

Far away the tail end of the Comparse parade was leaving the Piazza del Duomo as the head of the column entered the Campo itself and the civic judges keenly studied the turnout, comportment and flag-waving skills of the standard-bearers. Whoever won the coming horse-race, the best-accoutred Contrada team would be awarded the *masgalano*, the finely chased silver salver. It was important, and all present knew it. The tourist bent to examine his wife's ankle.

'Can I be of help?' said a quiet voice. The American started and turned round. The stranger stood above him, framed by the sun. The tourist stood up. The man was tall and rangy, with a calm lined face. They were both of an age, mid-fifties, and the stranger had greying hair. In faded canvas slacks and denim shirt he looked like a wanderer, a hippie but no longer young. His English was cultured but with a hint of an accent, probably Italian.

'I don't know,' said the American with some suspicion.

'Your wife has fallen, hurt an ankle?'

'Yup.'

The stranger knelt on the flagstones of the yard, eased off the sandal and slowly massaged the damaged ankle. His fingers were gentle and skilled. The man from Kansas watched, prepared to defend his wife if need be.

'It is not broken, but I am afraid it is twisted,' said the man.

'How do you know?' asked the husband.

'I know,' said the man.

'Yeah? Who are you?'

'I am the gardener.'

'The gardener? Here?'

'I tend the roses, sweep the yard, keep it right.'

'But it is the day of the Palio. Can't you hear?'

'I hear. It will need strapping. I have a clean T-shirt I could tear into strips. And cold water to stop the swelling.'

'What are you doing here on the day of the Palio?'

'I never see the Palio.'

'Why? Everyone goes to the Palio.'

'Because it is today. The second of July.'

'What's so special?'

'It is Liberation Day also.'

'What?'

'On this day, thirty-one years ago, the second of July 1944, Siena was liberated from German occupation. And something happened here, in this courtyard, something important. I believe it was a miracle. I'll go for the water.'

The American was startled. The man from Topeka was a Catholic: he went to mass and confession; he believed in miracles – if they were endorsed by Rome itself. Much of his entire summer tour of Italy was to see Rome at last. Siena was an afterthought. He gazed around the empty courtyard.

It was about twenty yards by thirty. On two sides it was bounded by high walls, twelve feet at least, with one arch, gates drawn open, through which he had entered. On the other two sides the walls were even higher, fifty feet or more, blank but for a few slits, topped with roofs, the outer walls of a massive building centuries old. At the far end of the yard, set into the wall of the huge edifice, was another door. It was made not of planks but entire beams bolted together to withstand attack and it was closed tight shut. The timber was ancient as the city itself, long bleached by sun save for a few dark blotches.

Along one side of the court, from end to end, ran a colonnade or cloister, the leaning roof supported by a row of stone columns and casting deep, cool shade inside. The gardener came back with strips of cloth and a pannikin of water.

He knelt again and firmly strapped with bandages the injured ankle, pouring water into the fabric to soak it and cool the flesh. The American's wife sighed with relief.

'Can you make it to the Palio?' asked the husband.

The wife rose, tested the ankle, winced. It pained her.

'What do you think?' asked the tourist of the gardener. He shrugged.

'The alleys are rough, the crowds dense and very rowdy. Without a ladder or a raised position you will see nothing. But there will be celebrations all evening. You will see the pageantry then, in every street. Or there will be another Palio in August. Can you wait on?'

'Nope. I've got cattle to run. Gotta go home next week.'

'Ah. Then . . . your wife could walk, but gently.'

'Can we wait a bit, honey?' she asked.

The tourist nodded. He glanced round the courtyard.

'What miracle? I don't see no shrine.'

'There is no shrine. There is no saint. Not yet. But one day, I hope.'

'So what happened here thirty-one years ago this day?'

THE GARDENER'S STORY

'Were you in the Second World War?' asked the gardener.

'Sure. US Navy. Pacific theatre.'

'But not here in Italy?'

'No. My kid brother was. He fought with Mark Clark.'

The gardener nodded, as if staring into the past.

'All through 1944 the Allies fought their way up the Italian peninsula, from Sicily to the far north and the Austrian border. All that year the German army fought and retreated, fought and retreated. It was a long retreat. At first they were the allies of the Italians, then after the Italian capitulation the occupiers.

'Here in Tuscany the fighting was very fierce. Field Marshal Kesselring commanded. Facing him were the Americans under General Clark, the British under General Alexander and the Free French under General Juin. By early June the fighting front had reached the northern border of Umbria and the south of Tuscany on this western sector.

'South of here the terrain is rugged, range after range of steep hills, valleys holding hundreds of rivers and streams. The roads wind along the mountainsides, the only possible passage for vehicles. They are easily mined and can be raked by gunfire from across the valley. Hidden spotters on the peaks of the hills can drop the artillery shells from behind them right onto the enemy with great accuracy. Both sides took heavy casualties.

'Siena became a big medical centre. The Wehrmacht's Medical Corps set up several hospitals here and they were always full. Towards the end even they overflowed and several nunneries and monasteries were requisitioned. And still the

Allied tide rolled on. Kesselring ordered all wounded well enough to be moved to be sent north. Columns of German ambulances rolled north day and night. But some could not be moved and had to stay. Many died of their wounds and are buried outside the city. The pressure on space eased for a while; until the last ten days of that month. Then the fighting redoubled, and it was close. In those last ten days a young German surgeon was drafted in here, fresh from college. He had no experience. He had to watch and learn and operate as he went along. Sleep was short, supplies running dry.'

There was a roar across the summer sky as, out of sight, the last of the parading Comparse entered the Piazza del Campo. Each of the rival Contrade was parading once round the giant sand racetrack laid over the cobblestones. An even louder shout greeted the arrival of the *carroccio*, the ox-drawn cart bearing the lusted-for banner itself, the object of the day's pageantry, the Palio.

'The German force in this sector was the Fourteenth Army, commanded by General Lemelsen. On paper it sounded great, but many of the units were exhausted by months of fighting and way under strength. The main contingent in it was General Schlemm's First Parachute Corps and Schlemm threw everything he had got from the sea to the mountains south of Siena. That was his right wing. On the left, further inland, the tired-out 90th Panzer Grenadier Division tried to hold off General Harmon's US First Armored.

'Right in the centre of Mark Clark's Fifth Army, and facing Siena city, were the Free French of General Juin. He was flanked by his own Third Algerian Infantry and Second Moroccan Infantry. These were the forces held by the Germans in five days of vicious fighting from the twenty-first to the twenty-sixth of June. Then the American tanks smacked through the panzers and Siena was outflanked, first on the east, then by the French on the west.

'Units of the retreating German companies pulled back, bringing their wounded with them. There were grenadiers, panzer men, Luftwaffe Field Division men and paratroopers. On the twenty-ninth of June, south of the city, there was one last and final clash before the Allied breakthrough.

'It was violent and hand-to-hand. Under cover of darkness the German stretcher-bearers went in and did their best. Hundreds of wounded, both German and Allied, were brought back into Siena. General Lemelsen pleaded with Kesselring for permission to straighten his line, seeing as he was outflanked on both sides and risked being encircled and captured with the entire First Parachute Corps inside Siena. Permission was granted and the paras pulled back into the city. Siena bulged with soldiers. So many were the wounded that this courtyard beneath the walls of the old nunnery was commandeered as a temporary shelter and field hospital for about a hundred of the last-arriving Germans and all the Allied wounded. The newly arrived young surgeon was given sole charge of it. That was on the thirtieth of June 1944.'

'Here?' said the American. 'This was a field hospital?'

'Yes.'

'There are no facilities here. No water, no power. Must have been rough.'

'It was.'

'I was on a carrier back then. We had a great sanatorium for the injured.'

'You were lucky. Here the men lay where the stretcher-bearers placed them. Americans, Algerians, Moroccans, British, Frenchmen and the hundred worst-injured Germans. They were really placed here to die. At the end there were two hundred and twenty of them.'

'And the young surgeon?'

The faded man shrugged.

'Well, he went to work. He did what he could. He had three orderlies assigned to him by the Surgeon-General. They raided local houses for mattresses, palliasses, anything to lie on. They stole sheets and blankets from all around. The sheets were just for bandages. There is no river running through Siena but centuries ago the Sienese built an intricate grid of underground aquifers to bring fresh water from mountain streams right under the streets. That provides access wells into the flowing water. The orderlies ran a bucket chain from the nearest right into the courtyard.

'A big kitchen table was taken from a nearby house and set up right there, in the centre, between the rose bushes, for operating. Drugs were scarce, hygiene shot to hell. He operated as best he could through the afternoon and into the dusk. When night fell he ran to the local military hospital and begged for some Petromax lanterns. By the light of these, he went on. But it was hopeless. He knew the men would die.

'Many of the wounds were terrible. The men were all in trauma. He was out of painkillers. Some patients had been torn by mines exploding under a comrade a few yards away. Others had shell or grenade fragments deep inside them. There were limbs shattered by bullets. Soon after dark the girl came.'

'What girl?'

'Just a girl. Local, an Italian girl, he presumed. A young woman, early twenties maybe. Strange-looking. He saw her staring at him. He nodded, she smiled, and he went on operating.'

'Why strange-looking?'

'Pale, oval face. Very serene. Short hair, not bobbed as in the fashion of those days, but sort of pageboy cut. Neat, not flirtatious hair. And she wore a kind of cotton shift of pale grey.'

'She helped out?'

'No, she moved away. She walked quietly among the men. He saw her take a cloth, dip it in one of the buckets of water and wipe their brows. He went on working as each new case was brought to the operating table. He went on even though he knew he was wasting his time. He was just twenty-four, hardly more than a boy himself, trying to do a man's job. Dog-tired, trying not to make mistakes, amputating with a bone-saw sterilized in grappa, suturing with domestic thread greased with beeswax, morphine running out, had to ration it. And they screamed, oh, how they screamed . . .'

The American stared at him hard.

'My God,' he whispered. 'You were that surgeon. You're not Italian. You were the German surgeon.'

The faded man nodded slowly.

'Yes, I was that surgeon.'

'Honey, I think the ankle's a bit better. Maybe we could still see the end of the show.'

'Quiet, hon. Just a few minutes more. What happened?'

In the Piazza del Campo the parade had left the arena and its participants had taken their places in the allotted stands fronting the palazzos. On the sand track only one drummer and one flag-bearer from each Contrada remained. Their task was to show their skill with the banner and staff, weaving intricate patterns in the air to the rhythm of the tambours, a final salute to the crowd before the race and a last chance to win the silver chalice for their own heraldic guild.

THE SURGEON'S STORY

'I operated through the night and into the dawn. The orderlies were as tired as I, but they brought the men to the table one by one and I did what I could. Before dawn she was gone. The girl was gone. I did not see her come and I did not see her go.

'There was a lull as the sun rose. The stream of

stretchers coming in through that arch let up and finally ceased. I was able to wash my hands and walk among the wounded to count those who had died in the night and ask that they be removed.'

'How many were there?'

'None.'

'None?'

'No man died. Not that night, nor as the sun rose on the morning of the first of July. In that corner over there were three Algerians. Chest and stomach wounds, one with shattered legs. I had operated on them all in the small hours. They were very stoical. They lay in silence, staring upwards, thinking perhaps of the dry hills of the Maghreb whence they had come to fight and die for France. They knew they were dying, waiting for Allah to come and call them to Him. But they did not die.

'Just there where your wife is sitting lay a boy from Austin, Texas. When he came in his hands were across his belly. I pulled them apart. He was trying to hold his own entrails inside himself through the torn stomach wall. All I could do was push the intestines back inside where they should have been, clamp and suture. He had lost a lot of blood. I had no plasma.

'In the dawn I heard him crying, calling for his mother. I gave him until noon, but he did not die. After dawn the heat increased even though the sun could not shine directly over those roofs. But I knew when it did, this place would become an inferno. I had the operating table moved under the cloister to the shade, but for the men outside there was little hope. What the blood loss and trauma had not done, the sun would do.

'Those under the cloister roof were the lucky ones. There were three Tommies there, all from Nottingham. One asked me for a cigarette. My English was very poor then, but that word is international. I told him that with lungs torn by shrapnel a cigarette, which he called a gasper, was the last thing he needed. He laughed and told me when General Alexander arrived, he at least would give him one. Crazy English humour. But brave too. They knew they were never going home, but could make silly jokes.

'With the stretcher-bearers back from the battle zone I commandeered three more. They were exhausted and truculent but thank God the old German discipline prevailed. They took over and my original three orderlies just curled up in a corner and passed out.'

'And the day went by?' said the tourist.

'The day went by. I ordered my new men to raid all the surrounding houses here for string, cords, ropes and more bedsheets. We strung the cords across the yard and draped the sheets over them with clothes pegs to create a bit of shade. And still the temperature rose. Water was the key. The suffering men croaked for water and my orderlies ran a bucket chain from the well to the yard, handing out cups as fast as they could. The Germans said "*Danke*", the French whispered "*Merci*" and the dozen Brits said "Ta, mate".

'I prayed for a cooling breeze or the setting of the sun. No breeze but after twelve hours of hell the sun set and the temperature dropped. In the mid-afternoon a young captain from Lemelsen's staff had come in by chance. He stopped, stared, crossed himself, muttered *"Du Liebe Gott,"* and ran. I chased after him, bawling that I needed some help here. He called over his shoulder, "I'll do what I can." I never saw him again.

'But maybe he did something. An hour later the Surgeon-General of the Fourteenth Army sent a handcart with medications. Field dressings, morphine, sulpha. Just as well. After sundown the last fresh casualties arrived, all German this time; about a score of them to bring the final number to around two hundred and twenty. And in the darkness, she came back.'

'The girl? The strange girl?'

'Yes. She just appeared, as the night before. Beyond the city walls the artillery seemed to have stopped at last. I presumed the Allies were preparing for their final, shattering push, the destruction of Siena, and I prayed we might be spared but knew it was hopeless. So it was quiet in the yard at last, apart from the groans and cries, the occasional scream, of men in pain.

'I heard the swish of her gown near me as I worked on a panzer grenadier from Stuttgart who had lost half his jaw. I turned and there she was, soaking a towel in the fresh-water butt. She smiled and began to move among the men on the ground, kneeling beside them, wiping their foreheads and gently touching their wounds. I called to her to leave the dressings alone, but she just went on.'

'She was the same girl?' asked the American.

'The same girl. None other. But this time I noticed something that I had not seen the previous night. It was not a shift that she was wearing but a sort of habit, as for a novice nun. Then I realized she must have come from one of the several convents in Siena. And there was a design on the front of the habit, dark grey on pale grey. It was of the cross of Christ but with a difference. One arm of the cross was broken and hung down at forty-five degrees.'

From the great piazza a new roar rolled across the roofs. The standard-bearers had finished their displays and the ten horses, sequestered until then in the courtyard of the Podesta, were being led out onto the sand. They had bridles but no saddles, for this is a bareback race. In front of the judges' stand the hoisting of the actual Palio for whose ownership they would run brought a further giant cheer.

In the courtyard the tourist's wife rose and tested her injured ankle.

'I think I can walk slowly on this,' she said.

'A few moments more, honey,' said her husband, 'then I swear we'll go and join the fun. And that second night?'

'I operated on the last twenty, the last of the Germans, then with my new equipment went back to try to make a better job of some from the night before. I had morphine, now. Antibiotics. Those most in pain I could at least help to die in peace.'

'And some did?'

'No. They hovered on the brink of death, but no

211

man died. Not that night. All night the young nun walked among them, saying not a word, smiling, swabbing their faces with fresh cool water from the well, touching their wounds. They thanked her, tried to reach out and touch her; but she smiled and eased away and moved on.

'For twenty-four hours I had been chewing Benzedrine to keep awake but in the small hours, with nothing more I could do and my supplies gone, the orderlies asleep over there by that wall, my smock, hands and face smeared with blood of other young men, I sat at the operating table where once a Sienese family had taken their meals, put my head in my hands and passed out. I was shaken awake by one of the orderlies as the sun rose. He had been scavenging, brought back a billy full of real Italian coffee, hoarded somewhere since the start of the war. It was the best cup of coffee I have ever had in my life.'

'And the girl, the young nun?'

'She was gone.'

'And the men?'

'I quickly did a tour of the whole courtyard, looking down at each. Still alive.'

'You must have been pleased.'

'More. Stupefied. It was not possible. My equipment was too little, the conditions too basic, the wounds too terrible and my skill too small.'

'This was July second, right? Liberation Day?'

'Right.'

'So the Allies threw in their final attack?'

'Wrong. There was no attack on Siena. Have you heard of Field Marshal Kesselring?'

'Nope.'

'In my view he was one of the most underrated commanders of the Second World War. He got his marshal's baton in 1940, but back then any German general could win on the Western Front. Being defeated, always in retreat against superior forces, is harder.

'There is one kind of general can lead a glorious advance, another kind can plan and execute a fighting retreat. Rommel was the first, Kesselring the second. He had to fight backwards from Sicily to Austria. By 1944 with complete control of the skies, better tanks, limitless fuel and supplies, the local population on their side, the Allies should have swept up Italy by the midsummer. Kesselring made them fight for every inch.

'But unlike some he was not a barbarian. He was cultured and he was a passionate lover of Italy. Hitler ordered him to blow the bridges of Rome across the Tiber. They were and remain architectural gems. Kesselring refused, which helped the Allied advance.

'While I sat here that morning with my coffee, Kesselring ordered General Schlemm to pull the whole First Parachute Corps out of Siena without firing a shot. Nothing was to be damaged, nothing destroyed. What I also did not know was that Pope Pius XII had interceded with Charles de Gaulle whose Free French were tasked to take the city and asked him not to destroy it. Whether there was a secret compact between Lemelsen and Juin we will never know. Neither said so, and both are dead now. But each received the same orders: save Siena.'

'Not a shot fired? Not a shell? Not a bomb?'

'Nothing. Our paras began the pull-out in the late morning. It went on all day. In the mid-afternoon there was one hell of a clatter of boots in that alley out there and the Surgeon-General of the Fourteenth Army appeared. Major General von Steglitz had been a famous orthopaedics man before the war. He too had been operating for days, but in the main hospital. He too was exhausted.

'He stood in the arch and stared around in amazement. There were six orderlies in here with me, two on water duty. He looked at my bloody smock and the kitchen table, now back out here in the light for better vision. He looked at the smelling pile of amputated limbs in that corner: hands, arms, legs, some still with the boots on.

'"What a charnel house," he said. "Are you alone here, Captain?"

'"Yessir."

'"How many wounded?"

'"About two hundred and twenty, *mein General*."

'"Nationalities?"

'"One hundred and twenty of our boys, about a hundred mixed Allies, sir."

'"How many dead?"

'"So far, sir, none."

'He glared at me, then snapped, "*Unmöglich*."'

'What does that mean?' asked the American.

'It means "impossible". Then he began to walk down the lines of mattresses. He did not need to ask, he could tell at a glance the type of wound, severity, chance of survival. There was a padre with him who knelt right there and gave the last rites to all who would die before sunrise. The Surgeon-General finished his tour and came back to this point. He stared at me for a long while. I was a mess: half-dead with tiredness, smeared with blood, smelling like a polecat, not a meal in forty-eight hours.

'"You are a remarkable young man," he said at last. "What you have done here cannot be done. You know we are pulling out?" I said I did. Word spreads fast in a defeated army.

'He gave his orders to the men behind him. Columns of stretcher-bearers came from the alley. Take only Germans, he told them, leave the Allies to the Allies. He walked among the German wounded, selecting only those who might be able to stand the long bumpy ride across the Chianti hills and up to Milan where they would at last get the best of everything. Those Germans he deemed to have no hope at all he told the stretcher-men to leave behind. When he had done, seventy of the Germans had been removed. That left fifty, and the Allies. Then he came back to me. The sun had dropped behind the houses, heading for the hills. The cool was returning. His manner was no longer brusque. He just looked old and ill.

'"Someone should stay behind. Stay with them."
'"I will stay," I said.

215

'"It will mean becoming a prisoner of war."

'"I know, sir," I said.

'"So, for you a short war after all. I hope we will meet again, back in the Fatherland."

'There was nothing more to be said. He walked into that arch, turned and threw me a salute. Can you imagine it? A general to a captain. I had no cap on, so I could not reply. Then he was gone. I never saw him again. He died in a bombing raid six months later. I was left alone here, with a hundred and fifty men, mainly scheduled to die if help did not come quickly. The sun went down, the darkness came, my lanterns were out of gas. But the moon rose. I began to pass out pannikins of water. I turned round, and she was back again.'

The sound in the Piazza del Campo was a continuous shout by now. The ten jockeys, small wiry men and all professionals, had mounted up. Each had been issued with his crop, a vicious quirt made from a dried bull's pizzle, with which they would hack not only at their own horses but at steeds and jockeys coming too close. Sabotage is part of the Palio race, which is not for the squeamish. The bets are mind-numbing, the lust to win beyond restraint and, once on the sand track, anything goes.

The lots had been drawn for the placing of the ten horses behind the thick rope that serves as a starting line. Each jockey, brilliantly garbed in the colours of his Contrada, had his round steel cap on, crop in hand, reins held tight. The horses skittered in anticipation as they entered their slots behind the rope. The starter or *mossiere* glanced up at the

Magistrato for the nod to drop the rope when the last horse was in place. The roar of the crowd sounded like a lion on the veld.

'She came back? The third night?'

'The third and the last. We worked as a sort of team. I spoke sometimes, in German of course, but she clearly did not understand. She smiled but said nothing, not even in Italian. We never touched. She tended the wounded men. I fetched more water and changed a few dressings. The Surgeon-General had left me fresh supplies, whatever he could spare for what he saw as a lost cause. By dawn they were gone.

'I noticed something else that third night that I had not seen earlier. She was a pretty girl but by the light of the moon I saw that she had a big black stain on the back of each hand, about the size of a dollar piece. I thought nothing of it, until years later. Just before dawn I turned again, and she was gone.'

'You never saw her again?'

'No. Never. Just after sunrise I saw flags begin to flutter from all those high windows over there. Not the eagle of the Reich, not any more. The Sienese had patched and stitched together the flags of the Allies, especially the tricolour of France. They broke out all over the city. About seven o'clock I heard footsteps coming up the alley outside. I was frightened. Remember, I had never seen an Allied soldier with a gun before, but Hitler's propaganda had taught us they were all murderers.

'After a few minutes five soldiers appeared in the

arch. They were dark and swarthy, uniforms so stained with earth and sweat I could hardly work out which unit they came from. Then I saw the Cross of Lorraine. It was the French. Except they were Algerians.

'They shouted some words at me but I did not understand. Either French or Arabic. I smiled and shrugged. I was wearing my bloody smock over my Wehrmacht shirt and trousers, but beneath the smock they must have seen my boots. Distinctive. Wehrmacht boots. They had taken heavy casualties south of Siena, and here I was, the enemy. They came into the yard, shouted and waved their rifles under my nose. I thought they were going to shoot me. Then one of the Algerian wounded called softly from that corner. The soldiers went over and listened while he whispered to them. When they came back their mood had changed. They produced a truly horrible cigarette and forced me to smoke it as a sign of friendship.

'By nine o'clock the French were flooding through the city, assailed on every side by ecstatic Italians, the girls smothering them with kisses, and I stayed here with my friendly captors.

'Then a French major appeared. He spoke a little English; so did I. I explained that I was a German surgeon, left behind with my charges, some of whom were French and most were Allies. He charged among the men on the ground, realized there were twenty of his fellow countrymen, apart from British and American Allies, and ran out into the alley shouting for help. Within an hour all the wounded had been taken to the by now almost empty main hospital, where only a few unmovable Germans remained. I went with them.

'I was held in the matron's room at gunpoint while a French colonel-surgeon examined them all, one by one. By this time they were on clean white sheets and relays of Italian nurses sponged them clean and spoon-fed them whatever nourishing foods they could take.

'In the afternoon the colonel-surgeon came to the room. He was accompanied by a French general, name of De Monsabert, who spoke English. "My colleague tells me that half of these men should be dead," he said. "What have you done to them?" I explained that I had done nothing but my best with the equipment and drugs that I had.

'They conferred in French. Then the general said, "We have to keep the records for the next of kin. Where are the dog tags of the ones who died – all nationalities?" I explained that there were no dog tags. Not a man brought into that courtyard had died.

'They talked again, the surgeon often shrugging his shoulders. Then the general said, "Will you give me your parole, and stay here to work with my colleague? There is much to be done." Of course I did. Where would I run? My country's army was retreating faster than I could walk. If I got away into the countryside the partisans would kill me. Then, from lack of food and sleep, I just passed out right on the floor.

'After a bath, twenty hours of sleep and a meal, I

was ready to work again. All the French wounded recovered by the French in the previous ten days had gone south to Perugia, Assisi, even Rome. Those in the Siena hospital were almost all from this courtyard.

'There were bones to be reset and plastered, sutures to be reopened and internal damage to be properly repaired. Yet wounds that ought to have gone septic and killed their owners were amazingly clean. Torn arteries seemed to have sealed themselves; haemorrhages had ceased to bleed. That colonel was an ace from Lyons; he operated and I acted as his assistant. We operated without a break for a night and a day and no man died.

'The tide of war rolled north. I was allowed to live with the French officers. General Juin visited the hospital and thanked me for what I had done for the French. After that I was assigned simply to look after the fifty Germans. After a month we were all evacuated south to Rome. None of the Germans would ever fight again, so repatriation was arranged through the Red Cross.'

'They went home?' asked the American.

'They all went home,' said the surgeon. 'The US Army Medical Corps took over their boys and shipped them out of Ostia back to the States when they were ready. The Virginians went home to the Shenandoah and the Texans to the Lone Star State. The boy from Austin who had cried for his mother went back to Texas, his innards still inside him, his stomach wall healed up.

'The French took theirs and brought them home

after the liberation of France. The British took theirs and took me with them. General Alexander was touring the hospital in Rome and heard about this courtyard in Siena. He said if I would extend my parole I could work in a military hospital in Britain with German wounded until the war ended. So I did. Germany had lost anyway. By the autumn of 1944 we all knew that. Peace came with the final surrender in May 1945 and I was allowed home to my native but shattered Hamburg.'

'Then what are you doing here thirty-one years later?' asked the American tourist.

The screams from the Piazza del Campo were clearly heard. One horse was down, leg broken, jockey unconscious as the remaining nine raced on. Despite the sand covering, there are bone-jarring cobbles beneath, the pace is frenzied and terrible crashes are frequent.

The faded man raised his shoulders and shrugged. He looked slowly around.

'What happened in this courtyard in those three days was, I believe, a miracle. But it was nothing to do with me. I was a younger and eager surgeon, but not that good. It was about the girl.'

'There will be other Palios,' said the tourist. 'Tell me about the girl.'

'Very well. I was sent back to Germany in the autumn of 1945. Hamburg was under British occupation. I worked at first in their main hospital and then the Hamburg General. By 1949 we had our own non-Nazi republic again and I moved to a private clinic. It prospered, I became a partner. I married a local girl, we had two children. Life became better, Germany prospered. I left and founded a small clinic of my own. I treated the new wealthy and became wealthy myself. But I never forgot this courtyard and I never forgot the girl in the nun's habit.

'In 1965 my marriage ended after fifteen years. The children were in their teens; they were distressed but they understood. I had my own money, I had my freedom. In 1968 I decided to come back here and find her. Just to say thank you.'

'So you found her again?'

'In a way. Twenty-four years had gone by. I presumed she was in her late forties, like myself. I supposed she was still a nun, or, if for any reason she had left the order, a middle-aged married woman with children of her own. So I came that summer of '68 and took a room at the Villa Patrizia and began my search.

'First I went to all the nunneries I could find. There were three, all different orders. I hired an interpreter and visited them all. I spoke to the Mothers Superior. Two had been there during the war, the third had come later. They shook their heads when I described the novice nun I was seeking. All summoned the oldest sister in the convent, but they knew of no such novice, then or ever.

'Of particular note was that habit she had worn: pale grey with a darker grey device stitched on the front. No-one recognized it. None of the orders had pale grey habits.

'I spread the net wider; perhaps she came from

an order outside the city, had been visiting relatives during that last week of German occupation in 1944. I roamed across Tuscany looking for the convent from which she came. No success. With my interpreter losing patience I researched all the types of habits used by orders of nuns, past and present. There were several of pale grey but no-one had ever seen the device of the cross with the broken arm.

'After six weeks I realized it was hopeless. No-one had ever heard of her, let alone seen her. She had come into this courtyard on three consecutive nights twenty-four years earlier. She had swabbed the faces of dying soldiers and comforted them. She had touched their wounds and they had not died. Perhaps she was one of those blessed with the gift of healing by touch. But then she had disappeared into the teeming mass of war-torn Italy, never to be seen again. I wished her well, wherever she was, but I knew I would never find her.'

'But you said you had,' remarked the American.

'I said "in a way",' the surgeon corrected. 'I packed to leave, but I tried one last recourse. There are two newspapers in this town. The *Corriere di Siena* and *La Gazzetta di Siena*. In each of them I took a quarter-page advert. It even had an illustration. I drew the device I had seen on her shift and this drawing appeared with the text of the advert. It offered a reward for any information that anyone could provide about this strange design. The morning I was due to leave, the papers appeared.

'I was in my room packing when the reception

rang to say there was someone asking for me. I came down with my bags. My cab was due in an hour. I never needed that cab and I missed my flight.

'Waiting in the hall was a little old man with a fuzz of white hair in the garb of a monk, a dark grey habit circled at the waist by a white rope, sandals on his feet. He had a copy of the *Gazzetta* in his hand, opened at the page of my own advert. We adjourned to the coffee lounge and sat down. He spoke English.

'He asked who I was, why I had placed the advert. I told him that I had been seeking a young woman of Siena who had helped me almost a quarter of a century earlier. He told me that his name was Fra Domenico and that he came from an order dedicated to fasting, prayer and learning. His own lifelong study had been the history of Siena and of its various religious orders.

'He seemed nervous, agitated, and asked me to narrate to him exactly how I had come across this particular design on a habit worn by a young woman in Siena. It's a long story, I told him. We have time, he replied, please tell me everything, so I did.'

The great piazza erupted in sound as one of the horses crossed the finish line just a half-length ahead of the next. The members of nine Contrade groaned in despair while those of the tenth, the Contrada called Istrice, the Porcupine, exploded in screams of joy. In the guildhalls of the losing nine the wine would flow that night but with much regretful shaking of heads and lectures on what might have been. In the guildhall of the Istrice District the celebrations would be a riot.

'Go on,' said the American, 'what did you tell him?'

'I told him everything. That was what he wanted, insisted on. From start to finish. Every tiny detail, over and over again. The cab came. I dismissed it. But with all that, I forgot one detail until the end. Then I remembered it. The hands, the girl's hands. At the end I told him about seeing, in the moonlight, the dark stains on the back of each hand.

'The monk went white as his snowy hair and began to run a rosary through his fingers, eyes closed, lips moving silently. I was a Lutheran then, I converted later. I asked what he was doing.

'"I am praying, my son," he replied. "What for, Brother?" I asked. "For my immortal soul and also for yours," he said. "For I believe you have seen the work of God." Then I begged him to tell me what he knew, and he told me the story of Catherine of Mercy.'

FRA DOMENICO'S STORY

'"Do you know anything of the history of Siena?" he asked.

'"No," I said, "almost nothing."

'"It is very long. This city has seen many centuries come and go. Some have been full of prosperity and peace, but most have seen war and bloodshed, dictators, feuds, famine and plague. But the two worst centuries were from 1355 to 1559.

'"These were two hundred years of endless, pointless and profitless warfare at home and abroad. The city was incessantly raided by marauding mercenary companies, the dreaded *condottieri*, and lacked firm government which could defend its citizens.

'"You must know there was no 'Italy' in those days, just a patchwork quilt of princedoms, dukedoms, mini-republics and city-states often lusting to conquer each other or actually at war. Siena was a city-republic, always coveted by the Dukedom of Florence, which eventually absorbed us under Cosimo the First of the house of Medici.

'"But that event was preceded by the worst period of all, 1520 to 1550, and that is the time of which I speak. The government of the city-state of Siena was in chaos, ruled by five clans called the Monti who feuded between each other until they had ruined the city. Up till 1512 one had dominated. Pandolfo Petrucci led the strongest of them all and ruled in a brutal tyranny but at least gave stability. When he died, anarchy was let loose inside the city.

'"The city government was supposed to be by the Balia, a permanent council of magistracy of which Petrucci had been a skilful and ruthless chairman. But every member of the Balia was also a member of one of the competing Monti and instead of collaborating to run the city, they fought each other and brought Siena to its knees.

'"In 1520 a daughter was born to one of the lesser scions of the house of Petrucci, which, even though

Pandolfo was dead, still ruled the roost on the Balia. But when she was four the house of Petrucci lost its hold on the Balia and the other four Monti fought unchecked.

'"The girl grew up as beautiful as she was pious and a credit to her family. They all lived in a large palazzo not far from here, protected from the misery and chaos of the streets outside. Where other rich and indulged girls became headstrong and wilful, not to say licentious, Caterina di Petrucci remained demure and dedicated to the Church.

'"The only rift with her father was on the question of marriage. In those days it was common for girls to wed as young as sixteen or even fifteen. But the years went by and Caterina rejected suitor after suitor to the chagrin of her father.

'"By 1540 a vision of hell was being wreaked upon Siena and the surrounding countryside; famine, plague, riots, peasant revolts and internal divisions harassed this city-state. Caterina would have been immune to most of this, protected by the walls of the palazzo and her father's guards, dividing her time between needlework, reading and attending mass in the family chapel. Then in that year something happened that changed her life. She went to a ball. She never arrived.

'"We know what happened, or we think we do, because there is a document written in Latin by her father confessor, an old priest retained by the Petrucci family for their spiritual needs. She left the palace in a coach with a lady-in-waiting and six bodyguards, for the streets were dangerous.

'"On her way her carriage was blocked by another which was drawn askew across the street. She heard shouting, a man screaming in pain. Against the wishes of her duenna she raised the blind and looked out.

'"The other coach belonged to a rival family among the Monti, and it seemed an old beggar had stumbled in the street, causing the horses to shy and swerve. The enraged occupant, a brutish young nobleman, had leapt out, seized a cudgel from one of his guards and was beating the beggar most savagely.

'"Without pausing, Caterina also jumped out into the mud and slime, ruining her silken slippers, and screamed at the man to stop. He looked up and she saw he was one of those young nobles her father had wished her to marry. He, seeing the shield of the Petrucci on her coach door, ceased what he was doing and climbed back into his carriage.

'"The girl squatted in the mud and held the torso of the filthy old beggar, but he was dying from his beating. Though such people must have been alive with parasites, stinking of mud and excrement, she held him in her arms as he died. The legend is that as she looked down into the exhausted, pain-racked face, smeared with mud and blood, she thought she saw the face of the dying Christ. Our old chronicler records that he whispered as he died, 'Look after my people.'

'"We will never know what really happened that day, for no eyewitnesses ever spoke of it. We just have the words of an old priest writing in a lonely monastic cell years later. But whatever happened, it changed her life. She went home and, in the court-yard of the palazzo, burned her entire wardrobe. She told her father she wished to renounce the world and enter a nunnery. He would have none of it and expressly forbade her.

'"Defying his will, something unheard of in those days, she toured the nunneries and convents of the city seeking admission as a novice. But messengers from her father had gone ahead of her and she was refused by them all. They knew the residual power of the Petrucci.

'"If her father thought that would stop her, he was wrong. She stole from the family treasury her very own dowry and, after negotiating secretly with a rival Monte, secured a long lease on a certain courtyard. It was not much; it belonged to and abutted the towering walls of the monastery of Santa Cecilia. The monks had no use for it: about twenty metres wide by thirty metres long, with a cloister running down one side and lying in the shadow of the high walls of stone.

'"To ensure that separation would be total, the Father Superior installed a great timber door of oaken beams in the only arch that led from the monastery into the courtyard and sealed it with heavy bolts.

'"In this yard the young woman set up a sort of refuge or sanctuary for the poor and the destitute of the streets and alleys. We would call it a soup kitchen today, but of course then there was no such thing. She cut off her long and lustrous hair and fashioned a simple shift of grey cotton, walking barefoot among the filth.

'"In that yard the poorest of the poor, the outcasts of society, the halt and the lame, the beggars and the dispossessed, the evicted pregnant serving girls, the blind and even the diseased, most feared of them all, could find sanctuary from the hell of the streets.

'"They lay in their filth, among excrement and rats, for they knew no different, and she swabbed and cleaned them, tended their wounds and sores, used her remaining dowry to buy food and then begged in the streets for money to keep going. Her family disowned her, of course.

'"But after a year went by the city's mood changed. People began to refer to her as Caterina della Misericordia, Catherine of Mercy. Anonymous donations began to arrive from the wealthy and the guilty. Her fame spread through the city and beyond the walls. Another young woman of good family gave up her wealth and came to join her. And then another, and another. By the third year all Tuscany had heard of her. More and worse, she came to the attention of the Church.

'"You must understand, signore, that these were terrible times for the Holy Catholic Church. Even I must say so; it had grown venal and corrupt on too long a diet of privilege, power and wealth. Many princes of the Church, bishops, archbishops and cardinals, led lives of earthly princes, dedicated to pleasure, violence and all the temptations of the flesh.

'"This had already created a reaction among the people, and they were finding new champions; it was a movement they called the Reformation. In northern Europe things were even worse. Luther had already preached his doctrine of heresy, the English king had broken with Rome. Here in Italy true faith was like a boiling cauldron. Just a few miles away in Florence the monk and preacher Savonarola had been burned at the stake after terrible tortures to make him recant, but even after his death the mutterings of rebellion went on.

'"The Church needed reform but not schism, yet many in power could not see it that way. Among them was the Bishop of Siena, Ludovico. He had most to fear because he had turned his palace into a scandal of carnal pleasures and gluttony, corruption and vice. He sold indulgences and granted final absolution to the rich only in exchange for all their wealth. Yet here in his own city, almost beneath his walls, lived a young woman who by her example put him to shame and the people knew it. She did not preach, she did not incite, as Savonarola had done, but he began to fear her nonetheless."'

From the judges' stand in the Piazza del Campo the treasured Palio was ceremoniously handed down to the leaders of the winning Contrada and the banners bearing the device of the porcupine waved frantically in triumph as they prepared to chant their way to the Victory Banquet.

'We've missed it all, honey,' said the American wife as she tested her damaged ankle again and found it much better. 'There'll be nothing left to see.'

'Just a tad longer. I promise we'll see all the celebrations and the pageantry. It lasts till dawn.

So what happened to her? What happened to Catherine of Mercy?'

'"The bishop's chance came the following year. It had been a summer of intense heat. The land parched, the streams ran dry, animal and human filth lay thick in the streets, the rats exploded in numbers. And then a plague came.

'"It was another incidence of the dreaded Black Death, which we now know as bubonic or pneumonic plague. Thousands fell ill and died. Today we know that this disease was spread by the rats and the fleas that lived upon them. But then people thought it was the visitation upon the people of an angry God, and an angry God must be appeased with a sacrifice.

'"By then, to distinguish herself and her three acolytes from other sisters in the city, Caterina had devised an insignia which all four wore on their habits: the cross of Jesus but with one broken arm to signify His grief for His people and the way they behaved to each other. We know about this because it was carefully described by the old father confessor who wrote down his memories years later.

'"The bishop declared this design to be a heresy and fomented a mob, many of them paid with coin from his own coffers. The plague, he decreed, had come from that courtyard, spread by the mendicants who slept there but thronged the streets in the daytime. People wanted to believe that someone was to blame for their sickness. The mob descended on the courtyard.

'"The old chronicler was not present, but he claims he heard what happened from many

232

sources. Hearing the mob coming, the three acolytes threw ragged blankets over their shifts and fled for safety. Caterina stayed. The mob burst in, beating the men, women and children they found there, hounding them out beyond the city walls to live or die on the starving countryside.

'"But they reserved their special rage for Caterina herself. She was almost certainly a virgin, but they held her down and violated her many times. Among them must have been soldiers of the bishop's guard. When they had done with her, they crucified her on the timber door at the end of the yard and there she finally died."

'That was the story,' said the faded man, 'that Fra Domenico told me in the hotel coffee room seven years ago.'

'That was it?' asked the American. 'There was no more that he had to say?'

'There was some more,' admitted the German.

'Tell me, please tell me everything,' asked the tourist.

'Well, in the words of the old monk, this is what happened.

'"The very night of the murder there came upon the city a terrible storm. Thunderheads rolled up at last beyond the mountains, so dark that the sun, then the moon and stars, were blotted out. Soon it began to rain. It was rain like no-one had ever seen. It had such a force and fury that it was as if all Siena were being subjected to a pressure hose. It went on all night and into the morning. Then the clouds rolled over and the sun came out.

'"But Siena had been cleansed. All the accrued filth had been scoured from every crack and crevice and washed away. Torrents ran down the streets and out through the venting holes in the walls to cascade down the mountainsides. With the water went the filth and the rats, washed away as the sins of a bad man in the tears of Christ.

'"Within days the plague began to abate, and soon passed away. But those who had taken part in the mob felt ashamed at what they had done. Some of them came back to the courtyard. It was empty and deserted. They took down the torn body from the door and wished to bury it in the Christian tradition. But the priests feared the bishop and his accusation of heresy. So a few braver souls took the body on a litter out into the countryside. They burned it and threw the ashes into a mountain stream.

'"The father confessor of the house of Petrucci, who wrote all this down in Latin, did not give the exact year, and even less the month and the day. But there is another annal which mentions the time of the Great Rain most exactly. It was in the year 1544, the month was July and the rain came on the night of the second day."'

CONCLUSION

'The day of the Palio,' said the American, 'and the Day of Liberation.'

The German smiled.

'The day of the Palio was fixed later, and the departure of the Wehrmacht was coincidence.'

234

'But she came back. Four hundred years later, she came back.'

'I believe so,' said the German quietly.

'To tend soldiers, like those who raped her.'

'Yes.'

'And the marks on her hands? The holes of cruci-fixion?'

'Yes.'

The tourist stared at the oaken door.

'The stains. Her blood?'

'Yes.'

'Oh my God,' said the tourist. He thought for a while, then asked, 'And you maintain this garden? For her?'

'I come every summer. Sweep the flags, tend the roses. It is just a way of saying thank you. Maybe she knows somehow. Maybe not.'

'It is the second day of July. Will she come again?'

'Perhaps. Probably not. But this I can guarantee to you. No-one, man, woman or child, will die in Siena this night.'

'There must be outgoings,' said the tourist. 'Costs ... to keep it going looking like this. If there is anything ...'

The faded man shrugged. 'Not really. There is an offertory box, over there on the bench by the wall. It is for the orphans of Siena. I thought she would have liked that.'

The American was as generous as all his race. He delved into his jacket and produced a thick billfold. Turning to the offertory box he peeled off half a dozen bills and stuffed them in.

'Sir,' he said to the German when he had helped his wife to her feet, 'I will leave Italy soon and fly back to Kansas. I will run my ranch and raise my cattle. But I will not forget, all my life, that I was here in this courtyard where she died, and I will recall the story of Caterina della Misericordia as long as I live. C'mon, honey, let's go and join the crowds.'

They left the courtyard and turned down the alley to the sound of the celebrations in the streets beyond. After a few moments a woman emerged from the deep dark shadows of the cloister where she had remained unseen.

She also wore stone-washed denim; her hair was braided in cornrows and ethnic beads hung from her neck. Slung across her back was a guitar. From her right hand dangled a heavy haversack and from her left her own tote bag.

She stood by the side of the man, fished a joint out of her top pocket, lit up, took a long drag and passed it to him.

'How much did he leave?' she asked.

'Five hundred dollars,' said the man. He had dropped the German accent and spoke in the tones of Woodstock and all points west. He emptied the wooden box of the bundle of dollars and pushed them into his shirt pocket.

'That's a great story,' said his partner, 'and I love the way you tell it.'

'I rather like it myself,' conceded the hippie modestly, as he hefted his rucksack and prepared to leave. 'And you know? They always fall for it.'

THE CITIZEN

The home run was always his favourite. In more than thirty years driving large aluminium tubes around the world for British Airways he had seen over seventy major cities, most of them capitals, and the original appetite had long faded.

Thirty years ago, bright-eyed and bushy-tailed, with the two rings of a Junior First Officer gleaming new on each sleeve, he had relished the far and foreign places. During the generous stop-overs he had explored the nightlife of Europe and the USA, taken the offered tours of the temples and shrines of the Far East. Now, he just wanted to get home to his house near Dorking.

Back then, there had been brief but torrid affairs with the prettiest stewardesses until Susan had married him and quite rightly put a stop to that sort of thing. Five thousand nights in hotel beds had long left only the desire to roll into his own and smell the lavender scent of Susan beside him.

A boy and a girl, Charles the honeymoon baby, now twenty-three and a computer programmer,

237

and Jennifer, at eighteen entering York University to read History of Art, had given him stability and an extra reason for coming home. With two years to retirement the prospect of swinging his hatchback into the drive on Watermill Lane and seeing Susan at the door waiting for him far superseded any appetite for foreign parts.

Across the aisle in the crew bus his stand-in captain was staring at the back of the driver's head. To his left, one of his two First Officers was gawping with still unsated curiosity at the bright neon sea of Bangkok as the city slipped away behind them.

Filling the rear of the crew bus, cool in the air conditioning, protected from the sticky heat outside, were the cabin crew: one Cabin Service Director and fifteen stewards, four male and eleven female. He had flown with them all from Heathrow two days earlier, and knew the CSD would handle everything from the door of the flight deck back to the tail fin. That was his job and he too was a veteran.

Captain Adrian Fallon's task was simply to fly another Boeing 747–400 Jumbo with over 400 passengers who paid his salary from Bangkok to London Heathrow, or, as his log book would soon record, from BKK to LHR.

Two hours before take-off the crew bus swerved into the airport perimeter, was nodded through by the guards on the gate and headed for the BA office. It was a long lead-time, but Captain Fallon was a stickler and the word from the BA office was that Speedbird One Zero, out of Sydney at 3.15 p.m.

238

(local) would be landing bang on time at 9.45 p.m. Bangkok local. In fact it was already on final approach.

A mile behind the crew bus there was a black limousine. It carried one passenger, seated in comfort in the rear behind the uniformed driver. Both car and driver came from the exclusive Oriental Hotel where the impeccably accoutred senior executive had been staying for three days. In the boot reposed his single suitcase, a hard-frame case in genuine leather with solid brass locks, the case of a man who travelled lightly but not cheaply. Beside him rested his attaché case, real crocodile.

In the breast pocket of his beautifully cut cream silk suit rested his British passport in the name of Hugo Seymour and the return half of a ticket from Bangkok to London, First Class of course. As Speedbird One Zero eased off the runway to begin its taxi roll towards the BA departure lounge, the limousine purred to a stop outside the check-in hall.

Mr Seymour did not push his own luggage on a trolley. He raised a manicured hand and a small Thai porter hurried over. Tipping the driver, the businessman nodded to his suitcase in the open boot, then followed the trotting porter into the check-in hall and pointed to the British Airways First Class desk. He had been exposed to the sticky heat of the tropical night for about thirty seconds.

It does not really take one hour and forty-five minutes for a First Class check-in. The young clerk behind the desk was attending to no-one else.

Within ten minutes the single hide suitcase was on its way to the baggage-handling area where its tags would clearly identify it as heading for the BA London flight. Mr Seymour had been issued with his boarding card and given directions to the First Class lounge, situated beyond passport control.

The uniformed Thai immigration officer glanced at the burgundy-coloured passport, then at the boarding pass and finally at the face through the glass screen. Middle-aged, lightly tanned, freshly shaved, iron-grey hair barbered and blow-dried; a soft and sweatless white silk shirt, silk tie from the Jim Thompson shop, the upper section of a cream silk suit from one of Bangkok's better tailors where they can run up a replica of Savile Row in thirty hours. He passed the identity document back under the glass screen.

'*Sawat-di, krab,*' murmured the Englishman. The Thai officer bobbed and smiled an acknowledgement at being thanked in his own language, usually impossible for foreigners.

Somewhere out of sight the disembarking passengers from Sydney to Bangkok were filing out of the Boeing and down the long corridors to Immigration. They were followed by the transit passengers until the aeroplane was empty and the cleaning staff could begin to scour the fifty-nine rows of seats, a task that would yield fourteen binliners of assorted garbage. Mr Seymour, his crocodile attaché case at his side, proceeded sedately to the First Class lounge where he was welcomed by two stunningly pretty Thai girls, seated and brought a glass of crisp white wine. He quietly buried himself in an article in *Forbes Magazine*, one among twenty passengers in a large, cool and luxurious lounge.

He had not seen, for he had not bothered to look, but as Mr Seymour presented himself at the First Class check-in desk he was just a few yards from Club Class check-in. The Boeing 747–400 in the BA seat configuration has fourteen First Class seats, of which ten would be occupied and four of these coming in from Sydney. Mr Seymour had been the first of the six boarding at Bangkok. All twenty-three Club Class seats would be full, with eighteen boarding in the Thai capital. These were the ones queuing a few yards from him in the check-in hall.

But beyond them were the Economy Class queues, now delicately referred to as World Traveller class. At these desks there was a seething mass of shuffling humanity. Ten desks were trying to cope with nearly 400 passengers. Among them were the Higgins family. They hauled their own baggage. They had come by coach, where the press of fellow travellers and the heat they generated had finally defeated the air-conditioning system. The World Travellers were dishevelled and sweaty. It took the Higginses nearly an hour to reach the departure lounge, with a brief visit to Duty Free, and to settle themselves in the No Smoking area. Thirty minutes to boarding. Captain Fallon and his crew were long on board, but even they were preceded by the cabin staff.

The captain and his crew had spent the usual

fifteen minutes in the office covering the necessary paperwork. There was the all-important flight plan which told him how long the flight would take, the minimum amount of fuel to be loaded and, over a number of pages, the details of the route he would be following tonight. All this information had been filed with the various air traffic control centres between Bangkok and London. A good long look at the weather for his route and in the UK revealed a quiet night ahead. He flicked quickly and with practised ease through the NOTAMs (Notices to Airmen), retaining the few pieces of information that affected him and disregarding the greater part which was irrelevant.

With the last piece of 'bumf' either retained or signed and handed back, the four pilots were ready to board. They were well ahead of their passengers, and the departers from Sydney were long gone. The cleaners were still on board, but that was the CSD's problem, and Mr Harry Palfrey would as usual cope with unflappable urbanity.

Not that the gang of Thai cleaners was the CSD's only concern. All the lavatories would be vented and scoured, then inspected. Enough food and drink for 400 passengers was being brought aboard and he had even managed a selection of the latest newspapers from London, just arrived from Heathrow on another jet. By the time Mr Palfrey was even halfway satisfied, his captain and crew were aboard.

In summer Captain Fallon would have been accompanied only by two First Officers, but this was late January and the winter headwinds would spin the flight up to thirteen hours, chock to chock, triggering a requirement for a relief captain.

Personally, Adrian Fallon thought it was unnecessary. At the rear of the flight deck, on the left-hand side, was a small room with two bunks and it was perfectly normal for the captain to leave the aircraft on automatic pilot and in control of two of the other pilots while he grabbed four or five hours' sleep. Still, rules are rules and there were four of them instead of three.

As the quartet marched down the last long tunnel to the almost empty aircraft Fallon nodded to the younger of his two First Officers.

'Sorry, Jim. Walkaround.'

The young man who had been staring at the delights of a vanishing Bangkok through the crew-bus windows nodded, opened the door at the end of the entry tunnel and slipped out into the sticky night. It was a chore they all disliked but it had to be done and it usually fell to the junior among them. If the jumbo jet were encased in a square box from nosetip to tail fin and wingtip to wingtip, that box would cover more than an acre. The walka-round man has to do exactly that; walk round the entire aircraft checking to see that all that ought to be there is there, and nothing else. A panel might be half-detached, a pool of liquid might indicate a leak, unspotted by the ground crew. To put not too fine a point on it, there are ground crews and ground crews; airlines prefer to have one of their own do the final walkaround check.

Sometimes the weather outside is way below freezing; or bathed in a tropical monsoon. Tough luck. In this case the eager beaver with three rings arrived back twenty minutes later damp with sweat and bearing several midge bites but otherwise fully functional.

Captain Fallon entered his domain by climbing the stairs from the entry level to the upper cabin, then walking forward through the flight-deck door. Within minutes the two captains and the remaining First Officer had their jackets off, hung behind the door of the rest room, and were in their seats. Fallon of course took the left-hand one and installed his senior First Officer to his right. The relief skipper kept out of the way by retiring to the bunk room to study the stock market.

When he began his career and graduated from the Belfast milk run to the long-hauls, Fallon was still in the days when he would have had a navigator and a flight engineer. Long gone. His engineer was now a bank of technology above his head and facing him from wall to wall; enough dials, clocks, levers and buttons to do whatever an engineer could do, and more. His navigator was confined to three Inertial Reference Systems, 'black boxes' which between them could accomplish all a navigator's duties and faster.

While the First Officer ran through the first of the five separate lists of checks, the Before Start checks, Fallon glanced at the load sheet which he would have to sign when all the luggage was confirmed aboard and the passenger list tallied with Mr

Palfrey's head-count. Every captain's nightmare is not so much the passenger on board with no luggage – that can follow on later; it is the luggage on board but a passenger who has decided to do a runner. The whole baggage hold has to be emptied until the rogue suitcases are found and expelled. They could contain anything.

The entire aircraft was still powered by its Auxiliary Power Unit, the APU, in truth a fifth jet engine of which few passengers knew anything. The APU on this giant aircraft is enough to power a small fighter by itself; its power enables everything on the aircraft to function independently of any source from outside – lights, air, engine-start, the lot.

In the World Traveller departure lounge Mr and Mrs Higgins and their daughter Julie were already tired and the child becoming fractious. They had left their two-star hotel four hours earlier and, in the manner of modern travel, it had been slog all the way. Luggage on board the coach, ensure that nothing has been left behind, queue and wait, sit in a tiny seat, traffic jams, worry about being late, more jams, decant from the coach at the airport, try to find luggage, child and trolley at the same time, line up in the milling crowd for check-in, queue and wait, security X-ray machines, body-search because the belt-buckle triggered the alarm, the child yelling at being separated from her dolly as it went through the X-ray, pick out some goodies in Duty Free, queue and wait ... and finally the hard plastic seats on the last stop before boarding.

Julie, clutching her dolly, made locally and a present from Phuket, was bored with the waiting and began to wander. A few yards away a man called to her.

'Hi, kid, nice doll.'

She stopped and stared at him. He was not like her father at all. He had cowboy boots with Cuban heels, soiled and ragged jeans, a denim shirt and ethnic beads. By his side was a small haversack. His hair was matted and probably unwashed and a straggly beard dangled from his chin.

Had Julie Higgins but known it, which at the age of eight she did not, the Far East is rife with Western backpackers and the man who had just addressed her was such a one. The Far East is like a magnet to thousands of them, partly because life there can be relaxed and cheap and also because in many cases there is easy access to the drugs they favour.

'She's new,' said Julie. 'I call her Pooky.'

'Great name. Why?' drawled the hippie.

'Because Daddy bought her in Poo-Ket.'

'I know it. Great beaches. You just vacationed there?'

'Yes. I swam with Daddy and we saw fishes.'

At this point Mrs Higgins jabbed her husband in the foot with one toe and nodded towards their daughter.

'Julie, come here darling,' Mr Higgins called out in a tone his daughter understood. It was one of disapproval. She trotted back towards them. Higgins glared at the hippie. It was a kind he loathed: footloose, dirty and almost certainly a user of drugs, the last person he wanted his daughter talking to. The hippie got the message. He shrugged, pulled out a pack of cigarettes, saw the No Smoking sign above his head and wandered off towards the smoking area before lighting up. Mrs Higgins sniffed. The public address system called for boarding to start, beginning with rows thirty-four to fifty-seven.

Mr Higgins consulted his boarding pass. Row thirty-four, seats D, E and F. Summoning his family around him, he checked they had all their carry-on pieces, and joined the final queue.

The 11.45 p.m. take-off time would not be met, but that was merely the published timetable, broadly speaking a work of fiction. What interested Captain Fallon was that he had a take-off slot from Bangkok Tower for five after midnight and he wanted to make it. In the modern world of civil aviation getting a take-off and landing slot was what counted. Miss your slot in Western Europe or North America and you could hang about for an hour waiting for another.

Not that a twenty-minute delay would matter. He knew he could make it up. Because of strong headwinds over Pakistan and the southern parts of Afghanistan his flight plan predicted a flight of 13 hours and 20 minutes. With London on GMT there was a seven-hour difference in time zones. He would be touching down in London about twenty past six on a bitter January morning with the outside temperature close to zero, a long call from Bangkok where the midnight thermometer was showing 26 degrees centigrade and humidity in the high nineties.

There was a knock on the cabin door; the CSD entered with the passenger manifest. He and his staff had done their head-count.

'Four hundred and five, skipper.'

It checked. Fallon signed off the load sheet and gave it to Palfrey, who went back down to hand it through the last remaining open door to the BA ground staff. Outside the mammoth flying machine the last of the courtiers were finishing their tasks of subservience. Baggage hold was closed, hoses disconnected, vehicles backed off to a respectful distance. The giant was going to start those four huge Rolls-Royce engines and roll.

In the First Class cabin Mr Seymour had allowed himself to be relieved of his beautiful silk jacket which was hung in the forward wardrobe. He kept, but loosened, the silk tie. A glass of champagne bubbled at his elbow and the CSD had endowed him with a fresh *Financial Times* and a *Daily Telegraph*. A snob to his boot heels, Mr Palfrey loved what he called 'the quality'. With even Hollywood stars resembling bag ladies, it was such a relief to look after the quality.

On the flight deck Fallon supervised the Cleared for Start checks. Glancing out and down he could see the tractor and, at its controls, that anonymous but vital minion sometimes referred to as Tractor Joe. Without him Speedbird One Zero was going nowhere because it was pointing straight at the terminal and could not turn round unaided.

From Bangkok Ground Control Fallon received his start-engines clearance. Simultaneously Tractor Joe's tiny but immensely powerful vehicle began to ease the 747–400 backwards and the four Rolls-Royce 524s came to life. Fallon needed no power from the ground for this; his APU would handle it all.

On Fallon's command, his co-pilot reached up to the overhead panel, pulled the start switch for number four engine, whilst with his other hand he operated the same number fuel-control switch. He repeated these actions three more times as he ripple-started the engines four three two and then one. Meanwhile the automatic fuel control brought the engines slowly up to 'idle'.

Tractor Joe was moving Speedbird One Zero round through ninety degrees so that her nose would be pointing to the taxi track while the wash of her jets would not blow away anything behind her. When he had done, he called up the flight deck on the headset he wore, the flex of which was still plugged in near to the aircraft's nose-wheel. He asked for parking brake.

He was right so to do; this Thai wanted to become an old man one day. To disconnect himself he had to descend from his tractor, walk to the nose of the jumbo and pull his flex from the socket. A Tractor Joe who disappears under the front wheel of a jumbo while doing this comes out like hamburger steak. Fallon put on the parking brake and gave the word. Thirty feet below him the Thai disconnected himself, stood back and held up the flag he had taken from the flex socket, as per procedure. Fallon gave him a grateful wave and the tractor drove off. Ground Control gave permission to roll and passed them over to Tower Control.

In Row 34 the Higginses were finally settled in. They had been lucky. Seat G was vacant so they had the whole row of four. John Higgins took D which was on one aisle; his wife had G at the other end of the row and on the other side aisle. Julie was between them, fussing over Pooky to ensure she was comfortable and able to enjoy a restful night.

Speedbird One Zero was rolling along the taxi way towards take-off point, her huge bulk steered solely by her nose-wheel, operated by the tiller under Fallon's left hand. Captain Fallon was in permanent contact with Tower Control. As he reached the far end of the main runway he asked for and got immediate take-off permission. That meant he could continue from taxi track to take-off without a pause.

The Jumbo turned onto the runway, lined its nose up with the centre line and high above the tarmac the captain eased the thrust levers forward then curled his fingers to press the toga (Take Off/Go Around) switches. The power in all four engines rose automatically to pre-set figures.

The passengers could feel the rumble increase in speed as the jumbo gathered pace. Neither they nor the crew in the cloistered calm of the flight deck could hear the manic scream of the four jets outside the hull, but they could feel the power. Far to one side the lights of the main terminal flashed by.

A touch on the controls brought the nose-wheel off the tarmac. The First Class passengers heard the first clunk beneath their feet, but this was simply the oleo leg extending as the weight came off. Ten seconds later the main undercarriage assemblies lifted off and she was airborne.

As she lifted clear of the ground, on Fallon's command his co-pilot selected the switch to bring up the entire undercarriage; a series of further clunks, then all the noise and the vibrations stopped. He climbed at 1,300 feet per minute to 1,500 feet, then eased the climb. As the speed increased Fallon called for the wing flaps to be retracted in sequence, from twenty degrees to ten, to five, to one, to zero and she was 'clean'.

John Higgins in 34 D finally loosed the rigid grip he had imposed on both his armrests. He was not a good flier and he hated take-off most of all, but he tried not to show his family. Glancing out into the aisle, he observed that the hippie was just four rows in front of them, in 30 C, across the aisle. The long passage stretched ahead of him to the bulkhead separating Economy from Club. Here there was a complete galley and four lavatories. He could see four or five stewardesses already up and about, preparing to serve the belated evening meal. It had been six hours since his last snack in the hotel, and he was hungry. He turned back to help Julie sort out her in-flight entertainment facility and find the cartoon channel.

Take-off at Bangkok is usually towards the north. Fallon eased the climbing airliner gently to port and looked down. It was a clear night. Behind them was the Gulf of Thailand on which Bangkok lay; ahead, across the width of the country, the Andaman Sea. Between lay Thailand, and the moon glinted off so many flooded rice paddies that the whole country seemed to be made of water. Speedbird One Zero climbed to 31,000 feet and levelled off, setting course for London, passing over Calcutta, Delhi, Kabul, Teheran, eastern Turkey, the Balkans and Germany on one of the several possible routes. He slipped Speedbird One Zero onto autopilot, stretched and right on cue one of the upper-deck stewardesses brought in the coffee.

In 30 C the hippie glanced at the small card offering the menu for the late-night dinner. His appetite was small; what he really lusted for was a cigarette. Thirteen hours of this, and another watching the carousel at Heathrow for his bigger rucksack, before he could slip outside and light up. And two after that before he could risk a decent joint.

'The beef,' he said to the smiling stewardess who stood beside him. The accent appeared American but his passport would say he was a Canadian called Donovan.

In an office in the west of London whose address is a fairly closely guarded secret, a phone rang. The man at the desk glanced at his watch. Five thirty and dark already.

'Yes.'

'Boss, BA Oh-One-Oh out of Bangkok is airborne.'

'Thanks.'

He put the phone down. William 'Bill' Butler did

not like to spend much time talking on phones. He did not talk much at all. He was known for it. He was also known as a good man to work for and a bad one to displease. What was not known by any of his subordinates was that he had once had a deeply loved daughter, the pride of his life, the girl who went to university on a scholarship and then died of a heroin overdose. Bill Butler did not like heroin. Even more he hated the men who trafficked in it. Which made him a bad enemy, and a formidable one, given the job he did. His department waged the endless war against hard drugs on behalf of HM Customs and Excise. It was known simply as 'the Knock', and Bill Butler made it his life's work to knock harder than any of them.

Five hours passed. The hundreds of packaged, reheated meals had been served, gobbled down (or left) and the plastic trays removed. The quarter-bottles of cheap wine had been quaffed and removed, or jammed into the pocket ahead of the knees. Aft of the bulkhead the heaving mass of Economy-Class humanity had finally settled down.

In the electronics bay below the First Class cabin, the two flight-management computers chatted electronically to each other as they absorbed information from the three Inertial Reference Systems, collected data from beacons and satellites, worked out the aircraft's position and directed the autopilot to make tiny movements of the controls to keep Speedbird One Zero on the preplanned track.

Far below lay the rugged land between Kabul and Kandahar. Away to the north in the mountains of the Panshir, the fanatical Taleban waged their war against Shah Masood, the last warlord to hold out against them. The passengers in the howling cocoon high above Afghanistan were shuttered against the blackness, the lethal cold, the engine noise, the cruel landscape and the war.

The window blinds were all down, the lights dimmed to a low glim, the thin blankets distributed. Most were trying to get some sleep. A few watched the in-flight movie; some were tuned in to the concert.

In seat 34 G Mrs Higgins was fast asleep, blanket up to chin, mouth half open, breathing gently. Seats E and F had been turned into one by the removal of the armrest, and Julie was spread out lengthways, blanket-warm, dolly clutched to chest, also asleep.

John Higgins could not sleep. He never could on aeroplanes. So, tired though he was, he thought back to their Far East holiday. It was a package, of course. An insurance clerk could not go as far as Thailand any other way, and even then it had involved scrimping and saving. But it had been worth it.

They had stayed at the Pansea Hotel on Phuket Island, far away from the tawdry goings-on at Pattaya – he had been most careful to check with the agency that all that side of things would come nowhere near his family. And it had been magical, they all agreed on that. They had rented bicycles and pedalled through rubber plantations and Thai villages in the interior of the island. They had stopped to marvel at red-painted, golden-roofed

Buddhist temples and seen the saffron-robed monks at their devotions.

From the hotel he had rented snorkel masks and fins for himself and Julie; Mrs Higgins did not swim, except gently in the pool. With these he and his daughter had swum out to a coral reef offshore, Julie with her water wings, he with a flotation belt. Beneath the water they had seen the scurrying fish: rock beauties and butterflies, four-eyes and sergeant-majors.

Julie had been so excited she raised her head to shout, in case her father had not seen them. But of course he had, so he gestured she should put her mouthpiece back in, before she took a gulp of water. Too late; he had to help her, spluttering and coughing, back to the beach.

There had been offers to give him a pupil's scuba-diving course in the hotel pool, but he had declined. He had read there might be sharks in the water and Mrs Higgins had squealed with horror. They were a family who wanted a nice adventure but not too much.

In the hotel shop Julie had found a doll in the form of a little Thai girl and he had bought it as a treat. After ten days at the Pansea, right below the stupefyingly expensive Amanpuri, they had completed the vacation with three days in Bangkok. There they had taken guided tours to see the Jade Buddha and the enormous Sleeping Buddha, wrinkled their noses at the stench coming off the Chao Praya River and choked on the traffic fumes. But it had been well worth it, the holiday of a lifetime.

On the seat-back in front of him was a small screen with a display of constant updates on their flight progress. He watched it idly. The figures were endless: time from Bangkok, distance covered, distance to destination, flight time ditto, outside temperature (a terrifying 76 below zero), speed of headwind.

Between the figures another image flashed up: a map of this part of the world and a small white aeroplane slowly jerking its way north-west towards Europe and home. He wondered if, like counting sheep, the mesmeric effect of the little plane might help him sleep. Then the jumbo hit a small patch of clear-air turbulence and he was wide awake, gripping the seat-arms.

He noticed that the hippie four rows ahead and across the aisle was also awake. He saw the man check his watch and begin to ease himself out of his blanket. Then the man stood up.

He glanced round as if to see if anyone was watching, then moved up the aisle towards the bulkhead. There was a curtain here, but it was only half-drawn and a shaft of light spilled out of the galley area, illuminating a patch of carpet and the two lavatory doors. The hippie reached the doors, glanced at each, but made no attempt to test them. No doubt both were occupied, though Higgins had seen no-one else move. The hippie leaned against one of the doors and waited.

Thirty seconds later he was joined by another man. Higgins was intrigued. The other man was quite different. He had a casual elegance and the appearance of wealth. He came from somewhere up front, Club or even First. But why?

In the light from the galley it was clear he wore the trousers of a cream suit, a silk shirt and a loosened tie, also of silk. His appearance reeked of First Class. Had he come this far back to relieve himself?

Then they began to talk: Mr Elegant and the hippie. It was low, earnest talk. Mainly the man from the front talked, leaning towards the hippie, who nodded several times in understanding. The body language said that the elegant man was giving a series of instructions and the hippie was agreeing to do what he was told.

John Higgins was the sort who kept an eye on neighbours and he was intrigued. If Mr Elegant wanted to go to the loo, there were five or six in First and Club. They could not all be occupied at this godforsaken hour. No, they had agreed to rendezvous at this point and at this time. Their conversation was no idle chit-chat, as of two men who chance to meet in a queue.

They parted. The man in the silk suit disappeared from view, heading back towards the front end. The hippie, without attempting to enter either of the lavatories, returned to his seat. John Higgins's mind was in a turmoil. He knew that he had witnessed something odd and yet significant but he could not work out what it was. He shut his eyes and feigned sleep as the hippie glanced round in the gloom to see if he had been watched.

Ten minutes later John Higgins believed he had his answer. Those two men had met by arrangement, a foreplanned rendezvous. But how had they agreed it? He was certain no elegant businessman in a cream silk suit had been in the Economy departure lounge. He would have stood out. Since boarding and seating, the hippie had not moved. He might have received a written note by the hand of a stewardess, but Higgins had never seen it happen, so that proved nothing.

But if not that, then there was only one explanation. The rendezvous at the point where Economy met Club, and at that precise moment of the night, could only have been agreed back in Thailand. But why? To discuss something? To exchange a progress report? For the elegant man to issue last-minute instructions? Was the hippie the businessman's PA? Surely not. Dressed like that? They were chalk and cheese. Higgins began to worry. More, he began to suspect.

It was eleven at night in London when the two covert talkers parted company. Bill Butler glanced at his sleeping wife, sighed and put out the light. His alarm was set for four thirty. Time enough; at that hour he could be washed, dressed, in his car and at Heathrow by five fifteen, a full hour before touchdown. After that it would be pot luck.

It had been a long day. When was it not? He was tired but still he could not sleep. His mind raced, and still the question was always the same. Was there anything else he could do?

It was a tip from one of his colleagues across the water in the US Drug Enforcement Administration, the formidable DEA, that had started the hunt.

Ninety per cent of the heroin consumed by addicts in the British Isles, and indeed most of Western Europe, was Turkish and therefore brown. It was a trade controlled with ruthless cunning by the Turkish mafia, among the most violent on the planet but extremely low-profile and unknown to most of the British public.

Their product came from the poppies of Anatolia: it looked like demerara sugar and it was mostly smoked or inhaled as fumes from a burning pinch on a tinfoil sheet held above a candle. The British addicts were not great injecters; the Americans were.

The Golden Triangle and hence the Far Eastern traffic did not produce this Turkish dope; it turned out Thailand White, like baking powder to look at, and usually 'cut' or mixed with similar white powder to dilute the quantity by twenty to one. This was what the Americans wanted.

So if a British gang could get hold of it on a regular basis and in reasonable quantities, the Cosa Nostra would be interested. Not to buy but to swap. The finest Colombian cocaine would exchange at three to one: six kilograms of coke against two of Thai White.

The DEA tip had come out of their Miami office. One of their underworld sources reported that three times in the last six months the Trafficante Family had sent a carrier or 'mule' over to Britain with six keys of Colombian pure and he had come back with two keys of Thai White.

Not enormous but steady, and each trip worth

£200,000 to the organizer at the British end. The quantities suggested to Bill Butler something other than ship or truck. Air. Passenger baggage. He tossed and turned and tried to grab four hours' sleep.

John Higgins could not sleep either. He had heard vaguely of that other, seamier side of the holiday paradise. He recalled reading an article about a mysterious place called the Golden Triangle: hillside after hillside growing *Papaver somniferum*, the opium poppy. The article had mentioned refining laboratories deep in the jungle along the border, impenetrable to the Thai army, where the opium toffee was reduced to base morphine and thence down again to powdery white heroin.

The passengers slept but John Higgins tossed in a welter of indecision. There could be several innocent explanations for that extraordinary meeting by the lavatory doors; his problem was that he could not think of one.

The little white plane on the screen was jerking its way into Anatolia, eastern Turkey, when John Higgins silently unbuckled himself, stood up and withdrew his attaché case from the rack above his head. No-one stirred, not even the hippie.

Seated again, he scoured his case for a plain sheet of white paper and a pen. The latter was easy; then he found four sheets of headed paper, purloined from his room at the Pansea Hotel. Carefully he tore off the sections with the Pansea logo and address, creating the plain paper he needed. Using his case as a writing desk, he began to pen a letter, writing in block capitals. It took him half an hour.

When he was done, the little white plane was edging over Ankara. He folded the sheets into the UNICEF charity envelope provided by BA and scrawled in heavy letters across the front: FOR THE CAPTAIN. URGENT.

He stood up, walked quietly to the curtains by the lavatory doors and had a peek into the galley. A young male steward had his back to him, preparing a breakfast tray for later. Higgins withdrew, unseen. A buzzer sounded. He heard the steward leave the galley and head forward. With the space empty, Higgins slipped through the curtain, placed the envelope upright between two coffee cups on the food-preparation area, and went back to his seat.

It was another half-hour before the steward noticed it as he made up more breakfast trays. He thought at first it was a donation to UNICEF, then spotted the writing, frowned, thought it over and finally went forward to find the Cabin Service Director.

'It was propped between two coffee cups, Harry. I thought I should bring it to you rather than go to the flight deck.'

Harry Palfrey twinkled benignly.

'Quite right, Simon. Well done. Probably a crank. Leave it to me. Now, the breakfast trays . . .'

He watched the young man walk away, noting the tight round buttocks beneath the uniform trousers. He had worked with a lot of stewards, bedded more than his share, but this one was drop-dead gorgeous. Perhaps at Heathrow . . . He looked at the envelope, frowned, thought of opening it but finally headed up the stairs and tapped on the door of the flight deck.

It was just a formality. The CSD can enter the flight deck at will. He walked straight in. The relief captain was in the left-hand seat, staring ahead at the lights of an upcoming coast. There was no sign of Captain Fallon. The CSD tapped on the door of the bunk room. This time he did wait.

Adrian Fallon opened up thirty seconds later and ran his fingers through greying hair.

'Harry?'

'Something a bit odd, skipper. Someone left this propped between two coffee cups in the mid-section galley. Never showed himself. Anonymous, I suspect.'

He held out the envelope.

Adrian Fallon's stomach turned over. In thirty years with the company he had never had a hijack and never a bomb-scare, but he knew several colleagues who had. It was the abiding nightmare. Now it looked as if he had one or the other. He tore open the envelope and, perched on the edge of the bunk, read it. The note began:

'Captain, I regret that I am unable to sign this, but I absolutely do not want to get involved. Nevertheless, I hope I am a dutiful citizen and feel I should let you know what I have observed. Two of your passengers have been behaving extremely strangely and in a manner that defies logical explanation.'

The letter went on to describe in detail what the

observer had seen and why it had seemed so odd as to rank as very suspicious. It ended:

'The two passengers concerned are a man who looks like a hippie: scruffy, disreputable, the sort probably no stranger to what are called exotic substances; he is seated in 30 C. The other I cannot place but he certainly came from First or Club Class.'

There was a description of the elegant man and finally the words:

'I hope I am not causing trouble, but if these two men are colluding with each other over some matter, it could be a matter about which the authorities would wish to be informed.'

Pompous ass, thought Fallon. What authorities, if not Her Majesty's Customs and Excise, and spying on his own passengers was something that stuck in his craw. He passed the letter to Harry Palfrey. The CSD read it and pursed his lips.

'Midnight assignation?' he suggested.

Fallon knew about Harry Palfrey, who knew he knew, so the captain chose his words.

'Nothing to indicate they fancied each other. And anyway, where could they have met before, if not Bangkok? So why not make a rendezvous in Heathrow? Why outside a loo door which they did not attempt to enter? Blast and damn. Harry, get me the passenger list, would you?'

While the CSD went on his errand, Fallon combed his hair, straightened his shirt and asked the relief captain, 'Current position?'

'Greek coast coming up. Something amiss, Adrian?'

'Hopefully not.'

Palfrey came back with the list. Seat 30 C was down to one Kevin Donovan.

'What about the other man? The elegant one?'

'I think I've seen him,' said Palfrey. 'First Class, seat 2 K.' He riffled through the passenger list. 'Down as Mr Hugo Seymour.'

'Let's confirm it before we jump anywhere,' said the captain. 'Slip down quietly and patrol both First and Club. Look for cream silk trousers coming out from under the blankets. Check in the wardrobes for a cream silk jacket to make up a suit.'

Palfrey nodded and padded downstairs. Fallon rang for a strong black coffee and checked the flight details.

The Flight Management System into which the route had been loaded before take-off nine hours earlier had ensured that Speedbird One Zero was right on track and schedule, passing over Greece four hours from touchdown. It was 2.20 a.m. London time and 3.20 a.m. Greek time and still pitch-black outside. There was broken cloud far below, showing the occasional twinkle of lights, and the stars were bright above.

Adrian Fallon was no more civically minded than the next man, and certainly less than the anonymous prat he was carrying in Economy, but he had a quandary. Nothing in the note indicated his command was in danger, and that being so his first reaction was to ignore it.

The trouble was, the British Airline Pilots' Association, BALPA, had a security committee and he was its vice-chairman. If anything *was* discovered at Heathrow, if either passenger Seymour or Donovan fell foul of the police or Customs for committing a pretty substantial offence, and word leaked out that he had been specifically warned about both passengers and had done nothing, the explanations would be difficult. A rock and a hard place. As Greece gave way to the Balkans he made a decision. Harry Palfrey had seen the note, not to mention the 'dutiful citizen' who had written it, and if anything blew up at Heathrow, who would stay silent to protect his rear end? So, better safe than sorry. He decided to transmit a brief non-panic forewarning, not to Customs and Excise but just to his own company duty officer yawning through the night shift at Heathrow.

To broadcast on the open channel would be to tell half the pilots heading towards Heathrow and there would be a score or more at that very moment, so he might as well take an ad in *The Times*. But BA airliners carry a gizmo called ACARS.

The Aircraft Communications, Addressing and Reporting System would enable him to send a message to BA (Ops) at Heathrow with some confidentiality. After that it would be thankfully out of his hands.

The CSD came back from below. It is Hugo Seymour, he said, no doubt about it. Right, said Fallon, and sent his brief message. They passed over Belgrade.

Bill Butler never received his four thirty wake-up alarm. At ten to four the phone rang. It was his duty man at Terminal Four, Heathrow. As he listened he slipped his legs from under the duvet and came awake fast. Twenty minutes later he was in his car, driving and calculating.

He knew all about decoys and anonymous denunciations. They were almost the oldest trick in the book. First, the anonymous phone call from a public booth somewhere in the city, denouncing someone on an incoming flight as being a carrier.

It was impossible for Customs to ignore the call, even though they might be 90 per cent certain the described tourist was simply an innocent, spotted and chosen at the point of departure. The caller would of course be a gang member based in London.

The described person would have to be intercepted while unnoticed in the throng the real carrier slipped past, looking innocent as the morning dew.

But a warning from the aircraft captain? That *was* new. A note from one of his own passengers? *Two* passengers denounced as suspicious? Somewhere behind all this was the organizing brain and it was Butler's job to pit his wits against that man and win. It could just be that this time an interfering busybody had thrown a spanner in the works.

He parked at Terminal Four and strode into the almost empty building. It was four thirty and a dozen huge jets in the livery of British Airways, which almost monopolized the fourth terminal, were heading in from Africa, the Orient and the Americas. In two hours the place would be bedlam again.

The six p.m. departures from New York, Washington, Boston and Miami, flying for seven hours downwind and adding five hours, would be meeting the flights from the east, flying for thirteen and subtracting seven. Within minutes, between six a.m. and six forty, the first hesitant off-boarded passengers would become a tidal wave. Ten members of his Knock team were also heading towards Terminal Four, weaving their way through the darkened lanes of the Home Counties. Butler needed to have his men at every stage of the disembarkation, immigration and customs hall process, but inconspicuously so. The last thing he wanted was a 'bottle-out'.

There had been such cases. The carrier, knowing exactly what his main suitcase contained, had simply lost his nerve and refused to collect his case. The carousel had gone on turning in the baggage hall and the customs officers had gone on watching, but that last single case was never claimed. How the carrier expected to face a bitter and angry gang boss was his own business and some no doubt failed to survive the experience. Butler wanted more than an abandoned suitcase. He wanted the carrier and the consignment at least.

According to instructions from West Drayton, Speedbird One Zero was moving across the Channel towards the coast of Suffolk. Her course was to bring her north of the airport, then a long, slow curve to port would line her up with the main runway, approaching from the west.

On the flight deck Adrian Fallon was back in the

left-hand seat, listening to the instructions from West Drayton, on course and on schedule. The 747 was down to 15,000 feet and Fallon could see the lights of Ipswich drifting towards them.

One of his two First Officers brought him a message received on the ACARS. It politely asked for the mysterious letter to be available at the door as soon as it opened, in the hand of the CSD and ready for collection. Fallon grunted in annoyance, took the two sheets of folded paper from his top shirt pocket and gave them to the First Officer, with instructions for Harry Palfrey. They crossed the coast. Six-oh-five.

In the three cabins there was that air of expectancy that always precedes a landing. Lights were long up, breakfast trays removed and stowed, video entertainment terminated. The cabin crew now had their jackets on, distributing passengers' jackets in First and Club. Window-seat occupants peered wearily out at the chains of lights passing beneath them.

Mr Hugo Seymour emerged from the First Class washroom, clean, shaved, combed and emitting the fragrance of an expensive Lichfield aftershave. Back in his seat he adjusted his tie, buttoned his waistcoat and accepted his cream silk jacket, folding it across his lap for later. His crocodile attaché case was between his feet.

In Economy the Canadian hippie shifted wearily and longed for a cigarette. Being in the aisle seat he could see nothing through the portholes and did not try.

The Higgins family four rows back was fully awake and ready for landing. Between her parents Julie was carefully telling Pooky of all the wonders she would be seeing in her new homeland. Mrs Higgins was packing the last of her paraphernalia into her carry-on bag. The ever-neat Mr Higgins had his plastic attaché case on his knees, hands folded on top. He had done his duty and felt the better for it.

On the seat-back the little white aeroplane finally jerked its way round the curve until its nose was pointing at Heathrow. The ensuing figures declaimed twenty miles to touchdown. It was six twelve.

From the flight deck the crew could see the still dark fields of Berkshire below them and the lights that illuminated Windsor Castle. The undercarriage went down; the flaps eased down in sequence to the full twenty-five degrees required. To a ground observer Speedbird One Zero appeared to be drifting, almost motionless, across the last miles to the concrete; in fact she was still flying at 170 knots, but slowing and dropping.

Adrian Fallon checked all his instruments yet again and acknowledged the instruction from Heathrow Tower that he was clear to land. Ahead of him a Boeing out of Miami had just cleared the runway and ten miles behind him was a Northwest carrier out of Boston. But their passengers would be going to Terminal Three. As for British Airways' dedicated Terminal Four, he would be the first of the morning. As his wing passed over the Colnbrook reservoir he went through 800 feet and the airspeed moved easily towards the 138 knots landing speed. At six eighteen Speedbird One Zero touched down.

Ten minutes later Adrian Fallon brought the huge jetliner to a final stop next to the mobile passenger tunnel, applied the parking brake and let the First Officer close her down. Power went from the main engines to the APU, causing a second-long flicker of the cabin lights, which then resumed burning brightly. Below him the cabin staff at the front end watched the gaping maw of the passenger tunnel move towards them and, as it clamped onto the side of the airliner, hauled back the door.

Standing immediately outside was a young man in the coveralls of the airport's technical staff. He spotted Harry Palfrey and raised an eyebrow.

'CSD?'

'The note?'

The young man nodded. Palfrey palmed him the two sheets of folded paper and he was gone. The CSD turned back with his practised beam to the First Class passengers waiting behind him.

'Goodbye, sir, and I hope you enjoyed the flight.'

They began to file past him. The eighth to go was the impeccable Mr Hugo Seymour, his sheer grooming singling him out at this dishevelled hour as very definitely one of the quality. Harry Palfrey genuinely hoped that some silly man in the back had not caused him any inconvenience.

After the First Class cabin was clear came the Club Class passengers, some from the rear, others tumbling down the stairs from the upper cabin. Right down the hull of the Boeing the Economy Class travellers, upright and jostling for space even with ten minutes left to wait, longed for their release like cattle from a pen.

The Immigration Hall is cavernous at that hour and the line of passport control officers waited behind their desks for the sea of humanity to come. Above and to one side is a mirrored wall, but it is a two-way mirror with a room behind it. Bill Butler stood in that room looking down.

There were ten passport officers below him, two for UK and European Union passports, eight for the rest of the world. One of his assistants had briefed them all. There was always co-operation between Immigration and Customs, and anyway the briefing had given another boring morning a little extra buzz. Of the First Class passengers only four were British, the rest Thai or Australian. The four UK citizens took only seconds to pass the necessary desk, and as the third received his passport back the immigration officer lifted her head slightly and nodded at the mirror. Bill Butler had the written note in his hand. Cream silk suit, only one. Hugo Seymour. He spoke quickly to a small communicator in his hand.

'Coming out now. Cream silk suit. Crocodile attaché case.'

Ranjit Gul Singh was a Sikh. He was also a Master of Arts from Manchester University and an officer of Customs and Excise, on attachment to the Knock. An observer that morning would have spotted his first qualification but not the other two. He was in the passage behind passport control, with a dustpan on a long handle and a brush. He took the message in a small earpiece no larger than a hearing-plug in his right ear. Seconds later a cream suit swished past his lowered head.

Officer Singh watched the businessman disappear into the men's lavatories halfway down the passage. He addressed his left sleeve in a low mumble.

'He's gone straight into the men's washroom.'

'Follow him, see what he does.'

The Sikh entered the washroom, flicking odd pieces of litter into his dustpan. The man in the cream suit was not entering a cubicle but washing his hands. Gul Singh produced a cloth and began to wipe out the bowls and the handbasins. The other occupant took no notice of him. The Sikh kept himself busy at his lowly task, but he checked to see if there was anyone hidden in the cubicles. Was this a rendezvous, a handover? He was still wiping and cleaning when the businessman dried his hands, picked up his attaché case and left. No contact had taken place. He told Bill Butler.

At that moment one of the passport officers at the desks for non-UK citizens nodded a shabby-looking hippie past him and raised his eyes to the mirrored wall. Butler took the signal and made a call on his communicator. In the passage leading to the customs hall a young woman who appeared to have disembarked from the aeroplane but had not, and who appeared to be adjusting her shoe,

272

straightened up, noted the jeans and denim shirt ahead of her and began to follow.

Hugo Seymour had emerged into the passage to find himself no longer alone but in a throng of Economy Class passengers. He's killing time, thought Bill Butler, losing himself in the mass. But why the stand-out-a-mile suit? That was when the anonymous call came. Butler took the report from the switchboard on his communicator.

'American-sounding voice,' said the operator. 'Tagged a Canadian hippie in jeans and denim shirt, long shaggy hair, wispy beard, but he's carrying a cargo in his haversack. Then hung up.'

'We're onto him,' said Butler.

'That was quick, boss,' said the admiring switchboard operator. Butler was striding down passages unknown to the public to take up position behind another two-way mirror, but this time in the customs area, specifically the Nothing to Declare Green Channel. If either of the suspects headed for the Red Channel, that would be a real surprise.

He was pleased the anonymous call had come through. It conformed to pattern. The hippie was the decoy, the obvious type. The respectable businessman would have the consignment. Not a bad trick, but this time, thanks to a dutiful citizen with insomnia, sharp eyes and a nosy disposition, it was not going to work.

The luggage from Bangkok was coming onto Carousel Six and over 200 people were already grouped around it. Most had acquired trolleys from the ranks at the end of the hall. Among the passengers stood Mr Seymour. His real hide hard-frame case had been one of the first to appear but he had not been there. The rest of the First Class passengers were gone. The hide case had already circled twenty times, but he made no eye contact with it, gazing instead at the delivery mouth by the wall whence the cases emerged from the baggage handling area beyond.

Ten yards away stood the hippie, Donovan, still waiting for his big black haversack. Just approaching the carousel, pushing not one but two trolleys, was Mr Higgins with his wife and daughter. Julie, on her first foreign journey, had insisted she wanted a trolley of her own for her single case and Pooky.

Piece by piece, the circulating bags were identified by their owners, hauled off the carousel and manhandled onto trolleys. The long shuffling column through the Green Channel had begun and was now swelled by travellers from two other jumbo jets, mainly Americans and some British returning from Caribbean vacations via Miami. A dozen uniformed customs men, looking deceptively bored, some in the carousel hall, others inside the channel, watched.

'There it is, Daddy.'

Several passengers looked round and smiled indulgently. There was no mistaking Julie Higgins's case. It was a medium-sized Samsonite, garishly decorated with decals of her favourite cartoon characters: Scooby Doo, Shaggy, Wile E. Coyote and the Roadrunner. Almost at the same time her parents' two holdall grips came along and the ever-neat John Higgins carefully stacked them so they would not fall off.

The hippie spotted his haversack, swung it onto his shoulders, disdained a trolley and began to stride to the Green Channel. Mr Seymour finally retrieved his hide suitcase, laid it on a trolley and followed. In the Green Channel Bill Butler stood behind his mirror and watched the tired, pre-dawn crocodile of humanity parading past the glass.

Inside the carousel hall an idle porter spoke briefly into his sleeve.

'Hippie first, coming now, silk suit ten yards behind.'

The hippie did not get far. He was halfway from the arch leading to the channel and the exit of blessed relief at the far end when two uniformed customs men stepped into his path. Polite of course. Deadly polite.

'Excuse me, sir, would you mind stepping this way?'

The Canadian exploded with rage.

'What the hell is this all about, man?'

'Just come with us, sir.'

The Canadian's voice rose to a shout.

'Now wait a fucking minute. Thirteen fucking hours on a plane and I don't need this shit, you hear?'

The queue behind him stopped as if shot. Then, in the manner of the British when someone is creating a scene, they tried to look the other way, pretend it was not happening, and continue to shuffle forward. Hugo Seymour was among them.

The Canadian, relieved of both his small and large haversack, still shouting and protesting, was hustled away through a side door to one of the search rooms. The shuffle resumed. The cream-suited businessman had almost made the exit arch when he too was intercepted. Two officers blocked his path and two more closed in behind.

At first he appeared not to realize what was happening. Then, beneath his tan, he went ashen grey.

'I don't understand. What seems to be the problem?'

'If you would just be kind enough to come with us, sir.'

He too was led away. Behind the one-way mirror Bill Butler sighed. Now, the big one. The end of the chase. The cases, and what they contained.

It took three hours, in two separate suites of rooms. Butler flitted between them both, growing ever more frustrated. When the Customs take luggage apart, they really find it all. If there is anything to find. They had both haversacks emptied and searched to the linings and the frames. Apart from several packs of Lucky Strikes there was nothing. That did not surprise Bill Butler. Decoys never carry anything.

It was Hugo Seymour who stunned him. They had the hide suitcase through the X-ray machine a dozen times. They measured for hidden compartments and found nothing. The same with the crocodile attaché case. It yielded a tube of Bisodol antacid tablets. Two of these were crushed and the powder chemically tested. The tests revealed

276

antacid tablets. He was stripped, clothed in a paper one-piece, and his clothes X-rayed. Then, naked, he was X-rayed himself to see if he carried any packages internally. Nothing.

Around ten o'clock, fifteen minutes apart, each had to be released. Seymour was by then loudly threatening legal action. Butler was not fussed by that. They usually did. That was because they had no idea of the real powers of Customs and Excise.

'You want them tailed, boss?' asked his gloomy Number Two. Butler thought about it and shook his head.

'It was probably a bum steer. If they are innocent patsies, we'll be following them for nothing. If they are not so innocent, I doubt if the controlling brains behind the Bangkok run will contact them before they have spotted the tail. Leave it. Next time.'

The Canadian, the first to be released, took the airport coach into London and checked into a seedy hotel near Paddington. Mr Hugo Seymour took a taxi and went to a far more expensive hostelry.

Just after two p.m. four men in various London streets received phone calls. Each was standing, as arranged, in a public phone booth. Each was told to report to an address. One of them made a call himself, then left for the rendezvous.

At four p.m. Bill Butler was sitting alone in his car outside a block of serviced apartments, the sort that could be rented by the week, or even the day.

At five past four the unmarked Transit van he had been awaiting drove up behind him and ten members of his Knock team spilled out. There was no time for briefing. The gang could have a lookout posted, though after watching for thirty minutes he had seen no lace curtain shift. He simply nodded and led the way through the doors of the block. There was a front desk but no-one manning it. He left two disappointed men to watch the lift doors and led the other eight up the stairs. The flat was on the third.

The Knock does not stand on ceremony. The rammer took off the door lock with a single smash and they were in: young, eager, very fit, adrenalin high. But no guns.

The five men in the rented drawing room put up no fight. They sat there, looking sandbagged by the suddenness and unexpectedness of the incursion. Butler came in last, very much the man in charge, while his team delved into inside pockets for identification. He took the glowering American first.

Later voice tests would show it was he who had made the call denouncing the Canadian hippie decoy to the Customs hotline at Heathrow Airport. The grip by his side contained six kilograms of what would turn out to be pure Colombian cocaine.

'Mr Salvatore Bono, I am arresting you on a charge of conspiring with others to import into this country a banned substance . . .'

When the formalities were over the man from Miami was cuffed and led away. Butler took the hippie next. As the surly Canadian was being taken out Butler called after his colleagues, 'My car. I want to talk to that one.'

Mr Hugo Seymour had changed out of his silk

suit and into tweed and slacks better adapted for an English day in late January. The second decoy. He, too, relieved of the block of fifty-pound notes totalling £10,000 that he had received for his role in the operation, went quietly. Butler turned to the remaining two.

The consignment was on the table between them, still in its carrying case, as it had come through Customs. The false bottom had been ripped out to reveal the cavity beneath, in which lay sylthane bags that, after verification, would reveal two kilograms of Thai White heroin. But the decals of Scooby Doo and Shaggy were plainly visible.

'Mr John Higgins, I am arresting you on a charge of importing, and of conspiring with others to import, into this country . . .'

The dutiful citizen had to be escorted to the bathroom where he threw up. When he was gone Butler turned to the last man, the organizer of the Bangkok dope run. He sat staring bleakly out of the window at the London sky, a sight he knew would in future be minimal.

'I've been after you for some time, chum.'

There was no reply.

'A nice scam. Not one decoy but two. And trotting along behind, avoiding the fracas in the Green Channel, innocent Mr Higgins with his dumpy wife and charming little daughter.'

'Get on with it,' snapped the middle-aged man.

'Very well. Mr Harry Palfrey, I am arresting you . . .'

Butler left his last two men to scour the rented

flat for any trace of evidence that might have been thrown away in the seconds when the door came down, and descended to the street. He had a long night of work ahead of him, but it was work he would enjoy. His Number Two was at the wheel of his own car, so he slid into the back beside the silent Canadian.

As the car drew away from the kerb, he said, 'Let's get some things straight. When did you first learn that Seymour was your partner in this double bluff?'

'Back there in the flat,' said the hippie.

Butler looked thunderstruck.

'What about the conversation in the middle of the night by the lavatory door?'

'What conversation? What lavatory? I had never seen him before in my life.'

Butler laughed, which he seldom did.

'Of course. Sorry about what they did to you at Heathrow, but you know the rules. I couldn't blow your cover, even there. Anyway, thanks for the phone call. Nice one, Sean. Tonight the beer's on me.'

WHISPERING WIND

Legend has always had it that no white man survived the massacre of the men under General Custer at the Little Bighorn, 25 June 1876. Not quite true; there was one single survivor. He was a frontier scout, aged twenty-four, name of Ben Craig.

This is his story.

It was the keen nose of the frontier scout that caught it first: the faint aroma of woodsmoke on the prairie wind.

He was riding point, twenty yards ahead of the ten cavalrymen of the patrol scouting forward of the main column down the western bank of Rosebud Creek.

Without turning round the scout raised his right hand and reined in. Behind him the sergeant and the nine troopers did the same. The scout slipped from his horse, leaving it to crop the grass in peace, and trotted towards a low bank between the riders and the creek. There he dropped to the ground and crawled to the crest, peering over the top while remaining hidden in the long grass.

They were camped between the ridge and the bank of the stream. It was a small camp, no more than five lodges, a single extended family. The teepees indicated Northern Cheyenne. The scout knew them well. Sioux teepees were tall and narrow; Cheyenne built theirs wider at the base, more squat.

Pictographs showing hunting triumphs adorned the sides and these too were in the Cheyenne manner.

The scout estimated the camp would contain between twenty and twenty-five persons, but the half-score of men were away hunting. He could tell by the ponies. There were only seven grazing near the lodges. To move such a camp, with the men mounted and the women and children, folded teepees and other baggage on travois there should have been almost twenty.

He heard the sergeant crawling up the bank towards him and gestured behind him for the man to stay down. Then the blue uniform sleeve with the three chevrons appeared beside him.

'What do you see?' said a hoarse whisper.

It was nine in the morning and already burning hot. They had been riding for three hours. General Custer liked to break camp early. But already the scout could smell the whiskey on the breath of the man beside him. It was bad frontier whiskey and the smell was rank, stronger than the perfume of the wild plum, cherry and the torrents of rambling dog roses that grew in such profusion along the banks to give Rosebud Creek its name.

'Five lodges. Cheyenne. Only the women and children in camp. The braves are away hunting across the creek.'

Sergeant Braddock did not ask how the scout knew this. He just accepted that he did. He hawked, ejected a squirt of liquid tobacco and gave a yellow-toothed grin. The scout slid down the bank and stood up.

'Let us leave them alone. They are not what we are looking for.'

But Braddock had spent three years on the plains with the Seventh Cavalry and had had depressingly little sport. A long and boring winter in Fort Lincoln had yielded a bastard son by a laundress and part-time whore, but he had really come to the plains to kill Indians and did not intend to be denied.

The slaughter took only five minutes. The ten riders came over the ridge at a canter and broke at once into a full gallop. The scout, mounted up, watched in disgust from the top of the ridge.

One trooper, a raw recruit, was so bad a horseman that he fell off. The rest did the butchery. All cavalry swords had been left behind at Fort Lincoln so they used their Colt revolvers or new-issue Springfield '73s.

When they heard the drumming of hooves the squaws attending the campfire and their cooking pots tried to find and gather their children before running for the river. They were too late. The riders were through them before they could reach the water, then turned and charged back through the lodges, shooting down anything that moved. When it was over and all the old people, women and children were dead, they dismounted and raided the teepees, looking for interesting loot to send home. There were several more shots from inside the lodges when still-living children were found.

The scout trotted the 400 yards from the ridge to the camp to examine the slaughter. There seemed

285

nothing and no-one left alive as the troopers
torched the teepees. One of the troopers, little more
than a boy and new to this, was bringing up his
breakfast of hard tack and beans, leaning out of the
saddle to avoid his own puke. Sergeant Braddock
was triumphant. He had his victory. He had found
a feathered war bonnet and affixed it to his saddle
near the canteen that ought to have contained only
spring water.

The scout counted fourteen corpses, tossed like
broken dolls where they fell. He shook his head as
one of the men offered him a trophy, and trotted
past the tents to the bank of the creek to give his
horse a brief drink.

She was lying half hidden in the reeds, fresh
blood running down one bare leg where the rifle
bullet had taken her in the thigh as she ran. If he
had been a mite quicker he would have turned his
head away and ridden back to the burning teepees.
But Braddock, watching him, had caught the direction of his glance and ridden up.

'What have you found, boy? Well, another
vermin, and still alive.'

He unholstered his Colt and took aim. The girl in
the reeds turned her face and stared up at them,
eyes blank with shock. The scout reached out,
gripped the Irishman's wrist and forced the pistol-
hand upwards. Braddock's coarse, whiskey-red
face darkened with anger.

'Leave her alive, she may know something,' said
the scout. It was the only way. Braddock paused,
thought and then nodded.

'Good thinking, boy. We'll take her back to the general as a present.'

He reholstered his pistol and went back to check on his men. The scout slipped off his horse and went into the reeds to tend to the girl. Luckily for her the wound was clean. At short range the bullet had gone through the flesh of the thigh as she ran. There was an entry wound and an exit hole, both small and round. The scout used his neckerchief to bathe the wound with clear creek water and bind it tight to stop the flow of blood.

When he had finished he looked at her. She stared back at him. A torrent of hair, black as a raven's wing, flowed about her shoulders; wide dark eyes, clouded with pain and fear. Not all Indian squaws were pretty in a white man's eyes, but of all the tribes, the handsomest were the Cheyenne. The girl in the reeds, aged about sixteen, had a stunning, ethereal beauty. The scout was twenty-four, Bible-raised, and had never known a woman in the Old Testament sense. He felt his heart pound and had to break the gaze. He swung her onto his shoulder and walked back to the ruined camp.

'Put her on a pony,' shouted the sergeant. He swigged again from his pannikin. The scout shook his head.

'Travois,' he said, 'or she'll die.'

There were several travois on the ground near the smouldering ashes of the teepees. Composed of two long, springy lodgepole pines, crossed over the back of a pony, with trailing ends spread wide and a stretched buffalo hide to carry the burden, the travois was a remarkably comfortable way of travelling, much easier on an injured person than the white man's cart, which bucked savagely at every rut.

The scout rounded up one of the straying ponies. There were only two left; five had stampeded into the distance. The animal reared and shied as he took its tethering rein. It had already caught the odour of white men and this smell could drive a pinto pony half wild. The reverse was also true: US cavalry horses could become almost unmanageable if they scented the body smell of Plains Indians.

The scout breathed gently into the animal's nostrils until it calmed down and accepted him. Ten minutes later he had the travois in place and the injured girl wrapped in a blanket on the buffalo hide. The patrol set off back up the trail to find Custer and the main body of the Seventh Cavalry. It was 24 June, year of grace 1876.

The seeds of the campaign of that summer across the plains of southern Montana dated back several years. Gold had been discovered at last in the sacred Black Hills of South Dakota and the prospectors poured in. But the Black Hills had already been accorded to the Sioux nation in perpetuity. Angered by what they saw as treachery, the Plains Indians responded by raids on prospectors and wagon trains.

The whites reacted with rage to such violence; tales of hideous barbarity, often fictitious or hugely exaggerated, fuelled the anger to boiling point, and the white communities appealed to Washington. The government responded by casually revoking the Treaty of Laramie and confining the Plains Indians to a series of meagre reservations, a fraction of what they had been solemnly promised. The reservations were in North and South Dakota territories.

But Washington also conceded the creation of a block known as the Unceded Territories. These were the traditional hunting grounds of the Sioux, still teeming with buffalo and deer. The block had its eastern border down the vertical line created by the western perimeters of North and South Dakota. Its western border was an imaginary line north–south, 145 miles further west, a line the Indians had never seen and could not imagine. To the north the Unceded block was bounded by the Yellowstone River, running through the land called Montana and into the Dakotas; to the south by the North Platte River in Wyoming. Here, at first, the Indians were allowed to hunt. But the westward march of the white man did not stop.

In 1875 the Sioux began to drift off the Dakota reservations and head west into the Unceded hunting grounds. Late that year the Bureau of Indian Affairs gave them a deadline: move back to the reservations by 1 January.

The Sioux and their allies did not contest the ultimatum; they simply ignored it. Most of them never even heard of it. They continued to hunt, and as winter gave way to spring they sought their traditional staples, the munificent buffalo and the gentle deer and antelope. In early spring the Bureau handed the matter over to the army. Its task: to find them, round them up and escort them back to the Dakota reservations.

The army did not know two things: how many there really were off reservation, and where they were. On the first matter, the army was simply lied to. The reservations were run by Indian agents, all white and many of them crooks.

From Washington they received allotments of cattle, corn, flour, blankets and money to distribute among their charges. Many swindled the Indians grossly, leading to hunger among the women and children, and thus the decision to return to the hunting plains.

The agents also had another reason for lying. If they declared that 100 per cent of those supposed to be on reservation were indeed there, they received 100 per cent allowance. As the percentage of those Indians accounted for dropped, so did the allocations and thus the agents' personal profits. In the spring of 1876 the agents told the army there were only a few handfuls of warriors missing. They lied. There were thousands and thousands of them missing, all gone west across the border to hunt the Unceded Lands.

As to where they were, there was only one way to find out. Troops would have to be sent into southern Montana to find them. So a plan was formulated. There would be three columns of mixed infantry and cavalry.

From Fort Lincoln in northern Dakota General

Alfred Terry would march west along the course of the Yellowstone River, the northern border of the hunting grounds. From Fort Shaw in Montana General John Gibbon would march south to Fort Ellis, then veer east along the Yellowstone until he met up with Terry's column coming the other way.

From Fort Fetterman, far to the south in Wyoming, General George Crook would march north, cross the headwaters of Crazy Woman Creek, cross the Tongue River and head up the valley of the Big Horn until he made rendezvous with the other two columns. Somewhere, between them, it was figured, one of them would find the main body of the Sioux. They all set off in March.

In early June Gibbon and Terry met up where the Tongue, flowing north, empties into the Yellowstone. They had not seen a single war bonnet. All they knew was that at least the Plains Indians were somewhere to the south of them. Gibbon and Terry agreed that Terry would march on westward and Gibbon, now united with him, would retrace his steps back to the west. This they did.

On 20 June the combined column reached the point where the Rosebud flows into the Yellowstone. Here it was decided that in case the Indians were up that particular watercourse, the Seventh Cavalry, which had accompanied Terry all the way from Fort Lincoln, should peel off and head up the Rosebud to the headwaters. Custer might find Indians, he might find General Crook.

No-one knew that on the 17th Crook had chanced into a very large concentration of mixed Sioux and Cheyenne and taken a beating. He had turned round, headed back south and was even then happily hunting game. He did not send any riders north to find and warn his colleagues, so they did not know there would be no relief coming up from the south. They were on their own.

It was on the fourth day of forced march up the valley of the Rosebud that one of the forward patrols returned with a tale of victory over a small village of Cheyenne, and one prisoner.

General George Armstrong Custer, riding proudly at the head of his column of cavalry, was in a hurry. He did not wish to halt the entire unit for one prisoner. He nodded in response to Sergeant Braddock's appearance and ordered him to report to his own company commander. Information, if any, from the squaw could wait until they made camp that night.

The Cheyenne girl remained on the travois for the rest of that day. The scout took the pony to the rear and tethered its lead rein to one of the wagons of the baggage train. The pony pulling the travois trotted along behind the wagon. As no scouting was now needed, the scout remained nearby. In the short time he had been with the Seventh he had decided he did not like what he was doing, he did not like either the company commander to whom he was attached or the company sergeant; and he thought the famous General Custer a bombastic ass. He did not have the vocabulary to phrase it that

292

way, and in any case he kept his thoughts to himself. His name was Ben Craig.

His father, John Knox Craig, had been an immigrant from Scotland, ousted from his small farm by a greedy laird. This hardy man had emigrated to the United States in the early 1840s. Somewhere in the east he had met and married a girl of Scottish Presbyterian stock like himself, and, finding few opportunities in the cities, had headed west to the frontier. By 1850 he had reached southern Montana and decided to try for his fortune by panning for gold in the wilderness around the foothills of the Pryor Range.

He was one of the first in those days. Life had been bleak and hard, with bitter winters in a timber shack by a stream at the edge of the forest. Only the summers had been idyllic, the forest teeming with game, trout brimming in the streams and the prairie a carpet of wild flowers. In 1852 Jennie Craig bore her first and only son. Two years later a small daughter died in infancy.

Ben Craig was ten, a child of the forest and the frontier, when both his parents were killed by a Crow war party. Two days later a mountain trapper called Donaldson had come across the boy, hungry and grieving amid the ashes of the burnt-out cabin. Together they had buried John and Jennie Craig beneath two crosses by the water's edge. Whether Craig Senior had ever put together a stash of gold dust would never be known, for if the Crow warriors had found it they would have scattered the yellow powder, thinking it to be sand.

Donaldson was older, a mountain man who trapped the wolf and beaver, bear and fox, and yearly took the pelts to the nearest trading post. Out of pity for the orphan, the old bachelor took him in and raised him as his own.

In his mother's charge Ben had only had access to one book, the Bible, and she had read him long passages from it. Though he was no dab hand at reading and writing he had retained tracts from what she called the Good Book in his head. His father had taught him to pan for gold, but it was Donaldson who taught him the ways of the wild, the call of the birds by name, the tracking of an animal by its spoor and how to ride and shoot.

It was with the trapper that he met the Cheyenne, who also trapped, and with whom Donaldson traded his store goods from the trading post. It was they who taught him their ways and their language.

Two years before the summer campaign of 1876 the old man was claimed by the same wilderness in which he had lived. He missed his mark while shooting an old cinnamon bear and the crazed animal clawed and mauled him to death. Ben buried his adoptive father near the cabin in the forest, took what he needed and torched the rest.

Old Donaldson had always said, 'When I'm gone, boy, take what you need. It will all be yours.' So he took the razor-sharp bowie knife and its sheath decorated in the Cheyenne manner, and the 1852 Sharps rifle; the two horses, saddles, blankets and some pemmican and hard tack for the ride. He needed no more. Then he came down from the mountains to the plain and rode north to Fort Ellis.

He was working there as hunter, trapper and horse-breaker in April 1876 when General Gibbon rode by. The general needed scouts who knew the land south of the Yellowstone. The pay offered was good, so Ben Craig signed on.

He was present when they reached the mouth of the River Tongue and met up with General Terry; he rode back with the combined column until they found again the mouth of the Rosebud. Here the Seventh Cavalry under Custer was detailed to go south up the course of the creek, and the call went out for anyone who could speak Cheyenne.

Custer already had at least two Sioux-speaking scouts. One was a black soldier, the only one in the Seventh, Isaiah Dorman, who had lived with the Sioux. The other was the Chief Scout, Mitch Bouyer, a half-blood, part French, part Sioux. But although the Cheyenne have always been regarded as first cousins and traditional allies of the Sioux, the languages are different. Craig put up his hand and was detailed by General Gibbon to join the Seventh.

Gibbon also offered Custer three extra companies of cavalry under Major Brisbin, but was turned down. Terry offered him Gatling machine guns, but he turned these down as well. When they set off up the Rosebud the Seventh was 12 companies of troops, 6 white scouts, over 30 Indian scouts, a wagon train, and 3 civilians, in all 675 men. These also included farriers, smiths and muleteers.

Custer had left his regimental band behind with

Terry, so when he made his final charge it would not be to the sound of his favourite march, 'Garryowen'. But as they moved down the river course, kettles, pots, cauldrons and ladles banging together from the sides of the chuck wagons, Craig wondered which band of Indians Custer hoped to catch by surprise. With the noise and the column of dust raised by 3,000 hooves, he knew they could be seen and heard several miles off.

Craig had had two weeks between the Tongue and the Rosebud to look at the famed Seventh and its iconic commander, and the more he saw the more his heart sank. He hoped they would not meet a large body of Sioux and Cheyenne prepared to fight, but feared they might.

All day the column rode south, following the course of the Rosebud, but saw no more Indians. Yet several times, when the wind blew off the prairie to the west, the cavalry horses became skittish, even panicky, and Craig was sure they had smelt something on the breeze. The burning teepees could not have gone unnoticed for very long. A high-rising column of smoke over the prairie could be seen for miles. The element of surprise was gone.

Just after four in the afternoon General Custer called a halt and made camp. The sun began to drop towards the distant and invisible Rockies. Tents for the officers were quickly established. Custer and his intimates always used the ambulance tent, the biggest and most spacious. Folding camp chairs and tables were set up, the horses watered in the stream, food prepared, campfires lit.

The Cheyenne girl lay silent on the travois and stared at the darkening sky. She was prepared to die. Craig took a canteen of fresh water from the creek and offered her a drink. She stared at him with huge dark eyes.

'Drink,' he said in Cheyenne. She made no move. He poured a small stream of the cool liquid onto her mouth. The lips parted. She swallowed. He left the pannikin beside her.

As dusk deepened a rider from B Company came down the camp looking for him.

When he was found the trooper rode back to report. Ten minutes later Captain Acton rode up. He was accompanied by Sergeant Braddock, a corporal and two troopers. They all dismounted and surrounded the travois.

All the frontier scouts attached to the Seventh, the six whites, the small group of Crows and the thirty or so Arikaras, known as the Rees, formed a group with a common interest. They all knew the frontier and the way of life.

Round the campfires in the evening, before turning in, it was customary for them to talk among themselves. They discussed the officers, starting with General Custer, and the company commanders. Craig had been surprised how unpopular the general was with his men. His younger brother Tom Custer, commanding C Company, was much better liked, but the most loathed of them all was Captain Acton. Craig shared this antipathy. Acton was a career soldier who had joined just after the

Civil War ten years earlier and risen in the Seventh in the shadow of Custer, the scion of a wealthy family back east. He was thin, with a chiselled face and a cruel mouth.

'So, Sergeant,' said Acton, 'this is your prisoner. Let's find out what she knows.

'You talk the savage's lingo?' he asked Craig. The scout nodded. 'I want to know who she is, what group she was with and where the main body of the Sioux is to be found. Right now.'

Craig bent over the girl on the buffalo hide. He broke into Cheyenne, using both words and numerous hand gestures, for the dialects of the Plains Indians had limited vocabulary and needed hand signals to make the meaning plain.

'Tell me your name, girl. No harm will come to you.'

'I am called Wind That Talks Softly,' she said. The cavalrymen stood around and listened. They could understand not a word, but could comprehend the shakes of the girl's head. Finally Craig straightened up.

'Captain, she says her name is Whispering Wind. She is of the northern Cheyenne. Her family is that of Tall Elk. Those were his lodges that the sergeant wiped out this morning. There were ten men in the village, including her father, and they were all away hunting deer and antelope east of the Rosebud.'

'And the main concentration of the Sioux?'

'She says she has not seen the Sioux. Her family came up from the south, from the Tongue River.

298

There were some more Cheyenne with them, but they parted company a week ago. Tall Elk preferred to hunt alone.'

Captain Acton stared down at the bandaged thigh, leaned forward and squeezed hard. The girl sucked in her breath but gave no cry.

'A little encouragement perhaps,' said Acton. The sergeant grinned. Craig reached out, took the captain's wrist and removed it.

'That will not work, Captain,' he said. 'She has told me what she knows. If the Sioux cannot be to the north, the way we have come, and they are not to the south and east, they must be to the west. You could tell the general that.'

Captain Acton plucked the restraining hand from his wrist as if it were infected. He straightened up, produced a half-hunter silver watch and glanced at it.

'Chow time in the general's tent,' he said. 'I must go.' He had plainly lost interest in the prisoner. 'Sergeant, when it is full dark take her into the prairie and finish her off.'

'Anything say we can't have a little fun with her first, Captain?' asked Sergeant Braddock. There was a gust of approving laughter from the other men. Captain Acton mounted his horse.

'Frankly, Sergeant, I don't give a damn what you do.'

He spurred his mount in the direction of General Custer's tent at the head of the camp. The others mounted likewise. Sergeant Braddock leaned down to Craig with a leer.

'Keep her safe, boy. We'll be back.'

Craig walked over to the nearest chuck wagon, took a plate of salt pork, tack and beans, found a box of ammunition, sat down and ate. He thought of his mother, fifteen years earlier, reading to him from the Bible by the dim light of a tallow candle. He thought of his father, patiently panning hour after hour to find the elusive yellow metal in the streams running down from the Pryors. And he thought of old Donaldson, who had only once taken off his belt to him, and then when he had been cruel to a captured animal.

Shortly before eight, with darkness now settled on the camp, he rose, returned his billycan and spoon to the wagon, and walked back to the travois. He said nothing to the girl. He just unhitched the two poles across the pinto pony's back and lowered the rig to the ground.

He picked up the girl from the floor and swung her effortlessly onto the pinto's back, handing her the tether rein. Then he pointed to the open prairie.

'Ride,' he said. She stared at him for two seconds. He slapped the pony on the rump. Seconds later it was gone, a sturdy, hardy, unshod animal that could find its own way across many miles of open prairie until it scented the odour of its own kin. Several Ree scouts watched curiously from fifty feet away.

They came for him at nine and they were angry. Two troopers held him while Sergeant Braddock hit him about the body. When he sagged they dragged him through the camp to where General Custer, by the light of several oil lamps and surrounded by a group of officers, sat at a table in front of his tent.

George Armstrong Custer has always been an enigma. But it is clear there were two sides to the man: a good and a bad, a light and a dark.

On his light side he could be joyous and full of laughter, addicted to boyish practical jokes, and pleasant company. He possessed an endless energy and enormous personal stamina, forever engaged in some new project, whether collecting wildlife from the plains to send back to zoos in the east, or learning taxidermy. Despite years of absence, he was unswervingly loyal to his wife, Elizabeth, on whom he doted.

After a drunken experience in his youth, he was teetotal, refusing even a glass of wine with dinner. He never swore and forbade profane language in his presence.

During the Civil War fourteen years earlier he had shown such blinding courage, such total absence of personal fear, that he had quickly risen from lieutenant to major-general, only agreeing to revert to lieutenant-colonel to stay in the smaller postwar army. He had ridden at the head of his men into withering curtains of fire, yet never been touched by a bullet. He was a hero to myriad civilians, yet was distrusted and disliked by his own men, excepting his own personal court.

This was because he could also be vindictive and cruel to those who offended him. Although himself unscathed, he lost more of his own men, dead and wounded, than any other cavalry commander in the war. This was put down to an almost crazy rashness. Soldiers tend not to warm to a commander who is going to get them killed.

He ordered the use of the lash frequently during the War of the Plains and sustained more desertions than any other commander in the West. The Seventh was endlessly being depleted by the nocturnal departure of deserters, or snowbirds as they were called. The unit had to be constantly replenished with fresh recruits, but he had little interest in training them to become efficient and drilled cavalrymen. Despite a long autumn and winter at Fort Lincoln, the Seventh was in a deplorable state in June 1876.

Custer possessed a personal vanity and ambition of awesome proportions, going out of his way to encourage personal glorification through newspapers whenever he could get it. Many of his mannerisms, the tanned buckskin suit, the flowing auburn curls, were to this end, as was the journalist Mark Kellogg, who now accompanied the Seventh Cavalry to war.

But as a commanding general he had two flaws that would kill him and most of his men in the next hours. One was that he constantly underestimated his enemy. He had the reputation of a great Indian-fighter and he believed it. In truth, eight years earlier he had wiped out a sleeping Cheyenne village, that of Chief Black Kettle on the Washita River in Kansas, surrounding the sleeping Indians in the night and butchering most of them, men, women and children, at sunrise. The Cheyenne had just signed a new treaty of peace with the white men, so they thought they were safe.

In the intervening years he had been involved in four small skirmishes with war parties. The aggregate losses for all four were not a dozen. Considering the hideous casualty lists of the Civil War, these brushes with local Indians were hardly worth a mention. Yet the readers back east were hero-hungry and the painted savage of the frontier was a demonic villain. Sensational newspaper reports and his own book, *My Life on the Plains*, had led to this reputation and the iconic status.

The second fault was that he would listen to no-one. He had some extremely experienced scouts with him on the march down the Rosebud, but he ignored warning after warning. This was the man before whom Ben Craig was dragged on the evening of 24 June.

Sergeant Braddock explained what had happened, and that there were witnesses. Custer, surrounded by six of his officers, studied the man in front of him. He saw a young man twelve years his junior, just under six feet tall, clad in buckskin, with curling chestnut hair and electric blue eyes. He was clearly Caucasian, not even a half-blood as some scouts were, yet his feet were clad in soft leather boots rather than stiff cavalry issue, and a single white-tipped eagle feather hung from a braided strand of hair at the back of his head.

'This is a very serious offence,' said Custer when the sergeant had finished. 'Is it true?'

'Yes, General.'

'And why did you do it?'

Craig explained the earlier interrogation of the girl and the plans for later that evening. Custer's face tightened in disapproval.

'I'll have none of that sort of thing in my command, not even with squaws. Is it true, Sergeant?'

At this point Captain Acton, sitting behind Custer, intervened. He was smooth, persuasive. He had personally conducted the interrogation. It had been entirely verbal, via the interpreter. There had been no infliction of pain on the girl. His last instructions were that she should be guarded through the night, but not touched, so that the general could make a decision in the morning.

'I think my troop sergeant will confirm what I say,' he concluded.

'Yessir, that's just the way it was,' said Braddock.

'Case proved,' said Custer. 'Close arrest until court martial. Send for the provost-sergeant. Craig, in letting this prisoner go, you have sent her to join and warn the main body of the hostiles. That is treason and a hanging offence.'

'She did not ride to the west,' said Craig. 'She rode to the east to find her own family, what's left of them.'

'She can still now warn the hostiles where we are,' snapped Custer.

'They know where you are, General.'

'And how do you know that?'

'They've been shadowing you all day.'

There were ten seconds of stunned silence. The provost-sergeant appeared, a big, bluff veteran called Lewis.

'Take this man in charge, Sergeant. Close arrest. Tomorrow at sun-up there will be a quick court martial. Sentence will be carried out immediately. That is all.'

'Tomorrow is the Lord's Day,' said Craig.

Custer thought. 'You are right. I will not hang a man on a Sunday. Monday it shall be.'

To one side, the regimental adjutant Captain William Cooke, a Canadian, had been scratching notes of the proceedings. These he would later stuff in his saddlebag.

At this moment one of the scouts, Bob Jackson, rode up to the tent. With him were four Rees and a Crow scout. They had been up ahead at sundown and were late in returning. Jackson was half white and half Piegan Blackfoot. His report brought Custer excitedly to his feet.

Just before sundown Jackson's native scouts had found traces of a large camp, many circular marks in the prairie where the teepees had stood. The trail from the camp headed west, away from the valley of the Rosebud.

Custer was excited for two reasons. His orders from General Terry had been to go right on up to the headwaters of the Rosebud, but then to use his own judgement if fresh information was available. This was it. Custer was now a free man to create and formulate his own strategy and tactics, his own battle plan, without having to follow orders. The second reason was that he at last seemed to have found the main body of the elusive Sioux. Twenty miles to the west lay another river in another valley: the Little Bighorn, flowing north to join the Bighorn and thence to the Yellowstone.

Within two or three days Gibbon's and Terry's combined forces would reach that confluence and turn south down the Bighorn. The Sioux were in a nutcracker.

'Break camp,' shouted Custer and his officers scattered to their units. 'We march through the night.' He turned to the provost-sergeant. 'Keep that prisoner beside you, Sergeant Lewis. Tethered to his horse. And close behind me. Now he can see what happens to his friends.'

They marched through the night. Rough country, harsh terrain, out of the valley, always climbing towards the watershed. The men and horses began to tire. They arrived at the divide, the high point between the two valleys, in the small hours of the morning of Sunday the 25th. It was pitch dark but the stars were bright. Soon after the divide they found a rivulet which Mitch Bouyer identified as Dense Ashwood Creek. It flowed westwards, downhill to join the Little Bighorn in the valley. The column followed the creek.

Just before dawn Custer called a halt, but there was no pitching of camp. The tired men rested in bivouac and tried to catch a few moments' sleep.

Craig and the provost-sergeant had been riding barely fifty yards behind Custer as part of the head-quarters troop. Craig was still mounted on his horse, but his Sharps rifle and bowie knife were with Sergeant Lewis. His ankles were tied with rawhide thongs to his saddle girth and his wrists behind him.

At the pre-dawn pause Lewis, who was a bluff, by-the-book but not unkindly man, untied the ankles and let Craig slide to the ground. His wrists remained tied, but Lewis fed him several slugs of water from his canteen. The coming day would again be hot.

It was at this point that Custer made the first of the foolish decisions he would make that day. He summoned his third-in-command, Captain Frederick Benteen, and ordered him to take three companies, H, D and K, and ride off into the badlands to the south to see if there were any Indians there. From a few yards away Craig heard Benteen, whom he judged to be the most professional soldier in the unit, protest the order. If there was a big concentration of hostiles up ahead on the banks of the Little Bighorn, was it wise to split the force?

'You have your orders,' snapped Custer and turned away. Benteen shrugged and did as he was bid. Of Custer's total force of about 600 soldiers, 150 rode away into the endless hills and valleys of the badlands on a wild goose chase.

Although Craig and Sergeant Lewis would never know it, Benteen and his exhausted men and horses would return to the river valley several hours later, too late to help but also too late to be wiped out. After giving his order, Custer broke camp again and the Seventh marched on down the creek towards the river.

At the hour of dawn a number of Crow and Ree scouts who had been out forward of the column came back. They had found a knoll near the confluence of

Dense Ashwood Creek and the river. Being familiar with the whole area, they knew it well. There were pine trees on it, and by climbing one an observer could finally see the whole valley ahead.

Two Rees had been up the trees and seen what they had seen. When they learned that Custer intended to continue, they sat down and began their death songs.

The sun rose. The heat began to come upon the day. Ahead of Craig, General Custer, who was wearing his cream buckskin suit, took off the jacket, rolled it and fastened it behind his saddle. He rode on in a blue cotton shirt, with his wide-brimmed cream hat shielding his eyes. The column came to the knoll.

Custer went halfway up and tried to spot with a telescope what lay ahead. They were on the bank of the creek, still three miles short of the confluence with the river. When he came down from the hill and conferred with his remaining officers, rumour buzzed through the column. He had seen part of a Sioux village with smoke rising from the cooking fires. It was now mid-morning.

Across the creek and east of the river there was a low range of hills which blocked the view of anyone at ground level. Still, Custer had found his Sioux. He did not know precisely how many there were and declined to listen to the warnings of his scouts. He determined to attack, the only manoeuvre in his personal lexicon.

The battle plan he chose was a pincer movement. Instead of securing the Indians' southern flank and waiting for Terry and Gibbon to close off the north, he decided to form both halves of the nutcracker with what was left of the Seventh Cavalry.

Tethered to his horse and awaiting court martial after the battle, Ben Craig heard him order his second-in-command, Major Marcus Reno, to take a further three companies, A, M and B, and continue west. They were to reach the river, ford it, turn right and charge the lower end of the village from the south.

He would leave one company to guard the mule train and the supplies. With his remaining five companies Custer would gallop due north, behind the range of hills, until he emerged at the northern end. Then he would ride down to the river, cross it and attack the Sioux from the north. Between Reno's three companies and his own five, the Indians would be trapped and destroyed.

Craig could not know what lay out of vision on the other side of the low hills, but he could study the behaviour of the Crow and Ree scouts. They knew, and they were preparing to die. What they had seen was the biggest concentration of Sioux and Cheyenne in one place that there had ever been or ever would be. Six great tribes had come together to hunt in partnership, and were now camped along the western bank of the Little Bighorn River. They contained between 10,000 and 15,000 Indians drawn from all the tribes of the plains.

Craig knew that in Plains Indian society a male was deemed to be a warrior between the ages of fifteen and mid to late thirties. One-sixth of any plains tribe were therefore warriors. Thus there were 2,000 of them down by the river, and they were not in a mood to be tamely driven back to any reservation when they had just heard that the plains to the north-west were teeming with deer and antelope.

Worse, and no-one knew this, they had met and defeated General Crook a week earlier and were not afraid of the blue-coated soldiers. Nor were they out hunting, like the menfolk of Tall Elk the previous day. In fact, on the evening of the 24th they had had a huge celebration of the victory over Crook.

The reason for the week's delay was simple: one week was the mourning period for their own dead from the fight with Crook on the 17th, and so the celebration could only take place after seven days. On the morning of the 25th the warriors were recovering from the dancing of the previous evening. They had not gone hunting and they were still in full body paint.

Even so, Craig realized this was no sleeping village like that of Black Kettle by the Washita. It was past noon when Custer split his forces for the last and lethal time.

The scout watched Major Reno depart, heading down the creek towards the river crossing. At the head of B Company Captain Acton gave a glance at the scout he had virtually condemned to die, permitted himself a thin smile and rode on. Behind him Sergeant Braddock sneered at Craig as he went by. Within two hours both would be dead and the remnants of Reno's three companies marooned on a hilltop trying to hold out until Custer could come back and relieve them. But Custer never came back and it was General Terry who would rescue them two days later.

Craig watched another 150 of the shrinking force head off down the creek. Though he was not a soldier, he had little faith in them. A full 30 per cent of Custer's men were raw recruits with minimal training. Some could just about manage their horses when they were calm, but would lose control in combat. Others could hardly manage their Springfield rifles.

Another 40 per cent, though of longer careers, had never fired a shot in anger at an Indian, nor met them in skirmish, and many had never even seen one except docile and cowed on a reservation. He wondered how they would react when a howling, painted horde of warriors came sweeping out to defend their women and children. He had the direst premonition and it turned out to be right. But by then it would be far too late.

There was a final factor he knew Custer had refused to bear in mind. Contrary to legend, Plains Indians held life to be sacred, not cheap. Even on the warpath they refused to take heavy casualties and after losing two or three of their best and bravest warriors would usually disengage. But Custer was attacking their parents, wives and children. Honour alone would forbid the menfolk to cease to fight until the last *wasichu* was dead. There could be no mercy.

As the dust cloud of Reno's three companies disappeared down the creek Custer ordered the baggage train to stay put, guarded by one company of his remaining six. With the others, E, C, L, I and F, he turned towards the north with the range of hills keeping him invisible to the Indians in the valley of the river, but they were also invisible to him.

He called over to the provost-sergeant, 'Bring the prisoner along. He can see what happens to his friends when the Seventh gets among them.'

Then he turned and trotted off to the north. The five companies fell in behind him, about 250 men in all. Craig realized Custer still did not perceive the danger, for he was bringing three civilians with him to watch the fun. One was the wispy, bespectacled journalist Mark Kellogg. More to the point, Custer had two young relatives along, for whom he must have felt responsible. One was his youngest brother, Boston Custer, aged nineteen, and the other was a sixteen-year-old nephew, Autie Reed.

The men were trotting two abreast, in a line nearly half a mile long. Behind Custer rode his adjutant, Captain Cooke, and behind him the general's orderly of the day, Trooper John Martin, who was also the regimental bugler. His real name was Giuseppe Martino; he was an Italian immigrant who had once been a butler for Garibaldi, and he still had only a limited command of English. Sergeant Lewis and the tethered Ben Craig were thirty feet behind Custer.

As they rode up into the hills, still keeping below

the crest, they could turn in their saddles and see Major Reno and his men crossing the Little Bighorn before attacking from the south. At this point Custer, noticing the glum faces of his Crow and Ree scouts, invited them to turn and ride back. This they did without waiting for a second invitation. They survived.

The troops rode like this for three miles until they finally cleared the crest to their left and could at last look down into the valley. Craig heard a sharp intake of breath from the big sergeant who held his horse's bridle and the murmured words: 'Sweet Jesus.' The far bank of the river was a great ocean of teepees.

Even at that distance Craig could make out the shapes of the lodges and the colours in which they were decorated, identifying the tribes. There were six separate villages.

When the Plains Indians travelled, they did so in column, tribe by tribe. When they stopped to camp, they settled in separate villages. Thus the whole encampment was long and narrow, six circles flowing down the riverbank on the other side of the water.

They had been travelling north when they had stopped several days earlier. The honour of breaking trail had been given to the Northern Cheyenne, so their village was the northernmost. Next to them came their closest allies, the Oglala Sioux. Close by the Oglala were the Sans Arc Sioux and then the Blackfeet. Second from the south were camped the Minneconjou and at the far south, even then being attacked by Major Reno, was the tail of the column, the village of the Hunkpapa, whose chief and supreme medicine man of the Sioux was the veteran Sitting Bull.

There were others present, lodged with their nearest relatives, elements of the Santee, Brulé and Assiniboin Sioux. What the Seventh could not see, now blotted out by the hills, was that Major Reno's attack on the southern end of Sitting Bull's Hunkpapa tribe was a catastrophe. The Hunkpapa had come swarming out of their lodges, many mounted and all fully armed, and counter-attacked.

It was almost two in the afternoon. Reno's men had been easily and skilfully outflanked to their left by pony-mounted warriors riding round them on the prairie and, with their flank turned, were being forced back into a stand of cottonwoods by the riverbank they had just crossed.

Many had dismounted from their horses in the trees, others had lost control and been thrown off. Some had lost their rifles, which the Hunkpapa gleefully took. Within minutes the remainder would have to stream back across the same river and take refuge on a hilltop, there to endure a thirty-six-hour siege.

General Custer surveyed what he could see, and from a few yards away Craig studied the great Indian-fighter. There were squaws and children to be seen about the camps but no warriors. Custer thought this a nice surprise. Craig heard him call to the company commanders, who had grouped round him. 'We will go down and make a crossing and capture the village.'

Then he summoned Captain Cooke and dictated a message. It was to, of all people, Captain Benteen, whom he had long sent off into the wilderness. The message Cooke scribbled said: 'Come on. Big village. Be quick. Bring packs.' He meant extra ammunition. This he gave to the bugler, Martino, who would live to tell the tale.

The Italian by a miracle did find Benteen, because that canny officer had given up his wild goose chase in the badlands, returned to the creek, and eventually joined Reno on the besieged hill. But by then there was no question of breaking through to the doomed Custer.

As Martino cantered back down the trail, Craig turned in his saddle to watch him. He saw twenty-four of Captain Yates's F Company also turn round and simply ride off without orders. No-one tried to stop them. Craig glanced back at Custer, up ahead. Did nothing penetrate that peacock head?

The general stood in his stirrups, raised his cream hat above his head and called to his troops, 'Hurrah, boys, we've got them.'

These were the last words the departing Italian heard, and he later reported them to the inquiry. Craig noticed that, like so many with fine auburn hair, Custer at thirty-six was developing a bald patch. Although nicknamed 'Long Hair' by the Indians, he had had it cropped short for the summer campaign. Perhaps for this reason the Oglala squaws later could not recognize him where he fell, and the warriors did not think him worth scalping.

After his salutation Custer spurred his horse

forward and the remaining 210 men followed. The ground ahead, leading down to the riverbank, was shallower and easier for a downhill charge. Half a mile later the column wheeled left, company by company, to descend the slope, ford the river and attack. At this point the Cheyenne village exploded.

The warriors came out like a cloud of hornets, painted in their battle colours, most naked from the waist up, screaming their high-pitched 'yip yip yip' cries as they rode to the river, splashed across and came up the eastern bank towards the five companies. The bluecoats stopped in their tracks.

Beside Craig, Sergeant Lewis reined in, and Craig heard again the muttered 'Sweet Jesus'. Hardly were they across the river than the Cheyenne threw themselves from their ponies and came forward and upward on foot, sinking into the long grass to become invisible, rising, running a few paces and dropping again. The first arrows began to fall among the cavalry. One buried itself in the flank of a horse, which whinnied in pain, rearing high and throwing its rider.

'Dismount. Horses to the rear.'

The shout was from Custer, and no-one needed a second bidding. Craig watched some of the soldiers unholster their Colt .45s, shoot their own horse straight through the forehead, and then use the body as a rampart. They were the smart ones.

There was no defensive cover on that hill. Not a rock or boulder behind which to hide. As the men jumped to the ground a few were detached from each company to take a dozen mounts by the bridle

316

and run them back to the crest of the ridge. Sergeant Lewis turned both his and Craig's horse and cantered them back to the ridge. There they joined the milling mob of cavalry mounts being held by a score of troopers. Before long the horses began to scent the Indians. They skittered and reared, pulling their handlers with them. From the saddle Lewis and Craig watched. After the first rush, the battle went quiet. But the Indians were not finished; they were simply moving to surround.

It was said later that the Sioux destroyed Custer that day. Not so. The Cheyenne did most of the frontal assault. Their cousins the Oglala Sioux deferred to them the honour of defending their own village, which would have been the first in Custer's attack, and acted in an assisting capacity, moving round the flanks to cut off any retreat. From his vantage point Craig could see the Oglala slipping through the long grass far to the left and right. Within twenty minutes there was no hope of retreat. The zipping bullets and hissing arrows began to fall closer. One of the horse-handlers took a falling arrow in the base of the throat and fell, choking and screaming.

The Indians had some rifles and even a few old flintlocks, but not many. By the end of the afternoon they would be substantially rearmed with new Springfields and Colts. Mainly, they used arrows, which for them had two advantages. The bow is a silent weapon; it does not give away the position of the firer. Many bluecoats died that afternoon with an arrow in the chest and never saw a target. The other advantage was that clouds of arrows could be fired high in the sky, to fall almost vertically on the cavalrymen. The effect was particularly damning on the horses. Within sixty minutes a dozen mounts had been hit by falling arrows. They broke away from the handlers, tearing the reins from the men's grasp, and galloped away down the trail. The others, uninjured, followed their example. Long before the men were dead, the horses were gone and all hope of escape gone with them. Panic began to run like wildfire through the crouching troopers. The few veteran officers and NCOs simply lost control.

The Cheyenne village belonged to Little Wolf, but by chance he was missing. When he returned an hour too late for the fight, he was roundly abused for not being there. In fact, he was the one leading the scout party that had been tracking Custer up the Rosebud and across the divide to the Little Bighorn.

In his absence leadership went to the next senior warrior, a visitor from the Southern Cheyenne called Lame White Man. He was in his mid-thirties, neither lame nor white. When a group of thirty troopers under an officer tried to make a break towards the river, he charged them alone, crushing their morale and dying a hero in the process. None of those thirty struggled back to the rings on the slope. Watching them die, their companions lost hope of survival.

From above, Lewis and Craig could hear the sounds of men praying and crying as they faced their death. One trooper, little more than a boy and blubbering like a baby, broke circle and came up the hill seeking one of the last two horses. Within seconds four arrows thudded into his back and he went down twitching.

The two men on horses were now within range, and several arrows whistled past. Perhaps fifty to a hundred men were still left alive on the slope below, but half of them must have taken an arrow or a bullet. Sometimes a warrior, seeking personal honour, would mount up and charge straight past the crouching soldiers, defying a hail of shot and, the marksmanship being what it was, riding away unharmed but covered in glory. And always the high-pitched screams.

Every soldier there thought they were war cries. Craig knew better. The charging Indian's cry was not for battle but for death, his own. He was simply confiding his soul to the care of the Everywhere Spirit.

But what really destroyed the Seventh Cavalry that day was their fear of being taken alive and tortured. Each soldier had been completely brainwashed with stories of the hideous ways in which captives of the Indians died. In the main they were wrong.

Plains Indians had no culture of the prisoner of war. They had no facilities for them. But an opposing force could surrender with honour if they had lost half their men. After seventy minutes Custer had certainly done this. But in Indian lore, if opponents just kept on fighting, they would normally be killed to the last man.

If a prisoner was taken alive, he would normally only be tortured in one of two cases: if he was recognized as one who had formally sworn never to fight the Indians of that tribe again, and had broken his word, or if he had fought with cowardice. In either case he was without honour.

In Sioux/Cheyenne culture the withstanding of pain with fortitude and stoicism could recover that honour. A liar or a coward should be given that chance, through pain. Custer was one who had once sworn to the Cheyenne that he would never fight them again. Two squaws of that tribe, recognizing him among the fallen, pushed steel awls through the dead eardrums so that he could hear better next time.

As the circle of Cheyenne and Sioux closed in, the panic ran like a brushfire through the surviving men. Battles in those days were never fought in good visibility; there was no smokeless ammunition. After an hour the hill was wreathed in a fog of powder smoke, and through the fog came the painted savages. Imagination ran riot. Years later an English poet would write:

When you're wounded and left on Afghanistan's
  plains,
And the women come out to cut up your
  remains,
Why, you rolls to your rifle and blows out your
  brains,
And you goes to your Gawd like a soldier.

None of the last survivors on that hillside would ever live to hear of Kipling, but what he described was what they did. Craig heard the first pistol shots as wounded men saved themselves the misery of torture. He turned to Sergeant Lewis.

The big man was white-faced beside him, both their horses running out of control. There was no escape back down the track; it seethed with Oglala Sioux.

'Sergeant, you'll not let me die like a tied pig,' the scout called to him. Lewis paused, thought, and his dedication to duty ended. He slipped from his horse, drew his knife and cut the thongs that tied Craig's ankles to his girth-strap.

At that moment three things happened in less than a second. Two arrows from a range of no more than a hundred feet thudded into the sergeant's chest. Knife in hand, he gazed at them with some surprise, then his knees buckled and he fell onto his face.

From even closer range a Sioux warrior rose from the long grass, pointed an ancient flintlock musket at Craig and fired. He had clearly used too much black powder in an effort to achieve increased range. Worse, he had forgotten to remove the ramrod. The breech exploded with a roar and a sheet of flame, shattering the man's right hand to pulp. If he had been firing from the shoulder he would have lost most of his head, but he was firing from the hip.

The ramrod came out of the barrel like a quivering harpoon. Craig had been facing the man. The ramrod took his horse full in the chest, penetrating to the heart. As the animal went down Craig, hands still cord-tied, tried to throw himself clear. He landed on his back, his head slammed into a small rock and he was knocked cold.

Within ten minutes the last white soldier on Custer's hill was dead. Though the scout was unconscious and never saw it, the end when it came was blisteringly fast. Sioux warriors would later relate that one minute the few dozen last survivors were still fighting and the next the Everywhere Spirit had simply swept them away. In fact most just 'rolled to their rifles' or used their Colt pistols. Some did the favour to wounded comrades, others to themselves.

When Ben Craig came to, his head sang and reeled from the blow by the rock. He opened one eye. He was on his side, hands tied behind, one cheek pressed to the earth. Grass blades were close to his face. As his head cleared he became aware of soft-shod feet moving all about him, of excited voices and occasional cries of triumph. His vision cleared also.

There were bare legs and feet in moccasins running across the hillside as Sioux warriors hunted for loot and trophies. One of them must have seen his eyes move. There was a yelp of triumph and strong hands jerked his torso upright.

There were four warriors round him, faces painted and contorted, still deranged by the killing frenzy. He saw a stone war club raised to smash out his brains. For one second as he sat and waited for death he wondered idly what lay on the other side of life. The blow did not fall. Instead a voice said, 'Stop.'

He looked up. The man who had spoken was astride a pony ten feet away. The dropping sun was to the right of the rider's shoulder and the glare reduced the image of the man to a silhouette.

His hair was undressed; it fell like a dark cloak around his shoulders and back. He carried no lance, nor yet a steel hatchet, so he was clearly not Cheyenne.

The pony the man rode moved a foot to one side; the sun went behind the shoulder and the glare fell away. The rider's shadow dropped over Craig's face and he saw more clearly.

The pinto pony was neither piebald nor skew-bald as most Indian mounts. It was a pale fawn, known as a golden buckskin. Craig had heard of that pony.

The man on it was naked but for a breechcloth around his waist and moccasins on his feet. He was dressed like a simple brave but had the authority of a chief. There was no shield on his left forearm, implying that he disdained personal protection, but from the left hand dangled a stone war club. Therefore, Sioux.

The war club was a fearsome weapon. Eighteen inches of haft, ending in a fork. Into the fork was rammed a smooth stone the size of a large goose egg. This was tied with hide thongs which would have been soaking wet when applied as lashings. Drying in the sun, they would shrink and tighten, so that the stone never fell. A blow from such a club would smash arms, shoulders or ribs, and crush the human skull like a walnut. It could only be used at close quarters, thus bringing much honour.

When he spoke again it was in the Oglala Sioux tongue, which being closest to Cheyenne the scout could understand.

'Why did you tie the *wasichu* like this?'

'We did not, Great Chief. We found him thus tied, by his own people.'

The dark gaze fell on the thongs still tied to each of Craig's ankles. The Sioux noticed, but said nothing. Sat, lost in thought. His chest and shoulders were covered with painted circles to represent hailstones and from his hairline a single black lightning bolt ran to his bullet-scarred chin. He wore no other ornamentation but Craig knew him by repute. He was looking at the legendary Crazy Horse, undisputed chief of the Oglala Sioux these past twelve years, since the age of twenty-six, a man revered for his fearlessness, mysticism and self-denial.

An evening breeze came off the river below. It ruffled the chief's hair, the long grass and the feather behind the scout's head, which came to rest on one buckskin shoulder. Crazy Horse noted this too. It was a sign of honour given by the Cheyenne.

'He lives,' ordered the war leader. 'Take him to Chief Sitting Bull for judgement.'

The warriors were disappointed to lose the chance of so much loot, but they obeyed. Craig was hauled to his feet and hustled down the hill to the river. As he went the half-mile he saw the aftermath of the massacre.

Across the slope the 210 men of the five companies, minus scouts and deserters, were strewn in the strange postures of death. The Indians were stripping them of everything in the search for trophies, then carrying out the ritual mutilations, different according to each tribe. The Cheyenne slashed legs so the dead man could not pursue them, the Sioux battered skulls and faces to pulp with stone clubs. Others severed arms, legs and heads.

Fifty yards down the hill the scout saw the body of George Armstrong Custer, naked but for his cotton ankle socks, marble white under the sun. He remained unmutilated save for the punctured eardrums and would be found that way by Terry's men.

Everything was being taken from pockets and saddlebags: rifles and pistols of course, with the copious supply of ammunition still remaining; tobacco pouches, steel-case watches, wallets with family photos, anything that could constitute a trophy. Then came the caps, boots and uniforms. The hillside swarmed with braves and squaws.

At the riverbank there was a cluster of ponies. Craig was hoisted onto one and he and his four escorts splashed through the Little Bighorn to the western bank. As they rode through the Cheyenne village the women came out to scream abuse at the one surviving *wasichu*, but they fell silent when they saw the eagle feather. Was this a friend or a traitor?

The group trotted down through the camps of

the Sans Arcs and the Minneconjou until they reached the village of the Hunkpapa. The camp was in uproar.

These braves had not faced Custer on the hill; they had met and driven back Major Reno, whose remnants were even then across the river, besieged on their hilltop, joined by Benteen and the mule train, wondering why Custer did not ride back down the hills to relieve them.

Blackfoot, Minneconjou and Hunkpapa warriors rode hither and thither waving their trophies taken from Reno's dead, and here and there Craig saw a blond or ginger scalp being waved aloft. Surrounded by screaming squaws, they came to the lodge of the great medicine man and judge, Sitting Bull.

His Oglala escorts explained the orders of Crazy Horse, handed him over and rode back to seek their trophies on the slope. Craig was roughly thrown into a teepee and two old squaws were instructed to watch over him with knives in their hands.

It was long after dark when he was sent for. A dozen braves came for him and dragged him out. Campfires had been lit and by their light the still-painted warriors were a fearsome sight. But the mood had calmed, even though a mile away, beyond the cottonwood stand and across the river, out of sight, occasional shots in the dark indicated that the Sioux were still crawling up the hill to Reno's defensive circle on the bluff.

In the entire battle, at both ends of the huge camp, the Sioux had taken thirty-one casualties.

Although 1,800 warriors had been involved and their enemies had been virtually wiped out, they felt the loss. Up and down the camps widows were keening over husbands and sons and preparing them for the Great Journey.

At the centre of the Hunkpapa village was one fire larger than the rest, and around it were a dozen chiefs, supreme among them Sitting Bull. He was then just forty but he looked older, his mahogany face even darker in the firelight and deeply lined. Like Crazy Horse, he was revered for once having had a great vision of the future of his people and of the buffalo of the plains. It had been a bleak vision: he had seen them all wiped out by the white man, and he was known to hate the *wasichu*. Craig was thrown down twenty feet to his left so that the fire did not block the view. They all stared at him for some time. Sitting Bull gave an order which Craig did not understand. A brave unsheathed his knife and moved behind Craig. He waited for the death blow.

The knife sliced through the cords binding his wrists. For the first time in twenty-four hours he could bring his hands to the front of his body. He realized he could not even feel them. The blood began to flow back, causing first a fiery tingle and then pain. He kept his face immobile.

Sitting Bull spoke again, this time to him. He did not understand, but replied in Cheyenne. There was a buzz of surprise. One of the other chiefs, Two Moon of the Cheyenne, spoke.

'The Great Chief asks why the *wasichu* tied you to your horse and your hands behind you.'

'I had offended them,' said the scout.

'Was it a bad offence?' For the rest of the interrogation Two Moon interpreted.

'The chief of the blue uniforms wanted to hang me. Tomorrow.'

'What had you done to them?'

Craig thought. Was it only the previous morning that Braddock had destroyed the lodge of Tall Elk? He started with that incident and finished when he was sentenced to hang. He noticed Two Moon nod at the reference to Tall Elk's lodges. He already knew. At each sentence he paused while Two Moon translated into Sioux. When he was done there was a brief murmured conference. Two Moon called to one of his men.

'Ride back to our village. Bring Tall Elk and his daughter here.'

The brave went to his tethered pony, mounted and rode away. Sitting Bull's questions resumed.

'Why did you come to make war against the Red Man?'

'They told me they had come because the Sioux were moving away from the reservations in the Dakotas. There was no talk of killing until Long Hair went crazy.'

There was another buzz of consultation. 'The Long Hair was here?' asked Two Moon. For the first time Craig realized they had not even known whom they were fighting.

'He is on the hillside across the river. He is dead.'

The chiefs conferred again for a while, then there was silence. A council was a serious thing and there was no need for hurry. After half an hour Two Moon asked, 'Why do you wear the white eagle feather?'

Craig explained. Ten years ago when he was fourteen he had joined a bunch of Cheyenne youths and they all went hunting in the mountains. They all had bows and arrows, save Craig, who had been allowed to borrow Donaldson's Sharps rifle. They had been surprised by an old grizzly, an evil-tempered veteran with hardly a tooth left in his head but the strength in his forepaws to kill a man with a single swipe. The bear had come out of a thicket with a mighty roar, and charged.

At this point one of the braves behind Two Moon asked to interrupt.

'I remember this story. It happened in the village of my cousin.'

Round the campfire there is nothing like a good story. He was invited to complete the tale and the Sioux craned to listen as Two Moon translated.

'The bear was like a mountain and he came fast. The Cheyenne boys scattered to the trees. But the small *wasichu* took careful aim and fired. The bullet passed under the bear's muzzle and struck him in the chest. He rose to his back feet, tall as a pine, dying but still coming forward.

'The white boy ejected the spent cartridge and inserted another. Then he fired again. The second bullet went into the roaring mouth, through the roof and blew out the brains. The bear took one more pace and fell forward. The great head came down so close that saliva and blood splashed the boy's knees. But he did not move.

329

'They sent a messenger to the village and braves came back with a travois to skin the monster and bring the hide to make a sleeping robe for my cousin's father. Then they held a feast and gave the *wasichu* a new name. Kills-Bear-With-No-Fear. And the eagle feather of a man who hunts. So it was told in my village a hundred moons ago before we were moved to the reservations.'

The chiefs nodded. It was a good story. A party on ponies rode up. Behind was a travois. Two men Craig had never seen before entered the firelight. By their dressed and plaited hair they were Cheyenne.

One was Little Wolf, who told how he had been hunting east of the river when he saw plumes of smoke rising over the Rosebud. He investigated and found the slaughtered women and children. While he was there he heard the bluecoat soldiers coming back, so he trailed them all day and night until they came to the valley of the camp. But he was too late for the great fight.

The other man was Tall Elk. He had returned from hunting after the main column had passed. He was still grieving over his murdered womenfolk and children when his daughter came back. She was wounded but alive. Together with his other nine braves they had ridden through the night and the day to find the camp of the Cheyenne, arriving just before the battle, in which they had taken part with a will. He personally had sought death on Custer's hill and had killed five *wasichu* soldiers but the Everywhere Spirit had not taken him.

The girl from the travois was the last to be heard. She was pale and in pain from the wound and the long ride from the Rosebud, but she spoke clearly.

She told of the massacre, and of the big man with the stripes on the arm. She did not understand his language but she understood what he wanted to do to her before she died. She told how the buckskin one had given her water, and eaten his meal, and set her on a pony and sent her back to her people.

The chiefs conferred. The judgement came from Sitting Bull but it was the verdict of them all. The *wasichu* might live, but he could not go back to his people. Either they would kill him, or he would tell them the position of the Sioux. He would be given into the care of Tall Elk, who could treat him as prisoner or as guest. In the spring he could go free or remain with the Cheyenne.

Around the fire there were grunts of approval from the braves. It was just. Craig rode back with Tall Elk to the teepee he had been given, and spent the night with two braves watching him. In the morning the great camp packed up to move. But scouts coming at dawn had brought news of even more bluecoats in the north, so they decided to go south towards the Bighorn Mountains and see if the *wasichu* came after them.

Having accepted him into his clan, Tall Elk was generous. Four uninjured cavalry horses were found and Craig took his pick. They were not much valued by the Plains Indians, who preferred their hardy ponies. This was because few horses could adapt to the harsh winters of the plains. They needed hay, which the Indians never gathered, and could rarely survive the winter on lichen, moss and willow bark like the ponies. Craig selected a tough-looking, rangy chestnut he thought might adapt and named her Rosebud after the place where he had met Whispering Wind.

A good saddle was easily found because the Indians never used them, and when his Sharps rifle and bowie knife were traced and identified, they were returned to him with some reluctance. From the saddlebags of his dead horse at the top of the slope he recovered his Sharps ammunition. There was nothing left to loot on the hillside. The Indians had taken all that interested them. They had no desire for the white man's paper and white sheets fluttered in the long grass where they had been thrown. Among them were Captain William Cooke's notes of the first interrogation.

The striking of the villages took all morning. The teepees came down, the utensils were packed, the women, children and baggage loaded onto the numerous travois and shortly after midday the departure began.

The dead were left behind, laid out in their teepees, painted for the next world, in their best robes, with the feathered bonnets of their rank. But in accordance with tradition all their household artefacts were scattered on the ground.

When Terry's men, coming up the valley from the north, discovered this the next day they would think the Sioux and Cheyenne had departed in a hurry. Not so: scattering the effects of the dead was the custom. They would all be looted anyway.

Ever after the Plains Indians would protest that they only wanted to hunt, not fight, but Craig knew the army would recover from its loss and come looking for vengeance. Not for a while, but come they would. Sitting Bull's grand council knew it too, and within a few days it was agreed the tribes should split up into smaller groups and scatter. This would make the job of the bluecoat soldiers harder and give the Indians a better chance of being able to winter in the wild and not be driven back to a half-starved winter in the Dakota reservations.

Craig rode with what was left of the clan of Tall Elk. Of the ten hunters who had lost their women-folk by the Rosebud, two had died at the Little Bighorn and two were injured. One, with a slight gash in the side, chose to ride. The other, who had taken a Springfield bullet through the shoulder at close range, was on a travois. Tall Elk and the other five would find new women. To enable this to happen, they had joined ranks with two other extended families, making a clan of some sixty men, women and children.

When the group decision to split up came to them, they met in council to decide where they should go. Most were for heading on south into Wyoming, hiding in the Bighorn Mountains. Craig was asked for his view.

'The bluecoats will come there,' he said. With a stick he drew the line of the Bighorn River. 'They will look for you here in the south, and here in the east. But I know a place in the west. It is called the Pryor Range. I was raised there.'

He told them about the Pryors.

'The lower slopes teem with game. The forests are thick and their branches blur the smoke rising from cooking fires. The streams are full of fish and higher there are lakes with many fish also. The *wasichu* never come there.'

The clan agreed. On 1 July they peeled away from the main party of Cheyenne and, guided by Craig, headed north-west into south Montana, avoiding General Terry's patrols, which were fanning out from the Bighorn but not that far west. In mid-July they reached the Pryors and it was still as Craig had said.

The teepees were shrouded by trees and invisible from half a mile away. From a nearby rock, today called Crown Butte, a watchman could see many miles, but no-one came. The hunters brought many deer and antelope from the forests and children fished fat trout from the streams.

Whispering Wind was young and healthy.

Her clean wound healed fast until she could run again, swift as a fawn. Sometimes he caught her eye as she brought food to the menfolk and always his heart hammered inside him. She gave no sign of what she felt, casting her glance downward when she caught him staring. He could not know that something in her belly seemed to melt and her ribcage wanted to burst when she took a glance from those dark blue eyes.

During the early autumn they just fell in love.

334

The women noticed. She would return from serving the men flushed, the front of her buckskin tunic rising and falling, and the older women would cackle with glee. She had no mother nor aunt left alive, so the squaws were from different families. But they had sons among the twelve unmarried and therefore eligible braves. They wondered which one had set the beautiful girl afire. They teased her to let them know before he was stolen by another, but she told them they were talking nonsense.

In September the leaves fell and the camp moved higher to be screened by the conifers. The nights turned chill as October came. But the hunts were good and the ponies cropped the last grass before turning to moss, bark and lichen. Rosebud adapted like the ponies around her and Craig would go down to the prairie and return with a sack of fresh grass, sliced in tufts with his bowie knife.

If Whispering Wind had had a mother she might have intervened with Tall Elk, but there was no-one, so eventually she told her father herself. His rage was terrible to behold.

How could she think such a thing? The *wasichu* had destroyed all her family. This man would go back to his people and there was no place for her. Moreover, the warrior who had taken the bullet in the shoulder at the Little Bighorn was now almost recovered. The shattered bones had finally knit. Not straight, but whole again. He was Walking Owl and he was a fine and brave warrior. He was to be her betrothed. It would be announced the next day. That was final.

Tall Elk was perturbed. It could be the white man felt the same. He would have to be watched day and night from now on. He could not go back to his people; he knew where they camped. He would stay the winter but he would be watched. And so it was.

Craig was suddenly moved to stay and sleep in a teepee with another family. There were three other single braves sharing the same lodge and they would stay alert if he tried to move during the night.

It was at the end of October that she came for him. He was lying awake, thinking of her, when a knife slowly and soundlessly slit one of the panels of the teepee. He rose silently and stepped through. She stood in the moonlight looking up at him. They embraced for the first time and the blazing heat flowed back and forth.

She broke free, stepped back and beckoned. He followed where she led, through the trees to a spot out of sight of the camp. Rosebud was saddled up, a buffalo robe rolled behind the saddle. His rifle was in its long sheath by the shoulder. The saddle-bags bulged with food and ammunition. A pinto pony was also tethered. He turned and they kissed and the cold night seemed to spin around him. She whispered in his ear, 'Take me to your mountains, Ben Craig, and make me your woman.'

'Now and for ever, Whispering Wind.'

They mounted up and walked the horses quietly through the trees until they were clear, then rode down past the butte and towards the plain. At sunrise they were back in the foothills. At dawn a small party of Crow saw them in the distance and turned north towards Fort Ellis on the Bozeman Trail.

The Cheyenne came after them; they were six, moving fast, travelling light with their rifles slung behind their shoulders, hatchets in waistbands, trade blankets beneath them, and they had their orders. The betrothed of Walking Owl was to be brought back alive. The *wasichu* would die.

The Crow party rode north and they rode hard. One of them had been with the army in the summer and knew that the bluecoats had posted a big reward for the white renegade, enough to buy a man many horses and trade goods.

They never made the Bozeman Trail. Twenty miles south of the Yellowstone they ran into a small patrol of cavalrymen, ten in all, commanded by a lieutenant. The former scout explained what they had seen, using mainly sign language, but the lieutenant understood. He turned the patrol south for the mountains, with the Crow acting as guides, seeking to cut the trail.

That summer the news of the massacre of Custer and his men had swept America like a blast of cold air. Far to the east the high and mighty of the nation had gathered at Philadelphia, the city of brotherly love, to celebrate the first centenary of independence on July the Fourth, 1876. The news from the western frontier seemed unbelievable. An immediate inquiry was ordered.

After the battle the soldiers of General Terry had

scoured the fatal hillside, seeking an explanation of the disaster. The Sioux and the Cheyenne were twenty-four hours gone and Terry was in no mood to pursue them. Reno's survivors had been relieved but they knew nothing beyond what they had seen as Custer and his men rode out of sight behind the hills.

On the hillside every scrap of evidence was gathered and stored, even as the decomposing bodies were hastily buried. Among those things collected were the sheets of paper stuck in the long grass. Among these were the notes taken by Captain Cooke.

None of those who had stood behind Custer when he interrogated Ben Craig was left alive, but the clerkish notes by the adjutant said enough. The army needed a reason for the disaster. Now they had one: the savages had been forewarned and were fully prepared. The unwitting Custer had ridden into a massive ambush. More, the army had a scapegoat. Incompetence could not be accepted; treachery could. A reward of $1,000 was posted for the taking of the scout, dead or alive.

The trail went cold, until a party of Crow saw the fugitive, with an Indian girl behind him, riding out of the Pryor Mountains in the last days of October.

The lieutenant's horses had rested, fed and watered through the night. They were fresh and he rode them hard to the south. His career was at stake.

Just after the sun rose Craig and Whispering

Wind reached the Pryor Gap, a defile of lowland between the main range and the single peak of West Pryor. They crossed the defile, cantered through the foothills of West Pryor and emerged into the badlands, rough country of grassy ridges and gullies that went west for fifty miles.

Craig had no need to use the sun for guidance. He could see his target in the far distance, glittering in the morning sun beneath a cold blue sky. He was heading for the Absaroka Wilderness, which he had hunted as a boy with old Donaldson. This was terrible country, a wilderness of forest and rocky plateaus where few could follow, and it ran upwards into the Beartooth Range.

Even from that distance he could see the icy sentinels of the range, Thunder, Sacred, Medicine and Beartooth Mountains. There a man with a good rifle could hold off an army. At a creek he paused to give the sweating mounts a few gulps of water, then pressed on towards the peaks that seemed to nail the land to the sky.

Twenty miles behind, the six warriors, eyes scanning the ground for the telltale marks of steel-shod hoofs, kept up a fast trot that saved their ponies' energy and could be maintained for mile after mile.

Thirty miles to the north the cavalry patrol pressed south to pick up the trail. They found it at noon just west of West Pryor Peak. The Crow scouts suddenly reined in and circled, staring at a patch of sun-hardened earth. They pointed down to the marks of steel horseshoes and the spoor of an unshod pony close behind. A short distance away were the traces of other ponies, five or six in all.

'So,' murmured the lieutenant, 'we have competition. No matter.'

He gave the order to continue westward, though the horses were beginning to tire. Half an hour later, cresting a rise in the plain, he took his telescope and scanned the horizon ahead. Of the fugitives there was no sign, but he saw a puff of dust and beneath it six tiny figures on pinto ponies trotting towards the mountains.

The Cheyenne ponies were also tiring but so, they knew, must be the mounts of the fugitives up ahead. The warriors gave their horses water at Bridger Creek, just below the modern village of Bridger, and half an hour's rest. One, ear pressed to the ground, heard the drumming of hoofs coming from behind, so they mounted up and rode on. After a mile their leader pulled away to one side, hid them all behind a knoll and climbed to the top to look.

At three miles he saw the cavalry. The Cheyenne knew nothing of any papers on a hillside, nor of any reward for the runaway *wasichu*. They presumed the bluecoats must be hunting them, for being off-reservation. So they watched and waited.

When the cavalry patrol reached the parting of the tracks it stopped while the Crow scouts dismounted and studied the ground. The Cheyenne saw the Crows point ever westward and the cavalry patrol continued in that direction.

The Cheyenne kept up with them on a parallel

track, shadowing the bluecoats as Little Wolf had shadowed Custer up the Rosebud. But in mid-afternoon the Crow spotted them.

'Cheyenne,' said the Crow scout. The lieutenant shrugged.

'No matter, let them hunt. We have our own quarry.'

The two parties of pursuers pressed on till night-fall. The Crow followed the trail and the Cheyenne shadowed the patrol. As the sun tipped the moun-tain peaks both groups knew they had to rest the horses. If they tried to go on their mounts would simply collapse beneath them. Besides, the ground was becoming harder and the trail more difficult to follow. In darkness, without lanterns, which they did not have, it would be impossible.

Ten miles ahead Ben Craig knew the same. Rosebud was a big, strong mare, but she had covered fifty miles carrying a man and equipment over broken ground. Whispering Wind was not a skilled rider and she too was at the end of her tether. They camped by Bear Creek, just east of the modern township of Red Lodge, but lit no fire for fear it might be seen.

As darkness fell the temperature plunged. They rolled themselves in the buffalo robe and in seconds the girl was fast asleep. Craig did not sleep. He could do that later. He crawled out of the robe, wrapped himself in the red trade blanket and kept watch over the girl he loved.

No-one came, but before dawn he was up. They ate, quickly, some dried antelope meat and a

341

quantity of corn bread she had taken from her teepee, washed down with creek water. Then they left. The pursuers were also up as the first light revealed the trail. They were nine miles behind and closing. Craig knew the Cheyenne would be there; what he had done could not be forgiven. But he knew nothing of the cavalry.

The land was harder, the going slower. He knew his pursuers would be catching up and he needed to slow them by disguising his trail. After two hours in the saddle the fugitives came to the confluence of two creeks. To the left, tumbling out of the mountains, was Rock Creek, which he judged to be impassable as a way into the real wilderness. Straight ahead lay West Creek, shallower and less rocky. He dismounted, tied the pony's tethering rein to the horse's saddle and led Rosebud by the bridle.

He led the small convoy off the bank at an angle towards Rock Creek, into the water, then doubled back and took the other waterway. The freezing water numbed his feet, but he pressed on for two miles over the gravel and pebbles. Then he turned to the mountains on his left and led the mounts out of the water into the dense forest.

The land now rose steeply beneath the trees and with the sun shut out it was chill. Whispering Wind was shrouded in her blanket, riding bareback at a walking pace.

Three miles behind, the cavalry had reached the water and stopped. The Crows pointed out the tracks seeming to lead up Rock Creek and after conferring with his sergeant the lieutenant ordered his patrol up the false trail. As they disappeared, the Cheyenne reached the two creeks. They did not need to enter the water to hide their tracks. But they chose the right creek and trotted up the bank, scanning the far side for signs of horses coming out of the water and heading for the high country.

After two miles they found the signs in a patch of soft earth across the creek. They splashed over and entered the forest.

At midday Craig arrived at what he thought he remembered from his hunting trip years before, a great open plateau of rock, the Silver Run Plateau, which headed straight to the mountains. Although they did not know it, they were now over 11,000 feet high.

From the edge of the rocks he could look down towards the creek he had followed and then quit. To his right, there were figures down there, where the two creeks split. He had no telescope but in the thin air visibility was extraordinary. At half a mile these were not Cheyenne; they were ten soldiers with four Crow scouts. They were an army patrol coming back down Rock Creek, having realized their error. That was when Ben Craig understood the army was still after him for liberating the girl.

He took his Sharps rifle from its sheath, inserted a single cartridge, found a rock to rest it on, set the sights at maximum elevation and squinted down into the valley.

'Take the horse,' old Donaldson had always said. 'In this country a man with no horse has to turn back.'

He aimed for the forehead of the officer's mount. The crash, when it came, echoed through the mountains, backward and forward like rolling thunder. The bullet took the lieutenant's horse just to the side of the head, high in the right shoulder. It went down like a sack, the officer with it. He twisted an ankle as he fell.

The troopers scattered into the forest, save the sergeant, who threw himself behind the downed horse and tried to help the lieutenant. The horse was finished but not dead. The sergeant used his pistol to put it out of its misery. Then he dragged his officer to the trees. No more shots came.

In the forest on the slope the Cheyenne dropped from their ponies to the carpet of pine needles and stayed there. Four of them had Springfields looted from the Seventh, but they also had the Plains Indian's lack of marksmanship. They knew what the young *wasichu* could do with that Sharps, and at what range. They began to crawl upwards. It slowed them down. One of the six stayed in the rear, leading all six ponies.

Craig cut the blanket into four pieces and tied one quarter round each of Rosebud's hoofs. The material would not last long between steel shoe and rock but it would hide scratch marks for 500 yards. Then he trotted south-west across the plateau towards the peaks.

It is five miles across the Silver Run and there is no cover. After two miles the frontiersman looked back and saw specks coming over the ridge onto the rock shelf. He trotted on. They could not hit him and they could not catch him. A few minutes later there were more specks; the cavalrymen had led their mounts up through the forest and were also on the rock, but a mile east of the Cheyenne. Then he came to the crevasse. He had not been this high before; he did not know it was there.

It is steep and narrow, Lake Fork, with sides wooded with pine and a freezing stream at the bottom. Craig turned along its edge and looked for a place where the banks were shallow enough to cross. He found such a place in the shadow of Thunder Mountain, but he had lost half an hour.

Pushing himself and the horses to the limit, he led them down the ravine and up the other side to another and last sheet of rock, Hellroaring Plateau. As he emerged from the gulley a shot whistled over his head. From across the ravine one of the troopers had seen movement among the pines. His delay had not only let his pursuers catch up, he had shown them the way across.

Ahead of him was another three miles of flat running before the towering palisades of Mount Rearguard, among whose jumbled rocks and caves no man on earth would ever take him. In the thin air two humans and two animals gasped for oxygen but still he pressed on. Darkness would come soon, and he would disappear into the peaks and ravines between Rearguard and Sacred and Beartooth Mountains. No man could follow a trail up here. Beyond Sacred Mountain was the watershed divide and after that it was downhill all the way into Wyoming. They would lose the hostile world, be married, dwell in the wilderness and live for ever. As the daylight faded Ben Craig and Whispering Wind left their pursuers behind and headed for the slopes of Mount Rearguard.

In the dusk they climbed above the rock plain and met the snowline where the whiteness of the peaks is never melted. There they found a flat ledge, fifty yards by twenty, and at the back a deep cave. A few last pines shrouded the entrance.

Craig hobbled the horses as darkness fell and they cropped pine needles beneath the trees. The cold was intense, but they had their buffalo robe.

The scout hauled his saddle and remaining blanket into the cave, loaded his rifle and laid it by his side, then spread the buffalo skin by the mouth of the cave. Craig and Whispering Wind lay on it and he pulled the other half over them both. Inside the cocoon the natural warmth of human bodies returned. The girl began to move against him.

'Ben,' she whispered, 'make me your woman. Now.'

He began to slip her buckskin tunic upwards over her eager body.

'What you are doing is wrong.'

It was utterly silent this high on the mountain, and though the voice was old and frail the words, in the Cheyenne language, were quite clear.

Craig, his hide shirt gone and bare-chested in the freezing cold, was at the entrance to the cave, rifle in hand, in a moment.

He could not understand why he had not seen the man before. He sat cross-legged under the pines at the edge of the flat rock. Iron-grey hair hung to his naked waist, his face was wrinkled and lined as a burnt walnut. He was of immense age and piety, a tribal shaman, a vision-quester come to the lonely places to fast, meditate and seek guidance from the infinite.

'You spoke, holy one?' The scout gave him the honorific title reserved for those of great age and wisdom. Where he came from, he could not guess. How he had climbed to these altitudes, he did not know. How he could survive the cold with no covering was not imaginable. Craig only knew that some vision-questers could defy all the known laws.

He felt the presence of Whispering Wind join him in the mouth of the cave.

'It is wrong in the eyes of Man, and of Meh-y-yah, the Everywhere Spirit,' said the old man.

The moon had not yet risen but the stars in the clean and bitter air were so bright that the wide rock ledge was bathed in a pale light. Craig could see the starlight glitter in the old eyes that fixed him from beneath the tree.

'Why so, holy one?'

'She is promised to another. Her intended fought bravely against the *wasichu*. He has much honour. He does not deserve to be treated like this.'

'But now she is my woman.'

'She will be your woman, man of the mountains. But not yet. The Everywhere Spirit speaks. She should go back to her people and her intended. If she does, you will one day be reunited and she will

347

be your woman and you her man. For ever. So says Meh-y-yah.'

He took a stick from the ground beside him and used it to help him rise. His naked skin was dark and old, pinched by the cold, with only breechcloth and moccasins to protect him. He turned and slowly walked through the pines and down the track until he was gone from view.

Whispering Wind turned her face up to Craig. There were tears running down her cheeks but they did not fall, freezing before they touched her chin.

'I must go back to my people. It is my fate.'

There was no arguing. It would have served nothing. He prepared her pony while she slipped on her moccasins and wrapped her blanket around her. He took her in his arms one last time and swung her onto the pony's back, handing her the rein. Silently she directed the pinto to the start of the track downwards.

'Wind That Talks Softly,' he called. She turned and stared at him in the starlight.

'We will be together. One day. It was spoken so. While the grass grows and the rivers run, I will wait for you.'

'And I for you, Ben Craig.'

She was gone. Craig watched the sky until the cold bit too deep. He led Rosebud deep into the cave and prepared an armful of pine needles for her. Then he pulled the buffalo hide deeper into the darkness, rolled himself in its folds and fell asleep.

The moon rose. The braves saw her coming towards them across the stone plain. She saw two campfires burning below the rim of the gulch where the pines grew and heard the low call of an owl from the fire to her left. She made her way there.

They said nothing. That would be for her father, Tall Elk. But they still had their orders. The *wasichu* who had violated their lodges must die. They waited for dawn.

At one in the morning great clouds swept over the Beartooth Range and the temperature began to drop. The men round both campfires shivered and wrapped themselves tighter in their blankets, but it was no use. Soon they were all awake, hurling more wood onto the fires, but still the temperature fell.

Both the Cheyenne and white men had wintered in the fierce Dakotas and knew what midwinter could do, but this was the last day of October. Too early. Yet the temperature fell. At two o'clock the snow began to fall like a white wall. In the camp of the cavalry the Crow scouts rose.

'We would go,' they said to the officer. He was in pain from his ankle but knew the bounty and the capture would transform his life in the army.

'It is cold, but dawn will soon come,' he told them.

'This is no ordinary cold,' they said. 'This is the Cold of the Long Sleep. No robe is proof against it. The *wasichu* you seek is already dead. Or he will die before the sun.'

'Then leave,' said the officer. There was no more tracking to be done. His quarry was on the mountain he had seen shimmering in the moonlight before the snow came.

The Crow mounted up and left, heading back

across the Silver Run Plateau and down the slopes to the valley. As they left, one gave the harsh call of a night bird.

The Cheyenne heard it and looked at each other. It was a warning cry. They too mounted up, threw snow on the fire and left, taking the girl with them. And still the temperature fell.

It was about four in the morning when the avalanche came. It fell from the mountains and moved a thick blanket of snow across the plateau. The advancing wall hissed as it slid towards Lake Fork, and when it fell into the ravine it took all before it. The remaining men and horses could not move; the cold had pinned them where they lay and stood. And the snow filled the creek until only the tops of the pines showed.

In the morning the clouds cleared and the sun returned. The landscape was a uniform white. In a million holes the animals of the mountain and forest knew that winter had come, and they should hibernate until the spring.

In his high cave, rolled in his buffalo robe, the frontiersman slept.

When he awoke he could not, as sometimes happens, recall where he was. In the village of Tall Elk? But he heard no sounds of the squaws preparing the morning meal. He opened his eyes and peered out from the folds of the buffalo fur. He took in the rough walls of the cave and the memories came back in a rush. He sat up and tried to clear his head of the last mists of sleep.

Outside he could see a white shelf of rock dusted with snow and it glittered in the sun. He emerged bare-chested and sucked in the morning air. It felt good.

Rosebud, still hobbled at the forelegs as he had left her, had come out of the cave and was nibbling at some young pine shoots at the edge of the shelf. The morning sun was to his right hand; he was staring north towards the distant plains of Montana.

He walked to the forward edge of the shelf, dropped to the ground and peered down towards Hellroaring Plateau. There were no signs of woodsmoke coming from Lake Fork. His pursuers seemed to have gone.

He returned to the cave, dressed in his buckskin suit and belt. Taking his bowie knife he went back to Rosebud and freed her front legs. She whinnied softly and nuzzled his shoulder with her velvet muzzle. Then he noticed something strange.

The soft green shoots upon which she fed were those of spring. He looked around. The last few hardy pines which survived this high were each pushing out pale green buds towards the sun. With a start of shock he realized that, like a creature of the wild, he must have hibernated through the bitter cold of winter.

He had heard it could be done. Old Donaldson had once mentioned a trapper who overwintered in a bear cave and did not die, but slept like the cubs beside him until winter passed.

In his saddlebags he found a last portion of wind-dried meat. It was hard to chew but he forced it down. For moisture he took a handful of powder snow, crushed it between his palms till it was water, then licked his hands dry. He knew better than to eat raw snow.

The bags also contained his round trapper hat of warm fox fur, and he pulled this onto his head. When he had saddled Rosebud he checked his Sharps rifle and the twenty cartridges that remained to him, slipped it into its sheath and prepared to leave. Heavy though it was, he rolled the buffalo robe that had saved his life and lashed it behind the saddle. When there was nothing left in the cave he took Rosebud's bridle and began to walk her down the track to the plateau.

He was not quite decided what to do, but he knew there would be plenty of game in the lower forests. With traps alone a man could live well down there.

He crossed the first plateau at a slow walk, waiting for a sign of movement or even a ranging shot from the edge of the crevasse. None came. When he reached the cleft there was no sign of his pursuers returning to continue the hunt for him. He could not know that the Crow had reported that all the bluecoat soldiers were lost in the blizzard and their quarry also must have died.

He found again the track down into Lake Fork and up the other side. The sun rose higher as he walked across the Silver Run until it was a full thirty degrees above the horizon. He began to feel warm.

He went down through the pine forests until the

broadleaf trees began and there he made his first camp. It was noon. With springy twigs and a yard of twine from his saddlebag he made a rabbit snare. It took an hour until the first unsuspecting rodent came out of its hole. He killed and skinned it, used his small box of tinder and flint to make a fire and enjoyed the roasted meat.

He spent a week camping at the edge of the forest and recovering his strength. Fresh meat was plentiful, he could tickle trout from the numerous creeks and water was all he needed to drink.

By the end of the week he decided he would leave for the plains, travelling by moonlight, hiding up in the day, and return to the Pryors, where he could build a shack and make a home. Then he could ask where the Cheyenne had gone and wait for Whispering Wind to be free. He had no doubt it would happen, for so it had been spoken.

On the eighth night he saddled up and left the forest. By the stars he headed north. It was the time of the high moon and the land was bathed in pale white light. After walking through the first night he camped by day in a dry creek where no-one would see him. He lit no more fires and ate meat he had smoked in the forest.

On the next night he turned to the east, where the Pryors lay, and soon crossed a long strip of hard black rock that ran away on each side. Just before dawn he crossed another one, but after that no more. Then he entered the badlands, hard country to ride but easy to hide in.

Once he saw cattle standing silently in the

353

moonlight and wondered at the stupidity of the settler who had left his herd untended. The Crow would feast well if they found them.

It was on the fourth morning of his trek that he saw the fort. He had camped on a knoll and as the sun rose he saw the fort in the foothills of the West Pryor Mountain. He studied it for an hour, alert for signs of life, the blare of a bugle on the wind, the smoke rising from the troopers' chow house. But there was no sign. As the sun rose he withdrew into the shade of a clump of bush and slept.

Over his evening meal he thought what he should do. This was still wild country and a man travelling alone was in constant danger. Clearly the fort was newly built. It had not been there the previous autumn. So the army was extending its control of the tribal lands of the Crow people. A year earlier the nearest forts had been Fort Smith to the east on the Bighorn River and Fort Ellis to the north-west on the Bozeman Trail. To the latter he could not go; they would recognize him there.

But if the new fort was not occupied by the Seventh, or men of Gibbon's command, there was no reason anyone would know him by sight, and if he gave a false name . . . He saddled Rosebud and decided to scout the new fort during the night and remain unseen.

He reached it in the moonlight. No unit flag flew from its pole, no chink of light came from within, no sound of human habitation. Made bolder by the silence, he rode to the front gate. Above it were two words. He recognized the first as 'Fort' because he

354

had seen it before and knew its shape. The second word he could not recall. It began with a letter made of two vertical poles with a sort of crossbar. On the outside of the high double gates was a chain and padlock to keep them closed.

He walked Rosebud round the twelve-foot-high stockade walls. Why would the army build a fort and leave it? Had it been attacked and gutted? Were all inside dead? But if so, why the padlock? At midnight he stood on Rosebud's saddle, reached up and locked fingers over the palisades. Seconds later he was on the walkway five feet below the parapet and seven feet above the ground inside. He looked down.

He could make out the quarters for the officers and the troopers, the livery stable and kitchens, the armoury and water barrel, the trade goods store and the forge. It was all there, but it was abandoned.

He came soft-footed down the steps inside, rifle at the ready, and began to explore. It was new, all right. He could tell by the joinery and the freshness of the sawcuts across the beams. The post commander's office was locked, but everything else seemed to be open to the touch. There was a bunkhouse for the soldiers and another for travellers. He could find no earth latrines, which was odd. Against the back wall, away from the main gate, was a small chapel and beside it in the main wall a door secured on the inside with a timber bar.

He removed this, stepped outside, walked round the walls and led Rosebud inside. Then he rebarred the door. He knew he could never defend the fort alone. If a war party attacked, the braves would come over the walls with the same ease as he. But it would serve as a base for a while, until he could discover where the clan of Tall Elk had gone.

In daylight he explored the livery stable. There were stalls for twenty horses, all the tack and feed a man could need and fresh water in the trough outside. He unsaddled Rosebud and gave her a brisk rub with a stiff brush while she feasted off a bin of oats.

In the forge he found a tin of grease and cleaned his rifle until the metal and wooden stock shone. The trade store yielded hunter's traps and blankets. With the latter he made a comfortable niche in the corner bunk of the cabin set aside for passing travellers. The only thing he was short of was food. But in the trade store he eventually found a jar of candies, so he ate them for his evening meal.

The first week seemed to fly by. In the mornings he rode out to trap and hunt, and in the afternoons he prepared the skins of the animals for future trade. He had all the fresh meat he needed and knew of several plants in the wilderness whose leaves made a nourishing soup.

He found a bar of soap in the store and bathed naked in the nearby creek, whose water, though icy, was refreshing. There was fresh grass for his horse. In the chow kitchen he found bowls and tin plates. He brought in dry fallen winter-wood for his fire and boiled water in which to shave. One of the things he had taken from Donaldson's cabin was his old cut-throat razor, which he kept in a slim steel case. With soap and hot water he was amazed at how easy it was. In the wilderness or on the march with the army he had perforce used cold water and no soap.

The spring turned to early summer and still no-one came. He began to wonder where he should turn to ask where the Cheyenne had gone and where they had taken Whispering Wind. Only then could he follow. But he feared to ride east to Fort Smith or north-west to Fort Ellis, where he would surely be recognized. If he learned the army still wanted to hang him, he would take the name of Donaldson and hope to pass unknown.

He had been there a month when the visitors came, but he was away in the mountains trapping. There were eight in the party and they came in three long steel tubes that rolled on spinning black discs with silver centres but were drawn by no horses.

One of the men was their guide and the other seven were his guests. The guide was Professor John Ingles, head of the faculty of Western History at the University of Montana at Bozeman. His chief guest was the junior senator for the state, all the way from Washington. There were three legislators from the Capitol at Helena and three officials from the Department of Education. Professor Ingles unlocked the padlock and the party entered on foot, staring about them with curiosity and interest.

'Senator, gentlemen, let me welcome you to Fort Heritage,' said the professor. He beamed with pleasure. He was one of those lucky men to possess limitless good humour and to be hopelessly in love with the very activity from which he made his living. His work was his lifelong obsession, a study of the Old West and the detailing of its history. He was steeped in knowledge of Montana in the old days, of the War of the Plains, of the native American tribes who had warred and hunted here. Fort Heritage was a dream he had nursed for a decade and coaxed through a hundred committee meetings. This day was the crowning moment of that decade.

'This fort and trading post is an exact replica, to the last and tiniest detail, of what such a place would have been at the time of the immortal General Custer. I have supervised every detail personally and can vouch for them all.'

As he led the party round the timber cabins and facilities he explained how the project had had its birth in his original application to the Montana Historical Society and the Cultural Trust; how funds had been found in the dormant Coal Taxes fund held by the Trust and allocated after much persuasion.

He told them the design was inch-perfect, made from local forest timber as it would have been, and how, in his pursuit of perfection, even the nails were of original type and steel screws banned.

His enthusiasm overflowing and infecting his guests, he told them: 'Fort Heritage will be an involving and deeply meaningful educational experience for children and young people not only from Montana but, I expect, from the surrounding states. Tour bus parties have already booked from as far away as Wyoming and South Dakota.

'At the very edge of the Crow Reservation, we have twenty acres of paddocks outside the walls for the horses and we will take a hay crop in due season to feed them. Experts will scythe the hay in the old-fashioned way. Visitors will see what life used to be like on the frontier a hundred years ago. I assure you this is unique in all America.'

'I like it, I like it a lot,' said the senator. 'Now, how will you staff it?'

'That is the crowning glory, Senator. This is no museum but a functioning, working 1870s fort. The funds run to the employment of up to sixty young people throughout the summer, right through all the main national holidays and above all the school vacations. The staff will be mainly young, and drawn from the various schools of drama in the principal cities of Montana. The response from the students wishing to work through the summer break and fulfil a worthwhile task at the same time has been impressive.

'We have our sixty volunteers. I myself will be Major Ingles of the Second Cavalry, commanding the post. I will have a sergeant, corporal and eight troopers, all students who know how to ride. Mounts have been loaned by friendly ranchers.

'Then there will be some young women, pretending to be cooks and laundresses. The mode of dress will be exactly as it was then. Other drama students will play the roles of trappers in from the mountains, scouts from the plains, settlers moving west to cross the Rockies.

'A real blacksmith has agreed to join us, so the visitors will see horses being shod with new shoes. I will take services in the post chapel over there and we will sing the hymns of those days. The girls will of course have their own dormitory and a group chaperon in the form of my faculty assistant, Charlotte Bevin. The soldiers will have one bunkhouse, the civilians the other. I assure you, no detail has been overlooked.'

'Surely there have to be some things that modern young people cannot do without. How about personal hygiene, fresh fruit and vegetables?' said a congressman from Helena.

'Absolutely right,' beamed the professor. 'There are in fact three areas of subterfuge. I will not be having any loaded firearms on the post. All handguns and rifles will be replicas, save a few that fire blanks and only under supervision.

'As to hygiene, you see the armoury over there? It has racks of replica Springfields, but behind a false wall is a real bathhouse with hot running water, toilets, faucets and basins and showers. And the giant butt for rainwater? We have underground piped water. The butt has a secret entrance at the back. Inside is a gas-operated refrigeration unit for steaks, chops, vegetables, fruit. Bottled gas. But that's it. No electricity. Candles and oil lamps only.'

They were at the door of the travellers' bunkhouse. One of the officials peered inside.

'It seems you have had a squatter,' he remarked.

They all stared at the blanketed bunk in the corner. Then they found other traces. Horse dung in the stable, the embers of a fire. The senator roared with laughter.

'Seems some of your visitors can't wait,' he said. 'Maybe you have a real frontiersman in residence.'

They all laughed at that.

'Seriously, Professor, it's a great job. I'm sure we all agree. You are to be congratulated. An asset to our state.'

With that they left. The professor locked the front gate behind him, still wondering about the bunk and the horse dung. The three vehicles ground down the rough tracks to the long strip of black rock, Highway 310, and turned north for Billings and the airport.

Ben Craig returned from his trapping two hours later. The first clue that his solitude had been disturbed was that the door in the main wall near the chapel had been barred from the inside. He knew he had left it closed but wedged. Whoever had done it had either left by the main gate or was still inside.

He checked the big gates but they were still locked. There were strange tracks outside which he could not understand, as if made by wagon wheels but wider with zigzag patterns in them.

Rifle in hand, he went over the wall, but after an hour of checking he was satisfied there was no-one else there. He unbarred his door, led Rosebud inside, saw her stabled and fed, then re-examined the footmarks in the main parade ground. There were marks of shoes and heavy hiking boots, and more of the zigzag tracks, but no marks of hoofs. And there were no shoe-marks outside the gate. It was all very odd.

Two weeks later the resident staff party arrived. Once again Craig was out tending his traps in the foothills of the Pryors.

It was quite a column. There were three buses, four cars with spare drivers to take them away and twenty horses in big silver trailers. When they were all unloaded the vehicles drove away.

The staff had changed back in Billings into the costumes appropriate for their roles. Each had a backpack of changes of clothing and personal effects. The professor had checked everything and insisted that nothing 'modern' be brought along. Nothing electrical or battery-operated was allowed. For some it had been a wrench parting with their transistor radios, but it went with the contract. Not even books published in the twentieth century were allowed. Professor Ingles insisted that a complete change by one entire century was vital, both from the point of total authenticity and from a psychological angle.

'With time you really will get to believe you are what you are, frontier people living in a crucial time in Montana's history,' he told them.

For several hours the drama students, having volunteered not only for a summer job that beat waiting tables but also for an educational experience that would help with their careers, explored their new environment with growing enthusiasm.

The cavalry troopers stabled their horses and fixed their sleeping quarters in the military bunkhouse. Two pin-ups, of Raquel Welsh and Ursula Andress, were tacked up and immediately confiscated. There was high good humour and a growing sense of excitement.

The civilian workers, the farrier, traders, cooks, scouts and settlers from back east, occupied the second large bunkhouse. The eight girls were marshalled to their own dormitory by Miss Bevin. Two covered wagons, prairie schooners, covered in white canvas and drawn by heavy draught horses, arrived and were parked near the main gate. They would prove a focal attraction for future visitors.

It was late afternoon when Ben Craig reined in Rosebud half a mile away and studied the fort with a rising sense of alarm. The gates were wide open. Scouting from that distance, he could make out two prairie schooners parked inside and people crossing the parade ground. The flag of the Union fluttered from the pole above the gate. He made out two blue uniforms. He had waited weeks to be able to ask someone where the Cheyenne had gone or been taken, but now he was not so sure.

After deliberating for half an hour, he rode in. He came through the gate as two troopers were about to close it. They glanced at him curiously but said nothing. He dismounted and began to lead Rosebud to the stable. Halfway there he was intercepted.

Miss Charlotte Bevin was a nice person, good-natured and welcoming in the American way, blonde, earnest and wholesome with a freckled nose and a wide grin. She gave Ben Craig the latter.

'Well, hallo there.'

It was too hot to be wearing a hat, so the scout bobbed his head.

'Ma'am.'

'Are you one of our party?'

As the professor's assistant and herself a post-graduate student, she had been involved in the project from the outset and had been present at the numerous interviews leading to the final selection. But this young man she had never seen.

'I guess so, ma'am,' said the stranger.

'You mean, you'd like to be?'

'I suppose I do.'

'Well, this is a bit irregular, you not being on the staff. But it's getting late to spend the night on the prairie. We can offer you a bed for the night. So stable your horse and I'll talk with Major Ingles. Would you come to the command post in half an hour?'

She crossed the parade ground to the command post and tapped on the door. The professor, in full uniform of a major of the Second, was at his desk immersed in administrative papers.

'Sit down, Charlie. Are the young people all settled in?' he asked.

'Yes, and we have an extra one.'

'A what?'

'A young man on a horse. Early to mid-twenties. Just rode in off the prairie. Looks like a local late volunteer. Would like to join us.'

'I'm not sure we can take any more on. We have our complement.'

'Well, to be fair, he has brought all his own equipment. Horse, buckskin suit, pretty soiled, saddle. Even had five animal pelts rolled behind his saddle. He's obviously made the effort.'

'Where is he now?'

'Stabling the horse. I told him to report here in half an hour. Thought you might at least take a look at him.'

'Oh, very well.'

Craig did not have a watch, so he judged by the fall of the sun, but he was accurate to five minutes. When he knocked he was bidden to enter. John Ingles had buttoned up his jacket and was behind his desk. Charlie Bevin stood to one side.

'You wanted to see me, Major?'

The professor was at once struck by the authenticity of the young man before him. He clutched a round fox-fur hat. An open, honest-looking nutbrown face with steady blue eyes. Chestnut hair that had not been trimmed for many weeks was held back by a leather thong in a ponytail, and beside it hung a single eagle feather. The buckskin suit even had the straggling hand-stitching he had seen before on the real thing.

'Well now, young man, Charlie here tells me you would like to join us, stay a while?'

'Yes, Major, I surely would.'

The professor made a decision. There was a bit of slack in the operating fund for the occasional 'contingency'. He judged this young man to be a contingency. He pulled a long form towards him, took a steel-nibbed pen and dipped it in the inkwell.

'All right, let us have a few details. Name?'

Craig hesitated. There had been not a hint of recognition so far but his name might ring a bell. But the major was plump and somewhat pale. He looked as if he had just come out to the frontier. Perhaps back east there had been no mention of the events of the previous summer.

'Craig, sir. Ben Craig.'

He waited. Not a hint that the name meant anything at all. The plump hand wrote in clerkish script: Benjamin Craig.

'Address?'

'Sir?'

'Where do you live, son? Where do you come from?'

'Out there, sir.'

'Out there is the prairie and then the wilderness.'

'Yes, sir. Born and raised in the mountains, Major.'

'Good Lord.' The professor had heard of families who lived in tar-paper shacks deep in the wilderness, but this was usually in the forests of the Rockies, in Utah, Wyoming and Idaho. He carefully wrote 'No Fixed Abode'.

'Parents' names?'

'Both dead, sir.'

'Oh, I'm sorry to hear that.'

'Gone these fifteen years.'

'So who raised you?'

'Mr Donaldson, sir.'

'Ah, and he lives . . .?'

'Also dead. A bear got him.'

The professor put down his pen. He had heard of no fatalities due to a bear attack, though some tourists could be remarkably careless with their picnic garbage. It was all a question of knowing the wild. Anyway, this handsome young man was clearly without family.

'No next of kin?'

'Sir?'

'Who should we contact in the event of . . . anything happening to you?'

'No-one, sir. No-one to tell.'

'I see. Date of birth?'

''Fifty-two. End of December, I think.'

'So you would be nearly twenty-five years old?'

'Yessir.'

'Right. Social Security number?'

Craig stared. The professor sighed.

'My, you do seem to have slipped through the net. Very well. Sign here.'

He turned the form around, pushed it across the desk and offered the pen. Craig took it. He could not read the words 'signature of applicant' but the space was clear enough. He stooped and made his mark. The professor retrieved the paper and stared in disbelief.

'My dear boy, my dear dear boy . . .' He turned the paper so Charlie could see it. She looked at the inky cross in the space.

'Charlie, as an educator I think you have a small extra task this summer.'

367

She flashed her wide grin.

'Yes, Major, I think I do.'

She was thirty-five years old, had been married once, not well, and had never had babies. She thought the young man from the wilderness was like a boy-child, naïve, innocent, vulnerable. He would need her protection.

'Right,' said Professor Ingles, 'Ben, go and get yourself settled in, if you are not already, and join us all at the trestle tables for the evening meal.'

It was good food, the scout thought, and plenty of it. It came on enamelled tin plates. He ate with the help of his bowie knife, a spoon and a wad of bread. There were several half-hidden grins around the table, but he missed them.

The young men he shared the bunkhouse with were friendly. They all seemed to be from towns and cities he had not heard of and presumed to be back east. But it had been a tiring day, and there was no light save candles to read by, so these were quickly blown out and they fell asleep.

Ben Craig had never been taught to be curious about his fellow man but he noticed the young men around him were strange in many ways. They purported to be scouts, horse-breakers and trappers, but seemed to know very little about their skills. But he recalled the raw recruits led by Custer and how little they too had known of horses, guns and the Indians of the Great Plains. He supposed nothing much had changed in the year he had lived with the Cheyenne or alone.

There were to be two weeks of settling in and

rehearsals in the schedule before the visitor parties began to arrive, and this time was dedicated to getting the fort in perfect order, practising routines and lectures by Major Ingles, mainly held in the open air.

Craig knew none of this and prepared to go out hunting again. He was crossing the parade ground, heading for the main gate which stood wide open each day, when a young wrangler called Brad hailed him.

'What you got there, Ben?' He pointed to the sheepskin sheath hanging forward of Craig's left knee in front of the saddle.

'Rifle,' said Craig.

'Can I see? I'm way into guns.'

Craig eased his Sharps out of the sheath and handed it down. Brad was ecstatic.

'Wow, that is a beauty. A real antique. What is it?'

'Sharps fifty-two.'

'That's incredible. I didn't know they made replicas of this.'

Brad sighted the rifle on the bell in the frame above the main gate. It was the bell that would be rung with vigour if any hostiles were spotted or their presence reported, and would warn outside working parties to hurry back. Then he pulled the trigger.

He was about to say 'Bang' but the Sharps did it for him. Then he was knocked back by the recoil. If the heavy bullet had hit the bell square on, it would have shattered it. Instead it hit at an angle and screamed off into space. But the bell still emitted a clang that stopped all activity in the fort. The professor came tumbling out of his office.

'What on earth was that?' he called, then saw Brad sitting on the ground clutching the heavy rifle. 'Brad, what do you think you're doing?'

Brad clambered to his feet and explained. Ingles looked sorrowfully at Craig.

'Ben, maybe I forgot to tell you, but there is a no-firearm rule on this base. I'll have to lock this up in the armoury.'

'No guns, Major?'

'No guns. At least not real ones.'

'But what about the Sioux?'

'The Sioux? So far as I know they are on the reservations in North and South Dakota.'

'But, Major, they might come back.'

Then the professor saw the humour. He gave an indulgent beam.

'Of course, they might come back. But not this summer, I think. And until they do, this goes behind a chain in the armoury.'

The fourth day was a Sunday and the staff all attended morning service in the chapel. There was no chaplain, so Major Ingles officiated. In mid-service he moved to the lectern and prepared to read the lesson. The big Bible was opened at the appropriate page with a marker.

'Our lesson today comes from the Book of Isaiah, chapter eleven, starting at verse six. Here the prophet deals with the time when God's peace shall come upon our earth.

' "The wolf also shall dwell with the lamb, and

370

the leopard shall lie down with the kid; and the calf and the young lion and the fatling together. And a little child shall lead them.

'"And the cow and the bear shall feed; their young ones shall lie down together, and the lion . . ."'

At this point he turned the page, but two of the ricepaper sheets had stuck together and he stopped, as the text made no sense. As he wrestled with his confusion a young voice spoke from the middle of the third row in front of him.

'"And the lion shall eat straw like the ox. And the sucking child shall play on the hole of the asp and the weaned child shall put his hand on the cockatrice's den. They shall not hurt nor destroy in all my holy mountain, for the earth shall be full of the knowledge of the Lord as the waters cover the sea."'

There was silence as the congregation stared open-mouthed at the figure in the stained buckskin suit with the eagle feather dangling from the back of his head. John Ingles discovered the remainder of the passage.

'Yes, precisely. Here endeth the first lesson.'

'I really do not understand that young man,' he said to Charlie in his office after lunch. 'He cannot read or write but can recite passages from the Bible that he learned as a child. Is he weird or am I?'

'Don't worry, I think I have figured it out,' she said. 'He really was born to a couple who chose to live in isolation in the wilderness. When they died he really was adopted, unofficially and probably illegally, by a single man, much older, and raised as the old man's son. So he really does have no formal education. But he has a huge knowledge of three things: the Bible that his mother taught him, the ways of the last remaining wilderness and the history of the Old West.'

'Where did he get that from?'

'The old man, presumably. After all, if a man died at age, say, eighty, only three years ago, he would have been born before the end of the last century. Things were pretty basic around here back then. He must have told the boy what he recalled or was himself told about the frontier days by survivors.'

'So why does the young man play the role so well? Could he be dangerous?'

'No,' said Charlie, 'none of that. He is just fantasizing. He believes he has a right to trap and hunt at will, like they used to in the old days.'

'Role-playing?'

'Yes, but then, aren't we all?'

The professor roared with laughter and slapped his thighs.

'Of course, that is what we're all doing. He just does it brilliantly well.'

She rose.

'Because he believes in it. The best actor of them all. You leave him to me. I'll see he comes to no harm. Incidentally, two of the girls are already making sheep's eyes at him.'

In the bunkhouse Ben Craig still found it odd that his companions, when they undressed for the night, stripped right down to brief shorts made of

372

cotton, while he preferred to sleep in the usual ankle-length white underwear. After a week this led to a problem and some of the young men spoke to Charlie.

She found Craig after log-hauling detail, swinging a long-handled axe as he reduced the cords of pine to splits for the kitchen range.

'Ben, could I ask you something?'

'Sure, ma'am.'

'And call me Charlie.'

'All right, Charlie, ma'am.'

'Ben, do you ever bathe?'

'Bathe?'

'Uh-huh. Strip right down and wash the body, all of it, not just the hands and face?'

'Why sure, ma'am. Regular.'

'Well, that's nice to hear, Ben. When did you last do that?'

He thought. Old Donaldson had taught him that regular bathing was necessary, but in creeks of melted snow there was no need to become addicted.

'Why, as recently as last month.'

'That's what I suspected. Do you think you could do that again? Now?'

Ten minutes later she found him leading Rosebud, fully saddled, out of the stable.

'Where are you going, Ben?'

'To bathe, Charlie, ma'am. Like you said.'

'But where?'

'In the creek. Where else?'

Every day he had wandered out into the

long-grassed prairie to perform the usual bodily functions. He washed face, arms and hands in the horse-trough. His teeth were kept white by an hour with the splay-ended willow twig, but he could do that as he rode.

'Tether the horse and come with me.'

She led him to the armoury, unlocked it with a key on her belt and took him inside. Beyond the racks of chained Springfields was the back wall. Here she found a pressure-operated release in a knothole and swung open the hidden door. There was a further room equipped with basins and bathtubs.

Craig had seen hot tubs before, during his two years at Fort Ellis, but they had been made of wooden staves. These were of enamelled iron. He knew tubs had to be filled by relays of buckets of hot water from the kitchen range, but Charlie turned a strange knob at one end and steaming water flowed out.

'Ben, I'm going to come back in two minutes and I want to find all your clothes, except the buckskin, which needs dry-cleaning, outside the door.

'Then I want you to get in with the brush and soap and scrub yourself. All over. Then I want you to take this and wash your hair with it.'

She handed him a flask with a green liquid that smelled of pine buds.

'Finally I want you to dress again from any underclothes and shirts you find in those shelves over there. When you are done, come back out. OK?'

He did as he was bid. He had never been in a hot bath before and found that it was pleasant, though he had trouble finding out how the faucets operated and nearly flooded the floor. When he had done, and shampooed his hair, the water was a dull grey. He found the plug at the bottom and watched it drain away.

He selected cotton shorts, a white T-shirt, and a warm plaid shirt from the racks in the corner, dressed, braided the eagle feather back into his hair and came out. She was waiting for him. In the sun was a chair. She carried scissors and a comb.

'I'm not an expert, but this will be better than nothing,' she said. 'Sit down.'

She trimmed his chestnut hair, leaving only the long strand with the feather untouched.

'That's better,' she said when she was done. 'And you smell just fine.'

She put the chair back in the armoury and locked it. Expecting warm thanks, she found the scout looking solemn, even miserable.

'Charlie, ma'am, would you walk with me?'

'Sure, Ben. Something on your mind?'

Secretly she was delighted at the chance. She might now begin to understand this enigmatic and strange product of the wilderness. They walked out through the gate and he led the way across the prairie towards the creek. He was silent, lost in thought. She forced back her desire to interrupt. It was a mile to the creek and they walked for twenty minutes.

The prairie smelt of hay-ready grass and several

times the young man raised his gaze to the Pryor Range, towering in the south.

'It's nice to be out on the range, looking at the mountains,' she said.

'It's my home,' he said and lapsed into silence. When they reached the creek he sat down at the water's edge and she gathered the folds of her full cotton dress about her and sat facing him.

'What is it, Ben?'

'Can I ask you something, ma'am?'

'Charlie. Yes, of course you can.'

'You wouldn't tell me no lies?'

'No lies, Ben. Just the truth.'

'What year is it?'

She was shocked. She had hoped for something revelatory, something about his relationship with the other young people in the group. She stared into the wide, deep blue eyes and wondered . . . she was ten years his senior but . . .

'Why, it's 1977, Ben.'

If she had expected a non-committal nod, it was not what she got. The young man leaned his head between his knees, covered his face with his hands. His shoulders under the buckskin began to shake.

She had only once seen a grown man cry. It was beside an auto wreck on the highway from Bozeman to Billings. She rocked forward onto her knees and placed her hands on his shoulders.

'What is it, Ben? What's the matter with this year?'

Ben Craig had felt fear before. Facing the grizzly,

on the slope above the Little Bighorn, but nothing like this awful terror.

'I was born,' he said at length, 'in the year 1852.'

She was not surprised. She knew there had been a problem. She wrapped her arms round him and held him to her bosom, stroking the back of his head.

She was a modern young woman, a girl of her time. She had read all about these things. Half the youth of the West was attracted by the East's mystic philosophies. She knew all about the theory of reincarnation, or at any rate the belief in it. She had read of some people's sense of déjà-vu, a conviction that they had existed before, long ago.

This was a problem, the phenomenon of delusion, that had been tackled, was even then being tackled, by the science of psychiatry. There was help, counselling, therapy.

'It's all right, Ben,' she murmured as she rocked him like a child. 'It's all right. Everything's going to be OK. If you believe that, it's fine. Spend the summer with us here at the fort and we'll live as they lived a hundred years ago. In the fall you can come back to Bozeman with me and I'll find people to help. You're going to be all right, Ben. Trust me.'

She took a cotton handkerchief from her sleeve and dabbed his face, overcome by her sense of compassion for the troubled young man from the hills.

They walked back to the fort together. Satisfied that her underclothes were modern and there were modern medications to hand in the event of cuts, bruises or illness, secure in the knowledge that the

Billings Memorial Hospital was only minutes away by helicopter, Charlie was beginning to enjoy the long cotton dress, the simple life and the routines of frontier-fort living. And now she knew that her doctoral thesis was a certainty.

'Major' Ingles's lectures were obligatory for all. Due to the warm late-June weather, he held them on the parade ground, the students on rows of benches in front of him, his easel and pictorial material to hand. Once he was lecturing on the real history of the Old West he was in his element.

After ten days he reached the period of the War of the Plains. Behind him he had draped large-scale photographs of the principal Sioux leaders. Ben Craig found himself staring at a blow-up of a photograph of Sitting Bull, taken in his later years. The Hunkpapa medicine man had been to Canada for sanctuary but had returned to throw himself and the remainder of his people on the mercy of the US Army. The picture on the easel was taken just before he was murdered.

'But one of the strangest of them all was the Oglala chief, Crazy Horse,' said the professor. 'For reasons of his own he never permitted himself to be photographed by the white man. He believed the camera would take his soul away. Thus he is the one man of whom there is no photograph. So we will never know what he looked like.'

Craig opened his mouth and shut it again.

In another lecture the professor described in detail the campaign that led to the fight at the Little Bighorn. It was the first time Craig learned what happened to Major Reno and his three companies, or that Captain Benteen had returned from the bad-lands to join them on the besieged hilltop. He was glad most of them had been rescued by General Terry.

In his final lecture the professor dealt with the round-up in 1877 of the scattered groups of Sioux and Cheyenne and their escort back to the reser-vations. When John Ingles called for questions Craig raised his hand.

'Yes, Ben.' The professor was pleased to take a question from his one pupil who had never crossed the threshold of a grade school.

'Major, was there ever mention of a clan chief called Tall Elk, or of a brave named Walking Owl?'

The professor was flustered. He had reference books back at the faculty to fill a truck and most of their contents were in his own head. He had expected a simple question. He searched his memory.

'No, I do believe no-one heard of them and no later witnesses among the Plains Indians men-tioned them. Why do you ask?'

'I have heard it said that Tall Elk split away from the main group, avoided Terry's patrols and win-tered right over there in the Pryor Range, sir.'

'Well, I have never heard of such a thing. If he did, he and his people must have been found in the spring. You would have to ask at Lame Deer, now the centre of the Northern Cheyenne Reservation. Someone at the Dull Knife Memorial College might know.'

Ben Craig memorized the name. In the fall he would find his way to Lame Deer, wherever that was, and ask.

The first visitor parties came at the weekend. After that the parties came almost daily. They came by buses mainly, and some in private cars. Some were groups in the charge of their teachers, others private family parties. But they all parked in an area half a mile away and out of sight, and were brought to the main gates in the covered wagons. It was part of Professor Ingles's 'getting in the mood' stratagem.

It worked. The children, and they were mainly children, were thrilled by the wagon ride, which was new to most of them, and in the last 200-yard approach to the gates could imagine they really were frontier settlers. They poured from the wagons in an excited throng.

Craig was detailed to work on his animal pelts, which were stretched on frames in the sun. He salted and scraped them, readying them for softening and tanning. The soldiers drilled, the smith pumped the bellows of his forge, the girls in their long cotton dresses washed clothes in big timber tubs and 'Major' Ingles conducted parties from activity to activity, explaining each function and why it was necessary in the life on the plains.

There were two Native American students who posed as non-hostile Indians living in the fort as trackers and guides, in the event the soldiery would need to respond to the emergency of a settler party out on the plains being attacked by an off-reservation war party. They wore cotton pants, blue canvas shirts, waist sashes and long black wigs under stovepipe hats.

The favourite attractions seemed to be the blacksmith and Ben Craig working on his pelts.

'Did you trap them yourself?' asked one boy from a school in Helena.

'Yep.'

'Do you have a licence?'

'A what?'

'Why do you wear a feather in your hair if you are not an Indian?'

'The Cheyenne gave it to me.'

'Why?'

'For bringing down a grizzly.'

'That's a wonderful story,' said the escorting teacher.

'No it's not,' said the boy. 'He's an actor just like all the rest.'

As each new wagonload of visitors arrived Craig scanned them for the glimpse of a cascade of black hair, the turn of a face, a pair of large dark eyes. But she did not come. July slipped into August.

Craig asked for three days to go back to the wilderness. He rode out before dawn. In the mountains he found a stand of osage cherry, took his hand-axe, borrowed from the smithy, and went to work. When he had cut, shaved and scraped the bow-stave he strung it with twine from the fort, as he had no animal tendons.

The arrows he cut from rigid and cue-straight ash saplings. The tail feathers from an inattentive wild turkey formed the flights. By a creek he found flint rocks and from these he chipped and knapped the arrowheads. Both Cheyenne and Sioux had used mainly flint or iron arrowheads, lodged into a cleft at the tip of the arrows and lashed in place with ultra-fine cords of skin.

Of the two the plainsmen feared the flint the more. The iron arrowheads could be withdrawn against the barb along with the arrow, but the flint variety generally broke off, involving deep and usually terminal no-anaesthetic surgery. Craig made four of them. On the third morning he took the buck.

When he rode back in the beast was across his saddlebow, the arrow still in the heart. He took the kill to the kitchen, hung, gutted, skinned and dissected the animal, finally offering the cook sixty pounds of fresh venison in front of a stunned audience of townsfolk.

'Something wrong with my cooking?' asked the chef.

'No, it's fine. I liked the cheese pie with coloured bits.'

'It's called a pizza.'

'Just figured we could do with some fresh meat.'

While the scout was washing off his hands and forearms in the horse trough the cook took the bloody arrow and walked quickly to the command post.

'It's a beautiful artefact,' said Professor Ingles as he handled it. 'I have seen them in museums, of course. Even the barred tail feathers from a turkey are clearly identifiable as Cheyenne work. Where did he get it?'

'He says he made it,' said the cook.

'Impossible. Nobody can knap flint like this any more.'

'Well, he has four,' said the chef, 'and this one was right in the animal's heart. Tonight I'm serving fresh venison.'

The staff ate it at a barbecue outside the stockade walls and enjoyed it.

Across the fire the professor watched Craig slicing slivers of cooked meat from a haunch with his razor-sharp bowie knife and recalled Charlie's assurance to him. Maybe, but he had his doubts. Could this strange young man ever turn dangerous? He noted that now four of his female students were trying to attract the untamed boy's attention, but his thoughts always seemed to be far away.

By the middle of the month the black dog of despair was beginning to overtake Ben Craig. Part of him tried to remain convinced that the Everywhere Spirit had not lied to him, not betrayed him. Had the girl he loved also been given the curse of life? None of the high-spirited group around him knew that he had already made a decision. If by the end of the summer he had not found the love for which he had obeyed the vision-quester's plea, he would ride back to the mountains and by his own hand go to join her in the spirit world.

A week later the two wagons rolled again through the gates and their drivers halted the sweating draught horses. From the first poured a gaggle of young and excited children. He sheathed his knife, which he had been honing on a stone, and walked forward. One of the grade-school teachers had her back to him. From her head to the middle of her back flowed a torrent of hair the colour of jet.

She turned. Japanese-American, round puppy face. The scout turned and strode away. His rage boiled up. He stopped, raised clenched fists to the sky and screamed.

'You lied to me, Meh-y-yah. You lied to me, old man. You told me to wait but you have cast me into this wilderness, an outcast of man and God.'

Everyone in the parade ground between the buildings stopped and stared. Ahead of him was one of the 'tame' Indians, walking away. This man also halted.

The old face, wizened and brown like a burnt walnut, ancient as the rocks of the Beartooth Range, framed by strands of snow-white hair, stared at him from beneath the stovepipe hat. In the vision-quester's eyes was an expression of infinite sadness. Slowly he shook his head. Then he raised his gaze and nodded silently, looking at a point beyond the young scout.

Craig turned again, saw nothing and looked back. Underneath his hat his friend Brian Heavyshield, one of the two Native American actors, was staring at him as if he had gone crazy. He turned back to the gate.

The second wagon was unloaded. A crowd of children milled around their teacher. Jeans, check shirt, baseball cap. She stooped to separate two scuffling boys, then wiped her shirtsleeve across her brow. The peak of her cap got in the way. She pulled the baseball cap off. A torrent of released dark hair tumbled down to her waist. Disconcerted by the sensation of someone staring, she turned towards him. An oval face, two huge dark eyes. Whispering Wind.

He could not move. He could not speak. He knew he should say something, walk towards her, anything. But he could not, he just stared. She flushed, embarrassed, broke the gaze and gathered her charges to begin the tour. An hour later they arrived at the stables, led by Charlie, their tour guide. Ben Craig was grooming Rosebud. He knew they would come. It was on the route.

'This is where we keep the horses,' said Charlie. 'Some are cavalry mounts, others belong to the frontiersmen who live here or are just passing through. Ben here is looking after his horse Rosebud. Ben is a hunter, trapper, scout and mountain man.'

'Want to see all the horses,' yelled one of the children.

'All right, honey, we'll see all the horses. Just don't get too close to the hooves in case they kick out,' said Charlie. She led the youngsters down the line of stalls. Craig and the girl were left facing each other.

'I'm sorry I stared, ma'am,' he said. 'My name is Ben Craig.'

'Hi. I'm Linda Pickett.' She held out her hand. He took it. It was warm and small, the way he remembered.

'Could I ask you something, ma'am?'

'Do you call every female ma'am?'

'Guess so. Way I was taught. Is it bad?'

'Kind of formal. Like from a long time ago. What did you want to ask?'

'Do you remember me?'

Her brow furrowed.

'I don't believe so. Have we met?'

'A long time ago.'

She laughed. It was the sound he recalled from around the campfires at Tall Elk's lodges.

'Then I must have been too young. Where was it?'

'Come. I'll show you.'

He led the puzzled girl outside. Beyond the timber palisades the peaks of the Pryor Range rose in the south.

'Do you know what those are?'

'The Beartooth Range?'

'No. They are further west. Those are the Pryors. That was where we knew each other.'

'But I've never been into the Pryor Range. My brothers used to take me camping as a kid, but never there.'

He turned and looked into the beloved face.

'You are a schoolteacher now?'

'Uh-huh. In Billings. Why?'

'Are you going to come back here again?'

'I don't know. There are other parties scheduled to come later. I might be assigned. Why?'

'I want you to come again. Please. I must see you again. Say you will.'

Miss Pickett flushed again. She was too beautiful not to have been in receipt of many passes from boys. Usually she brushed them aside with a laugh that conveyed the message but gave no offence. This young man was strange. He did not flatter, he did not smile invitingly. He seemed solemn, earnest, naïve. She stared into the frank, cobalt eyes and something fluttered inside her. Charlie came out of the stable with the children.

'I don't know,' said the girl, 'I'll think about it.'

An hour later she and her party were gone.

It took a week, but she came. One of her colleagues at the school was called away to the bedside of a relative. There was a vacancy in the escort group and she volunteered. The day was hot. She wore a simple cotton print frock.

Craig had asked Charlie to check the visitor roster for him, looking for a booking from the school.

'You have your eye on someone, Ben?' she asked archly. She was not disappointed, recognizing that a relationship with a sensible girl could enormously help his rehabilitation to the real world. She was pleased by the speed with which he was learning to read and write. She had procured two simple books for him to read, word by word. After the fall she thought she could find lodgings for him in town, a job as store clerk or table waiter, while she worked on her thesis about his recovery.

He was waiting when the wagons unloaded their cargoes of children and teachers.

'Will you come walk with me, Miss Linda?'

'Walk? Where?'

'Out to the prairie. So we can talk.'

She protested that the children needed her attention, but one of her older colleagues gave her a broad wink and whispered that she should take time for her new admirer if she wished. She wished.

They walked away from the fort and found a jumble of rocks in the shade of a tree. He seemed tongue-tied.

'Where do you come from, Ben?' she asked, aware of his shyness, quite liking it. He nodded towards the distant peaks.

'You were raised over there, in the mountains?' He nodded again.

'So what school did you go to?'

'No school.'

She tried to assimilate this. To spend a whole boyhood hunting and trapping, never to go to school . . . It was too strange.

'It must be very quiet in the mountains. No traffic, no radios, no TV.'

He did not know what she was talking about but presumed she referred to things that made noise, other than the rustle of the trees and the call of the birds.

'It's the sound of freedom,' he said. 'Tell me, Miss Linda, have you heard of the Northern Cheyenne?'

She was surprised but relieved at the change of subject.

'Of course. In fact my great-grandmother on my mother's side was a Cheyenne lady.'

He swung his head towards her, the eagle feather danced in the hot breeze, the dark blue eyes fixed her, pleading.

'Tell me about her. Please.'

Linda Pickett recalled that her grandmother had once shown her an old photograph of a wizened crone who had been her own mother. Even with the passing years the large eyes, fine nose and high cheekbones indicated the old woman in the faded monochrome snapshot had once been very beautiful. She told what she knew, what her now-dead grandmother had told her as a little girl.

The Cheyenne woman had once been married to a brave and there had been a baby boy. But about 1880 an epidemic of cholera on the reservation had taken the brave and the boy away. Two years later a frontier preacher had taken the young widow as his wife, braving the disapproval of his fellow whites. He had been of Swedish extraction, big and blond. There were three daughters, the youngest Miss Pickett's own grandmother, born in 1890.

She in turn had married a Caucasian and produced a son and two daughters, the younger girl born in 1925. In her late teens it was that second daughter, Mary, who had come to Billings seeking work, and had found it as a clerk in the newly established Farmers' Bank.

Working at the next booth was an earnest and industrious teller called Michael Pickett. They married in 1945. Her father had not gone to the war due to short-sightedness. There were four elder brothers, all big blond lads, and then Linda in 1959. She was just eighteen.

'I don't know why, but I was born with a streak of jet black hair down my head, and dark eyes, nothing like my mom and pa. So there you are. Now you.'

He ignored the invitation.

'Do you have marks on your right leg?'

'My birthmark? How on earth do you know?'

'Please let me see it.'

'Why? It's private.'

'Please.'

She paused awhile, then tucked up her cotton skirt to reveal a slim golden thigh. They were still there. Two puckered dimples, the entry and exit holes of the trooper's bullet beside Rosebud Creek. Irritated, she pulled her skirt back down.

'Anything else?' she asked sarcastically.

'Just one. Do you know what *Emos-est-se-haa'e* means in the Cheyenne language?'

'Heavens no.'

'It means Wind That Talks Softly. Whispering Wind. May I call you Whispering Wind?'

'I don't know. I suppose so. If it pleases you. But why?'

'Because it was once your name. Because I have dreamed about you. Because I have waited for you. Because I love you.'

She flushed deep pink and rose to her feet.

'This is madness. You know nothing about me, nor I of you. Anyway, I am engaged to be married.'

She stalked off to rejoin her group and would talk to him no more.

But she came back to the fort. She wrestled with her conscience, told herself a thousand times she was being crazy, a fool, out of her mind. But in that mind she saw the steady blue eyes holding hers and convinced herself that she should tell this lovelorn young man that there was no point in their ever meeting again. At least, that was what she told herself she would do.

On a Sunday, a week before school resumed, she caught a tour bus from the centre of the town and alighted at the parking lot. He seemed to know she was coming. He was waiting on the parade ground, as he had every day, with Rosebud saddled up.

He helped her up behind him and rode out to the prairie. Rosebud knew her way to the creek. By the glittering water they dismounted, and he told her how his parents had died when he was a boy and a mountain man had adopted him as his own and raised him. He explained that instead of the school of books and maps he had learned the spoor of every animal of the wild, the cry of every bird, the shape and character of every tree.

She explained that her own life was quite different, orthodox and conventional, planned out. That her fiancé was a young man of good and immensely wealthy family who could give her everything a woman could need or want, as her mother had explained. So there was no point . . .

Then he kissed her. She tried to push him away, but when their lips met the strength went out of her arms and they slipped helplessly round the back of his neck.

His mouth did not smell of alcohol or stale cigars, as did that of her fiancé. He did not grope her body. She smelt the odour of him: buckskin, woodsmoke, pine trees.

In a tumult she broke away and began to walk back to the fort. He followed but did not touch her again. Rosebud ceased cropping and walked behind.

'Stay with me, Whispering Wind.'

'I cannot.'

'We are destined for each other. It was so spoken, a long time ago.'

'I cannot answer. I have to think. This is crazy. I am engaged.'

'Tell him he will have to wait.'

'Impossible.'

There was a prairie schooner leaving the gates, heading for the out-of-sight parking lot. She diverted her course, boarded it and went inside. Ben Craig mounted Rosebud and walked after the wagon.

At the parking lot the passengers disembarked from the wagon and boarded the bus.

'Whispering Wind,' he called, 'will you come back?'

'I cannot, I am going to marry someone else.'

Several matrons looked with displeasure at the young horseman with the wild appearance who was clearly importuning a nice young girl. The doors closed and the driver started the engine.

Rosebud gave a frightened whinny and reared high on her back legs. The bus began to move, picking up speed on the rough road that would lead back to the blacktop highway. Craig touched Rosebud in the flanks and rode after it, canter developing to gallop as the bus accelerated.

The mare was terrified of the monster beside her. It snorted and roared at her. The force of the wind increased. Inside the coach the passengers heard a shout.

'Whispering Wind, come with me to my mountains and be my wife.'

The driver glanced in his rear-view mirror, saw the flaring nostrils and wildly rolling eyes of the horse, and pressed the gas. The bus bucked and jolted on the rough road. Several matrons screamed as they clutched their plump offspring. Linda Pickett rose from her window seat and tugged at the sliding pane.

The bus was slowly outpacing the galloping horse. Rosebud was stricken with panic but trusted to the firm knees that pressed her ribs and the grip on her rein. A dark head came out of a window. Down the slipstream came her reply.

'Yes, Ben Craig, I will.'

The horseman reined in and was lost to view in the dust.

She wrote her letter carefully, not wishing to provoke an outbreak of his temper, which she had felt before, but just to make her meaning regretfully clear. When she had finished her fourth draft, she signed it and posted it. Nothing was heard for a week. The meeting, when it came, was short and brutal.

Michael Pickett was a pillar of his community, president and chief officer of the Farmers' Bank of Billings. Starting as a humble teller just before Pearl Harbor, he had risen through the ranks to the post of assistant manager. His hard work, orthodoxy and conscientiousness had caught the eye of the founder and owner of the bank, a lifelong bachelor with no kin.

On retirement this gentleman had offered to sell his bank to Michael Pickett. He wanted someone to continue his tradition. Loan finance was raised and the buyout went through. In time most of the purchasing loans were repaid. But in the late Sixties there had been problems: overextension, foreclosures, bad debts. Pickett had been forced to go public and raise survival capital by offering stock on the market. The crisis had been ridden through and liquidity returned.

A week after the arrival of his daughter's letter Mr Pickett was not invited but summoned to a meeting with the fiancé's father at his home, the impressive Bar-T Ranch on the banks of the Yellowstone River south-west of Billings. They had met before, at the time of the betrothal, but in the Cattlemen's Club dining room.

The banker was shown into a huge office with polished timber floors and expensive panelling, adorned with trophies, framed certificates and the heads of prize bulls. The man behind the expansive desk did not rise or greet. He gestured to a single vacant chair facing him. When his guest was seated, he stared at the banker without a word.

Mr Pickett was discomfited. He thought he knew what it was about.

The rancher and tycoon took his time. He unwrapped a large Cohiba, lit up and when it was drawing well pushed a single sheet of paper across his desk. Pickett read it; it was his daughter's letter.

'I'm sorry,' he said. 'She told me. I knew she had written. I had not seen the letter.'

The rancher leaned forward, admonitory finger raised, angry eyes set in a face like a side of beef beneath the Stetson he always wore, even in his office.

'No way,' he said. 'No way, you get it? No way any girl treats my boy like this.'

The banker shrugged.

'I'm as disappointed as you,' he said. 'But young people . . . sometimes they change their mind. They are both young, maybe a bit overhasty?'

'Talk to her. Suggest she has made a bad mistake.'

'I have talked to her. So has her mother. She wishes to call off her engagement.'

The rancher leaned back and glanced about the room, thinking how far he had come since his early days as a simple wrangler.

'Not when it comes to my boy,' he said. Retrieving the letter, he pushed a sheaf of papers across the desk. 'You had better read these.'

William 'Big Bill' Braddock had indeed come a long way. His grandfather had come west from Bismarck, North Dakota, where he had been born, albeit out of wedlock, to a cavalry soldier who had died fighting on the plains. The grandfather had taken a job in a store and kept it all his life, neither rising nor being dismissed. His son had followed in his humble footsteps, but the grandson had taken a job on a cattle ranch.

The boy was big, hard, a natural bully and given to settling disputes with his fists, almost inevitably to his own advantage. But he was also smart. After the war he had spotted the early beginnings of a company opportunity: the refrigerated truck, capable of delivering prime Montana beef hundreds of miles from where it had been raised.

He struck out on his own, starting with trucks, moving into slaughtering and butchering, until he controlled the whole business from the ranch gate to the barbecue. He created his own name brand, Big Bill's Beef, free-range, juicy, field-fresh and in your local supermarket. When he moved back into ranching, the missing link in the beef chain, it was as the boss.

The Bar-T, bought ten years earlier, was a rebuilt showpiece and the most impressive mansion along the Yellowstone. His wife, a subdued wisp of a woman almost invisible to the naked eye, had produced him one son, but hardly a chip off the old block. Kevin was in his mid-twenties, much indulged, spoiled and terrified of his father. But Big Bill doted on his scion; nothing was too good for his only son.

Michael Pickett finished the papers pale and shaken.

'I don't understand,' he said.

'Well, Pickett, it's pretty plain. I have spent a

week buying up every marker you owe in this state. That means I now hold the majority stock. I own the bank. And a packet it has cost me. All because of your daughter. Pretty, I'll say that, but stupid. I don't know or care who this other guy she's met is, but you tell her to drop him.

'She writes back to my son and admits she made a mistake. Their engagement resumes.'

'But if I can't persuade her?'

'Then you tell her she will be responsible for your complete destruction. I'll take your bank, I'll take your house, I'll take everything you've got. Tell her you won't be able to get a cup of coffee on credit in this county. You hear?'

As he drove down to the highway Michael Pickett was a broken man. He knew Braddock was not joking. He had done this before to men who had crossed him. Pickett had also been warned that the nuptials would have to be advanced to mid-October, a month away.

The family conference was unpleasant. Mrs Pickett was accusatory and wheedling by turns. What did Linda think she was up to? Had she any idea what she had done? Marriage to Kevin Braddock would bring her, at a stroke, all the things others worked a lifetime to achieve: a fine house, spacious grounds to raise the kids, the best schools, a position in society. How could she throw it all away for a silly infatuation with an out-of-work actor pretending to be a frontier scout for the duration of a summer work assignment?

Two of her brothers who lived and worked

locally had been called to attend. One suggested he go out to Fort Heritage and have a man-to-man talk with the interloper. Both young men suspected a vengeful Braddock could ensure that they too lost their jobs. The brother who spoke was on the state government payroll, and Braddock had powerful friends in Helena.

Her distraught father polished his thick-lensed eyeglasses and looked miserable. It was eventually his misery that convinced Linda Pickett. She nodded, rose and went to her room. This time she wrote two letters.

The first was to Kevin Braddock. She admitted she had developed a silly, girlish crush on a young wrangler she had met, but that it was over. She told him she had been foolish to write him the way she had, and asked for his forgiveness. She wished their engagement to resume and looked forward to becoming his wife before the end of October.

Her second letter was addressed to Mr Ben Craig, c/o Fort Heritage, Bighorn County, Montana. Both letters were posted the following day.

Despite his obsession with authenticity Professor Ingles had made two other concessions to modernity. Though there were no telephone lines to the fort, he kept in his office a radio/telephone powered by rechargeable cadmium/nickel batteries. There was also a postal service.

The Billings post office had agreed to deliver all mail for the fort to the office of the town's principal tour bus company, and they had agreed to send the satchel of mail needing delivery with the driver of their next bus out. Ben Craig received his letter four days later.

He tried to read it, but had trouble. Thanks to Charlie's lessons he had become accustomed to capital letters and even lower-case print, but the cursive handscript of the young woman defeated him. He took the letter to Charlie, who read it and looked at him with pity.

'I'm sorry, Ben. It's from the girl you took a fancy to. Linda?'

'Please read it to me, Charlie.'

'"Dear Ben,"' she read, '"two weeks ago I did something extremely foolish. When you shouted to me from your horse, and I shouted back from the bus, I think I said that we could be married. Back home I have realized how stupid I was.

'"In truth I am engaged to a fine young man whom I have known for some years. I find that I simply cannot break off my engagement to him. We are to be married next month.

'"Please wish me luck and happiness in the future, as I wish to you. With a farewell kiss, Linda Pickett."'

Charlie folded the letter and handed it back. Ben Craig stared at the mountains, lost in thought. Charlie reached out and placed her hand over his.

'I'm sorry, Ben. It happens. Ships that pass in the night. She clearly developed a girlish crush on you, and I can understand why. But she has made her decision to stay with her fiancé.'

Craig knew nothing of ships. He stared at his mountains, then asked: 'Who is her betrothed?'

'I don't know. She doesn't say.'

'Could you find out?'

'Now, Ben, you are not going to cause any trouble?'

Long ago Charlie had had two young men come to blows over her. She found it rather flattering. But that had been then. She did not want her untamed young protégé heading into a fist-fight on account of a chit of a girl who had come three times to the fort to mess with his vulnerable affections.

'No, Charlie, no trouble. Just curious.'

'You're not going to ride into Billings and start a fight?'

'Charlie, I just want that which is mine, in the eyes of man and the Everywhere Spirit. As it was spoken long ago.'

He was talking riddles again, so she persisted.

'But not Linda Pickett?'

He thought for a while, chewing on a grass stem.

'No, not Linda Pickett.'

'You promise, Ben?'

'I promise.'

'I'll see what I can do.'

In college at Bozeman Charlie Bevin had had a friend who had become a journalist and moved to work on the *Billings Gazette*. She called her and asked for a quick check of the back issues for any mention of the announcement of an engagement involving a young woman called Linda Pickett. It did not take long.

Four days later the mail package brought her a cutting from the early summer. Mr and Mrs

Michael Pickett and Mr and Mrs William Braddock had been pleased to announce the engagement of their daughter Linda and son Kevin. Charlie raised her eyebrows and whistled. No wonder the girl did not intend to break her engagement.

'That must be the son of Big Bill Braddock,' she told Craig. 'You know, the beefsteak king?'

The scout shook his head.

'No,' said Charlie with resignation, 'you just hunt your own. Without a licence. Well, Ben, the father is very rich indeed. He lives on a big spread up north of here, near the Yellowstone. Do you know the river?'

Craig nodded. He had ridden down every inch of the southern bank with General Gibbon, from Fort Ellis to the junction with the Tongue, far east of Rosebud Creek, where they turned back.

'Could you find out when the wedding will be, Charlie?'

'You remember your promise?'

'I do. No Linda Pickett.'

'That's right. So what do you have in mind? A little surprise?'

'Uh-huh.'

Charlie made another phone call. September slipped into October. The weather remained fine and mild. The long-range forecast suggested a real Indian summer, with fine sunny weather until the end of the month.

On the 10th a copy of the *Billings Gazette* arrived with the tour bus. With the school term well under way, the flow of visitors was easing fast.

In the paper from her friend Charlie found an entire column from the writer of the social diary. She read it out to Craig.

In breathless prose the diarist described the forthcoming nuptials of Kevin Braddock and Linda Pickett. The ceremony would be at the magnificent Bar-T Ranch south of Laurel Town on 20 October. Given the continuing clement weather, the ceremony would take place on the expansive lawns of the estate at 2 p.m. before an invited thousand guests who would include the social cream and business elite of the state of Montana. She went on like this to the bottom of the page. Ben Craig nodded and memorized.

The next day the post commander addressed them all on the parade ground. The Fort Heritage summer experience would close for the winter months on 21 October, he said. It had been an outstanding success and messages of congratulations had flowed from educators and legislators across the state.

'There will be much hard work to do in the four days prior to closure,' Professor Ingles told his young team. 'Salaries and wages will be paid out on the day before. We have to get the facility cleaned, stored and ready for the hard winter before we go.'

Afterwards Charlie took Ben Craig aside.

'Well, Ben, we're coming to the end,' she said. 'When it's over we can all go back to wearing our normal clothes. Oh, I suppose those are your normal clothes. Well, you have a wad of dollars coming. We can go into Billings and get you some sneakers, jeans, a selection of sports shirts and a couple of warm jackets for the winter.

'Then I want you to come back to Bozeman with me. I'll find you nice lodgings and then introduce you to some people who can help you.'

'Very well, Charlie,' he said.

That evening he tapped on the professor's door. John Ingles was sitting at his desk. A wood-burning pot-bellied stove glowed in the corner to take the chill off the evening air. The professor welcomed his buckskin-clad visitor warmly. He had been impressed by the lad, by his knowledge of the wild and the old frontier and the fact that never once had he slipped out of character. With his knowledge and a college degree, the professor could have found him a post on campus.

'Ben, my boy, how can I help you?'

He expected to be able to dispense some fatherly advice for the future.

'Would you have a map, Major?'

'A map? Well, good Lord. Yes, I suppose I do. Which area?'

'Here at the fort, and north to the Yellowstone, please, sir.'

'Good idea. Always useful to know where one is, and the surrounding country. Here.'

He spread the map out on the desk and explained. Craig had seen campaign maps before, but they were mostly blank except for landmarks noted by a few trappers and scouts. This one was covered with lines and blobs.

'Here is the fort, on the north side of West Pryor Mountain, facing north to the Yellowstone and south to the Pryors. Here is Billings, and here is where I come from, Bozeman.'

Craig ran his finger the hundred miles between the two towns.

'The Bozeman Trail?' he asked.

'Quite right, that's what it used to be called. A blacktop highway now, of course.'

Craig did not know what a blacktop highway was, but thought it might be the long strip of black rock he had seen in the moonlight. There were dozens of smaller towns shown on the large-scale map and, on the southern bank of the Yellowstone, at the confluence with Clark's Creek, an estate marked Bar-T Ranch. He reckoned it to be a tad to the west of a line due north from the fort and, cross-country, twenty miles. He thanked the major and handed back the map.

On the night of the 19th Ben Craig turned in early, just after chow time. No-one thought it odd. All the young men had spent the day cleaning up, greasing metal parts against the winter frosts, storing tools in secure cabins for next spring. The others in the bunkhouse came to bed around ten and quickly fell asleep. None noticed that their companion, beneath his blanket, was fully clothed.

He rose at midnight, slipped his fox hat on his head, folded two blankets and left without making a sound. No-one saw him cross to the stable, let himself in, and start to saddle Rosebud. He had made sure she had a double ration of oats for the extra strength she would need.

When she was ready he left her there, let himself into the smith's forge and took the items he had noted the previous day: a hand-axe with belt sheath, a jemmy and metal cutters.

The jemmy took the hasp and padlock off the armoury door, and once inside the cutters made short work of the chain threaded through the trigger guards of the rifles. They were all replicas but one. He took his Sharps '52 model back and left.

He led Rosebud to the small rear door by the chapel, unbarred it and walked out. His two blankets were under his saddle, the buffalo robe rolled and tied behind. The rifle in its sheath hung forward of his left knee and by his right knee hung a rawhide quiver with four arrows. His bow swung from his back. When he had walked his horse half a mile from the fort in silence he mounted up.

In this manner Ben Craig, frontiersman and scout, the only man to survive the massacre at the Little Bighorn, rode out of the year of grace 1877 and into the last quarter of the twentieth century.

By the setting of the moon he reckoned it was two in the morning. He had time to walk the twenty miles to the Bar-T Ranch and save Rosebud's energy. He found the pole star and headed a few degrees to the west of the due-north path it indicated.

The prairie gave way to farmland and here and there he found posts in his way, with wire strung between them. He used the cutters and walked on.

He crossed the line from Bighorn into Yellowstone County, but he knew nothing of that. At dawn he found the banks of Clark's Creek and followed the curving stream north. As the sun tipped the hills to the east he spied a long stretch of bright white post-and-rail fencing and a sign announcing: 'Bar-T Ranch. Private Property. Keep out.' He deciphered the letters and walked on until he found the private road leading to the main gate.

At half a mile he could see the gate, and beyond it an enormous house surrounded by magnificent barns and stables. At the gate there was a striped pole across the road and a guardhouse. In the window was a low night light. He withdrew another half-mile to a stand of trees, unsaddled Rosebud and let her rest and crop the autumn grass. He rested through the morning but did not sleep, remaining alert like a wild animal.

In truth the newspaper diarist had underestimated the splendour Big Bill Braddock planned for his son's wedding.

He had insisted that his son's fiancée undergo a thorough examination at the hands of his family doctor, and the humiliated girl had had no choice but to concede. When he read the full report, his eyebrows rose.

'She's what?' he asked the doctor. The medical man followed where the sausage finger pointed.

'Oh yes, no question about it. Completely intacta.'

Braddock leered.

'Well, lucky young Kevin. And the rest?'

'Flawless. A very beautiful and healthy young woman.'

The mansion had been transformed by the most fashionable interior designers money could hire into a fairy-tale castle. Out on the acre-sized lawn the altar had been set up twenty yards from the rail fence, facing the prairie. In front of the altar were row upon row of comfortable chairs for his guests, with an aisle down the centre for the loving couple to walk, Kevin first, attended by his best man, she and her nincompoop father to join them to the strains of the Bridal March.

The buffet banquet was to be laid out on trestle tables behind the chairs. No expense had been spared. There were pyramids of champagne glasses in Stuart crystal, oceans of French champagne of an eyebrow-raising marque and all vintage. He was determined his most sophisticated guest would not find a single detail amiss.

From Seattle arctic lobster, crab and oysters had been flown on ice. For those who preferred something stronger than champagne there was Chivas Regal by the crate. As he clambered into his four-poster the night before the wedding, Big Bill was worried only about his son. The boy had been drunk again and would need an hour in the shower to shape up in the morning.

To entertain his guests further, as the married couple changed for their departure on honeymoon to a private island in the Bahamas, Braddock had planned a Wild West rodeo right next to the gardens. These troupers, like the caterers and their staff, were all hired. The only people Braddock did not hire were the security detail.

Obsessive about his personal security, he maintained his own private army. Apart from three or four who stayed close to him at all times, the rest worked as wranglers on the ranch, but they were trained in firearms, had combat experience and would follow orders to the letter. They were paid to do so.

For the wedding he had brought all thirty of them into close proximity to the house. Two manned the guard post on the main gate. His personal protection detail, headed by an ex-Green Beret, would be near him. The rest posed as stewards and ushers.

Throughout the morning a stream of limousines and luxury coaches detailed to pick up guests from the airport at Billings cruised up to the main gate, were checked and passed through. Craig watched from deep cover. Just after midday the preacher arrived, followed by the musicians.

Another column of catering vans and the rodeo performers came through a different gate, but they were out of sight. Shortly after one, the musicians began tuning up. Craig heard the sound and saddled up.

He turned Rosebud's head towards the open prairie and rode round the perimeter fence until the guardhouse dropped out of sight. Then he headed for the white rails, moving from a trot to a canter. Rosebud saw the rails approaching, adjusted her stride and sailed over. The scout found himself in a large paddock, a quarter-mile from the outlying barns. A herd of prize longhorn steers grazed.

At the far side of the field Craig found the gate to the barn complex, opened it and left it that way. As he moved through the barns and across flagstoned courtyards two patrolling guards hailed him.

'You must be part of the cabaret?'

Craig stared and nodded.

'You're in the wrong place. Go down there and you'll see the rest of them at the back of the house.'

Craig headed down the alley, waited till they had moved on, then turned back. He headed for the music. He could not recognize the Bridal March.

At the altar Kevin Braddock stood with his best man, immaculate in white tuxedo. Eight inches shorter than his father and fifty pounds lighter, he had narrow shoulders and wide hips. Several zits, to which he was prone, adorned his cheeks, partly masked by dabs of his mother's face powder.

Mrs Pickett and the Braddock parents sat in the front row, separated by the aisle. At the far end of that aisle Linda Pickett appeared on the arm of her father. She was ethereally beautiful in a white silk wedding gown flown from Balenciaga in Paris. Her face was pale and set. She stared ahead with no smile.

A thousand heads turned to look as she began the walk down the aisle to the altar. Behind the rows of guests serried ranks of waiters and waitresses stood watching. Behind them appeared a lone rider.

Michael Pickett delivered his daughter to stand

beside Kevin Braddock, then seated himself beside his wife. She was dabbing her eyes. The preacher raised his eyes and voice.

'Dearly beloved, we are gathered here this day to join this man and this woman in Holy Matrimony,' he said when the music of the march had faded. If he saw the rider facing him fifty yards down the aisle he may have been puzzled but gave no sign. A dozen waiters were nudged aside as the horse moved forward several paces. Even the dozen bodyguards round the perimeter of the lawn were staring at the couple facing the preacher.

The preacher went on.

'. . . into which holy estate these two persons present come now to be joined.'

Mrs Pickett was sobbing openly. Braddock glared across at her. The preacher was surprised to see a slow tear well from each of the bride's eyes and flow down her cheeks. He presumed she too was overcome with joy.

'Therefore, if any man can show any just cause why they may not lawfully be joined together, let him now speak, or else hereafter for ever hold his peace.'

He raised his eyes from the text and beamed at his congregation.

'I so speak. She is betrothed to me.'

The voice was young and strong, and it carried to every corner of the lawn as the horse surged forward. Waiters were knocked flying. Two body-guards launched themselves at the horseman. Each took a flying kick in the face and went backwards

410

among the last two rows of guests. Men shouted, women screamed, the preacher's mouth was a perfect O.

Rosebud moved from trot to canter to gallop in seconds. Her rider reined her back in and hauled the bridle to his left. With his right arm he reached down, encircled the slim, silk-clad waist and pulled the girl up. For a second she swung across the front of his body, then slipped behind, threw a leg over the buffalo roll, clamped her arms around him and hung on.

The horse charged past the front row, cleared the white rail fence and galloped away through the belly-high grass of the prairie beyond. The scene on the lawn degenerated into utter chaos.

The guests were all upright, screaming and shouting. The longhorn herd trotted round the corner and onto the trim grass. One of Braddock's four men, seated far down the row from his master, ran past the preacher, drew a handgun and took careful aim at the disappearing horse. Michael Pickett let out a shout of 'No-o-o-o', threw himself at the gunman, seized his arm and jerked it upwards. The gun fired three shots as they wrestled.

That was enough for the congregation, and the steers. All stampeded. Chairs crumbled, salvers of lobster and crab were tossed aside to spill on the lawn. A local mayor was thrown through a pyramid of Stuart crystal and went down in an expensive shower of trash. The preacher dived under the altar, where he met the bridegroom.

Out on the main driveway two patrol cars from

411

the local sheriff's office were parked, with four troopers. They were there to guide traffic and had been invited in for a snack lunch. They heard the shots, glanced at each other, threw their burgers away and ran for the lawn.

At the edge of the lawn one of them cannoned into a fleeing waiter. He jerked the man upright by his white jacket.

'What the hell just happened here?' he demanded. The other three stared open-mouthed at the bedlam. The senior deputy listened to the waiter and told one of his colleagues: 'Get back to the car and tell the sheriff we have a problem here.'

Sheriff Paul Lewis would not normally have been in his office on a Saturday afternoon, but he had paperwork he wanted to clear before starting the new week. It was twenty after two when the head of the duty deputy came round the office door.

'There's a problem out at the Bar-T.'

He was holding a phone in his hand.

'You know, the Braddock wedding? Ed is on the line. Says the bride's just been kidnapped.'

'Been WHAT? Put him on my line.'

The red light flashed as the transfer came through. He snatched the handset.

'Ed, Paul. What the hell are you talking about?'

He listened while his man at the ranch reported. Like all peace officers, he loathed the idea of kidnapping. For one thing it was a filthy crime, usually directed at the wives and children of the rich; for another it was a federal offence and that meant the Bureau would be all over him like a rash. In thirty years of service to Carbon County, ten of them as sheriff, he had known three takings of hostages, all resolved without fatalities, but never yet a kidnapping. He presumed a team of gangsters with fast cars, even a helicopter, were involved.

'A lone horseman? Are you out of your mind? Where did he go? . . . Over the fence and away across the prairie. OK, he must have hidden a car somewhere. I'll call in some out-of-county help and block the main roads. Look, Ed, get statements from everyone who saw anything: how he got in, what he did, how he subdued the girl, how he got away. Call me back.'

He spent half an hour calling in reserves and arranging patrol cars on the main highways out of Carbon County, north, south, east and west. The Highway Patrol troopers were told to check every vehicle and every trunk. They were looking for a beautiful brunette in a white silk dress. It was just after three when Ed called back from his car at the Bar-T.

'This is getting very weird, chief. We have near twenty statements from eyewitnesses. The rider got in because everyone thought he was part of the Wild West rodeo show. He was dressed in buckskin, riding a big chestnut mare. He had a fur-trapper's hat, a feather hanging from the back of his head and a bow.'

'A bow? What kind of a bow? Pink ribbon?'

'Not that kind of a bow, chief. A bow as in bow and arrow. It gets stranger.'

'It can't. But go on.'

413

'All the witnesses say when he charged up to the altar and reached down for the girl, she reached up to him. They say she seemed to know him and wrapped her arms round him as they went over the fence. If she hadn't she'd have fallen off and be here now.'

A huge weight lifted off the sheriff. With a bit of luck he did not have a kidnap, he had an elopement. He began to grin.

'Now are they all sure about that, Ed? He didn't hit her, knock her cold, throw her over his saddle-bow, hold her prisoner as he rode?'

'Apparently not. Mind you, he has caused an awesome amount of damage. The wedding ceremony was wrecked, the banquet pretty smashed up, the bridegroom pissed and the bride gone.'

The sheriff's grin widened.

'Why, that's terrible,' he said. 'Do we know who he is?'

'Maybe. The bride's father said his daughter had a kinda crush on one of those young actors they've had out at Fort Heritage all summer, posing as frontiersmen. You know?'

Lewis knew all about the fort. His daughter had taken his grandchildren out for a day and they had loved it.

'Anyway, she broke off her engagement to Kevin Braddock because of this. Her parents persuaded her she was crazy and the engagement resumed. They say he's called Ben Craig.'

The deputy went back to his statement-taking, and Sheriff Lewis was about to try to contact

Fort Heritage when Professor Ingles came on the line.

'This may be nothing,' he began, 'but one of my young staff has quit and run. During the night.'

'Did he steal anything, Professor?'

'Well, no, not as such. He has his own horse and clothes. But he also has a rifle. I had confiscated it for the duration. He broke into the armoury and took it back.'

'What does he need it for?'

'Hunting, I hope. He's a nice young man but a bit wild. He was born and raised in the Pryor Range. His folk seem to have been mountain people. He never even went to school.'

'Look, Professor, this could be serious. Could this young man turn dangerous?'

'Oh, I hope not.'

'What else is he carrying?'

'Well, he has a bowie knife, and a hand-axe is missing. Plus a Cheyenne bow and four arrows with flint heads.'

'He took your antiques?'

'No, he made them himself.'

The sheriff counted to five, slowly.

'Would this by chance be Ben Craig?'

'Yes, how did you know?'

'Just keep helping, Professor. Did he start a love affair with a pretty young schoolteacher from Billings who came out to the fort?'

He heard the academic conferring with someone in the background called Charlie.

'It seems he developed a deep affection for such

415

a girl. He thought she accepted him, but I am informed she wrote him to break it all off. He took it badly. He even asked where and when her wedding would take place. I hope he hasn't made a fool of himself.'

'Not quite. He's just snatched her from the altar.'

'Oh my God.'

'Look, could he switch from horse to car?'

'Heavens, no. He can't drive. Never been in one. He'll stay on his beloved horse and camp out in the wild.'

'Where will he head?'

'Almost certainly south, to the Pryors. He's hunted and trapped there all his life.'

'Thank you, Professor, you've been most helpful.'

He called off the roadblocks and telephoned the Carbon County helicopter pilot, asking him to get airborne and check in. Then he waited for the inevitable call from Big Bill Braddock.

Sheriff Paul Lewis was a good peace officer, unflappable, firm but kindly. He preferred to help people out rather than lock them up, but the law was the law and he had no hesitation in enforcing it.

His grandfather had been a soldier with the cavalry who had died on the plains, leaving a widow and baby son at Fort Lincoln. The war widow had married another soldier who had been posted west into Montana. His father had been raised in the state and married twice. By the first marriage in 1900 there had been two daughters. After his wife's death he had married again and at the mature age of forty-five had sired his only son in 1920.

Sheriff Lewis was in his fifty-eighth year and would retire in two more. After that, he knew of certain lakes in Montana and Wyoming whose cut-throat trout would benefit from his personal attention.

He had not been invited to the wedding and entertained no sense of puzzlement as to why not. Four times over the years he or his men had investigated drunken brawls involving Kevin Braddock. In each case the bartenders had been well recompensed and had preferred no charges. The sheriff was pretty relaxed about young men in fist-fights, but less so when Braddock Junior beat up a bar girl who had refused his rather peculiar tastes.

The sheriff had thrown him in the slammer and would have proceeded with charges on his own, but the girl suddenly changed her mind and recalled that she had simply fallen downstairs.

There was another piece of information the sheriff had never divulged to anyone. Three years earlier he had had a call from a friend on the Helena City force. They had been at police college together.

The colleague related that his officers had raided a nightclub. It had been a drug bust. The names and addresses of all present had been taken. One was Kevin Braddock. If he had had any drugs he had got rid of his stash in time and had to be released. But the club had been exclusively gay.

The phone rang. It was Mr Valentino, Big Bill Braddock's personal lawyer.

'You may have heard what happened here this afternoon, Sheriff. Your deputies were present minutes later.'

'I heard not all went according to plan.'

'Please do not patronize, Sheriff Lewis. What happened was a case of brutal kidnap and the criminal must be caught.'

'I hear you, Counsellor. But I have a sheaf of statements from guests and catering staff to the effect that the young lady co-operated in mounting the horse and that she had had a love affair with this young man, the horse-rider, before. That looks to me more like an elopement.'

'Weasel words, Sheriff. If the girl had wished to break off her engagement there was nothing to stop her. This girl was snatched with physical force. The criminal committed trespass to get in here, kicked two of Mr Braddock's staff in the face and did an impressive amount of malicious damage to private property. Mr Braddock intends to press charges. Will you bring this hooligan in, or shall we?'

Sheriff Lewis did not like being threatened.

'I hope you and your client are not thinking of taking the law into your own hands, Counsellor? That could be most unwise.'

The lawyer ignored the counter-threat.

'Mr Braddock is deeply concerned for the safety of his daughter-in-law. He is within his right to search for her.'

'Was the wedding ceremony complete?'

'Was it what?'

'Are your client's son and Miss Pickett actually married in law?'

'Well . . .'

'In that case she is not your client's daughter-in-law. She is no relation.'

'Until further information she is still my client's son's fiancée. He is acting as a concerned citizen. Now are you going to bring this hooligan in? There is always Helena.'

Sheriff Lewis sighed. He knew how much influence Bill Braddock had with some legislators in the state capital. He was not afraid of that either. But this young man, Ben Craig, had undoubtedly committed offences.

'As soon as he can be traced, I'll be there,' he said. As he put the phone down he thought it might be wise for him to get to the lovebirds before Braddock's men. His helicopter pilot came on the line. It was nearly four, with two hours to go before sundown and the fading of the light.

'Jerry, I want you to find the Bar-T Ranch. Then fly south towards the Pryors. Keep an eye open in front and to both sides.'

'What am I looking for, Paul?'

'A lone rider, heading south, probably for the mountains. There's a girl mounted up behind him in a white wedding dress.'

'Are you putting me on?'

'Nope. Some saddle-bum just snatched the fiancée of Bill Braddock's son from the altar.'

'I think I like the guy already,' said the police officer as he left the Billings Airfield area.

'Just find him for me, Jerry.'

'No sweat. If he's there I'll find him. Out.'

The pilot was over the Bar-T five minutes later

419

and set his course due south. He maintained 1,000 feet, low enough to give him a good view of any moving rider below him and high enough to cover a ten-mile-wide swathe to left and right.

To his right he could see Highway 310 and the rail line running south towards the village of Warren and on into Wyoming via the flat country. Ahead he could see the peaks of the Pryors.

In case the rider had tried to evade detection by veering west across the road, Sheriff Lewis asked the Highway Patrol to cruise down the 310 and keep an eye open on both sides of the road for the torso of a rider above the prairie grass.

Big Bill Braddock had not been idle. Leaving his staff to cope with the anarchy on his lawn, he and his security men had gone straight to his office. Never a man known for his good humour, those around him had still not ever seen him in such a towering rage. For a while he sat at his desk in silence. There were a dozen grouped round him, waiting for orders.

'What do we do, boss?' asked one eventually.

'Think,' snarled the rancher. 'Think. He's a man alone on a horse, heavy-laden. Limited range. Where would he go?'

The former Green Beret, Max, studied a wall map of the county.

'Not north. He'd have to cross the Yellowstone. Too deep. So, south. Back to that replica fort in the hills?'

'Right. I want ten men, mounted and armed. Go south, spread out over a five-mile front. Ride like hell. Overtake him.'

When the ten wranglers were saddled up he addressed them outside.

'You each have radiophones. Stay in touch. If you see him, call for back-up. When you corner him, get the girl back. If he attempts to threaten her, or you, you know what to do. I think you know what I mean. I want the girl back, no-one else. Go.'

The ten riders cantered out the main gate, fanned out and broke into a gallop. The fugitive had a forty-minute start but he was carrying two riders and saddlebags, a rifle and heavy buffalo hide.

Inside the ranch lawyer Valentino reported back.

'The sheriff seems pretty relaxed about it all. But he is going to mount a search. Patrol cars on the roads and probably a helicopter,' he said.

'I don't want him to get there first,' snapped Braddock. 'But I do want to know what information he gets. Max, get to the radio shack. I want a band-sweep of every police channel in the county. Permanent listening watch. Get my own helo up in the air. Get ahead of the riders. Find the bastard. Guide them to him. We'll need more than one. Rent two more out of the airport. Go. Now.'

They were all wrong. The professor, the sheriff, Braddock. The frontiersman was not heading for the Pryors. He knew that was too obvious.

Five miles south of the ranch he had stopped, taken one of his saddle blankets and wrapped it round Whispering Wind. It was bright red but it hid the glaring white of the dress. But he had never heard of helicopters. After the halt he slanted south-west towards where he recalled having crossed a long strip of black rock the previous spring.

At a mile, he could make out a row of upright posts with wires strung between them. They ran across his front as far as the eye could see. They were the phone lines running above the Burlington rail line that paralleled the highway.

At half past three Jerry called in from his hovering Sikorsky.

'Paul, I thought you said there was a lone rider? There's a goddamn army down here.'

Braddock's pursuers, thought the sheriff.

'What do you have, exactly, Jerry?'

The voice crackled over the distance.

'I count at least eight riders abreast, galloping south. Ranch hands by the look. And they're travelling light. Also, there's another helo, up ahead, hovering over the foothills, close to that replica fort.'

Lewis swore softly. He wished now he were with the helicopter instead of stuck in an office.

'Jerry, if the fugitives are up ahead, try and get to them first. If Braddock's hoods get to the boy he won't be worth squat.'

'You got it, Paul. I'll keep looking.'

In the ranch house the head of the radio operator came round the door.

'Mr Braddock, sir, the sheriff's helicopter is right over our own team.'

'That makes an eyewitness,' said Max.

'Tell my boys to keep looking,' snapped Braddock. 'We'll sort out any court case later.'

Sheriff Lewis was glad he had stayed in overall control in his office when a call came through at five minutes before five. An excited voice shouted, 'Got 'em.'

'Speaker, identify.'

'Car Tango One. On the Three-Ten. He just crossed the highway, riding south-west. Caught a glimpse before he went behind some trees.'

'Where on the Three-Ten?'

'Four miles north of Bridger.'

'Confirm the target is now west of the highway,' ordered Lewis.

'That is affirmative, Sheriff.'

'Stay on the highway in case he doubles back.'

'Ten-four.'

Sheriff Lewis studied his wall map. If the rider continued on his track he would come up against another rail line and the much bigger Interstate 212 running right through the mountains to Park County, Wyoming.

There were two Highway Patrol cars cruising the interstate. He asked them to move further south and keep their eyes open for someone trying to cross from east to west. Then he called up his helicopter pilot.

'Jerry, he's been seen. Well to your west. He just crossed the Three-Ten riding south-west. Can you get over there? About four miles north of Bridger. He's back in open country again.'

'OK, Paul, but I'm going to have a fuel problem soon and the light is fading fast.'

The sheriff looked again at the tiny community of Bridger.

'There's an airstrip at Bridger. Go to the limit of your fuel, then put down there. You may have to spend the night. I'll tell Janey.'

In the ranch house it had all been heard. Max studied the map.

'He's not going for the Pryors. Too obvious. He's heading for the Wilderness and the Beartooth Range. He figures to ride right through the range into Wyoming and lose himself. Clever. That's what I'd do.'

Braddock's operator told the ten horsemen to turn due west, cross the highway and resume looking. They agreed to that, but forbore to warn him that they had ridden their mounts so hard for fifteen miles that they were in danger of breaking down. And darkness was closing in.

'We should get a couple of cars with men in them down the interstate,' said Max. 'He'll have to cross it if he wants to make the Wilderness.'

Two big off-road vehicles were despatched with eight more men in them.

Approaching the interstate, Ben Craig dismounted, climbed a tree on a small knoll and studied the barrier. It was raised above the plain and a train track, another spur of the Burlington line, ran beside it. Occasionally a vehicle would pass, heading north or south. All around him were the badlands, rough country of creeks, rocks and ungrazed prairie grass, belly-high to a horse. He descended and from his saddlebag took his packet of steel and flint.

There was a light breeze from the east, and when

the fire took hold it spread to cover a mile-wide front and moved towards the road. Billows of smoke rose into the darkening sky. The breeze bore them west, faster than the advancing fire, and the road disappeared.

The patrol car five miles to the north saw the smoke and came south to investigate. As the smoke thickened and darkened the patrolmen stopped, a mite too late. Within seconds they were enveloped in the clouds. There was nothing for it but to back up.

The tractor-trailer heading south for Wyoming tried really hard to avoid the tail lights when the driver saw them. The brakes worked perfectly and the semi stopped. The one behind it was not so lucky.

Tractor-trailers are very adaptable, until they jackknife. The second rig hit the first and both performed that manoeuvre, slewing across the centre line and blocking the highway in both directions. Given the escarpments on both sides, driving around the blockage was not an option.

The patrol officers were able to make one radio call before they had to quit their vehicle and join the truck drivers further up the road, out of the smoke pall.

The message was enough. Fire trucks and heavy lifting gear soon headed south to cope with the emergency. It took all night but they had the road open again by dawn. Messages flashed to Wyoming halted all traffic south of the mountains. Only those already on the road were marooned for the night.

In the confusion, invisible in the smoke, a single rider trotted across the highway and into the wild country to the west. The man had a kerchief across his face and the girl who rode behind him was shielded by a blanket.

West of the highway the rider dismounted. The muscles beneath Rosebud's gleaming coat were trembling with exhaustion and there were ten miles yet to the cover of the timber. Whispering Wind eased herself forward into the saddle but she was half her lover's weight.

She slipped the blanket from her shoulders and sat shimmering white in the dusk, her unleashed hair flowing to her waist.

'Ben, where are we going?'

For answer he pointed to the south. In the last rays of the setting sun the peaks of the Beartooth Range rose like flames above the forest line, sentinels of another and better life.

'Through the mountains, into Wyoming. No-one will find us there. I will build you a cabin and hunt and fish for you. We will be free and live for ever.'

Then she smiled, for she loved him very much, and believed his promise, and was happy again.

Braddock's personal pilot had had no choice but to turn back. His fuel was low and the ground below was too dark to make out details. He landed at the ranch on the last of his reserve.

The ten riders limped into the little community of Bridger on their exhausted horses and asked for lodgings. They ate at the diner and made beds in their own saddle blankets.

Jerry put the sheriff's helicopter down at Bridger airstrip and was offered a bed for the night by the manager.

At the ranch it was the former Green Beret who took over the planning. Ten of the private army were stranded at Bridger with exhausted horses; eight more were marooned in their vehicles upstream of the blockage on the interstate. Both sets would be there all night. Max faced Bill Braddock and the remaining twelve. He was in his element, planning a campaign, just like in Vietnam. A large map of the county adorned the wall.

'Plan One,' he said. 'Cut off the pass – literally. Right here there is a deep cleft or defile running right through the range into Wyoming. It is called Rock Creek. Beside it runs the highway, twisting and winding until it emerges on the south side.

'He may try to ride along the grass edging the highway to avoid the high country on either side. As soon as the blockage on the interstate is clear, our boys need to race down here, overtaking everything in their path, and stake out the road at the state line. If he appears, they know what to do.'

'Agreed,' growled Braddock. 'Supposing he tries to ride through during the night?'

'He can't, sir. That horse of his must be on its last legs. I figure he crossed the road because he is heading for the forest, then the mountains. As you see, he has to penetrate the expanse of the Custer National Forest, climbing all the way, crossing the defile called West Fork and then more climbing to emerge on this plateau, the Silver Run. Hence Plan Two.

'We use the two rented helicopters to overfly him, picking up the ten men at Bridger on their way. These men are set down in a skirmish line across this plateau. When he emerges from the forest onto the rock, he'll be a sitting target for men crouching behind boulders halfway across.'

'Order it,' said Braddock. 'What else?'

'Plan Three, sir. The rest of us enter the forest on horses at dawn behind him and flush him upwards to the plateau at the top. Either way, we'll hunt him down like game.'

'And if he turns on us in the forest?'

Max smiled with pleasure.

'Why, sir, I am a jungle-trained fighter. There are three or four others who did time in 'Nam. I want them all with us. If he tries to make a stand in the timber, he's mine.'

'How do we get the horses down there with the road blocked?' asked one of the others.

Max's finger traced a fine line on the map.

'There's a small secondary road. Runs from the Billings highway fifteen miles west of here, through the badlands to terminate here at Red Lodge, right at the neck of the Rock Creek defile. We drive them down in trailers through the night, mount up at dawn and go after him. Now I suggest we sleep for four hours and rise at midnight.'

Braddock nodded his agreement. 'One other thing, Major. I'm coming with you and so is Kevin. Time we both saw the end of the man who humiliated me today.'

Sheriff Lewis also had a map, and he had come to

similar conclusions. He asked for co-operation from the town of Red Lodge and was promised a dozen mounts, fresh and saddled, for sunup. Jerry would refuel at the same time and be ready for take-off.

The sheriff checked with the emergency service working on the interstate and was told they would have a clear road by four in the morning. He asked that his own two cars be allowed through first. He could be at Red Lodge by four thirty.

He had no trouble finding volunteers even for a Sunday. Policing a county of peaceable folk can be short of really eventful days, but a true manhunt usually set the adrenalin running. Apart from Jerry above him, he had on call a private pilot with a high-wing spotter plane and would have ten men with him for the ground pursuit. That should be enough for one rider. He stared long and hard at the map.

'Please don't go into the forest, kid,' he murmured. 'You could be awfully hard to find in there.'

As he was speaking Ben Craig and Whispering Wind made it to the forest line and disappeared into the trees. It was pitch dark under the canopy of the spruce and lodgepole pine. Half a mile in, Craig made camp. He relieved the tired Rosebud of her saddle, the girl, rifle and blankets. Among the trees Rosebud found a rill of fresh water and juicy pine needles. She began to rest and recover.

The scout lit no fire but Whispering Wind needed none. She curled in the buffalo robe and fell asleep. Craig took his axe and trotted away. He was gone six hours. When he returned he catnapped for an hour, then broke camp. He knew that somewhere up ahead was the creek where he had delayed the cavalry and the Cheyenne a long time ago. He wanted to cross it and gain the farther bank before his pursuers could come within rifle range.

Rosebud was fresher, if not fully recovered from her marathon of the previous day. He led her by the bridle. Despite her rest the strength was flowing out of her, and they had many miles to go to reach the safety of the peaks.

He marched for an hour, sensing his direction from the stars glimpsed through the treetops. Far away to the east, above the sacred Black Hills of Dakota, the sun pinked the sky. He came to the first defile across his path, the precipitous gully called West Fork.

He knew he had been here before. There was a way across if only he could find it again. It took an hour. Rosebud drank from the cool water and, slipping and scrabbling for a foothold, they clambered up the far bank to the high ground.

Craig gave Rosebud a further rest and found a hidden place where he could stare down at the creek. He wanted to see how many were coming after him. They would be on fresh horses, that was sure, but something was different. These pursuers had strange metal boxes that flew in the sky like eagles beneath whirling wings and they roared like bull moose in the rut. He had seen these flying boxes over the badlands the day before.

True to their promise the emergency services cleared the interstate for traffic just after four in the

430

morning. Guided by a Highway Patrol officer, Sheriff Lewis's two cars threaded through the tangle of gridlocked vehicles to the head of the line and set off for Red Lodge fifteen miles to the south.

Eight minutes later they were overtaken by two large off-road trucks travelling at dangerous speed.

'Shall we go after them?' asked the police driver.

'Let them go,' said the sheriff.

The off-roads roared through the waking township of Red Lodge and headed into the canyon where the interstate bordered Rock Creek.

The gulch became narrower and the slopes more vertical, with a clear drop of 500 feet into the creek on the right-hand side and the sheer face of the wooded mountains on the left. The hairpin bends became tighter and tighter.

The leading vehicle came round the fifth hairpin too fast and too late to see the freshly felled pine lying across the road. The body of the off-road made it to the southern side but the four wheels remained on the north. There were five men in the truck and they had ten legs between them. Four were broken, to which could be added three arms, two collarbones and a dislocated pelvis.

The driver of the second vehicle had a clear choice: to pull right and drop into the creek or pull left into the mountainside. He pulled left. The mountain won.

Ten minutes later the least injured man was staggering back up the highway to seek help when the first tractor-trailer came round a bend. The brakes were still working perfectly. It stopped in time but jackknifed. Then the trailer, as if in silent protest at these indignities, rolled sedately onto its side.

Sheriff Lewis and his party of seven deputies had arrived in Red Lodge to be met by the local officer with a string of borrowed horses. There were also two Forest Rangers. One of them spread a map over the hood of a car and pointed to the landmarks in the Custer National Forest.

'The forest is bisected, east to west, by this creek, the West Fork,' he said. 'This side of the fork there are tracks and campsites for summer visitors. Cross the creek and you are into real wilderness. If your man has done that, we will have to go in there after him. It's no-vehicle country, which is why we have the horses.'

'How dense is it in there?'

'It's thick,' said the ranger. 'What with the warm weather the broadleaf trees are still in foliage. Then comes the pine forest, then the rock plateau all the way to the high peaks. Can your man survive in there?'

'From what I hear, he was born and raised in the wilderness,' sighed the sheriff.

'Not a problem, we have modern technology,' said the other ranger. 'Helicopters, spotter planes, walkie-talkies. We'll find him for you.'

The party was about to leave the cars and move off when a message came through from the sheriff's office. It was a patch-through from the air traffic controller at Billings Field.

'I have two big helos waiting for take-off,' said the man in the control tower. He and Sheriff Lewis had known each other for years. They fished trout together, and there are few stronger bonds.

'I'd have let them go but they have been rented by Bill Braddock. They have filed flight plans for Bridger. Jerry says you have a problem down there. Something about the Bar-T wedding? It's on all the morning news.'

'Stall them. Give me ten minutes.'

'You got it.' To the waiting helicopter pilots the controller said, 'Clearance delayed. We have an incomer joining the circuit.'

Sheriff Lewis recalled Jerry telling him about a skein of armed riders heading south from the ranch in pursuit of the runaways. They would logically have been caught by the darkness far from home and would have spent the night in the open prairie or at Bridger. But if they were recalled to the ranch, why not ride there on rested horses? He asked for a call to another friend, the head of the FAA in Helena. The official came on the line after being woken in his home.

'This had better be good, Paul. I like my Sundays.'

'I have a little problem with two runaways who have decided to head into the Absaroka Wilderness. I'm going in with a party of deputies and a couple of rangers to bring them back. There are some concerned citizens around here who seem to want to turn it into a turkey shoot. And the media will be along later. Could you declare the Wilderness area off limits for today?'

'Sure.'

'There are two helos at Billings Field waiting take-off.'

'Who's in the tower at Billings?'

'Chip Anderson.'

'Leave it to me.'

Ten minutes later the helicopters received a call from the tower.

'Sorry about that. The incomer turned away. You are cleared for take-off, subject to the FAA Exclusion Zone.'

'What Exclusion Zone?'

'The whole Absaroka Wilderness up to five thousand feet.'

In matters of air space and in-air safety the word of the Federal Aeronautics Administration is law. The hired pilots had no intention of losing their licences. The engines were switched off and the rotors slowly wound down.

Big Bill Braddock and his remaining ten men had arrived in the pre-dawn along the secondary road that approached Red Lodge from the north-west. Five miles from the town, on the edge of the forest, they unloaded the horses from the trailers, checked their weapons, mounted up and went into the trees.

Braddock also had portable transceivers and was in touch with his radio room at the ranch. As dawn lightened the canopy of trees above the riders he learned he had ten men being stretchered off the interstate in the middle of Rock Creek and another ten stranded at Bridger without air transport to bring them over the fugitives to the rock plateau. The major's Plans One and Two were history.

'We'll go get the bastard ourselves,' growled the cattleman. His son, ill at ease in the saddle, took a swig from his hip flask. The posse rode into the forest in a quarter-mile-wide chain, scanning the ground for fresh hoof marks. After thirty minutes one of them found the spoor, the marks of Rosebud's hoofs and, leading them, the footprint of what could have been a moccasin. Using his communicator, he called the others over to join him. After that they followed as a group. A mile behind, Sheriff Lewis and his party rode in.

It took the sharp eyes of the rangers less time, ten minutes.

'How many horses does this man have?' asked one.

'Just the one,' said Lewis.

'There's more than one set of tracks here,' said the ranger. 'I count four at least.'

'Damn the man,' said the sheriff. He used his transceiver to call his office and ask for a phone-through to Counsellor Valentino at his private home.

'My client is profoundly worried for this young lady's safety, Sheriff Lewis. He may have mounted a search party. I assure you he is entirely within his rights.'

'Counsellor, if any harm comes to these young people, if either of them is killed, I'm going to be looking at murder in the first. You just tell your client that.'

He switched off before the lawyer could protest.

'Paul, this guy has kidnapped a girl and he does

have a rifle,' murmured the senior deputy, Tom Barrow. 'Seems we may have to shoot first and ask questions afterwards.'

'There's a mass of statements that the girl jumped on his horse,' snapped Lewis. 'I do not want to blow some kid away for a mess of broken glass.'

'And two kicks in the face.'

'All right, and two kicks in the face.'

'And a prairie fire, and a closedown of the inter-state.'

'All right, the list's getting a bit long. But he's up there alone with a pretty girl, an exhausted horse and a rifle dated 1852. Oh yes, and a bow and arrow. We have all the technology, he has none. Keep a sense of proportion. And keep following those tracks.'

Ben Craig lay invisible in the undergrowth and watched the first horsemen arrive at the creek. From 500 yards he could pick out the towering figure of Big Bill Braddock and the much smaller one of his son, who squirmed in the saddle to ease the chafing of his backside. One of the men beside Braddock was not in western clothes but in camouflage uniform, jungle boots and beret.

They did not have to scout around for the path down the steep slope to the water, nor the path on which to scramble up the other side. They had simply followed Rosebud's tracks, as he knew they would. Whispering Wind could not walk in her silken slippers, and Rosebud could not conceal her tracks in soft ground.

He watched them make their descent into the

bubbling clear water and there pause to drink and splash their faces in relief.

No-one heard the arrows and no-one saw where they came from. By the time they had emptied their rifles into the trees above the far bank, the bowman was gone. Soft-footed and trackless, he slipped through the forest to his horse and his girl and led them on and upwards towards the peaks.

The arrows had found their marks, entering soft flesh, penetrating to the bone and snapping off the flint tips. Two men were down, yelling in pain. Max, the Vietnam veteran, raced up the southern bank, threw himself flat and scanned the undergrowth into which the attacker had vanished. He saw nothing. But if the man had still been there his covering fire would have protected the party in the creek.

Braddock's men helped the injured back up the way they had come. They screamed all the way.

'We'll have to get them out of here, boss,' said one of the bodyguards. 'They need hospitalization.'

'All right, let them mount up and go,' said Braddock.

'Boss, they can't mount up. And they can't walk.'

There was no help for it but to cut branches and make two litters. When this was done another four men were needed to carry the poles of the makeshift stretchers. With six men and an hour lost, the Braddock party reassembled on the far bank, protected by the gun of Major Max. The four carriers began to tramp back through the forest. They did not know a travois would have been easier and saved more manpower.

The sheriff had heard the fusillade and feared the worst. But in this density of cover it would have been foolish to gallop forward for fear of meeting a bullet from the other party. They met the stretcher-carriers coming back down the trail created by so many horses.

'What the hell happened to them?' asked the sheriff. The Braddock soldiers explained.

'Did he get away?'

'Yep. Major Max got across the creek but he was gone.'

The stretcher-bearers continued back towards civilization and the sheriff's posse hurried forward to the creek.

'And you guys can wipe those smiles off your faces,' snapped the sheriff, who was fast losing patience with the young woodsman somewhere up ahead of him. 'No-one is going to win this fight with bows and arrows. For God's sake, it's 1977.'

Each of the wounded men they had just seen was lying face down on his litter with a Cheyenne turkey-feathered arrow sticking vertically out of the left buttock. The sheriff and his men crossed the creek, slipping, sliding, hauling on their horses' bridles, until they were assembled on the far bank. There would be no more picnic sites for campers up here. This was the landscape when the world was young.

But Jerry was up in his helicopter, 1,000 feet above the canopy of trees, quartering the wilderness until he found the parties of horsemen crossing the creek. This narrowed his line of search. The fugitives had to be up ahead of the followers, somewhere on or near the line from the crossing to the mountains ahead.

He was having a problem with part of his technology. Because of the density of the foliage he could not raise Sheriff Lewis on his walkie-talkie. For his part the sheriff could hear his pilot calling but could not make out what he said. The static was too loud and the words broke up.

What Jerry was saying was: 'I've got him. I've seen him.'

He had in fact caught a glimpse of a lone horse, led by the bridle, with the blanket-shrouded figure of a girl on its back. The fugitives had been crossing a small clearing in the forest when the helo, sweeping across the sky tilted to one side to give the pilot the best downward vision, had caught them for a second in the open. But it was only a second; then they were back under the trees again.

Ben Craig stared up through the canopy at the monster chattering and clattering above him.

'The man in it will be telling the hunters where you are,' said Whispering Wind.

'How can they hear, with all that noise?' he asked.

'Never mind, Ben. They have ways.'

So did the frontiersman. He eased the old Sharps from its sheath and slipped in one long, heavy-grain round. To get better vision, Jerry had dropped to 600 feet, just 200 yards up. He hovered, slightly nose down, gazing for another small clearing they might have to cross. The man below him sighted carefully and fired.

The heavy slug tore through the floor, went between the pilot's spread thighs and made a starred hole in the bulbous canopy past his face. Seen from the ground the Sikorsky performed one wild, crazy circle, then hauled away to one side and upwards. It did not relent until it was a mile to one side and a mile high.

Jerry was screaming into his microphone.

'Paul, the bastard just drilled me. Right through the canopy. I'm out of here. I have to go back to Bridger and check the damage. If he'd hit the main rotor assembly I'd be a goner. The hell with this. The gloves are off, right?'

The sheriff heard none of this. He had heard the distant boom of the old rifle and seen the helicopter giving a ballet performance up against the blue sky; he had seen it head for the horizon.

'We have the technology,' murmured one of the rangers.

'Stow it,' said Lewis. 'The boy's going inside for years. Just keep moving, rifles at the ready, eyes and ears alert. We have a real manhunt on here.'

Another hunter had heard the rifle shot, and he was much closer, about half a mile. Max had proposed that he scout forward of the main party.

'He's walking a horse, sir, which means I can move faster. He won't hear me coming. If I get a clear shot I can bring him down with the girl several feet away.'

Braddock agreed. Max slipped away forward, dodging quietly from cover to cover, eyes ahead and to each side, covering the bush for the slightest movement. When he heard the rifle shot it gave him a clear line to follow, about half a mile ahead and slightly to the right of his trail. He began to close in.

Up ahead Ben Craig had holstered his rifle and resumed his march. He had but a half-mile left to go before the forest gave way to the rock sheet known as the Silver Run. Above the trees he could see the mountains coming slowly closer. He knew he had slowed his pursuers but not turned them back. They were still there, still following.

A bird called, high in the trees behind him. He knew the bird and he knew the call, a repeated toc-toc-toc that faded as the bird flew away. Another responded, the same call. It was their warning call. He left Rosebud to graze, moved twenty feet off the trail left by her hoofs and trotted back through the pines.

Max flitted from cover to cover, following the hoof marks, until he came to the clearing; with his camouflage uniform and black-streaked face he was invisible in the gloom beneath the trees. He studied the clearing and grinned when he saw the glitter of the brass cartridge in the middle of it. Such a silly trick. He knew better than to run forward to examine it, and take the bullet from the hidden marksman. He knew the man must be there. The too-obvious bait proved it. Inch by inch he studied the foliage on the other side.

Then he saw the twig move. It was a bush, a large and dense bush across the clearing. The gentle breeze moved the foliage, but always the same way. This branch had moved the opposite way. Peering at the bush he made out the faint tawny blur six feet above the ground. From the previous day he recalled the fox fur trapper's hat on the rider's head.

He was carrying his preferred weapon of choice, the M-16 carbine: short-barrelled, light and utterly dependable. His right thumb slipped the catch silently to 'automatic' mode and then he fired. Half a magazine tore into the bush; the tawny blur vanished, then reappeared on the ground where it had fallen. Only then did Max break cover.

The Cheyenne never used stone war clubs. They preferred hatchets, with which they could slash sideways and downwards from a horse's back, or throw with accuracy and speed.

The flying axe hit the major in the right bicep, shearing through the muscle and shattering the bone. The carbine fell from a nerveless hand. He stared down, white-faced, and pulled the axe from his own limb and when the bright red blood gushed, clamped his left hand over the gash to staunch the flow. Then he turned and ran down the path whence he had come.

The scout let drop from his left hand the fifty-foot thong with which he had tweaked the branch, recovered his axe and his hat and ran on to find his horse.

Braddock, his son and remaining three men

found the major leaning up against a tree, breathing deeply, when they caught up.

Sheriff Lewis and his party had heard the fusillade of carbine fire, the second that day, but quite different from the fugitive's single-shot rifle, and rode in fast. The senior ranger looked at the shattered arm, said, 'Tourniquet,' and broke open his first-aid pack.

While he dressed the mangled flesh and bone Sheriff Lewis listened as Braddock told him what had happened. He stared at the rancher with contempt.

'I ought to arrest the lot of you,' he snapped. 'And if it wasn't for the fact we are one hell of a long way from civilization, I would. As of now, you butt right out of this, Mr Braddock, and stay out.'

'I'm seeing this thing through,' shouted Braddock. 'That savage stole my son's girl and has seriously injured three of my men—'

'Who should not even have been here. Now, I'm going to bring this boy in to face charges, but I am not looking for any fatalities. So I want your weaponry, I want it all and I want it now.'

Several rifles swung in the direction of Braddock and his party. Other deputies collected the rifles and handguns. The sheriff turned to the ranger who had done his best for the major's arm.

'What do you reckon?'

'Evacuation, quickly,' said the ranger. 'He could ride back with an escort to Red Lodge, but it's twenty hard miles, with West Fork in the middle. A tough ride, he might not make it.

'Up ahead is the Silver Run Plateau. The radios should work there. We could call up a helo.'

'Which do you advise?'

'Helo,' said the ranger. 'That arm needs surgery without delay or he'll lose it.'

They rode on. In the clearing they found the discarded carbine and the cartridge. The ranger studied it.

'Flint arrows, a flying hatchet, a buffalo gun. Who the hell is this guy, Sheriff?'

'I thought I knew,' said Lewis. 'Now I don't think I do.'

'Well,' said the ranger, 'he sure ain't an out-of-work actor.'

Ben Craig stood at the edge of the forest and stared ahead at the shimmering flat plain of rock. Five miles to the last, hidden creek; two more across the Hellroaring Plateau and a last mile up the face of the mountain. He stroked Rosebud's head and her velvet-soft muzzle.

'Just one more before the sun goes down,' he told her. 'One more ride and we will be free.'

He mounted up and urged the horse into a canter over the rock. Ten minutes later the pursuers reached the plateau. He was a speck on the rock face a mile away.

Clear of the trees the radios functioned again. Sheriff Lewis made contact with Jerry and learned the fate of the little Sikorsky. Jerry was back at Billings Field and had borrowed a larger Bell Jetranger.

'Get down here, Jerry. Don't worry about the

sniper. He's over a mile away, out of range. We have an emergency evacuation. And that civilian volunteer with the Piper Cub? Tell him I need him and right now. I want him over the Silver Run Plateau, no lower than five thousand feet. Tell him he's looking for a lone horseman heading for the mountains.'

It was past three and the sun was moving west towards the peaks. When it slipped behind Spirit Mountain and Beartooth Mountain the darkness would come fast.

Jerry and the Bell got there first, clattering out of the blue sky to land on the flat rock. The major was helped aboard and one deputy went with him. The police pilot took off, radioing ahead to Billings Memorial to ask for a landing in the parking lot and major surgery and trauma teams to be on standby.

The remaining riders set off across the plateau.

'There's a hidden creek he probably doesn't know about,' said the senior ranger, moving up beside the sheriff. 'It's called Lake Fork. Deep, narrow, steep-sided. There's only one way down and up the other side that could be passable for a horse. Take him ages to find it. We could close up and take him there.'

'And if he's waiting in the trees, with that rifle sighted on us? I don't want to lose one or two of you guys to prove a point.'

'So what shall we do?'

'Hang loose,' said Lewis. 'He has no way out of the mountains, not even down into Wyoming, not with air surveillance.'

'Unless he marches through the night.'

'He has an exhausted horse and a girl in white silk wedding slippers. He's running out of time and he ought to know it. Just keep him in sight at about a mile and wait for the spotter plane.'

They rode on with the tiny distant figure in their view. The spotter plane came just before four. The young pilot had had to be called from his work in Billings, where he had a job with a camping store. The tops of the trees that clothed the steep banks of Lake Fork came into view.

The voice of the pilot crackled out of the sheriff's radio set.

'What do you want to know?'

'There's a lone rider up ahead of us, with a blanket-wrapped girl mounted behind. Can you see him?'

The Piper Cub, high above, winged off towards the creek.

'Sure can. There's a narrow creek over here. He's entering the trees.'

'Stay clear. He has a rifle and he's a crack shot.'

They saw the Piper climb and bank over the creek two miles ahead.

'Right. But I can still see him. He's off the horse and leading it down into the creek.'

'He'll never get up the other side,' hissed the ranger. 'We can close up now.'

They broke into a canter, with Braddock, his son and his remaining three gunmen with empty holsters coming behind them.

'Stay out of range,' warned the sheriff again. 'He

can still fire from through the trees if you get too close. He did it to Jerry.'

'Jerry was hovering at six hundred feet,' the pilot crackled over the air. 'I'm doing one hundred and twenty knots at three thousand feet. By the by, he seems to have found a way up. He's climbing out onto the Hellroaring Plateau.'

The sheriff glanced at the ranger and snorted.

'You'd think he's been here before,' said the bemused ranger.

'Maybe he has,' snapped Lewis.

'No way. We know who moves up here.'

The posse reached the rim of the canyon, but the screen of pines blocked the vision of the exhausted man tugging his horse and its burden out on the other side.

The ranger knew the only path down into the creek, but the hoof marks of Rosebud showed that their quarry knew the same. When they emerged onto the second plateau the fugitives were again a speck in the distance.

'It's getting dark and fuel is low,' said the pilot. 'I have to go.'

'One last circle,' urged the sheriff. 'Where is he now?'

'He's made the mountain. He's off and leading again. Climbing the north face. But it looks like the horse is breaking down. It's stumbling all over the track. I guess you'll have him at sunup. Good hunting, Sheriff.'

The Piper turned in the darkening sky and droned away back to Billings.

'Do we go on, boss?' one of the deputies asked. Sheriff Lewis shook his head. The air was thin, they were all sucking in the oxygen, night was falling fast.

'Not in the dark. We camp here till daylight.'

They made camp in the last of the trees above the creek, facing the mountains to the south, so close in the fading light they seemed to tower above the specks on the rock that were men and horses.

They broke out thick, warm sheepskin jackets and pulled them on. Bundles of old dead branches were found beneath the trees, which soon burned bright and warm. At the sheriff's suggestion Braddock, his son and his remaining three men camped a hundred yards away.

It had never been intended to spend the night so high on the plateau. They had not brought bedrolls and food. They sat on horse blankets round the fire, propped against their saddles, and dined on candy bars. Sheriff Lewis stared into the flames.

'What are you going to do tomorrow, Paul?' asked Tom Barrow.

'I'm going to go forward to the mountain alone. No guns. I'm going to fly a flag of truce and take the loudhailer. I'm going to try to talk him down from that mountain, with the girl.'

'That could be dangerous. He's a wild kid. He might try to kill you,' said the ranger.

'He could have killed three men today,' mused the sheriff. 'He could have, but he didn't. He must realize he can't protect the girl up there in a siege. I figure he probably won't shoot down a peace officer under a white flag. He'll listen first. It's worth a try.'

Chill darkness wrapped the mountain. Pulling, hauling, tugging, urging and pleading, Ben Craig led Rosebud up the last stretch and onto the shelf of flat rock outside the cave. The horse stood trembling, eyes dull, while her master took down the girl from her back.

Craig gestured Whispering Wind towards the old bear cave, untied the buffalo robe and spread it for her. He eased off the quiver with its two remaining arrows, took the bow from his back and laid them down together. He unhitched the rifle sheath and laid the weapon beside the bow. Finally he loosened the girth and removed the saddle and the two bags.

Relieved of her burdens, the chestnut mare took a few steps towards the scrubby trees and the sere foliage beneath them. Her back legs gave way and she sat on her rump. Then the front legs buckled. She rolled onto her side.

Craig knelt by her head, took it on his lap and stroked her muzzle. She whinnied softly at his touch and then her brave heart gave out.

The young man too was racked by tiredness. He had not slept for two days and nights, hardly eaten, and had ridden or marched nearly a hundred miles. There were things yet to do and he drove himself a little further.

At the edge of the shelf he looked down and saw below and away to the north the twin campfires of the pursuers. He cut branches and saplings where the old man had sat and made a fire. The flames lit the ledge and the cave, and the white silk-clad figure of the only girl he had ever loved or ever would.

He broke open the saddlebags and prepared some food he had brought from the fort. They sat side by side on the rug and ate the only meal they had had together or ever would.

He knew that with his horse gone the chase was almost over. But the old vision-quester had promised him that this girl would be his wife, and that it was so spoken by the Everywhere Spirit.

Down on the plain the conversation among the exhausted men withered and died. They sat in silence, faces lit by the flickering flames, and stared at the fire.

In the thin air of the high peaks the silence was total. A light zephyr came off the peaks but did not disturb the silence. Then there was a sound.

It came to them through the night, borne by the cat's-paw wind off the mountain. It was a cry, long and clear, the voice of a young woman.

It was not a cry of pain or distress but that wavering, ebbing cry of one in such an ecstasy that it defies description or repetition.

The deputies stared at each other, then lowered their heads to their chests and the sheriff saw their shoulders twitch and shake.

A hundred yards away Bill Braddock rose from beside his fire as his men sought not to catch his eye. He stared at the mountain and his face was a mask of rage and hatred.

At midnight the temperature began to drop. At first the men thought it was the night chill becoming colder due to the high altitude and thin atmosphere. They shivered and drew their sheepskins tighter. But the cold went through their jeans and they huddled closer to the fire.

Below zero and still falling; the deputies looked at the sky and saw thick clouds begin to blot the peaks from sight. High on the side of Mount Rearguard they saw a single speck of a fire; then it faded from view.

These were Montana men, accustomed to the bitter winters, but the last ten days of October were too early for such cold. At one o'clock the rangers estimated it was twenty degrees below zero, and still plunging. At two they were all up, thoughts of sleep gone, stamping to keep the circulation going, blowing on hands, hurling greater piles of branches onto the fire, but to no effect. The first fat flakes of snow began to fall, hissing into the fire, diluting its heat.

The senior ranger went over to Sheriff Lewis, teeth chattering.

'Cal and me reckon we should move back to the shelter of the Custer Forest,' he said.

'Will it be warmer there?' he asked.

'It might be.'

'What the hell is happening here?'

'You'll think me crazy, Sheriff.'

'Indulge me.'

The snow thickened, the stars were gone, a freezing white wilderness was moving towards them.

'This place is the meeting point of the Crow lands and the Shoshone Nation. Years ago warriors fought and died here, before the white man came. The Indians believe their spirits still walk these mountains; they think it is a magical place.'

'A charming tradition. But what's with the damn weather?'

'I said it sounded crazy. But they say that sometimes the Everywhere Spirit comes here too, and brings the Cold of the Long Sleep, against which no man can stand. Of course, it's just a weird climatic phenomenon, but I think we should move out. We'll freeze before sunup if we stay.'

Sheriff Lewis thought and nodded.

'Saddle up,' he said. 'We're riding out. Go tell Braddock and his men.'

The ranger came back through the blizzard a few minutes later.

'He says he's going to pull into the shelter of the creek but no further.'

The sheriff, the rangers and the deputies, shuddering with cold, recrossed the creek and rode back across the Silver Run Plateau to the dense pines of the forest. The temperature inside the trees rose to zero. They built more fires and survived.

At half past four the white mantle on the mountain broke away and swept down to the plain, a quietly seething tidal wave that moved like a wall over the rock, tumbled into the narrow creek and filled it to the brim. Half a mile into the Silver Run it finally stopped. The skies began to clear.

Two hours later Sheriff Paul Lewis stood at the

edge of the forest and looked to the south. The mountains were white. The east was pink with the promise of a bright new day and the sky was indigo, turning duck-egg blue. He had kept his radio next to his body all night for warmth and it had worked.

'Jerry,' he called, 'we need you down here, with the Jetranger, and fast. We've had a blizzard and things look bad ... No, we're back at the edge of the forest, where you evacuated the mercenary yesterday. You'll find us all there.'

The four-seater came whirling out of the rising sun and settled on the cold but snow-free rock. Lewis put two deputies into the rear and climbed up beside his pilot.

'Go back to the mountain.'

'What about the sharpshooter?'

'I don't think anyone's going to be shooting right now. They'll be lucky if they are alive.'

The helicopter retraced the line the posse had ridden the previous day. Lake Fork Creek was marked only by the tops of some pine and larch. Of the five men inside there was no sign. They flew on towards the mountain. The sheriff was looking for the spot where he had seen the pinprick of a camp-fire in the sky. The pilot was nervous, staying wide and high; no hovering at 600 feet.

Lewis saw it first. The inky black mark on the face of the mountain, the mouth of a cave, and in front of it a snow-dusted shelf of rock wide enough to take the Jetranger.

'Take her down, Jerry.'

The pilot came in carefully, scanning for movement among the rocks, a man taking aim, the flash of a gun using out-of-date black powder. Nothing moved. The helo settled on the shelf, blades turning fast, ready for a getaway.

Sheriff Lewis jumped from the door, handgun at the ready. The deputies clambered out with rifles, dropping to the ground to cover the cave mouth. Nothing moved. Lewis called out.

'Come on out. Hands high. No harm will come to you.'

There was no reply. Nothing stirred. He ran a zigzag course to the side of the cave mouth. Then he peered round.

There was a bundle on the floor and nothing more. Still cautious, he moved in to investigate. Whatever it had once been, probably an animal skin of some kind, it was rotted by age, the fur gone, strands of hide holding it together. He lifted the mouldy skin away.

She lay underneath in her white silk wedding dress, a cascade of frosted black hair about her shoulders, as if asleep in her bridal bed. But when he reached to touch, she was cold as marble.

Holstering his gun and mindless of any crouching gunman, the peace officer scooped her up and ran outside.

'Get those sheepskins off and wrap her,' he shouted to his men. 'Get her into the back and keep her warm with your own bodies.'

The deputies tore off their warm coats and shrouded the body of the girl. One climbed into the

454

rear seats with the young woman in his arms and began to chafe her hands and feet. The sheriff pushed the other man into the spare front seat and shouted at Jerry: 'Get her to the clinic at Red Lodge. Fast. Warn them you're coming with a near-death hypothermia. Keep the cabin system at maximum all the way. There may be a tiny chance. Then come back for me.'

He watched the Jetranger hammer away across the plateaus of rock and the huge spread of forest that led out of the wilderness. Then he explored the cave and the shelf in front of it. When he was done he found a rock, sat and stared north at the almost unbelievable view.

In the clinic at Red Lodge a doctor and a nurse began to work on the girl, stripping away the chilled wedding dress, chafing hands and feet, arms, legs and ribcage. Her surface temperature was below frostbite level and her core temperature into the danger zone.

After twenty minutes the doctor caught a faint beat deep inside, a young heart fighting to live. Twice the beat stopped; twice he pumped the ribcage till it came back again. The body core temperature began to rise.

Once she stopped breathing and the doctor forced his own breath into her to make the lungs resume. The temperature in the room was at sauna level and the electric blanket wrapping her lower limbs was at maximum.

After an hour an eyelid trembled and the blue colour began to ebb from the lips. The nurse checked the core temperature: it was above danger level and rising. The heartbeat steadied and strengthened.

In half an hour Whispering Wind opened her large dark eyes and her lips whispered, 'Ben?'

The doctor offered a short prayer of thanks to old Hippocrates and all the others who had come before him.

'It's Luke, but never mind. I thought we might have lost you there, kid.'

On his stone the sheriff watched the Jetranger returning for him. He could see it miles away in the still air and hear the angry snarl of its rotors clawing at the atmosphere. It was so peaceful on the mountain. When Jerry touched down Sheriff Lewis beckoned to the single deputy in the front seat.

'Break out two blankets and come over here,' he shouted when the rotor blades had slowed to idling speed. When the deputy joined him he pointed and said, 'Bring him too.'

The young man wrinkled his nose.

'Aw, Sheriff . . .'

'Just do it. He was a man once. He deserves a Christian burial.'

The skeleton of the horse was on its side. Every scrap of skin, flesh, muscle and sinew had long been picked clean. The hair of tail and mane had gone, probably for nesting material. But the teeth, ground down by the tough forage of the plains, were still in the jaw. The bridle was almost dust, but the steel bit glittered between the teeth.

The brown hoofs were intact and on them the

four shoes nailed in place long ago by some cavalry farrier.

The skeleton of the man was a few yards away, on his back, as if he had died in his sleep. Of his clothes there was almost nothing left, scraps of rotten buckskin clinging to the ribs. Spreading one blanket, the deputy began to place the bones upon it, every last one. The sheriff returned to those things the rider had once possessed.

Wind and weather over countless seasons had reduced the saddle and girth to a pile of rotten leather, and also the saddlebags. But among the mess gleamed the cases of a handful of brass cartridges. Sheriff Lewis took them.

There was a bowie knife, brown with rust, in the remains of a beaded scabbard which crumbled at the touch. What had once been the sheepskin sheath of a frontier rifle had been torn away by pecking birds, but the firearm lay in the frost, clogged with the rust of years, but still a rifle.

What perplexed him were the two arrows in their quiver, the stave of osage cherry, tapered at both ends and notched to take the string, and the axe. All appeared to be almost new. There was a belt buckle and a length of tough old leather that had survived the elements still attached to it.

The sheriff took them all, wrapped them in the second blanket, gave a last look round to see there was nothing left, and climbed aboard. The deputy was in the back with the other bundle.

For the last time the Jetranger lifted away into the sky, back over the two plateaus and on to the green mass of the National Forest under the morning sun.

Sheriff Lewis looked down at Lake Fork, choked in snow. There would be an expedition to bring back the cadavers but he knew no-one had survived. He stared down at the rock and the trees and wondered about the young man whom he had pursued across this unforgiving land.

From 5,000 feet he could look down to Rock Creek on his right and see that the traffic was flowing again on the interstate, the fallen pine and the wreckage cleared. They passed over Red Lodge and Jerry checked with the deputy who had remained there. He reported the girl was in intensive care but her heart still beat.

Four miles north of Bridger as they followed the highway home, he could see a hundred acres of fire-blackened prairie, and twenty miles further he looked down at the tonsured lawns and prize longhorns of the Bar-T Ranch.

The helicopter crossed the Yellowstone and the highway west to Bozeman, dipped and began to lose height. And so they came back to Billings Field.

' "Man that is born of woman hath but a little time to live." '

It was late February and bitter cold in the small cemetery at Red Lodge. In the far corner was a fresh-dug grave and above it, on two crossbars, a simple and cheap pine coffin.

The priest was muffled against the chill, the two sextons punched their gloved hands as they waited. One mourner stood at the foot of the grave in snow boots and a quilted coat, but bareheaded. A cape of raven hair flowed about her shoulders.

At the far edge of the graveyard a big man stood under a yew and watched but did not approach. He wore a sheepskin coat against the cold, the insignia of his office pinned to the front.

It had been a strange winter, mused the man under the tree. The widowed Mrs Braddock, appearing more relieved than bereaved, had emerged from her isolation and taken over the chairmanship of Braddock Beef Inc. She had a hair and facial makeover, wore smart clothes and went to parties.

She had visited the girl in hospital, liked her and offered her a cottage, rent-free, on the ranch and a job as private secretary. Both had been accepted. By deed of gift she had returned to Mr Pickett the controlling stock of his bank.

'"Earth to earth, ashes to ashes, dust to dust,"' intoned the priest. Two snowflakes, drifting on the breeze, settled on the black mane of hair like the blossoms of the wild dog rose.

The sextons took the cords, kicked out the crossbars and lowered the coffin into the grave. Then they stood back and waited again, eyeing their shovels jammed into the pile of fresh earth.

In Bozeman the forensic pathologists had taken their time and done what they could. They established the bones must have been those of a man just under six feet tall, almost certainly of great physical strength.

There were no breaks in the bones, nor any signs

of wounds that might have caused death, which was presumed to have been from exposure.

The dentists had been intrigued by the teeth: straight, white and even, not one cavity. They put the young man in his mid-to-late twenties.

The scientists had taken over the non-human fragments. Carbon-14 tests had revealed the organic matter, buckskin, leather, fur, to have dated from a period put firmly in the mid-1870s.

The abiding enigma was the quiver, arrows, bow and axe. The same tests proved these were quite recent. The accepted solution was that a party of Native Americans had visited the cave just recently and left their trophies for the man who had died there long ago.

The bowie knife was buffed and restored, dated by its bone handle and donated to Professor Ingles, who had hung it in his office. The sheriff had claimed the old rifle. It too had been professionally restored and hung on the wall behind his desk. He would take it into retirement with him.

'"In the certain knowledge of the Resurrection and the Life Hereafter. Amen."'

Relieved of their waiting, the sextons restored their circulation by shovelling the earth into the grave. The priest had a few words with the sole mourner, patted her on the arm and hurried away to find warmth in his presbytery. She did not move.

After a single and singularly unrevealing statement from the girl in hospital, the manhunt had petered out. The press had speculated that the man must have ridden off the mountain in the night and vanished into the wilds of Wyoming, leaving her to die in the cave.

The sextons filled the grave, quickly made a border of mountain rocks round the earth and filled the space with four sacks of tan gravel.

Then they tipped their fur hats to the girl, took their shovels and left. The big man moved quietly forward until he stood just behind and to one side of her. She made no move. She knew he was there and who he was. He took off his hat and held it by his side.

'We never did find your friend, Miss Pickett,' he said.

'No.'

She held a flower in front of her, a single long-stemmed red rose.

'I guess we never will now.'

'No.'

He took the rose from her fingers, stepped forward, stooped and placed it on the gravel. At the head of the plot was a timber cross, donated by the good people of Red Lodge. A local craftsman had branded some words into the timber with a hot iron before varnishing. They read:

> HERE LIES
> A FRONTIERSMAN
> DIED IN THE MOUNTAINS
> CIRCA 1877
> KNOWN ONLY UNTO GOD
> R.I.P.

The man straightened up.

'Is there anything I can do? You need a ride home?'

'No. Thank you. I have my car.'

He replaced his hat, tipped the brim to her.

'Good luck to you, Miss Pickett.'

He walked away. His car, bearing the livery of the County Sheriff's Office, was parked outside the cemetery. He raised his eyes. To the south-west the peaks of the Beartooth Range glittered in the sun.

The girl stayed a while longer. Then she turned and walked towards the gate.

A slight breeze from the peaks caught her, blowing open the long quilted coat and revealing the four-month bulge of her belly.

THE END

ICON
by Frederick Forsyth

Russia, 1999, poised to collapse in an economic and social meltdown of hyper-inflation, chaos, corruption and crime. Elections loom and a single charismatic voice rings out across the land. Igor Komarov claims he will crack down on crime, eliminate corruption and restore the glory.

But a secret document, stolen from his desk, leaves those in the West who read it pale and shaken. If the Black Manifesto is true, this man is no saviour of the nation, but a new Adolf Hitler.

Jason Monk, ex-CIA, goes back to the city to which he said he would never return. He finds a world of poverty and luxury, of politicians, gansters, private armies, prostitutes and priests. The American has a double task: stop Komarov and prepare for an icon worthy of the Russian people.

Icon is the master storyteller at his very best, a novel with all the Forsyth hallmarks of intricate political realism, stunning suspense and a narrative that will leave you breathless.

'Forsyth's narrative surges along with great power; the story is terrifying and timely; and the vendetta between Monk and Komarov grips you to the end'
Daily Telegraph

'One of his best works for a long time'
Sunday Times

0 552 13991 2

A SELECTED LIST OF FINE WRITING
AVAILABLE FROM CORGI

THE PRICES SHOWN BELOW WERE CORRECT AT THE TIME OF GOING TO PRESS. HOWEVER
TRANSWORLD PUBLISHERS RESERVE THE RIGHT TO SHOW NEW RETAIL PRICES ON COVERS
WHICH MAY DIFFER FROM THOSE PREVIOUSLY ADVERTISED IN THE TEXT OR ELSEWHERE.

All Transworld titles are available by post from:
Bookpost, PO Box 29, Douglas, Isle of Man, IM99 1BQ
Credit cards accepted. Please telephone 01624 836000,
fax 01624 837033, Internet http://www.bookpost.co.uk
or e-mail: bookshop@enterprise.net for details.
Free postage and packing in the UK. Overseas customers: allow
£1 per book (paperbacks) and £3 per book (hardbacks).